A KILLING IN PARADISE

Dylan Kasper: Book Two

Elliot Sweeney

WILDFIRE

First published in paperback in 2024 by
WILDFIRE
an imprint of HEADLINE PUBLISHING GROUP

1

Cataloguing in Publication Data is available from the British Library

ISBN 978 1 4722 9272 8

Typeset in 11/14.25pt Bembo Book MT Pro by Jouve (UK), Milton Keynes

Printed and bound in Great Britain by Clays Ltd, Elcograf S.p.A.

HEADLINE PUBLISHING GROUP
an Hachette UK Company
Carmelite House
50 Victoria Embankment
London
EC4Y 0DZ

www.headline.co.uk
www.hachette.co.uk

'Always make the audience suffer as much as possible.'

– Alfred Hitchcock

For my parents, Jane and Jim

Prologue

It was weeks later, when my wounds had healed, and the stories about Nate Willoughby were finally beginning to fade from public interest, that the nightmares came.

By then it was mid-March. Mornings were brighter, days longer, sweetened with the warming hints of spring; trees, naked weeks prior, were blossoming leaves and fruit buds. All seemed well.

Yet amidst life, the pall of death spread through my mind like a sarcoma. Each night I woke soaked with sweat, a tangle of air in my chest, the images pulsating like wounds.

My landlady, a retired psychiatrist, tells me that post-traumatic shock of this kind is not uncommon. As a former policeman I know first-hand how certain scenes encountered in the line of duty will always remain in the darker recesses of memory. The first attender to a gang rape or child murder will testify to this. And when my daughter's suicide ended my career with the Met, I thought I'd experienced all life could throw.

But nothing could have prepared me for those two weeks at the start of this year. The things I saw, did, and what I learned I was capable of. Perhaps the nightmares are my mind's way of making sense of it all. Or perhaps they are my punishment.

Rather than talk in abstracts and swerve details, I will stick to the facts and leave the opinions for others. In January, an evil came into our lives of the kind the professionals struggle to explain.

This is a story I perhaps shouldn't share. But it's one I'm struggling to contain.

Chapter 1

We were midway into the second round when the blood hit the ring floor.

It came from the nose of Patience Mensah, the fiery boxer I'd ventured out to see fight on this cold January evening. She'd stepped in too hard, caught a mean uppercut from her opponent, and then reeled back to the ropes. The crowd roared as Patience's legs buckled and the other girl, blonde, ripped, trained at one of those pricey clubs in the City, saw the opening and piled in.

'Damn,' Mani said, wincing beside me from his chair. 'That's Patience's lot, I'd say.'

Perhaps. But when she glanced back at the hecklers, her eyes still bore a spark of rage. Patience wasn't throwing in the towel yet.

I drank some Export from the can, paid for by Mani. As were the tickets for tonight's inter-borough bout, and pretty much everything else. He'd called that morning, asked me to join him. I'd seen Patience training at Savages, my local gym, and knew she'd be worth the jaunt. Hard of wallet and short on plans, I agreed.

Pretty fast, I realised Mani wasn't himself; avoiding eye contact, acting cagey. He'd started smoking again too, never a good sign, for Mani's consumption of cigarettes was generally a measure of his stress levels.

But I figured what the heck – he'd get to explaining whatever was on his mind when he was ready. Till then I was having a decent time watching these two girls beat the crap out of each other.

'Thirty seconds left till the end of the round,' Mani said.

'That's a lifetime in boxing,' I said.

Sure enough, there was more drama in the ring. Again, Patience stepped in too hard, and another jab caught her, this time to the ribs, winding her. The crowd whipped up an octave. Her opponent dived in with the punches, and Patience raised her gloves, protecting her chin. The blows rocked her.

'C'mon, girl,' Mani said, his hands fists. 'Dig deep.'

Ten seconds before the bell, Patience lunged forward for a clinch. Although bruised, she had something left in the can, but the other fighter was breathless. Patience snuck in two close suckers to her liver and was loading up more when the ref stepped in, drew them apart. But it was enough to send the girl to her corner with something to think about.

Mani looked over. 'Patience don't really live up to her name, huh, Kasper?'

'*Im*-patient would be better,' I said. 'Then again, what's in a name? I share mine with a friendly ghost.'

Mani grinned. 'You enjoying yourself?'

'Indeed I am,' I said, looking around, taking in our setting.

The community hall, situated between Tottenham and Hackney, was two-thirds capacity, a hundred or so barrel-bellied geezers and track-suited kids from the flats. The floor was rough concrete, the ceiling corrugated metal, the seating nothing more than a load of foldup chairs rammed around the makeshift ring. Beers and Cokes were the sole refreshments, paid for with cash, no cards, definitely no tick. The smell of sweat, lager and flatulence reeked. Madison's Square it was not.

'So, how's life?' Mani said. 'You still seeing that nurse from the dating app?'

I shook my head. 'She dropped me out just before Christmas when she found out what I do for work. Or *don't* do, I should say.'

'You're joking?'

'Afraid not. I mean, what's not to like about an ex-plod turned out-of-work PI?'

'Beats me,' Mani said, grinning some more. 'After you got those crooked cops sent away last year, I figured you'd be flooded with job offers, and pretty women.'

'You'd think so, right? But the only work I've had in the last few weeks was photographing a cheating husband meeting his bit on the side in a McDonald's car park. And my own love life's about as exciting as that same McDonald's car park.'

Mani chuckled, rolled his head back, and his necklace sparkled, a simple gold crucifix I'd never seen him without.

It was a tonic, joking about my current woes, but truth-be-told they were no laughing matter: like it or not, I needed to make a few lifestyle changes sharpish, or else I'd sink.

This wasn't the time to berate myself though. Right then, all I really wanted was to let my hair down with a mate.

Although I'd known Mani – aka Emmanuel Meads, church-going father of three – for less than a year, it seemed longer, perhaps because of the circumstances in which we'd met. Last spring I'd investigated the death of a troubled young man who put himself under a train Mani was driving. When that case got messy and the bodies stacked up, Mani helped me dispose of a psychopathic cat killer's corpse by feigning another suicide. I guess you could say I owed him one.

'What do you reckon Pat's chances are of pulling this fight back?' he said.

'Fair,' I said. 'Her opponent's quicker, but your girl has guts. She just needs to keep that temper in check, wait for the opening, then—' I brought my fists together.

Mani nodded. 'She's a good kid, but she's had a tough life. I know her family. I tell you that?'

'You hadn't,' I said, sensing we were close to what was playing on his mind.

A leggy blonde with curves in all the right places held up a Round Three placard, momentarily sidetracking me. Patience was first on her feet, smacking her gloves, her eyes fizzing.

Mani leaned over. 'I told Patience 'bout you. That you're a private investigator, looking for work. She's keen to meet after the fight.'

The bell sounded. Patience piled in.

I looked at Mani. 'Why's she want to meet me?'

Before he could answer, the crowd erupted.

I glanced back at the ring. Patience had connected a southpaw to the other girl's chin, enough to spin her one-eighty. Her mouth guard hit the floor, chattering like a castanet.

'Whoa!' Mani said, grabbing my shoulder. 'You see that!'

It was a blinding punch that sent the girl floundering like a drunkard.

Patience wasn't taking chances though. She charged in a right, stepped in to deliver a second.

No need. The girl's legs went to rubber and the ref pulled the plug.

The crowd erupted.

Patience raised her gloves, punched air.

Mani was on his feet, clapping. His crucifix dallied around his neck, the silver glinting against the flashing cameras.

With the fights all finished and the hall emptying, Mani and I sank another beer at the makeshift bar and he filled me in.

Patience, it turned out, was the older sister of Kwame Mensah, a fourteen-year-old petty criminal who'd been murdered on Paradise Estate five nights prior.

'Here,' Mani said, passing me his phone, 'read this.'

It was Tuesday's *Gazette*. I remembered reading the article the morning it came out – this year's first stabbing, but certainly not its last, the teenager killed on northeast London's version of the Bronx. The piece featured a mug shot of Kwame, taken from a previous arrest. The malt-skinned boy with narrow cornrows and sharp cheekbones was a ringer for his sister.

'Police are putting his death down as knife crime,' Mani said. 'Kids killing kids. Gang beefs. He's another statistic.'

'That's what the article suggests,' I said, handing back the phone.

'I know Patience and Kwame from church. They got dragged there by their parents when they were little.'

'Where're the parents now?'

'Their mum died from cancer eleven years back. They reckon she got it breathing asbestos in those rotten flats. And their dad, he got killed last year.'

'Killed? What happened?'

'Colin had mental problems. Stopped his meds, started shouting weird stuff around the estate, thinking the government was putting thoughts into his head. Police rocked up. When Colin refused to pipe down, one of them tasered him, the rest piled in. He died right there in front of Patience and Kwame. Heart failure brought on by asphyxiation. No one got charged, even disciplined. Maybe you read about it?'

I had, and remembered being disturbed, but not surprised, to read of another vulnerable man's death caused by police over-restraint.

'Anyway,' Mani said, 'after that, Patience and Kwame were two angry kids, alone on Paradise. I tried to help, popping round, offering what I could. But they were struggling. Specially Kwame. Patience had her boxing. But he was falling into crime.'

'Police got a perp for his killing?'

Mani shook his head. 'There's a witness saw him get chased by a gang of boys with knives. Given he had a record, the Met's ruled out alternatives. Gang crime. The case is open-shut.'

'You think the police might be right on this one?'

'What do you reckon?'

'I reckon you wouldn't have suggested me to Patience if you thought it was that straightforward.'

Mani drew his lips together. There was more.

'What?' I said.

'Patience discovered something yesterday. It's pretty messed up, man.'

'What did she find?'

Mani swigged from his can. I noticed his hands had started trembling.

'C'mon,' he said. 'Be easier if you saw it for yourself.'

Patience Mensah was sitting on a bench at the far end of a steamy, sweaty, but otherwise empty changing room. She was clad in a silky black post-fight gown that had *Pat the Bulldozer* embroidered on the front. She didn't stand as we came in. Just looked up, searing me with a Black and Decker stare.

'Pat,' Mani said, 'what a fight, girl.'

She grunted.

'This is the friend I was telling you 'bout.' He gestured over towards me. 'Name's Dylan Kasper.'

We considered each other. She had small dark eyes, a stubby fighter's nose, and cheekbones you could sharpen a pencil on. Five-eight, lean and as ripped as cable wire, her chest was flat, shoulders square, glutes thick and solid. Her left eyebrow was mousing a little, and her nostril was packed with gauze. Despite the war-wounds, she had a steely presence, striking, handsome, intimidating too, and not exuding the welcoming vibe I expect from a potential client.

'Good to meet you,' I said.

'Yeah,' she replied.

I offered a hand. She took it. As handshakes go, it was a firm one.

'I seen you training at Savages,' she said, her voice, all street-edge and front.

'And I've seen you too,' I said. 'You've been putting in the hours. Nice work tonight.'

'Yeah,' she repeated. 'Mani tell you about my kid brother?'

'He did. Sorry for your loss.' Lines like this were about as much use as a cat-flap in a submarine, but you still had to say them. 'I gather you wanted to talk?'

'Me?' Patience said, frowning.

Mani stepped in, said, 'I thought you could tell Kasper what's been going on.' He looked between us keenly. 'I reckon he can help you.'

The penny dropped then – Patience and I had been misled

about each other. She hadn't been keen to meet me; and I wasn't made up to chat with her either. Mani, however, was gunning for us to speak. Why?

She kept up her stare. Finally, she said, 'You reckon you can help then?'

'Depends. What do you need help with?'

'What you think? To find out what happened to Kwame.'

'How about the police? You speak with them?'

'Police are racist liars. They killed my father.'

'Yeah, I heard. But there's a few decent officers still.'

'How do you know?'

'I used to be one.'

She looked at Mani, kissed her teeth. 'Why'd you bring a fed here, man?'

Mani gave an exasperated sound. 'Give Kasper a chance, Pat. I can vouch for him. Besides, who else is there?'

She returned to me. 'How come you left the police?'

I shrugged. 'Oh, the hours, the crappy pay. Plus, I got bored of wearing a tit on my head.'

A flicker of a smile lit her face, but it faded fast, and the eyes stayed hard.

Right then, I was pretty sure the police were right about her brother's killing, and it was nothing more than a beef turned ugly. Paradise was a cesspit of crime, notorious for tragedies that went unspoken, unresolved. It was a bleak reality, but a sign of the iniquitous times we were in.

I was tempted to say as much but held back, for I couldn't ignore what was in front of me – a kid torn up with grief and desperate for answers about her brother's death. I guessed I knew something about that. It was coming up to six years since my daughter died, aged fourteen too.

'Why don't you start from the beginning,' I said. 'Tell me what went down with Kwame.'

She shrugged. 'After Dad died, things got tough. Me and Kwame, we didn't have no money, no clue about life. Gas and electric bills hit the roof, the bills kept stacking up. Rent arrears, utilities, all that.'

'What did you two do to make ends meet?'

'My plan was to sack off the boxing, get a regular job, try to sort things out legit. But Kwame, he wanted me to keep on fighting. He reckoned I could go all the way.' She looked at her fists. 'So, *he* tried earning. My stupid brother became man of the house.'

'How'd he earn?'

'How you think? Thieving. Breaking an' entering, snatching stuff outta people's hands.'

'Whereabouts?'

'These ends, mostly. Kwame never strayed too far from the nest. Just saw the opportunity, an' took it, not thinking of no consequences.'

'What stuff did he go for?'

'Laptops, phones, anything electronic you can flog. He stole bare numbers. We didn't make much money, but it was enough to keep us going.' She paused. 'Till Monday. When he got killed.'

'OK. Talk me through Monday. What happened?'

'Day before, he told me he was stopping the crime. I figured it was a new year's resolution, some shit like that. But he said to me, "Sis, I'm onto something big. This thing will earn us a packet."'

'Did he tell you what the thing was?'

'Nah, he said it was a secret. It was better if I didn't find out. He was acting all secretive. I just left him to it. I wish I'd paid more attention.'

'Mani mentioned a witness who saw your brother getting chased?'

Patience kissed her teeth again. 'Trust me, that story's full of holes.'

'OK,' I said, 'I'm hoping you told this to the police? Even if you don't trust them, this is still a live investigation.'

She hesitated, looked again at Mani.

'Go on,' Mani said, 'show Kasper, Pat.'

Patience looked at the floor. Beneath the bench was a small Lonsdale bag, zipped up. I hadn't noticed it until now. She pulled it out, placed it beside her on the bench.

'If you see what's in that,' she said, 'you can't un-see it. Get me?'

When Mani said Patience had discovered something, I assumed it had been information, or a hunch. Not hard evidence.

I wondered if the bag contained drugs, maybe weapons. It wouldn't be the first time a kid got killed for nicking off big leaguers. And if that was the case, it should all go straight to the authorities, no question.

'What's in there?' I said.

Before opening the bag, Patience rose from the bench and walked to the door, bolting the top lock, the bottom one, checking we couldn't be interrupted. Then she came back, unzipped it.

I looked at Mani. He'd started rubbing the crucifix around his neck.

Patience reached in, removed a small item wrapped in a sweat towel and placed it on the bench. Carefully, she pulled the towel away.

It wasn't drugs or weapons, or anything like that.

It was a digital camcorder. Slick, handheld, not top end, but a fairly decent one from the looks of it.

'I found this in Kwame's drawer,' she said, 'along with this.'

She handed me a scrunched piece of paper. I flattened it, read the clumsy, heavily scrawled capitals:

HEY SIS

IF SOMETHING HAPPENS TO ME, DESTROY THIS
THING.

LOVE U

KWAME

I handed her back the note, pointed at the camcorder. 'But you didn't destroy it.'

She shook her head.

'It's stolen?'

'What do you think?'

'I think it is.'

The changing room wasn't steamy anymore. A draft was cutting through the air, and I felt a vague foreboding that came with it. If I'd paid attention to it, maybe I'd have made my excuses and left right then.

But I didn't.

'Go on,' Mani said, 'let Kasper see what's recorded on that thing.'

I looked at him, her, and the camcorder again. 'There's a home movie on it?'

'Yeah,' she said.

'Something to send to *You've Been Framed*, right?'

She shook her head. 'I ain't never watched no home movie like this. See what you think.'

She removed a laptop from the bag, booted it up, looked at Mani.

'Kill the lights,' she said.

Chapter 2

It took a moment for my eyes to adjust to the darkness in the changing room. Patience's laptop screen shone like a beacon; the only illumination in the space.

She removed an SD card from the camcorder and inserted it into a side port of the laptop, tapped a few buttons, turned it on the bench so it was facing me. Then she stood against the wall, facing me too. Mani followed suit. Now, neither could see what I could. It was just me and the screen.

'You're not watching?' I said.

'Already seen it,' Patience said.

'Same,' Mani said.

'Hit play when you're ready,' she said.

I moved the cursor, pressed the button. The screen flickered to life.

The first shot was blank fuzziness for maybe ten seconds. Then a director's clapboard appeared. **RED ROSE PRODUCTIONS** was chalked in capital letters on it, along with the date, **JANUARY 1**ST – six days ago.

'Action,' said a man off camera, and the board snapped shut.

First, there was a close-up shot of velvet fabric. I could hear

15

breathing, and a light gargling sound like a garden water feature.

Then the frame panned back, slowly revealing the velvet to be drapes, hung floor to ceiling. It had the feel of art-house cinema, like the kind of Derek Jarman stuff my landlady, Dr Steiner, sometimes goes in for: the light crisp, the focus steady, the silences stretched. I was about to say as much when the shot glided right, revealing the woman.

She was lying on a double bed. A blanket covered her to the shoulders. She was smiling a loose, languorous kind of smile, and looking directly at the camera.

'You brought me here to see a porno?' I said, towards Patience and Mani.

'Just watch,' Patience said.

The woman had dimply cheeks and muddy brown hair; dark red lipstick was lacquered to her mouth, and large hoop earrings hung from her ears, their stones distinctive, refracting the light in spears of green.

The focus stayed with her, the camera moving slowly, seductively around the contours of her concealed body. Her limbs appeared to be splayed out beneath the blankets in an X-shape. She kept the smile, her eyelids half-mast, like a cartoon dog's, with dim, crepuscular pupils.

Another minute or so passed in this way. The gargling in the background continued.

Then a second figure appeared from the left and stopped by the bed. He was head-to-toe in black – black bovver boots, black combats, a tight black long-sleeve and a black latex stocking over his head containing slits for eyes and a wider hole for the mouth. This was a very big man, tall, thick, broad-shouldered, his trunk-like arms folded across his barrel chest.

'Hello, Mandy,' said a voice off camera, male, middle-English, confident. 'We're delighted to have you in our first Red Rose film of the new year. Are you well?'

The woman nodded, the earrings sparkling as she moved her head. 'I'm fine,' she said, her accent strong, East European. 'We're filming now, yes?'

'We are. Please try not to swear.'

She giggled. 'I'm a little nervous.'

'Relax. You're doing brilliantly. Tell us a bit about yourself.'

She said she was seventeen, a good ten years off, and that she was born and raised in Buckingham to a 'nice English family'; all corny crap, definitely scripted.

'And what do you do for a living?'

'I'm a working girl. And an adult film actress.'

'Well, isn't that astonishing. Would you mind telling us what life is like for a girl in this trade?'

More giggling, which led her into a meandering account of her sex life: a few bondage interests, things she enjoyed with toys, nothing kinkier. While she spoke, the big man remained mute, staring down at her.

The film made me uncomfortable. Like with a lot of smut, there was a fakery to it, and the presence of Mani and Patience watching me watching it seemed to magnify this feeling.

In a different context I'd have switched off already. But I reminded myself that the camcorder was in the possession of a kid who got murdered. Like it or not, I was seeing this to the end.

'It's hot in here,' the voice off camera said.

'Yes,' the woman – Mandy – replied. 'Too warm.'

The big man sprang to life. He leaned over, took the blanket in both hands, and in one deft movement, he whisked it from her body.

'Ah,' the voice said, 'there you are.'

There, indeed. She was naked, her ankles and wrists strapped to the bedrails with wire cord, rendering her prone. She wasn't svelte or shaved like your typical sex model; hers was a lived-in body, legs on the heavier side, her belly a marsupial pouch. Her left breast was slightly bigger than the right, the areolas large, walnut coloured. There were nicks and bruises on her arms and legs. From a distance, they looked like track marks.

Despite this exposure, she seemed unperturbed. Clearly, this wasn't the first time she'd bared all.

'Am I meant to say anything now?' she said. 'Or do we just, you know, do it?'

'Such haste!' the voice said. 'Let's talk a bit more. There's no rush. Once we start, we may get carried away.'

The big man grunted, his first sound.

'We're going to have some fun,' she said, looking up him. 'I've been a bad girl.'

He grunted again.

'Yes,' the voice hissed, 'I think you have been bad. In fact, you've been a stupid whore, haven't you, Mandy?'

For a moment, her eyes wavered to the camera, and the person behind it. 'That wasn't in the script—'

'Shh,' he cut in, the voice light, playful. 'I'm just improvising.'

'Oh,' she said, a little uncertainly. 'Could you ask him to loosen the wires, please. My wrists are starting to hurt.'

'I'm afraid not.'

'Why?'

'Because you might misbehave. Let's take a closer look at you.'

Footsteps clicked from off camera, and then someone else appeared, another male, strolling towards the bed. The focus zoomed in on him.

Like the big man, he was dressed in black – black boots,

trousers, long-sleeve shirt, and the same black mask with three slits — yet physically, the two were opposites. He was lean and wiry, carrying the graceful movements and ectomorphic strength of a matador. In his right hand he carried a single red rose.

He came around the bed, stopping next to the bigger man who towered above. The improbable pair stood together, gazing down at this naked woman.

Slowly, the small man leaned over her face, so close their brows almost touched. I thought he was about to kiss her.

'Poor girl,' he said, his clipped voice identifying him as the man off camera.

My pulse rose, and my mouth tasted gummy.

He placed the rose next to her head. Then he cupped her breasts, one in each hand.

'Your fingers are cold,' she said.

He didn't answer, just slid upwards, stroking her neck, before finding her cheeks, her hair, finally her ears. It was like watching a conductor weave out the gentlest melody, a prelude for the climax. With immense tenderness, he held her earrings.

'No,' I said in a gasp, and realised I'd been holding my breath. 'Something's wrong.'

Too late.

'Do it,' the big man said, a gruff, expressionless voice.

'Do what?' the woman said, giggling again.

'Relax, Mandy,' the small man said. 'This may feel a little funny.'

She stared up.

He turned to the camera. Electricity crackled in his eyes.

Then, with a swift sharp recoil of both hands, he tore the hoop earrings through the flesh of her earlobes, and she started screaming.

★

That screaming would go on for five and a half of the longest minutes I've endured.

As the woman's ears gushed red, she writhed and gyrated, making the bed frame clang and thud on the floor. But it was useless. She was bound.

The small man stepped back, holding the earrings up to the camera, speaking to the big man, their words inaudible over the din.

The big man nodded and took over, pushing her torso down with one hand, slapping her face with the other. As she stared aghast, the small man reached off camera and came back with tools that he handed to the big man – a blunt mallet, followed by a cricket bat, then an iron – all experimented with, one by one.

'Jesus Christ,' I said.

Thwack!

She howled. Although repulsed, I couldn't take my eyes off the screen.

Thwack!

I could smell the rust of blood, the sweat, the wretched tang of terror. The big man's body throbbed.

Thwack!

Her eyes bulged manically, fury and fear scoring her bloodied face. The small man kept talking, giving instructions, his lips thin and red, smiling through his mask.

I tried to protect myself, separating from what I was seeing, retreating into my mind. But the sound clawed me back, reaching inside me and reverberating under my skin.

Eventually, she began to ebb. Shock, exhaustion, the damage taking hold. Her chest hissed. Pink bubbles blew from her nostrils. A milky caul glazed her eyes.

The big man stepped back, tired too, his shirt damp. He rubbed his slick hands together, like a carpenter after a day's work.

To the camera, the small man said: 'Well, I don't think Mandy will be misbehaving anymore. But in Red Rose tradition, we must be sure.'

He put the earrings into his pocket. Then he reached off camera and returned holding a kitchen knife, small and triangular, the kind used for slicing root vegetables. He gave it to the big man.

At the glint of metal, the woman's eyes refocused. A pall fell over her expression. She tried to speak, but the fight was over.

'Goodnight, Mandy.'

The big man put the knife to her throat, and cut.

It felt like I'd been punched in the heart.

Her neck opened like a grin and her limbs grew taut, the right foot quivering, a final paroxysm. Then she was still.

The big man rubbed the knife clean with a hanky.

'Thanks for watching,' the small man said. 'Wishing you a happy new year. See you next time.'

The picture fizzled out.

Silence.

I took a moment, waited for my breathing to settle.

It wouldn't.

Through the gloom I looked up, breathing through my mouth.

The whites of Mani's wide eyes were visible. 'Told you it was messed up,' he said.

Patience was staring too, her pupils aimed at me like arrow-tips. 'Well?'

'Well, what?' I said back.

'That was real, right?'

'I don't know what that was. But I'm pretty sure my life hasn't been enriched from seeing it.' I tried to keep my voice normal, but it wavered, and my breath kept juddering out.

'C'mon,' Patience said, 'they killed that girl.'

'You can't make calls like that,' I said, trying to sound convincing. 'Special effects, CGI – they're convincing. All sorts can be done these days, trust me.'

She shook her head. 'Trust me, *that* was a murder.'

I didn't know how to respond.

'Can you put the lights back on?' I said.

Mani walked over, flicked the switch. The changing room flooded with lurid brightness. I blinked a few seconds as my eyes adjusted, and then looked around.

Everything was the same as before: Mani, Patience, the changing room.

But something was irretrievably changed.

I looked at Patience. 'OK,' I said, 'let's agree for a moment that film *was* real. How do you think your brother's death is related to it?'

'Simple. Kwame stole this thing, and those two men killed him.'

'Explain how you got there.'

She stepped forward and lifted the camcorder. 'There's only the one film on the memory card. According to the digital display, it was made on New Year's Day just after one in the morning. You heard the man at the end, wishing us a happy new year.'

'So?'

'So, Kwame got killed January third, two nights later. What if he nicked this thing, saw what was on it, and figured he'd blackmail that pair.'

'Does that sound like the sort of thing your brother would do?'

'He was dumb enough to try it. Like I told you, those last couple of days he was nonstop about his secret moneymaking idea. He knew this thing was hot, that's why he wrote me the note. And he was right. It was hot enough to get him killed. Don't tell me that's all coincidence, man.'

She had a point. But I didn't want to say this aloud. Right then I didn't know what I was thinking. The film – real or not – had left a pretty deep impression. I could've done with some time to take stock.

'Kasper,' Mani said, his voice tight.

I looked over. He resembled a soldier who'd never come back from the trenches.

'Now I know why you've had a face on you all night,' I said.

He nodded. 'You ever seen anything like that before?'

I took a moment. 'Executions and fatal accidents caught on film, yes. But nothing—' I was finding it hard to pick my words, '—nothing that *staged*.'

'Is there a name for these kinds of films?'

'When I was a kid, they used to call them snuffs. I guess that's what it could be.'

'Snuffs,' Patience said. 'Isn't that something rich people smoke?'

'The term's got more than one use. They feature real-life killings. Before the internet, there used to be a few dodgy ones on VHS doing the rounds. And when I was a copper, I heard about a few more seized from fetish pornographers that looked like the real deal. But forensics always proved the killings were faked, made for the shock value. That's why you need to hold fire on making claims about this. Hopefully it's fake, too. To be honest, I figured snuffs were a dying trend.'

'Well, someone's still interested,' Mani said.

'For real,' Patience said. 'So what happens now? It's clear you don't wanna help. Any tips, Mr ex-copper?'

'Yeah,' I said. 'How about taking your brother's advice and destroying that thing?'

'Screw you,' she said, her voice high with indignation. 'It's the only lead I got on whoever killed him.'

'Then go to the police. Give them that camcorder, the letter, tell them what you told me. They could run tests, get forensics. You never know, there might be fingerprints, DNA, ways to link that thing to—'

'No police,' she broke in. 'I'll sort this out myself.'

She meant it too. Her hatred for the London Met ran deep, and no amount of persuading was going to change that.

'Just make some enquiries, Kasper,' Mani said. 'You're good at that kinda thing.'

'Enquiries about what? Who killed Kwame? Or who made that film? They might be two separate things.'

'They're not,' Patience said.

'You're an investigator,' Mani said, 'so investigate. You know what's right and what's fishy.'

'Fishy?' I shook my head. 'I wouldn't know where to start on a job like this. And just say it *did* turn out the film is real and there *is* a connection with it and what happened to Kwame, what then?'

'What do you think?' Patience said. 'Find those men and kill them.'

There it was: good, old-fashioned revenge. An eye for an eye. Blood for blood.

And for me, the final straw.

'Sorry,' I said to Mani. 'I'm off. Thanks for a memorable night.'

I got to my feet, marched to the door, unbolted the lock.

Mani called after me, but I wasn't interested. Right then I wanted to get out of that changing room and as far away from this whole nasty business as I could get.

I stepped into the hall. Cold air blustered against my face.

'Please, Kasper!' Patience cried. 'Those two bastards killed that woman, and my brother. They'll do it again, too. You know it!'

The small man's voice from the film repeated in my head:

'See you next time . . .'

I looked back.

Patience was sitting on the bench, slumped over her knees, head bowed, eyes tightly shut, mouth corkscrewed, holding the emotion in, but only just.

I stepped back in, closed the door with my heel.

'*Three* bastards,' I said, and moved towards them both.

She opened her eyes. They were bloodshot. 'Huh?'

'Someone else was there, Patience. Operating the camcorder. You could tell from the way the picture moved when the small man appeared, and the way it cut at the end.'

She and Mani exchanged looks. They hadn't thought of this.

I rubbed my brow. I wasn't getting out of this as easily as I hoped.

'OK,' I said.

'OK what?' Mani said.

'I'll have a snoop, see what turns up.'

'Thanks, man.'

'But understand, I'm no avenging angel.'

'Got it.'

'Now let's talk money.'

No one spoke.

'What, you think I work for free?'

'I can give you this,' Patience said, and reached into her bag, pulled out her trophy from tonight's win. 'When I get my next dole money, that's yours too.'

I looked at the trophy. It was small, plastic, made of tin, and would've got five quid at a push at Cash Converters. 'This is getting better and better.' I shook my head. 'Keep your money and your trophy. We'll call this *pro bono*.'

'What's that mean?'

'It means I'm a mug.' I breathed deeply. 'You've got one day for free.'

'That all?'

I couldn't help smiling. 'At the rate I'm giving you, I don't think you're in the position to haggle. Tomorrow, I'll make enquiries. I'll report back in the evening, and you can decide what to do. That's the best I can offer. I've got my own problems too. Take it or leave it.'

She looked at Mani. He nodded.

'You're on,' she said.

'Good.'

'Anything else you need to know?' Mani said.

'This witness,' I said, 'the one who saw Kwame getting chased.'

'What about him?' Patience said.

'You said his statement's full of holes. How'd you know this?'

She scowled. 'The man's a lying, lowlife criminal. He runs the café down by the cemetery. The place is a front for drug dealing.'

'He's not Terry Kinsella, by any chance?'

'You know him?' Mani said.

'In a manner of speaking.' I thought back to my policing days, the last time I crossed paths with Terry, and what a constitutionally dishonest creep he'd been back then. Leopards and spots came to mind. 'OK,' I said, 'that's useful to know.' I pointed at the camcorder. 'Can I take that? Might be useful.'

Without a word, Patience placed it in the gym bag and handed it over.

'OK,' I said, tossing the bag over my shoulder, shaking her hand again. There wasn't much else to say. 'Talk tomorrow, Patience.'

Mani and I left the community hall together and headed through the car park where he'd left his tatty old Astra.

It was a harsh night, the kind in January that demands your attention. I was wearing the warmest thing I owned, my late father's black leather jacket, quilted inside and with a shearling collar. Even so, the cold cut through.

Mani bought us a couple of instant coffees from a popup stand, and I loaded mine with UHT and sugar. We leaned by the gate, and he sparked a Marlboro.

'Sorry about all that,' he said, breathing out a cloud.

'You should be,' I said. 'Getting me here on false pretences was a shoddy move.'

'You're entitled to be pissed off with me. But Kwame's murder . . . seeing that film . . .' He drew heavily on the smoke. 'I had to do something, Kasper. And if I'd told you what to expect, you wouldn't have come.'

'It would've been nice to have had the choice, mate.'

Mani looked at the gym-bag, inside of which was the camcorder. 'You think that film's real, don't you? Admit it.'

'I hope it isn't,' I said. 'That's all I'm admitting.'

Mani nodded. 'Look, I appreciate you agreeing to this, especially now. You've not been having the best time with your business and personal life. Plus, you're coming up to the anniversary of your girl's death, right?'

'What's your point?' I said, a little sharper than intended.

'My point is, maybe this job will give you a bit of focus, help you get through a crappy time of year.'

'That's really considerate of you,' I said, no attempt to mask my sarcasm.

'I'm just saying—'

'I'm just saying, drop it. You got me out tonight, paired me and Patience knowing damn well we'd both struggle saying no to the other. That's a sneaky move, especially from a man of God.'

Rather than answer, he blew out another plume, then stubbed the butt on the ground.

'C'mon,' he said. 'Let's get out this cold.'

Soon as we were inside the Astra, Mani fired the engine. Hot air pumped from the vents, and light gospel came from the speakers. A photo of Mani's wife and kids was tacked to the dash, each of them dressed to the nines in Sunday bests.

Mani placed his coffee beside the photo and sparked a fresh Marlboro. I shoved the bag containing the camcorder between my legs and drank some coffee. Little granules hadn't dissolved properly. It tasted lumpy and bitter.

'You need any help tomorrow?' Mani said.

'No.'

'Yeah, I'd probably cramp your style. And I'm not expecting no miracles neither.'

'Phew.'

'But I meant what I said back there.'

I looked over at him.

'You got a talent for this kind of thing.'

'Snuff films are a little bit outside of my expertise. And working for free definitely isn't my bag.'

'Yeah, well,' he said, taking in smoke, 'you got into this line of work for more than just the money. Don't pretend different.'

I shook my head. 'I'm strictly business. And after tomorrow

I'm out unless Patience can pay me my daily rate plus expenses. I'm not running a charity.'

Neither of us spoke. I finished my coffee; Mani smoked his cigarette.

Then he lowered the window, flicked out the butt. Sparks danced on the pavement, then vanished in the darkness.

'I'll drive you home,' he said, and pushed into first gear.

'Cheers,' I said. 'Don't know about you, but I could use a hot shower.'

Chapter 3

I slept poorly.

Each time I shut my eyes the images from the film resurfaced, of dimply skin, red roses, hoop earrings and necks sliced open, the whole lot bleeding together into a Rorschach. I found myself in the film-set, locked under the lens watching the whole thing on repeat, there with the two masked men and the woman bound to the bedframe.

The feeling of enclosure was stifling, like the walls were closing in. But the sounds were the worst. The punches, blows and gargles, the thud of the bedframe as the woman writhed like an electrocuted cat; the calm voice from the small man as he pondered which tool to use next on her, and her screams as the big man then pulped and beat her with it – these and a barrage more assaulted the inside of my skull like a jackhammer left on in a bank vault.

Around five a.m., I got up. My loft room was dark, the predawn casting only a wispy grey light, and the cold was relenting. I turned on the bedside lamp and looked around.

Patience's sports bag was by the door. I didn't want to think about the camcorder inside it. Right then, I didn't want to think about any of this.

31

Unsure what to do, but needing to do something, I pulled on some joggers and a long-sleeve, and headed out, running laps around the wetlands beneath the raggy clouds, stopping to pound out push-ups on the ice crusted lawns. By lap four, thin rays of light were beginning to cut through the sky. My chest was raw, pulse racing, the intensity good, enough to distract me from my head.

Back home, I showered, dressed and by seven was in the kitchen brewing coffee.

My landlady, Dr Steiner, was a late riser, and I could hear light snores from her room. Today was her sixty-eighth birthday, and half a dozen cards had arrived for her. I considered bringing them to her along with her coffee and today's *Guardian*, but decided to let her sleep in. That evening she had a gathering planned. I'd see her then.

To be honest, an encounter with Dr Steiner didn't fill me with glee. Although cancer had curtailed her career as a psychiatrist, she remained a shrewd reader of human beings, and would know in an instant that all was not well. If I told her about the snuff film and what I'd agreed to do, she'd suggest that getting involved was a bad idea; she'd say I should hand everything to the police and be done with it.

And she'd probably be right.

I had a quick breakfast with Tommy, her pointer-cross puppy, lobbing him a bacon rasher as I scrolled through today's online *Gazette*.

Within minutes of reading, I'd lost my hunger.

Pages one and two described an ongoing trial of two north London policemen charged with circulating crime scene photos for salacious pleasure. I flicked to the sports pages instead, hoping to be cheered up by Spurs' latest good fortunes. No such luck.

The club was floundering, with rumors of financial mismanagement doing the rounds.

In the job section, an ad caught my attention. The security enforcer post was nightclub bouncing dressed up to sound fancy, but given my meagre finances and CV, I couldn't afford to be fussy.

I poured a second coffee and emailed the firm an expression of interest. After hitting send, I sat back and looked at Tommy, who was studying my leftovers studiously. I slid him the plate.

As he devoured them, I thought about my plan for the day. Realising I didn't have one, I went upstairs, booted up my laptop, took a moment to get my head into gear, and then watched the film from start to finish, trying to stay objective, and not get pulled into the savagery.

Impossible.

A second dose didn't give away any fresh clues, but reinforced how choreographed, how thought out, how finely executed the whole thing was. These men weren't amateurs. They were skilled. Skills like these only come about through experience.

And right at the end, the small man's closing line: 'See you next time.'

Next time.

It could be a fake. That was what I'd told Mani and Patience last night. And that was the assumption I should've been working with.

But Mani was right. Already, I knew in my heart what this was. Out there at that very moment, the men responsible for this monstrosity were roaming.

Killers. That tiny percentage of the population who'd crossed that irreversible line. I'd encountered my fair share of lowlifes, gangsters, and volatile criminals who needed to be kept away.

But murderers, who pre-meditated and orchestrated their crime, were something quite alien.

I started the film again. When the woman's face came into view, I hit pause, then zoomed in as close as possible before the pixelation blurred.

With a bit of experimentation, I was able to capture a decent enough headshot of her on my phone's camera. Even though the two men's faces were hidden behind masks, I did the same for them. Then I closed the laptop and considered where to begin.

I had no idea where the camcorder was stolen from. The two murderers were masked and unidentifiable.

I had a possible name for the woman – Mandy – and she said she was a sex worker. But that wasn't much to go on. London was a big city. Women in this line worked all over. How could I narrow it down?

Paradise Estate. Kwame Mensah was murdered there. Terry Kinsella, the witness, had his café there. And the place was a haunt for vice, as I well knew.

As much as the prospect didn't fill me with glee, that's where I had to go.

I buttoned my leather and wheeled my bike out the house. With the morning sky now a dappling grey and the headwind pushing hard, I pedalled away from the leafy house I lived in as a middle-ager, and back towards my roots.

Believe it or not, back in the fifties when Paradise Estate was first built, it was a sought-after place to live. A sprawling post-Blitz housing project spanning an impressive mile-and-a-half squared, Paradise was capable of housing ten thousand plus, and was considered a modernist and radical solution to condensed social living, complete with a shopping parade, a pub, a primary school, even a cemetery.

And from a distance, the silhouette of the blocks and ziggurats still looked attractive, if your tastes ran to the more utilitarian edges of architecture. Then again, if you're far enough away, they say a nuclear bomb looks kind of attractive too.

As I pedalled past the south entrance towards the stark tower-blocks, townhouses and flats, I felt a cold run through me that came from more than the time of year. Putrid greys and margarine beiges made up the cladding of these once austere buildings. The thin daylight magnified their decline, spotlighting the poverty, neglect, drawing out the fetid litter and blocked drain smells.

The looming towers and blocks cast sweeping shadows, and I could feel the anger corralled within each building. Flat after flat, sheet metal on some windows, chipboard over others, padlocks on the doors; smashed glass, mulchy cardboard, soiled mattresses, shopping trolleys, abandoned white-goods and splintering chipboard dumped out in porches; cider and beer cans, discarded contraceptives, drugs paraphernalia, even a few budget Christmas decorations were strewn across the paving, sodden in the new-year cold.

Following my mother's untimely death when I was a baby, my father moved us to Paradise for a fresh start. Dad was a misanthropic Pole who'd escaped the Warsaw ghetto as a kid, and he did his best to instil in me the same survivor instincts that had kept him alive. But on Paradise, raising a kid was a different kind of struggle to those he had endured; and after a group of older boys decided to take out their sadism and boredom on me, aged seven, he decided to relocate us again, to stay with his brother out east, where we remained.

Years later, as a headstrong copper, my vocation drew me back to Paradise. By then, the estate had become synonymous with vice, gangs, drugs, illegal immigrants, stabbings, shootings and unhappy endings; the local school had been forcibly closed after several damning Ofsted reports, and the cemetery, empty in my childhood, was hemmed with tenants gone before their time, and had seen countless funerals, including my father's.

Officially, the role of the police was to work with communities to reduce crime and disorder; but our unspoken remit was more about containment, keeping the undesirables within the perimeter of the estate where they'd be out of sight and mind, and preventing any spillages into the rest of the borough.

My departure from policing should've severed any ties with the estate once and for all. But Paradise is like a scab – try as I did to ignore it, I couldn't help picking.

In recent years, my reasons for returning were of a more personal nature. Paradise was a red-light zone, and although seeing prostitutes wasn't a habit I was comfortable with, since my daughter's death, these encounters had helped me through many a tough night. At an hourly rate, I'd breathe the same air as an anonymous woman, and feel something other than my own emptiness.

If the internet dating caught on or I patched things up with my ex, Diane, I'd like to think this habit would cease. Till then it was a go-to, and about all the intimacy I could handle.

As I came to the midpoint of the estate, I dismounted my bike and proceeded on foot. The sky was spitting, keeping most of the locals indoors, but before long the first faces emerged, hunched pensioners, single mums pushing buggies, a couple of raggedy working girls, plus the pre-requisite addict types and squatters, all wearing get out my way expressions. None stopped to chat.

Further in, I spotted a phalanx of teenage boys: six or seven of them stood in the doorway of a block. Their puppy-fat faces defied their predatory eyes.

Despite the inhospitality, I persevered, approaching maybe a dozen people. I used the same line, asking if they'd known a kid called Kwame Mensah, and flashed his mug-shot photo on my phone.

No surprises. The same stony silence met me each time: an elderly Caribbean gent feigned deafness before shuffling off; an overweight woman on a mobility scooter made out she didn't speak English and flagged me away; a scrawny male, riven with scars, seemed convinced I was a dealer until I gave him one of my business cards. The rest just blanked me or told me where to go.

Before long, I was at the spot where Kwame had been stabbed, an alleyway situated at the right corner of an open-plan square, nestled between two walls, sealed at one end by a wheelie-bin.

Normally there'd be flowers or photos or trinkets marking the scene of a death, especially one so recent, and where the victim was young.

Nothing like that here – just a cut of police tape stuck to the gum-pasted paving, flapping like a kite tail in the wind.

A rat appeared over the rim of the wheelie bin, sniffed around, then plunged its upper body into the open lid amongst the litter. Only its hind legs and tail showed, flickering back and forth.

It dawned on me that kids like Kwame had the odds against them from the word go. Some might claim he made poor choices, that he needed better role models, self-discipline.

Bollocks. Truth was, if my father had kept us living in Paradise,

I'm pretty sure I'd have gone down the crime route. And with a temper like mine, maybe I'd have gotten jacked with a knife down some rat-infested alley too.

I tried picturing the night of Kwame's death. It would've been dark, for there were no streetlights round here. The alley where he fell was thin, narrow. Why stab him there? Had he been hiding? Or had his killer been talking to him, and then stuck a blade in by surprise?

I thought about the witness – Terry Kinsella.

As a kid, I'd known Terry's stalwart mum. Irene Kinsella, a hardy Dubliner and the proprietor of Kinsella's Café, was a woman who went the extra mile for those in need, but took no shit from those trying it on. Something of a legend around the estate for her indomitable personality, generosity, not to mention her artery-blocking fry-ups, Terry, her only child, was undoubt-edly a disappointment, for apart from their surname, the two appeared to have little in common.

Back when I was a rookie copper, Terry was a cowardly crook, a grass and an informer, a degenerate, a peddler, and a sycophant. Paradise produced its fair share of criminals, but Terry was a con-stitutionally immoral villain who took slime to a new level, the kind who'd rob a granny's pension book, then invite himself over for tea to help her look for it.

Following Irene's death, Terry took over the café, and it soon became a base for drug dealing, money laundering, and all manner of dodgy dealings. Several times there'd been plans to raid his premises, but surprise-surprise, they never materialised, and everyone on the force all knew why – if Terry was feeding Paradise's locals a steady supply of narcotics, there was less chance of them venturing off the estate and causing a real headache for the outside world.

A reunion with Terry wasn't an alluring prospect. But short of other ideas, and quite fancying a cuppa, I decided to head to the café and find out what he knew.

Kinsella's Café was situated in the north fringes of Paradise, fifty yards to the right of the cemetery.

The parade of shops hadn't changed – a chicken shop, a convenience store, an offy, a bookie, a launderette, and the café. I passed two boys, six or seven, playing with toy guns while a woman, presumably their mum, stood in the launderette and watched forlornly.

I couldn't see any lights on inside the cafe, but music was playing – Artic Monkeys' first album. Wheeling my bike, I walked towards the entrance. A man and a woman emerged, both pale, skittish, gaunt. Drug addicts, no question.

'Terry about?' I said.

They stared at me, my bike, then back at me. 'He's in there,' the woman said. 'Upstairs.'

'Want us to mind your bike?' said the man.

I thanked him for the offer, told him he was fine, and went in.

The café layout was a far cry from Irene Kinsella's bustling days. There were no staff members, and the only customers were two men at a window table, both nursing cups of grey tea, their pallor matching their drinks. Druggy types too, with flat expressions, flatter eyes, no doubt awaiting a score from Terry.

Clustered around the cracked lino flooring were cheap plastic chairs and Formica tables, the surface splayed with tubs of gloopy red and brown sauce and bowls of crusty sugar. The reek of recycled fat cloyed in the warm, still air.

The toilets were to the left, with an **OUT OF ORDER** sign pinned to the door. If memory served right, those toilets had been out of order last time I'd been here, a good half decade back. To the right there was an open-plan kitchen, where Irene's famous fries used to get cooked. Leaning on the counter was a blackboard with the café's menu chalked on: meagre combinations of cooked breakfast items, lasagnes, curries and bologneses, everything served with chips.

I gave the two men a nod. One was stocky, his face lopsided by a zigzag scar. His mate, shorter, scrawnier, wore a rusty red beard, had blackened teeth and a long, weasel chin.

I leaned my bike by the door and wandered through. The once florally decorated café was sparsely furnished, the walls flaking, windows smeary, a limp light buzzing overhead. The only things to look at were the mishmash of framed Polaroids hanging from the crumbly plasterwork, Terry's 'wall of fame' as I once heard it described. The photos were pitiful, a pastiche of Terry's delusions of grandeur, showing him with minor celebs who must've fallen badly off the beaten track to end up in this ropey café. In each, he was clinging to the individual, an obsequious grin slathered across his face. I was staring at one of these snaps when the main man pushed through another door marked **STAFF ONLY** accompanied by a cloud of cannabis smoke.

'Here you are, lads,' he said to the two men, holding a couple of tiny, cling-filmed parcels in his palm. Then his eyes shot to me. Immediately, the bags of drugs vanished into his jeans pocket.

'Terry,' I said. 'Remember me?'

He had a face like a stubbed cigar, with a flat wedged nose, glazed stupid eyes, heavy grey stubble, and hair – what little remained – that receded back in a flimsy, oatmeal barb. He'd bloated even more than I remembered, most of it around his midriff, where fat swelled through his stained t-shirt and rippled over the hem of his jeans like bread dough.

He squinted at me, pulled on a smeary pair of specs, and recognition kicked in. 'PC Kasper,' he said, the voice a grizzly husk. 'As I live an' breathe. You plain clothes now?'

I shook my head. 'I left the police a few years back.'

'That so?' He grinned yellowly and looked past me at the two men. 'Boys, this fella was one of the only decent coppers out there. Back when we was kids, he used to carry me mam's shopping home for her. A good egg.'

I smiled at the two men. They stared balefully.

'So how's business?' I said. 'Judging by the photos hanging up, you've got a few well-off customers dropping by.'

He shrugged. 'If only. Trade's worse, and getting worser.'

'Can't think why. But you were always resourceful, with your fingers in a few pies, not to mention a bit of contraband in your trouser pocket. Know what I mean?'

'Haven't a clue.' He smirked. 'Anyway, if you aren't a copper no more, what is this, a social visit?'

'Kind of. I'm gasping for a brew. But I also wanted to ask a question or two.'

'About what?'

'Kwame Mensah.'

'Who?'

I repeated the name. 'He's the boy who got stabbed on Monday.' I held up my phone, and the photo of Kwame from the newspaper. 'That's him. I gather you may've witnessed something?'

Terry stared at the photo. He took a bruised roll-up perched behind his ear and lit it. 'What's your interest?' he said, smoke spraying from his nostrils.

'I'm working as a private investigator these days. Been asked to have a look.'

'Who by?'

'Kwame's big sister.'

Terry had another hit of smoke, looked at the photo again, then me. 'Said you wanted a brew, didn't you, Kasper?'

The banter had ended. Now, Terry was tetchy.

'A brew sounds good,' I said, realising this wasn't going to be straightforward.

'Pound fifty.'

He waddled to the kitchen. I followed. Behind me, the two men's eyes felt like knives stabbing my back.

'Don't know what to tell you,' Terry said, removing a couple of mugs from the sink, inspecting them. 'I've tried to put that night out my memory. It's upsettin', you know.'

'Sure,' I said, 'but give it a go.'

He shook his head. 'Maybe it's not the best idea you coming here, dredging up nasty stuff. You're not old bill. You're just Joe Public, like me.'

'Indeed I am,' I said. 'But this Joe's got plenty friends on the Met. It wouldn't take long for them to rock up here. And given that cloud of skunk that accompanied you earlier, not to mention the two bags of gear you pocketed when I came in, my guess, they'd find more than just bacon and burgers upstairs.'

In truth, I hadn't many mates left with the police, and getting them to zip over to Kinsella's Café to snoop around for drugs would be quite a feat, as Terry well knew.

His rubbery lips thinned, and his eyes narrowed. 'Police wouldn't bother comin', Kasper. You know as well as me. What happens in Paradise stays here.'

'Maybe,' I said. 'But are you willing to risk it? Surely it'd be easier just to tell me what you remember, then I'll disappear.'

After a long minute, he said, 'It's like what I said in my witness statement.'

'Repeat that to me.'

He plonked teabags into the mugs with the finesse of a bin man lobbing sacks. 'I seen the kid get chased by a bunch of other kids. They all bolted down an alley an' stuck him. A pack of hyenas, they were.'

He poured hot water from an urn into the mugs, dolloped in milk and slid one over, the teabag sloshing in the beige liquid like a drowned corpse. I placed some coins on the counter.

'What were they like,' I said, 'these kids?'

'Young.' Terry took the coins, counted them. 'With big, fuck-off knives. That boy musta been into some bad stuff to be chased like that. But you live by the sword, you die by it. Unnerstand?'

I told him I did and drank some tea. It tasted like warm dishwater.

'These hyena boys,' I said. 'Where'd they go after stabbing Kwame?'

Terry reached for the sugar bowl, and started heaping teaspoons into his mug. Six in total. 'Hell should I know? I was hiding, scared outta my wits. You hear stories, of witnesses getting targeted.' He took a loud slurp, then added a seventh teaspoon for good measure.

'You do hear stories,' I said, 'and fair play for coming forward like you did. Your mam would've been proud. A lot of people aren't that brave.'

Terry grinned. 'Just doin' my bit.'

'Where were you hiding?'

The grin quivered. 'What kinda question's that?'

'A reasonable one. See, I've just come from the murder scene.

Apart from the alleyway where Kwame died, it's an open-plan square. Not many spots where a man of your . . . stature could conceal himself.'

Terry looked as if he was working out a sum. When the sum flummoxed him, he withdrew a brown pill bottle from his jeans, twisted the lid, shook some pills out, looked at them. 'Can't remember,' he said.

'Any chance these boys did see you?'

'Nah,' he said, and gobbled what he held, washed down with tea. 'It was pitch dark. No way they noticed me.'

'Had you met Kwame before that night?'

'Never.'

'Did he call out to you? "Help!" or something like that?'

Terry shook his head, cautiously now. 'The kid didn't see me.'

'But you saw him? And the hyenas who murdered him?'

'Course. Where you going with this?'

'It just doesn't add up to me, that's all.'

'What doesn't?' Terry slapped the pill pot on the counter hard enough for a couple to jump out.

'If it was too dark for anyone to notice you, how'd you see the whole thing so clearly? These are young men with keen eyes, and you're an old stoner with thick, grubby specs.'

A rim of sweat gathered around Terry's brow. 'God, you ask a lot of questions. What's this? The French inquisition?'

'Spanish.'

'Huh?'

'Never mind. Sorry, Terry. No big deal.'

I looked at the other two. They hadn't moved.

'Yeah, well,' he said, 'it feels like you're making out I done summat wrong.'

'Have you?'

'What?'

'Done something wrong?'

He shook his head; the sweat was slug-trailing down his temple now. 'I'm just a local businessman. I thought I'd do the right thing by saying what I saw.'

I nodded.

'Look, Kasper, you were always straight with me.' He leaned across the counter. I could smell his musty body odour and fetid breath. 'That boy got killed 'cause of the life he led. Drugs. Knives. Gangs. End of.'

'I wish it was that simple,' I said.

'Huh?'

Sod it, I thought. Let's roll the dice, see what comes up.

'It's possible Kwame got caught up in some heavy stuff and was murdered because of it.'

'What's that mean?'

'The disappearance of a woman.'

I reached for my phone, scrolled to the photos I'd taken from the film, held up the woman's face. 'That's her,' I said. 'She may've gone by the name of Mandy.'

'How do you know that?'

'Because that's what she called herself in a film she's in, in which this duo appear to murder her.' I swiped to the image of the two masked men.

Terry stared at my phone. He was entirely still.

'Never seen any of these people,' he said.

'I never said you had,' I replied, returning the phone to my pocket.

He looked at me. 'Murdered? You're serious?'

'The film could be a fake. But real or not, it's a mystery why Kwame had it stashed away. And I'm wondering if it got him killed.'

I pushed my tea aside and leaned closer to Terry, keeping the two men in my periphery. 'So why don't you cut the crap?' I said. 'And tell me the truth about that night.'

Terry stepped back, held up his hands. 'Look, Kasper, you need to understand something.'

'Enlighten me.'

'First off, you can't go 'round making orders. Second of all, I haven't a clue what you're bleating on about.'

'Really?'

'You think I'm lying about what I seen?'

'I think you are, Terry. Those trotters of yours are covered in grime.'

The chairs scraped behind me. When I turned, the pair were standing.

'Terry,' I said, 'tell these clowns to sit down or else they'll get hurt.'

'What did you call us?' the weasel one said.

I repeated.

'Get him outta here, boys!' Terry yelled. 'There's a coupla free bags in it, you hurt him proper.'

'Last chance to back down,' I said.

No such luck. They approached, one left, one right, both serious. I raised my guard.

Scarface made the first move; a clumsy right.

I stepped back. The punch whistled past harmlessly.

Next, they both lunged, weasel trying a poorly judged rugby tackle, scar face a combination that missed wildly. I dodged both, putting a table between us.

They kept trying, kept missing, and after a minute they were both gasping.

'C'mon!' Terry hissed. 'I want him outta my café!'

When they tried again, I stepped in, barging weasel with my shoulder, and cracking scar face's brow with an elbow. Both stumbled, cascading into chairs. I followed with a jab to each of their jaws, not hard enough to do anything serious, but with sufficient oomph to send them down.

Scar face keeled back and landed star shaped. Weasel crumpled, cross-legged and said 'Ugh'.

I looked at Terry. He'd taken a frying pan from the sink and held it behind his head like a tennis racket. As his hands trembled, bits of lard fell like rubble.

'Come near me,' he yelled, 'an' I'll kill you! I mean it!'

'Oh, Terry,' I said, laughing a little, 'even for you, this is a pretty sorry state.'

'I don't know nothin' about no missing women, I'm telling you!'

His face was beetroot and glossy. Why was he so rattled?

Part of me was itching to see what came out if I really pumped for information. But apart from brute force and lame police threats, I had nothing really to barter with. The threat of calling the police didn't stand up. And if I stayed much longer, more of Terry's pals would turn up, and eventually there'd be someone who meant business.

Besides, I was only doing this investigation for a day, and wasn't getting paid a penny. Best call it quits and report back.

'All right,' I said. 'I'll go. Sorry to have upset you.'

'Yeah,' Terry said, my retreat giving him some balls. 'I am upset. What did you expect? Comin' here, laying down the law! Bloody liberty!'

'Like I said, I'm just trying to help the dead kid's sister get some closure.'

'Well, here's your closure! Come here again, you'll regret it!

I'll be ready, Kasper! And I'll have some proper muscle with me too!'

'Sure, Terry,' I said.

The pair had mostly recovered, and were using furniture to help them stand, groaning as they did, staring at me hatefully.

Terry ignored them. His eyes stayed fixed on me.

I walked back through the café, took my bike, and wheeled it towards the door. 'Nice seeing you,' I said, pushing through.

'Piss off!' he bellowed.

And off I pissed.

Chapter 4

I cycled away from Kinsella's Café, my pulse riding high from the scuffle, and my head full of fresh questions. Why had Terry fobbed off the police about Kwame's murder? Had Kwame been involved in Terry's dealings from his café, and killing him was a way to keep it under wraps? In that case, Terry had to be a suspect for the kid getting knifed, surely?

I rolled with this idea but couldn't make it work. Terry was a lowlife, but he was too puffy and out of shape to go around knifing teens in narrow alleyways. Someone else killed Kwame.

But my biggest bugbear wasn't this. It was Terry's expression. When I told him Kwame's death could be linked to a snuff film and showed him the photos from the film, he didn't turn red or rub his nose like liars do on TV. He just stared.

But he recognised the woman, maybe the men too, and knew more than he'd let on.

I braked abruptly, the tyres screeching. I was getting deeper into this than I'd have liked. My task was to have a one-day snoop and report back this evening. After that, job done.

I checked my watch. Three p.m. Perhaps I should call it quits now? I'd made inroads, certainly more than the police had. And I wasn't getting a penny for my troubles.

But trouble was my business.

Kwame, Terry, and the woman on the film were stuck together, and Paradise was the glue. I wanted to find out why, and needed someone with an ear to the ground.

She answered on the third ring.

'Hello, Dylan.' It was never Kasper, always my first name, spoken with that soft, smoky voice that still held a hint of East European. 'I haven't heard from you in a long time.'

'Hi, Lisa,' I said. 'Are you working?'

'Of course,' she said. 'Paradise's best known working girl.'

'And its finest,' I added. 'I'm nearby. Can I come over?'

'It's early. I'm not ready for business yet.'

'I can hang around.'

She paused. 'For you, I'll make an exception. Half an hour. Give the usual knock at the door. You remember it?'

I told her I did and hung up.

Then I started pedalling in the direction of Lisa's block out on the southern perimeter of Paradise, my heart rate already ticking with anticipation.

Of the dozen or so prostitutes whose numbers I had saved, Lisa tended to be my first choice. Sometimes we did the deed; other times we just chatted, and she let me hold her and we'd nap on the bed till my time was up. With her, it wasn't just physical; OK, that played a part; but there was something about *her* too.

Lisa was older for being on the game, somewhere in her mid-thirties. As far as I was aware she was without a pimp, kids, or addictions to feed. She'd turned tricks on the estate for years: I remember her from back when I was a uniform, her small, curvy body, and those dark, sensuous eyes that were impossible to forget.

She had a past, that much was clear. Her body was riddled with nicks, scars, and several burns where the skin glistened like varnished wood; occasionally, when she dozed off in my arms, she'd wake with a start after a nightmare caught her.

Yet she wasn't worn and weather-beaten by trauma; she retained a quiet intelligence and dark humour that captured me in ways I couldn't untangle.

Lisa was also a mainstay of Paradise, and a matriarch figure for many newer girls on the beat, a fact that might be handy right about now.

To kill time, I cycled loops around the estate, staring up at a cloudy grey sky that kept threatening to rain and kept not raining. Thirty minutes of this, the decision got made, and as the drizzle broke, I took this as my cue to head over to hers.

Blackened foil and Martel bottles fashioned into crack-pipes lay discarded around the weed-infested towpath that led to her block, along with nappy bags, tin cans and all kinds of nameless detritus. To the left, a junkie couple were crouching beneath a parapet, the woman holding a spoon, the man trying to light a match below it. It was the pair I'd seen earlier, leaving Kinsella's Café after scoring. They glanced at me, then away, making no attempt to conceal their drug use.

Years back, someone had wrenched the door to Lisa's block wide open, meaning anyone could wander in. As a precaution, she had a secret knock code that she shared with clients.

After some deliberation, I chained my bike to a lamppost and walked in, taking the narrow flight towards a small landing where there were three bedsitters. Lisa's was to the right.

I gave her door the 3-2-3 knock.

'Come, Dylan,' she said, and the door clicked open.

The room hadn't changed since my last visit – a double bed covered in a leopard print throw; a bedside table; a small faux leather settee; a gnarled dressing table upon which two tumblers of sweet cheery brandy rested, an aperitif that had become habitual whenever I visited.

Lisa was sitting on the bed, hands in her lap. She was wearing a lacy black outfit that pushed some things up and held others in place. Heavy mascara, rouge lipstick and sparkly gold earrings, the clip-on kind that I'd never seen her without. Starched blonde hair parted down the middle, forming an oval around those wistful eyes.

She was tiny, five foot nothing, and from a distance could've passed for a teenager. But close-up was another story, and when she spoke it was pure adult.

'Nice to see you again,' she said.

'And you.'

It was. Lisa was attractive – no, she was beautiful – and I could feel a throbbing in my gut.

Slowly she stood, came towards me, and stopped close enough for me to smell her.

'Your hands,' she said. 'They're bleeding. What have you done?'

She reached for them, turned them palms down. A few knuckles were frayed and swollen from the punches I'd thrown earlier. I hadn't noticed.

'Nothing,' I said. 'It's fine.'

She rubbed the sores gently. Her touch stirred me. My temptation was to reach out, pull her hips up close. Instead, I took my hands away, leaned against the windowsill and folded my arms.

A flicker of confusion glanced across her face. 'How do you

want me?' she said, unzipping the rear of her outfit, just enough to get a glimpse.

I shook my head. 'Not today.'

She hesitated. 'Something wrong?'

'Lisa, I want to talk with you. About a woman you might know. It's important.'

Her eyes narrowed. 'What woman?'

'I'm a private investigator. Did I ever tell you that?'

'No.'

'I'm trying to find someone who may be in your line of work.'

'A working girl?' She feigned disappointment, a hand over her mouth. 'You want her for company? Not me?'

'No, I've never met her.' I got out my phone, swiped to the photo. 'That's her,' I said, holding it up. 'She might go by the name Mandy.'

Lisa looked at the screen, then me. 'Why do you want to find her?' Her voice was edged with caution.

No point lying. 'This photo came from a film she was in. It was made recently. Take another look. Please.'

Her eyes retuned to the photo, stayed with it longer.

We were quiet.

'Well?' I said.

'I don't know,' Lisa said. 'Sorry.'

'You're sure?'

'Yes. But . . .' She faltered.

'But what?'

'There is someone she looks like.'

'Who?'

'I think her name is Mina. No . . . Minka.'

'How'd you know her name?'

'I met her once. I'd have forgotten her, but her sister, Baba . . . she's been asking questions around Paradise, looking for her too.'

My breath caught. 'This Minka's gone missing?'

Lisa nodded. She stepped back to the bed, sat on the mattress, placed her elbows on her knees and leaned forward, exposing her cleavage.

I came and sat next to her. The springs creaked under my weight.

'What can you tell me about her?' I said.

'Not much. She started working round here a few weeks ago.'

'And now?'

'Now, she's gone. Maybe she left. Many girls, they come and go. It's normal.'

'Lisa,' I said, 'did Minka have a pimp or sugar daddy?'

'I don't know.'

'What about drugs? You think she used?'

'Probably. Most girls do.'

'How about porn films, BDSM, that kind of thing? You ever hear about her making them?'

Lisa drew back, stared quizzically. 'Dylan, please, I never knew her well. No more questions.'

I'd overstepped. 'Sorry,' I said.

Far off, the banshee wail of a siren rose and fell. Out there at that moment, people were running, chasing, robbing, chiselling, a city steeped in divisions keeping the rich rich, and people like Lisa interned to bedsits like this one.

'Send me the photo,' she said, quietly. 'I can show it to Baba, ask if it is her sister. OK?'

'Thank you,' I said, and zapped it over.

Lisa's phone vibrated on the bedside table. She leaned for it, checked the arrival of my message. The movement brought out the swell of her breasts, and I heard my breath catch.

She must've sensed something, for she glanced round, a look to her eyes.

'Is there time?' I said.

She nodded.

It was functional, nothing more.

And after, my desire was replaced with a plunging sorrow, as if I'd just made a terrible mistake for which there could be no coming back.

'What's wrong, Dylan?' Lisa said, naked beside me, spooning against my back.

'Nothing,' I said. 'I just didn't plan on coming here for that.'

She played with a few strands of my chest hair. 'This is why you see me. It's OK. I like you.'

'Why do you like me? It can't be for my looks.'

'It's because you are a good man, Dylan. You try to help people, like you are helping to find this girl. You are handsome, too. The way a grizzly bear is.'

'Thanks,' I said. 'Grr.'

She laughed and ran her finger along my forearm, tracing scars mapping my skin. She never asked about them; likewise, I never asked about her scars. But I suppose they gave us a nameless connection.

'Here,' she said, and reached for one of the brandies, handing it to me, taking the other for herself. 'Cheers.'

We clinked, and I drank mine in one. It tasted warm, syrupy, and potent.

Lisa took a small sip.

'Aren't you smoking?' I said. 'Normally you have a cigarette straight after . . .'

Smiling, she reached to the bedside table again, held up a posh looking silver vape. She brought it to her lips, inhaled. The fluid bubbled.

'I quit cigarettes on December thirty-first,' she said proudly through a cloud of thick vapour. 'Now, I am on this.'

'Well done,' I said. 'I think.'

Blackcurrant clung in the air, superseding the briny scent of sex.

'I am making changes this year,' Lisa said. 'Stopping smoking is the start.'

'What else?'

'Soon, I will leave the UK. I have money saved, enough for a new life.'

'Where will you go?'

'I don't know. But there's nothing here for me. Just bad memories.'

I thought about this. 'Whatever you decide, that's great.'

'Thank you.'

'You're going alone?'

She smiled. 'You want to come with me, Dylan?'

It was a crazy idea, one we both knew could never work. But in that moment, crazy sounded good.

I wanted to tell her this, but before I could her phone pinged, throwing us back into the present.

She took the handset. 'My next client,' she said, reaching for her lace bra. 'He's waiting.'

I dressed fast, paid her with what little cash I still had. Wordlessly, she took the notes, made them disappear.

'I will let you know what I hear,' she said, zipping up her outfit.

I went to the door, opened it, felt a draft of biting air.

Halfway out, I turned. 'Lisa?'

She looked up from making the bed.

'Be careful.'

I felt stupid straight away, acting all paternal after what we'd just done.

Lisa didn't laugh though. She just smiled and said, 'Bye, Dylan.'

I descended the stairs two at a time, stepped out of the broken block door and back out. The sky was slate grey, and the air damp from the drizzle.

As I turned up my leather, I locked eyes with a baldish man hovering in the shadows of the block. He was wearing a rumpled suit and was chugging on a smoke.

'Finished?' he said.

'All yours,' I replied.

He grinned and scurried past and up to her flat. Watching him, a tiny part of my inner being fragmented and blew away.

Time to go. I had enough new information to give Patience and Mani, and I didn't fancy being in Paradise after dark when the creatures of the night came out.

But fate had other ideas.

A few minutes of scouring revealed that my bike had been stolen.

Lying in its place was the chain, neatly carved in two with an angle grinder, left like a chewed carcass.

'Dammit,' I said. I'd been through a lot with that bike.

Probably nicked by the junkies I'd seen earlier. I looked around in case the culprits were still lurking.

No such luck. They were long gone.

Sullenly, I started walking, hoping to find bus stop that would take me home.

But a few steps in, I halted again.

'Dammit,' I repeated. 'Dammit to fuck.'

I was angry. Not just because of my bike.

I was angry because in only a few hours I'd dug up more on Kwame Mensah's murder than the Met had found in the best part of a week. I was angry because Lisa and hundreds like her were stuck in bedsits, interned in a scummy lifestyle that men like me helped maintain.

But most of all I was angry because this whole investigation stank, and I'd only just scraped the surface. A woman had been butchered on video. A fourteen-year-old kid had been stabbed to death. And no one was doing anything about it.

Chill, Kasper, I told myself. Look at the positives.

I'd made progress, found a name for the snuff victim, and proved that Terry Kinsella's story was codswallop. Now, time to step back.

Tonight, I'd give the lot to Patience and Mani, and urge them to take it to the police. Hell, I'd even go with them, make sure things got handled right. And then I'd focus on getting some actual paid work, and my life into a semblance of order.

There. Decision made.

I should've felt better. But I didn't. And as I boarded a bus, took a seat downstairs, and watched the jagged silhouette of Paradise fade, that anger still simmered.

A text from Dr Steiner came as a distraction:

Kasper, come home!
You wouldn't dare leave your decrepit landlady alone on her birthday?

Her party. I'd forgotten about it.

I wasn't in the mood for shenanigans. But I had to show my face or else I'd never hear the end of it, and so replied:

On my way. Had some transport problems.

Then, as a passing thought, I sent another text:

Is it OK to bring a couple of friends?

Immediately Dr Steiner replied:

The more, the merrier.

I called Mani, told him to swing by the house with Patience.
'You found something, right Kasper?'
'Think so,' I said. 'We'll have a bit of birthday cake, and I'll fill you both in.'
'Sweet,' Mani said.
'Yeah,' I said, 'sweet,' swallowing down a taste like ashes in my mouth.

Chapter 5

An hour later I was back home, sitting around a dining table strewn with wine and beer bottles, an overflowing ashtray, and the remnants of Dr Steiner's birthday cake.

A few of her friends had attended earlier. Mainly ex-colleagues, plus a former girlfriend with whom she remained amicable. But they'd all slipped off, leaving only myself, the doctor, Mani, Patience, and Suzanna McGovern.

Suzanna – or Suzi as she liked to be called – was the seventeen-year-old daughter of Paddy, my late employer and friend. Last spring, Paddy's pub had burned down in an arson attack sparked to send me a message, and he died in the flames. In the months since, Suzi and I had forged an unlikely friendship.

Despite the age gap spanning five decades, she and Dr Steiner had forged a friendship too. Both were fiercely intelligent, cantankerous, and, following Suzi's coming-out two months prior, proud lesbians.

Suzi's plan was to finish up her A-levels, then go to Central St Martin's to study a degree in Fine Art, her passion. She'd no doubt excel, for she had her head screwed on tighter than a snare drum, was talented, funny, subtle, original, and blessed with exquisite half-Asiatic looks, with prominent bones and eyes that shone with fierce intelligence from behind her hipster glasses.

Presently, she was digging into a slice of cake while describing the earbashing she'd received from a couple of right-on friends about a college piece she'd submitted. Said work, which presently rested on the mantel, was a papier mâché doll's house, incorporating a father, wife and two children, a bland domestic scene bastardized with lurid pornographic cutouts she'd pasted into the diorama, the smut juxtaposing with the bland middle-Englishness to show the seediness lurking beneath domesticity. It was shocking, memorable, and, in my uneducated opinion, quite brilliant.

'And what business have these friends of yours to cast aspersions on this masterpiece?' Dr Steiner said, leaning across the table, pointing a lit Dunhill at the work.

'They said it reinforces the misogyny inherent in society,' Suzi said between mouthfuls, 'by minimizing sexual exploitation into the realms of banality' – chomp-chomp – 'and commoditizing women's bodies in the process.' A sliver of cream stuck to her lip. She rubbed it off with the back of her hand. 'Bollocks, right?'

'Apt choice of words,' Dr Steiner said. 'Your friends are probably jealous of your talents, and your capacity to speak the truth in ways they can't fathom.' She gave a wink and turned to Patience. 'What do you think, dear? Does the girl's work speak to you?'

Patience, who'd played with her cake and barely uttered a word since she arrived, looked at the doll's house and shrugged heavily.

I thought she was going to remain mute, but her eyes flitted up to Suzi, and she said, 'Don't listen to your mates. I think it's wicked.'

Suzi beamed.

From there, she and Patience began nattering, first about Netflix, then Insta, Tik Tok, before discovering a mutual regard for Dave, a performer they both thought was 'sick'.

'To be honest,' I said, leaning in, 'I always preferred Chas.'

They looked at each other: Patience frowned; Suzi rolled her eyes. Then they laughed, the first time I'd seen Patience lower her guard.

Dr Steiner gave an approving nod and reached for her Dunhills. Two bouts of cancer, the second requiring the removal of intestine and the fitting of a stoma bag hadn't quelled her fondness for the cancer sticks.

'Mind if I have one of those?' Mani said. 'I'm smoked out.'

'By all means,' she said, and passed the deck. 'So nice to meet a fellow masochist.' Then she looked at me. 'You haven't told me where you've been today. I'm assuming that's why your friends have graced us with their company, and why you have a face like a lost war.'

I went for a smile. 'Actually, I've been at Paradise Estate.'

'And what possible reason might you have to visit that armpit of the borough?'

Patience looked over, her face stern again. 'He's investigating my kid brother's murder. Kwame got stabbed at the start of the week. Our family's from that armpit.'

'Hm,' Dr Steiner said, 'my condolences, Patience, on both counts.' She stared at her from over her glasses, and said, 'You know how fortunate you are to have Kasper working for you?'

Patience looked nonplussed. 'Why? Man's an ex-copper.'

'True. But you have much in common.'

'Huh?'

'Didn't he tell you he's from Paradise as well?'

Patience shot me a look, her eyebrow raised.

'I was raised there till age seven,' I said.

She held the look and rubbed her nose. 'Why'd you leave?'

'Something happened.' I hesitated, but there was no way out of this. 'Some boys decided to play a trick.'

'What trick?' Suzi said, leaning across the table. 'I never heard this story.'

'Me neither,' Mani said.

Dr Steiner smiled wryly.

'It's no big deal,' I said. 'You know some of the townhouses around Paradise have underground rooms?'

'Yeah,' Patience said, 'big cellars, mostly used by the junkies.'

I nodded. 'Well, a group of older boys I was keen to impress decided it'd be funny to coax me into one of those rooms with the promise of some football cards. Instead, they locked me in and left me.'

'Did you escape?' Patience said.

I shook my head. 'I tried, punching the door till my hand was bleeding. It was pitch dark. I was trapped.'

'What happened?'

'After a few hours they let me out. They told me it was a joke, no big deal. They even gave me the cards to keep. I never told anyone about it, including my dad. He didn't ask what happened. But he knew I was different.'

'What was different?' Mani said.

'An anger was planted in me. And in a place like Paradise, anger can get you killed.'

Patience nodded slowly. 'For real.'

What I didn't say, but what still returns to my dreams, is the sense of enclosure I felt in that loamy basement, squatting against the wall, hot salty tears dripping onto my bloody fists, my sobs reverberating against the metal in flutter echoes.

It was my first experience of powerlessness; and it was the first time, but not the last, when I was sure I would die.

I drained my Heineken and went to get another from the fridge. On my return, the conversation had picked up, and Suzi was laughing, slapping a knee.

'What's funny?' I said.

'Patience thought you were my *dad*.'

I took the head off my beer. 'Thankfully, I have no claim on this one.'

'You had a kid, though?' Patience said. 'Right?'

'Where'd you hear that?'

'From a mate at Savages. They said something happened, an' you don't talk about it.'

I took a moment. 'I had a daughter. She died.'

'How?'

'Suicide. She was fourteen.'

'Same age as Kwame.' Patience pursed her lips. 'Sorry, man. I had no idea.'

'See,' Mani said, looking between Patience and me, 'Dr Steiner's right, you two are peas in a pod.'

I looked at Patience, saw the change.

Dr Steiner added, 'If I'd known my birthday conversations would be so morbid, I'd have locked myself away with a bottle of sherry and the latest Ian Rankin.'

Suzi grinned, and began asking Patience about her training regime, upcoming bouts, and then they were off again. Suzi looked rapt, her elbows on the table, hands making a V-shape with her chin balanced in them neatly, her eyes wide, rarely blinking.

A text message drew me away. It was Lisa:

Call me.

Immediately, I made my excuses, went upstairs to my loft, rang her.

'Hello, Dylan,' she said, her smoky voice sounding close to the receiver.

'Hey.' I could still smell her hair and feel the imprint of her body next to mine.

'I showed the photo to Baba, like I said I would.'

'And?'

'She says it's Minka. Her sister.'

'She's certain?'

'Yes.'

I took a moment, letting this settle. In a court of law, this wasn't proof positive that the film was a snuff or the woman in it was this Minka; but in my mind, it cemented it.

'Baba wants to meet you,' Lisa went on. 'I said I'd ask, and maybe we can go together.'

I drew in breath, held it. Then I said, 'I don't think I can, Lisa.'

'Why not?'

'I was only making enquiries today. From tomorrow, I'm done with this case. But I'll pass this on to my client. She can contact Baba and go from there.'

Lisa sighed. 'No one else, Dylan. Baba wants to meet *you*. I told her she can trust you, you're a good man. Please.'

Around ten, Dr Steiner retired to bed. I told Mani and Patience to wait at the house while I walked Suzi the ten-minute route back to her aunt's flat off the highroad.

As soon as I was back, they were on at me.

'Well?' Mani said.

'Tell us about today,' Patience said. 'What did you find out?'

'Let's talk on the patio,' I said. 'I don't want to discuss this stuff inside.'

The three of us stood in the biting cold on Dr Steiner's flagstone patio, and I described the day's findings.

When I'd finished, Patience said, 'See. That's proof. The film isn't fake. Kwame got killed 'cause of it.'

'Let's not jump ahead of ourselves,' I said. 'But it's clear that there's more to his death. Terry Kinsella's story is made of sand. And this Minka lead needs following up.'

'All this in one day?' Mani said, and looked at Patience. 'Told you Kasper was good, huh?'

She nodded. 'So where's this leave us? I mean, what happens now?'

They both looked at me. Expectation glimmered in their eyes.

During the walk back from Suzi's, I'd pre-rehearsed my exit speech: they should go to the police, and insist the case get reopened with this newfound evidence.

That would've been the clever thing to say.

Instead, I said, 'I'm going to find the people responsible, and take them out of play.'

Yeah, that's how clever I was.

No one spoke.

I said, 'I think the words you're looking for are thank you.'

Patience's eyes reddened. She reached for my hand, shook it vigorously. 'Thank you.'

'You're welcome. But before I get cracking, you need to know a couple of conditions.'

'Go on?'

'I've got limits. Things I *won't* do. Killing's one of them. The men on that film belong behind bars, but that's as far as I'll take it. If you want a hitman, look elsewhere.'

She hesitated, then nodded. 'Fair enough. What else?'

'At some point, I'll need to involve the police.'

She made a hissing sound, like a pricked inner-tube.

'This is serious crime, Patience. I promise, I'll keep the law at arm's length, only let them in when I'm certain it'll lead to arrests. But you're going to have to suck that up. Otherwise, I'm out.'

Another, longer pause. 'Yeah, OK,' she mumbled.

'What about payment?' Mani said. 'You'll want something for this, right?'

I shrugged. 'We both know I'm doing this for more than money.'

He grinned. 'Don't mind me asking, what made you come round? Last night, you were set to shut the door after a day's work.'

I thought about this.

'I don't know,' I eventually said. 'Maybe it's because the stuff I saw today on Paradise bothered me. People left there to rot. It's not right.' I looked at the moon. It was a waxing crescent, bleached bone yellow, with wispy clouds writhing before it. 'Maybe it's a little bit to do with my daughter too.'

'What do you mean?'

'The anniversary of her death's coming up. Six years. I'm pretty sure she wouldn't be too happy with me walking away from this thing.'

'Neither would my kid brother,' Patience said.

'Or the girl from that film,' Mani added. 'Minka.'

A chill dashed across my face, and I shivered. I felt a jolt of fear.

'Now let's get inside,' I said. 'It's damn cold.'

Chapter 6

I rose early, keen as mustard to crack this case open.

First up, research.

Getting a handle on snuff movies in the twenty-first century seemed a good start. Not the obvious way to begin a Sunday, but needs must.

There were a zillion companies using the Red Rose moniker, but I couldn't find one that catered in torture porn. No surprises there.

In fact, there was little about snuffs in general in the current digital age. What I'd told Mani and Patience appeared to be true – since the dawn of the internet, these notorious films had all but snuffled out, pun intended, becoming things of video nasty folklore.

Instead, the web was flooded with enough real-life gore and carnage to keep the most sadistic appetite sated. Footage caught on CCTV, surveillance cameras or captured by opportunistic mobile phone users, all abhorrent in nature, and accessible to anyone with a basic knowledge of computers.

I dipped my toe in for a taster. Within minutes, I'd watched a chimp being garrotted, prisoner-of-war beheadings, disloyal wives getting stoned; there were road-rage punch ups, shopping mall stabbings, and shootouts in suburban car parks and a high-school.

From what I could ascertain, the uploaders' motive for sharing these clips was to score social media praise and viewing hits, with no regard for the exploitative nature of the material.

One series really turned my guts. Bum Fights were real-life scraps between homeless people who were offered cash incentives to beat seven shades out of each other. As they piled in, you could hear the laughter of the filmmakers off camera, high, preppy tones, rich kids doing it for a giggle.

Forty-five minutes was ample. I slammed my laptop shut.

These films reeked of the shock factor, but the brutality was banal and pathetic. None had the arthouse hallmarks of the film I'd seen. Even in its un-edited form, the Red Rose movie was professionally done; the camera was steady; the lighting and sound dagger-sharp; it had a script, props, if props included mallets and knives; thought had gone into its creation.

More than this, it seized the viewer. Beginning with the artsy intro, hammy dialogue, luring the viewer into a false sense of security before pummelling them with the gore. Sick as it was to accept, a degree of talent went into its making.

I took the camcorder from the bag. It was a Sony model. Google revealed it was old, released over a decade back – top end in its day, now superseded – a digital recorder favoured by serious moviemakers, not your typical home user. First-hand, it would've set you back several thousand quid. These days they retailed on eBay for a couple of hundred, tops.

Maybe I could trace the retailer by its serial number and find the owners? A few minutes' searching quashed that idea. This model had been a popular bit of kit, sold in umpteen places around the world, and there was a decent second-, even third-hand market for them.

Instead, I returned to Kwame Mensah, speculated where he might've acquired it. According to Patience he was an opportunistic thief, seeing, snatching, and zipping off.

I needed to know more about Kwame and his death. After some deliberation, I rang Diane McAteer. She was a DS based at Holborn nick, my ex, and one of the shrewdest police officers I'd ever known. We'd met years back as coppers. I was still married, and we began seeing each other on the sly. Quickly, it became clear Diane was going places with her career, whereas my insubordination would always keep me in uniform. Despite our differences, we had something going, and an understanding that at some point we'd settle.

Then my daughter killed herself. That kind of put a kibosh on things.

She answered on the third ring: 'Well, hello, and to what do I owe the pleasure?'

I smiled at her voice. 'How's tricks, Diane?'

'Fair-to-middling. You?'

I told her I was fine – my first lie – and then got to it. 'Kwame Mensah. Heard the name?'

'He's the boy who was knifed out on Paradise last week?'

'The very same. Don't suppose you could give me a peek of his case files?'

'Want to say why?'

'I've been asked to look into the killing.'

'Who's your client?'

'The kid's big sister. She thinks you lot have made some assumptions.'

'She wouldn't be the first to think that.'

'I told her I'd have a dig, see what comes up. What do you reckon?'

Diane hesitated. We both knew that for a serving officer to share intel on a live case with a civilian was a serious breach of the law and could land her in a heap of trouble.

'How about I offer an incentive?' I added.

'Hit me.'

'If I get a bite on something, you get first dibs on the collar.'

'You onto something big?'

'Possibly.'

'Tomorrow morning,' she said. 'Coffee's on you.'

A little after eleven, I was outside Edmonton Green Train Station. Earlier, I'd exchanged a few texts with Lisa, and arranged for her to take me to meet Baba, the woman who claimed the snuff film victim was her sister Minka.

Church bells clanged in the distance, and families kitted out in their Sunday best meandered past the gum-pasted street. I was stiff and cold, and wondering if I'd been stood up, when a slight figure appeared from the turnstiles and spoke in a familiar husky voice.

'Hello, Dylan. Sorry I'm late.'

I tried to hide my shock, for away from Paradise – and dressed as she was in a sexless navy windbreaker, old jeans and tatty All-Stars – Lisa looked profoundly normal, nothing like the mock-up Barbie I'd been with yesterday. A Spurs cap was hiding her starched blonde hair, its rim masking her eyes. The only recognisable feature was her sparkly earrings, and that voice.

'This way,' she said, and began down the high street.

Walking alongside Lisa was an uncomfortable experience. This was a woman I'd paid for, someone I'd known intimately;

yet in the grey hues of morning, it dawned on me that I knew barely a thing about her.

Added to that, we were going to chat to the sister of a prostitute who'd gone missing and may've been carved up on film. Strange didn't come close.

'Baba doesn't speak good English,' Lisa said, as we turned onto a dusty old road of terraced houses. 'I will help to translate.'

'Does she know what you do for a living?'

''Course.'

'Did you tell her how I came to have that photo?'

'No.'

'What about how you and I know each other?'

'I said you are a friend, someone I trust. Baba won't be scared. Her fear is the police.'

'Why?'

'She's like many of us. No visa. No passport. Police can deport us. We cannot trust them. Understand?'

I indicated I did.

A few minutes later we arrived. It was a two-up two-down situated on an unremarkable strip of terraces. Over the years, profit-hungry landlords had converted a lot of these properties into HMOs — houses of multiple occupancy — filleting the original layout, turning every inch into rentable dwelling space irrespective of the cramped conditions and lack of communal areas.

My guess, this house fit the bill. Externally, it looked in particularly bad nick, the roof shingles dislodged, windowsills cracked and peeling.

There wasn't a bell, so Lisa tapped the letterbox. From inside, a woman shouted in a European language, Romanian or Bulgarian at a guess. A moment later the door opened.

Facing us was a small, squat, butch woman; five-four, every inch of it tough. She had a crop of shapeless brown hair and a steeped, Clint Eastwood chin. She was wearing scuffed boots and a paint-spattered t-shirt. Military tats marked her arms, and her right pinky was missing. Her hands were calloused, with mis-aligned knuckles that bore scabs; the left was clutching a can of Monster, the right, a half-smoked roll-up. Late thirties I'd say, but her bad teeth, hardy complexion and mistrustful eyes made her seem older, worldlier, bitterer too.

Lisa said something in the same foreign language. The woman said something back, her voice low and gravelly, like a tractor engine purring.

'Baba,' Lisa said, pointing at me, 'this is Dylan Kasper.'

Baba put the cigarette into her mouth and offered a hand, her grip cold and strong.

'Come,' she said, and stepped back, guiding us into a tight, unlit hall, and directly left into a bedroom.

I'd seen bigger prison cells. Judging by the sealed-up fireplace, it had once been part of a lounge, but the erection of a stud-wall through its middle put an end to that.

There was little furniture, for there wasn't the space – a single bed, a fold-up chair, a TV placed on the chair and a chest of draw-ers. A ring heater glowed orange, and on a hearth above the fireplace rested a solitary photo. It showed a girl, twelve or thir-teen. Her brown hair was plaited. She had braces on her teeth. She was smiling. It was the smile the woman on the video wore as she gazed up at the two masked men.

Baba closed the door to the room, leaned against the wall by the window, placed the can between her boots. Several fist-sized dents marred the plastering. That was where those scabs on her knuckles came from, I figured.

Lisa sat on the bed. I stood beside the doorframe, folded my arms.

Lisa said something. Baba nodded, pulled out a smartphone, held it up. It showed the photo I'd taken of the woman in the film.

'Minka,' Baba said, pointing at the screen; then she pointed to the photo of the teenager above the hearth. 'My sister.'

I nodded.

'Where is she?'

'That's what I want to talk to you about,' I said, and pulled out my notebook and pen.

With Lisa's help I asked a load of questions. It was slow going, but over the next half hour I got a pretty good sense of things.

Baba and Minka's backstories were grimly predictable. Two years ago they were stowed in a cargo lorry going to Dover, fed the age-old lie that the shores of England were paved with gold. Baba, not long out of the army, was doing her best to care for her wayward kid sister. Like many, they headed for London, paid cash to rent rooms off grid with other foreign nationals, and spent their first year working, Baba painting, decorating, working on sites, Minka waitressing and dancing, both sending whatever they could back home to help support the family.

Last February, Minka's boss asked for her NI number. When she failed to produce it, she got sacked. Word spread on the scene that she was illegal: she couldn't find work and fell behind on her rent.

A helpful boyfriend suggested she could earn fast cash by turning a trick or two. Another even more helpful boyfriend introduced her to street drugs to make those tricks pass more bearably.

Six months later, Minka was working a beat and had a habit

the size of Kilimanjaro. Baba tried to intervene, pleading with Minka to abstain, but to no avail: she ended up using on the sly. Just before Christmas the landlord found drugs paraphernalia, hit the roof and demanded Minka leave. From there she took to Paradise, squatting and tricking, before her disappearance a week ago.

I looked at Lisa, knew she could sense the shame that rose through me as I heard this. It was only by fluke I hadn't approached Minka for business myself.

Baba rubbed her temple and spoke towards the floor. 'I wanted to help Minka,' she said. 'But the drugs, they are so strong.' She made fists of her hands to exemplify the addictive bind. 'I was angry. My sister, working as prostitute. Bringing shame.'

'Do you know where she scored her drugs?'

''Course. The fat man in the café.'

'Terry Kinsella?'

'Yes. I go to Paradise, asking questions.'

'Did you speak to Terry?'

'I try to, yes. I say, where is my sister? I show him a photo of her. I say, you sell my sister drugs. Bastard liar say he knows nothing.'

'Did he,' I said, and stored this away. Now, I had hard proof that Terry lied yesterday about not recognising the girl in the photo. He'd be due another visit.

'Baba,' I said, 'does the name Kwame Mensah sound familiar?'

'No.'

'How about Red Rose Productions?'

'No.'

I was lining up another question, but Lisa flicked her head at me, her eyes saying to slow down. Looking back at Baba, I saw why. A mist had fallen over her. She was back to looking at the photo above the hearth of Minka as a child.

'Describe her, Baba,' I said. 'Your little sister, Minka.'

She told me of a happy girl from Vaslui; while Baba joined the military, Minka became a forthright, opinionated teenager who loved gymnastics, dancing, acting, nightlife. She wanted to study, but poverty, intensified by their father's casino habit and mother's chemotherapy, put an end to that. And when Minka got arrested for shoplifting, their mother knew it could be the start of a downward spiral, and paid smugglers her savings to get her girls to the UK.

'That was a mistake,' Baba said. 'I wish we never come to this country. Minka was better at home.'

'When did you last see Minka?'

'New Year's Eve.'

The night before the film got made. 'How was she then?'

'Happy.'

'Did she say why she was happy?'

'She tell me she is sorting her life. That she has a new job, performing. Good money.'

A tingle rose in my belly. 'What was this performing job?'

'She wouldn't say. A secret. A friend of hers helped find it.'

'Was the friend Terry Kinsella, by any chance?'

'I don't know.'

'And was the job performing on camera?'

Baba stared.

'Adult stuff, Baba? Sex films? Porn?'

Lines appeared across her brow, and her eyes became rheumy. She looked at Lisa, and back at me. 'I think so. I never ask. I should have. But I was ashamed. Now, I am too late.'

Too late. Christ, I knew how that felt.

I scribbled the last of this down and put my notebook in my pocket.

Lisa looked at her watch surreptitiously. She needed to get back.

Baba said something in their native language again.

'What's that?' I asked.

Lisa said, 'Baba said you think Minka is dead.'

There were many times as a copper I'd had the misfortune of delivering the news every family dreads. Experience helps with the wording, but it never gets easier.

I cleared my throat, said, 'Yes, Baba. I think she's dead.'

The silence blared like a foghorn.

'Please,' Baba said. 'How did she die?'

No way to sugarcoat it. 'She was murdered. The photo you saw came from a film the killers made showing her death.'

She stared, and began breathing unsteadily, as if she were hyperventilating, and her body grew taut and swollen, giving the appearance that her clothes had shrunk. She made fists, raised them. For an awful second her expression resembled her sister Minka's as she was tortured to death, and she turned to the wall, ready to punch it.

'No,' I said.

She froze mid throw, her arm shaking.

Then something slackened. She breathed out heavily, her eyes filled, and the first tear plopped to the cracked laminate flooring.

'Why would anyone hurt my baby sister?' Baba said.

'I don't know.'

'Dylan will find the men who did it,' Lisa said.

Baba stared. 'You will?'

'I'll try.'

'And you will kill them?'

I couldn't blame her for asking, just like I couldn't blame Patience for asking either. Christ, if I were in their position, I'd want the same thing too.

But I wasn't prepared to lie to appease their feelings, not over something this serious.

'No, Baba,' I said, as gently as I could. 'I won't be killing anyone.'

'Why? They kill my sister!'

'It won't help.'

'How do you know this?'

'Because I've been somewhere similar to you.'

'What?'

In as few words as possible, I told her about Rosie: aged just fourteen, my little girl left for school, took herself to the local rail station, and when her train approached, she stepped out onto the tracks.

Baba's mouth fell open and her hands unclenched.

Although the circumstances of Rosie and Minka's deaths were poles apart, something connected us now, a shared, unnatural loss.

'Dylan,' Lisa said, looking at her watch again.

'We need to go, Baba,' I said. 'Is there anything else you can think of?'

She shook his head.

'Then thanks. If I get a hit, I'll let you know.'

Lisa stood.

I went to the door, took the door handle, turned it, let Lisa out ahead of me. Then I looked over my shoulder a final time.

Baba was gazing at the wall. The bones behind her face had become apparent, and the shadows around her eyes looked even deeper than before.

*

79

We walked back to the train station.

Neither Lisa nor I were in the chitchat mood. Hardly surprising. Talking about death does that.

But when we got to the turnstiles, she said, 'I never knew about your daughter.'

I shrugged. 'It's not the kind of thing I talk about much.'

'But it brings you pain. And it's why you have those scars on your body. You punish yourself. Yes?'

I shrugged again. 'For a good few years after Rosie died, hurting myself seemed the only way I could feel anything. But I've learned better ways of coping these days.'

'I understand,' Lisa said. 'I am the same. We have both suffered.'

This newfound intimacy made me uncomfortable. We were crossing a line here, delving into our backstories.

'Do you have someone in your life now?' she said. 'I've never asked before.'

'I'm tight with my landlady. I've got a mate called Mani who drives trains. And I'm close with a young woman called Suzi, a bright kid. Like my daughter was.'

Lisa smiled. 'But you don't have a woman?'

I shook my head. 'I've tried dating. Apps and things. It hasn't worked out.'

We looked at each other.

Lisa said, 'Maybe we can talk another time. You and me. Just two normal people having a conversation.'

'I'd like that,' I said.

She turned, started for the turnstiles.

A thought suddenly caught me. Before I'd mulled it over, I reached for her sleeve, said, 'Lisa, please stop seeing clients. Just till this is over.'

She stared, incredulously. 'Why?'

'Because there's men out there hurting women like you.'

Her eyes drooped, and she shook her head. 'Oh, Dylan, I must work.'

'You don't have to.'

'They won't come for me. I'm nobody.'

'That's exactly why they might go after you.'

'You cannot ask this question again.'

I was trying to think of a comeback, a way around this, but she beat me to it. Standing on tiptoe, Lisa planted a kiss on my cheek. It was an astonishing kiss, and it threw me completely.

'Bye,' she whispered into my ear.

I watched her go into the station, down the escalator, and she fell out of view. I stayed there, staring at the spot where she'd been, wrapped in a fuzzy afterglow, letting it all sink in.

I had my victim's name confirmed. Minka Petrova. And I knew Terry Kinsella was a barefaced liar.

Perhaps there was enough for the police to launch a full-scale murder investigation?

Not yet. Going to the authorities would mean Lisa and Baba would both get dragged in, interrogated, quite possibly deported too. I didn't fancy having that on my conscience.

But the real reason for keeping hold of this was that I didn't want to hand over control yet. Not till I knew a hundred per cent who those killers were, and that they were going away. For now, I'd stay on the sharp edge of this case, keeping the police at arm's reach, and doing things my way.

I reached for my phone, found Patience in my contacts, called her.

'Kasper,' she said. 'What's up?' I could hear iron clanging in the background, the pounding of pads. She was training.

'I was thinking of heading over to Terry Kinsella's Café, giving him another squeeze.'

'How come?'

'He bullshitted me yesterday. I want to know why. Problem is, he told me he'd have some reinforcements if I came knocking again. I thought it might be good to have a bit of extra clout too. Want to come with?'

'Hell yeah,' she said. 'When were you thinking?'

'You free now?'

'Now's good.'

Chapter 7

Paradise again.

In the last hour the sky had opened, pouring a cold rain that smacked onto the paving. When it became ferocious, I sheltered under a parapet at the south entrance, waiting for it to calm. From here, I could take in the silhouette of the tower blocks, grey and bleak, all sharp edges and corners that seemed to vibrate through the strum.

After ten minutes, it turned to a drizzle. I popped my collar and moved around the puddles into the estate, and in the direction of Kinsella's Café.

Patience was leaning against the gating of Paradise Cemetery, partially sheltered beneath the naked branches of a weeping willow, her arms folded over her chest. She was wearing Nike trainers, an Everlast tracksuit and a baseball cap. Rainwater dribbled down its rim.

She gave me a nod, said, 'I been here twenty minutes. The café's closed. No sign of the fat man. Reckon he's done a runner?'

'Maybe,' I said. 'But Terry's not really the running kind.'

'So what's the plan?'

'We'll have a snoop. It's possible he's holed up in there.'

'And what if he is?'

'Let me do the talking. You just act mean. Can you manage that?'

Her eyes fizzed with the same explosive anger I'd seen in the ring, and told me all I needed to know.

'All right,' I said. 'Let's take a look around.'

The weather must've scared off the locals, for the area was devoid of life. Patience was right – the café was closed, its metal shutters drawn, the lights off.

I peered through the side windows, but they were daubed with years of grime. I tried the handle of the back door. Locked. A recce to the rear was a no-show too, revealing only a load of rusty oil drums and a large wheelie-bin overflowing with sacks spilling rancid foodstuffs.

'What do you think?' Patience said.

'Not sure.'

'This mean we're heading home empty handed?'

She sounded disappointed. As was I. If Terry really had bolted, then I had no other leads. I stared up at the café wall, squinting. There was a narrow rectangular window above the back door, single-glazed, partially open. A cat burglar's dream.

'I'm going through that,' I said. 'Hold the bin steady.'

I hiked onto the bin, careful not to slip on the wetness, then climbed up to the sill. After a little experimentation I managed to reach inside the window without losing footing and fully unlatch it. Then, using a drainpipe to shimmy further, I clambered up, pushing the window fully ajar, making space enough to snake in and drop to the floor, scraping both shins in the process, landing on my hands in a tumble.

Patience followed suit. She made the whole process look a

damn sight easier. We stood side by side, catching our breath, taking it in.

The café was gloomy, listless. Apart from the rattle of rain there was silence.

I breathed through my nose. The same odor of refried cooking fat lingered.

But something else lingered too. A sweet, sickly smell I'd smelled before.

Using my phone's torch, I moved into the main body of the café, amongst the grubby tables and chairs. A few feet from the kitchen, my heart became a tight ball. I knew what was waiting.

'Stay put,' I said.

'Why?' Patience said, behind me.

I didn't answer, just went to the counter, shone the light beam over.

Terry was collapsed on his side. He was dressed in the same grubby jeans and t-shirt he'd had on yesterday. One hand was hidden under his flabby tummy, the other flopped over his torso. His thick lensed glasses were skewed on his face, and his eyes were open, staring into the void.

He'd spilled a cup of tea as he fell, for there was ceramic shattered around him, and light brown liquid with globules of sugar sticking to the lino. Dotted around him were pills, too many to count, spilling from brown bottles, the kind you get from a pharmacy. I remembered him munching from one of these bottles yesterday.

Fighting back the nausea, I squatted down, felt his neck.

Stone cold. No pulse.

My guess, he'd died not long after my visit, and had been here since.

There was a handwritten note in his right hand. I put light to it. Scrawled in block capitals, it read:

I CAN'T GO ON ANYMORE

I picked up one of the pill bottles. It was half full. The label indicated the meds were benzodiazepines, strong tranquillizers. I shoved it into my pocket and stood.

Something had pushed Terry over the edge. Whatever it was, he'd taken it with him before I could find it out.

'Shit,' I said, as this realisation sank in.

I was about to start looking about when Patience screamed.

My torchlight tracked across the ceiling, and I looked her way. She was behind the counter, staring at Terry's body, eyes huge, skin bloodless.

'Oh my days!' she said. 'What the fuck, Kasper! That man dead?'

'Very.'

The steel had gone from her, and she looked like what she was – a scared kid, way out of her depth.

'Don't look at him,' I said, 'and don't touch anything.'

She nodded, said, 'OK, OK.'

I went further into the kitchen.

'Kasper, man,' Patience said, 'let's just split.'

'No,' I said. 'I need to search this place. You go if you want.'

She flung her hands up in exasperation, but she stayed put.

My temptation was to turn the lights on, but that could attract attention. Instead, I scanned around with my torch, moving crates and boxes, opening the fridge and freezer, not knowing what I was looking for, doing my best to keep Terry's corpse out of my vision.

After what felt an age all I'd turned up was some greying potatoes and a load of out-of-date bacon and cheese. Down on my knees, I shone my torch beneath the ovens. Apart from a deluge of rotten vegetables, crumpled foil and the clawing remnants of a decomposing rodent, there was nothing.

I stood. To the rear left of the café was the staff room Terry had emerged from yesterday.

'I'm going to have a peek in there,' I said, and tried the door.

To my surprise, it opened. Pine steps led up.

As I ascended, the smells of must, cannabis, sweat and the cold wafted down. Another door was at landing level, hanging ajar. I pushed it open, stepped onto a dim landing. It was narrow, strewn with dirty clothes; to the left was a solitary room.

I pushed open the door to this room. It clanked against something metal. I shone my torch inwards, made out a small space, scant of light. I found a switch on a wood beam. A snick, and a low hung bulb sparked on.

It was a square loft, fuzzy with motes; dank, un-insulated, unfurnished, and deathly quiet. Against the far-facing wall was a desk covered in papers and invoices, bank statements, unopened letters, plus used tea-mugs, dog-ends, loose tobacco crumbs. I picked a few random documents. The letters were utility bills and invoices, revealing Terry hadn't been the shrewdest bookkeeper, and was in quite a bit of debt. Not that he'd be bothered now.

To the adjacent wall there was a filing cabinet, the old metal kind. I was opening the top drawer when Patience yelled up, 'Kasper, what you doin'?'

'One minute,' I shouted.

Fast, I searched. The top drawer contained more bills, rammed in higgledy-piggledy, some addressed to Terry, others to various men and women with Paradise postcodes, and in no discernible order. Beneath those, more plastic pill bottles, a sizable mound of squidgy cannabis resin, and fifty or so cling-filmed baggies containing lumps of white and brown powder, crack and smack without question.

The middle drawer was much the same: papers, drugs, random crap.

The third drawer was a different story.

Polaroid photos were inside on a dark velvet fabric, folded away neatly. My head catapulted back to the snuff film, and the opening shot – velvet drapes, swishing, before the camera pulled away.

The feeling of restriction intensified in my throat. With a shaking hand, I reached for the photos. These weren't like the ones on the café shop floor. Terry didn't feature in any.

But a number of women did. Nineteen in total. On the rear of each there was a date and a name, scrawled in the same handwriting as Terry's suicide note.

I skimmed through, saying the names in my head.

Dawn. Polly. Leanne. Lucia. Mandy . . .

Mandy.

It was Minka Petrova, Baba's sister, the woman from the film.

I looked around the room, seeing it in a new light. Was this where the snuff was made, and where Kwame stole the camcorder from?

Suddenly I was breathing hard.

I stuffed the photos into my pocket, turned, headed for the door. Halfway out, I froze.

Propped by the wall was a bedframe. That's what I'd heard the door clank against. It was dull metal and had no distinguishable features. It could've been any bedframe.

But I knew what it was. And where I'd seen it.

'C'mon!' I said, thundering downstairs. 'We need to go! Now!'

Patience was by the main entrance to the café. She had regained composure, no longer shocked, more intrigued by Terry's wall, and the framed photos mounted.

'Patience!' I said.

She glanced over. 'Find anything?'

'Enough to prove Terry was up to his eyeballs.'

'Bastard.' Her eyes flitted to the kitchen where his corpse lay. 'He got off easy.'

Maybe. But his suicide had created a ton of new questions. And I wasn't going to answer them in this death-soaked café.

While I was thinking this, Patience returned to the pictures. As she stared, she tilted her head.

'Patience!' I said again.

She nodded, followed.

And we got the hell out of there.

Chapter 8

We walked fast from the café, back into Paradise. My focus was entirely inward, trying to make sense of what I'd just seen.

The photos, the velvet drape, the bedframe, it all proved Terry was involved far deeper than I'd first thought. But how?

I was angry – with Terry for being dead, and with myself for not moving on him sooner. If I'd squeezed him harder for information yesterday, maybe I'd have found stuff out. Now there were three deaths and a bunch of fresh questions.

'Where you goin', Kasper?' Patience said. She had her hood raised, cap down, eyes to the ground.

'Don't know,' I answered. 'I need to think.'

'Well, let's think this way.' She cut down an alley much like the one where her kid brother was killed.

I followed. A moment later we were outside a block.

'I'm home,' she said.

Hers was the ground-floor flat on a stretch of tawny three-tier buildings. The front window was boarded with plywood, and a chunk of cladding dangled from the doorframe hinge like a wobbly tooth.

'Come in,' she said. 'Dry off, have a drink.'

Something in her voice told me she needed to talk, to help make sense of what we'd seen.

But right then, I needed to be alone.

'Another time,' I said.

She hesitated, then nodded.

'You've seen dead bodies before?' I said.

'I had to identify Kwame last week,' she said. 'There was Dad before him. And when we were kids, Mum too.' She paused. 'What got you so spooked in that café?'

No point lying. 'I think the snuff film was filmed there.'

She nodded, said, 'That statement the fat man fed the police, about Kwame getting chased by a bunch of boys. It was made-up, right?'

'Yeah.'

'Reckon he killed my brother, Kasper?'

'No. Terry was a liar, but not a killer. When I saw him yesterday, he was scared, holding back.'

'Scared of you finding out?'

'Maybe. Or the two men from that film, wanting to keep him quiet about these.'

I pulled the photos from my pocket, masking them from the drizzle, and told Patience where I'd found them.

'The most recent one is Minka,' I said. 'The girl from that film we saw.'

'What about these others? Who're they?'

I didn't answer.

'You think they're dead?'

'Don't know,' I said, and returned the photos to my pocket. 'Will you be OK?'

Patience shrugged. 'Guess so.'

We'd both just lied to each other, and both knew it too.

I took a couple of steps away, then hesitated. Something else was tapping in my head amidst the maelstrom of shock. 'What were you looking at?'

Patience hadn't moved from the spot. 'Huh?' she said.

'Right before we left, you were staring at those pictures on the café wall.'

She looked confused. 'I was just doin' my best to ignore that dead man lying on the floor.'

This made sense. But still, there'd been a look about her. 'Maybe we should go back, take another look at—'

'Screw that, man,' she broke in, 'I ain't going there. Look, Kasper, I can't think straight.'

No shit. Her skin was pale, eyes wide, her mind reliving where we'd just been. Although she was a mean fighter, the girl was in shock, and had a rough night ahead.

'All right,' I said, 'sit tight. Soon as I know what's what, I'll be in touch.'

We shook hands, and I left her.

Halfway home, I found a payphone and called 999.

In a muffled voice I told the operator I'd seen someone collapsed in Kinsella's Café, and suggested they send a patrol team over sharpish. When the woman started asking for my name and address, I hung up and legged it home.

Up in my loft room, I placed all the photos of the women on the floor, ordered chronologically from the dates Terry had written on them. I looked at each, staying with Minka the longest, for hers was the face I knew best.

Now that she had a name, a sister I'd met, and a backstory, her fate seemed even more abhorrent. I thought of the photo on

Baba's wall showing her kid sister Minka, smiling, her braced teeth exposed. A girl with dreams . . .

I reached for the Bushmills, sloshed a couple of fingers into a teacup. I drank deeply, took a moment for my nerves to settle. Then I returned to the photos.

Each was a head and upper body shot taken against a gloomy bricked background, most likely the café wall. All the girls were staring straight at the lens, smiling a saccharine smile, their eyes red-dots from the camera flash; all were pretty, early to mid-twenties; but already they bore that hardened look street life engrains.

According to the information on the rear, the earliest photo was taken nine years back, November 14th, and showed a muddy haired, whey-skinned girl. Her name was Tammy. The most recent was Minka, taken December 29th last year, three days before the snuff was made, and five before Kwame got knifed.

Maybe these photos were audition shots? Terry took snaps of girls who came to the café, then showed them to his snuff movie mates for approval. He'd been the third man, a talent scout for the two killers, luring unsuspecting girls to act in what they thought were sex films. That's what Minka thought she was appearing in. Had the other eighteen women fallen foul to the same fate?

'Christ,' I said, as the idea grew wings.

A moment later it was airborne, and I had a full-blown theory. Kwame broke into Terry's café, expecting money or drugs, and instead found a snuff film-set and a camcorder. Not thinking, he took it. After watching what was filmed on it, he realised it was hot and tried to sell it back to Terry in a misguided blackmail bid.

Bad move, Kwame.

Terry told his friends, and they did away with poor Kwame. They'd have known a petty criminal from Paradise found dead wouldn't cause a ruckus, especially if Terry made up a story about witnessing kids with knives chasing him.

Now, Terry was dead too. And I'd hit a wall.

I checked my watch. It was only quarter to five, but I felt like I'd been at this for weeks. The sky was dark, getting darker, and the rain was back with a vengeance.

Something to take my mind off things sounded good. Maybe a hot bath, a nature documentary about fluffy animals, then bed.

But my feet had other ideas. Half an hour later I was on a barstool at Doyle's, a shady boozer off the High Road. The pub, which smelled like a wet mongrel, was the hangout for widowers, wanderers, misanthropes, miscreants, plus one or two loonies who I vaguely recognised from McGovern's, the watering hole I pulled pints at before it burned down last year. Right then, the place fit my mood to a tee.

I took the head off a Guinness and stared at the limned grain of the bar, trying to make sense of what I was feeling.

No two-ways, I was in a dark place. The violence of the snuff, the discovery of Terry's corpse, the photos in his office . . . it was all churning away. Then there was the anniversary of Rosie's suicide coming up.

But that wasn't all.

Truth be told, I was scared. I'd never done anything like this before, working a case so big, and relying on my own wits. Was I a loony too?

Three pints and several house whiskeys later, I concluded that I was.

Good going, Kasper.

Kwame had the right idea. That camcorder should've just been destroyed. Instead, I had it, along with the photos of nineteen women presumed dead.

A copy of today's *Gazette* lay on the bar. I reached for it, hoping for a distraction.

Fat chance.

The case against the two serving police officers accused of sharing crime scene photos had snowballed. Now, it turned out they'd also stolen a heap of child porn from evidence suites and re-circulated these images on the dark web's pay-per-view channels. Pillars of society.

A clang of the last orders bell drew me back. A gaunt barman started collecting empties, prodding a couple of old boys muttering into their pints. He said something to me about drinking up, and I stood, aware that the booze had done what it was meant to do, sanding my edges.

But as I stepped into the cold spitting rain, I knew the monkey was close to my back. Sure enough, back home, as I peeled off my clothes, dumped them in a pile and lay on my bed, I could smell its fetid breath.

Perhaps I should just throw in the towel. I'd call Mani, tell him I wasn't up to this, return the camcorder to Patience and let them handle it. The idea sounded good.

But that's all it was – an idea. One way or another I was in this thing till it was over.

'Over,' I said aloud.

What, precisely, would 'over' look like?

Having the men who made the snuff behind bars? Or more? 'Kill them.'

That's what Patience asked of me. Baba too.

If it came to it, could I? Did I really have it in me to take a life?

'Yeah you do,' a small, unfamiliar voice said, and as a curtain of sleep fell, I realised it came from me.

Chapter 9

The next morning, my eyes seemed to have iron filings attached to their lids, and bags – scratch that, suitcases – hanging beneath them. How much had I put away the previous night?

Quite a bit, I concluded.

To compound matters, I was due to meet Diane McAteer later that morning to talk over Kwame Mensah's murder; I didn't reckon she'd be too enamored by me stinking like a used beer mat.

I forced myself up and out, jogging to the New River green, stopping on the muddy banks that overlooked the power plants to knock out the push-ups and burpees until my muscles fizzed with lactic acid.

Back home, my breathing was aerobic, my heart pumping fresh oxygenated blood. A few coffees in, I felt half-human.

I checked the local news online, hoping to find out if Terry's body had been discovered yet. Nothing on the digitals, but a local Twitter page gave mention of a police incident at a café on the fringes of Paradise. That had to be it. Would Diane have heard about Terry's death?

I showered, changed into a plain grey shirt and newish jeans, and headed her way to find out.

Forty minutes later, she and I were at a resplendent Scandinavian café out in Finchley, near to where she'd bought an equally resplendent flat the previous year.

Diane was wearing a signature black mac, pinstripe power-suit and statement heels. As always, each item appeared to be cut and finished specifically for her. A few years back she'd straightened her afro, now wearing it tightly pulled back, and she had a signature sharp, melon-y perfume accompanying her.

She'd brought Murphy along too, her vast female lurcher-cross, the mother of Dr Steiner's puppy, Tommy, who looked more like a baby stallion than a dog. On a given day, Diane *or* Murphy alone had the presence to turn eyes; together they were formidable, and I was aware of the stares that came from onlookers, male, female, children alike.

Diane and I reconnected last spring following a case we were involved in. That brief dalliance culminated in an awkward night together from which I bolted, opting for the safe anonymity of a working girl, a move I'd regretted since. Since then, things between us had been amicable, and strictly platonic.

She ordered an oat latte and a pastry that looked like a ceramic tortoise. I opted for coffee, black, and one of the pastries too, which I demolished with three judicious bites.

'Here,' Diane said, handing me an A4 folder. 'The highlights from Kwame Mensah's murder investigation. Read it and weep.'

'Cheers,' I said. 'Hope this didn't cause you a headache to get.'

'You were in luck. Another case I'm working on drew me to the major incident suite at Hendon yesterday, so I caught a peek at this while there. I'll need them back once you finish.'

I nodded, scanning through. The pages were printouts from the *Holmes Two* police database, bearing the familiar insignia on each sheet. For a homicide enquiry, especially one that was still technically ongoing, the content was surprisingly thin.

I skipped to the crime scene photos, eleven in total. All showed a kid slumped in the Paradise alleyway where I'd stood the day before yesterday. They say death ages the face, but sometimes in the young it's the reverse. Kwame looked cherubic, with milky skin, downy bum fluff, and a wide, innocent mouth. His whole belly was slick was blood, and his tracksuit bottoms bore a dark wet stain around the crotch area where his bladder must've emptied, pre- or post-mortem, I couldn't tell.

The notes indicated that the only possessions on him were a bunch of house keys and a flyer for the inter-borough boxing bout Patience was due to fight in last Friday where I met her. No weapons were found. No cash.

No camcorder either.

Notes also indicated he'd been stabbed once – a precise wound – and died from mass haemorrhaging. An elderly gent found him and called it in.

In a couple of stills you could see an ambulance and police officers in the background, along with a cluster of onlookers – curious locals, oddballs, addicts, and insomniacs – huddled behind the police tape. Amongst these, his pasty skin, bulbous tummy and gormless grin giving him away, was Terry Kinsella.

Next, I went to the investigative report. To say it was patchy was an understatement. Terry's statement was all they had to go on, with no effort to consider alternatives. He described seeing Kwame chased by a 'pack of hyenas', a carbon copy of the story he'd weaved me. Like Mani said, as far as the police were concerned, Kwame was another statistic, his death open and shut.

I handed Diane the folder back.

'Well?' she said.

I shrugged. 'That's a pretty shoddy investigation.'

'What do you expect?'

'A few more lines of enquiry, for a start.'

'Acknowledged. But Kwame was a poor teenager involved in crime who got murdered on Paradise. Don't expect Poirot to be assigned the case.'

'Crikey,' I said, taken aback. 'I didn't expect to hear you talking like that.'

She shrugged. 'What, you think just because I'm a black copper from humble stock, I'm not blind to the realities that go on in areas like this?'

'To be honest, Diane, I don't know what I'm thinking.' I drank some coffee. 'How about suspects? Anyone?'

'None.'

'Is that normal in a murder like this?'

'Very. You know how it is. There's no leads. Killings like this hardly get a peek in the press the way a murder in an affluent place will. Plus people don't trust the police. Especially people from Paradise.'

She had a point. This mistrust of the Met was a depressing reality, the causes multifarious. 'OK,' I said. 'Anything in these forensics jump out to you?'

Diane shrugged. 'Not especially. Single stab wound, a sharp blade, delivered close range. No defence wounds.'

'Wouldn't that cast doubt on the witness account that Kwame was chased by his assailants?'

'It *could*,' she corrected. 'I figured you'd pick up on that, so did some digging. As that report states, the key witness who alleged seeing Kwame get chased was none other than Terry Kinsella, Paradise's mainstay drug dealer. Remember him?'

I nodded.

'Unfortunately, Terry was found yesterday. Apparent suicide.'

I nodded some more.

'It's quite a coincidence, you ask me to look into this, and then he rocks up dead.'

I turned my attention to the table.

'Don't act coy, Kas. I've heard the 999 call reporting a man collapsed in the café. A male's voice. Muffled, but sounds quite a bit like you.'

No getting out of this. 'OK,' I said. 'Guilty.'

'Guilty of what?'

'I broke into Terry's café yesterday and found him that way.'

'Why in Christ's name did you do that?'

'I went to ask some questions.'

'Questions about what?'

'What he claimed he saw. I think he was involved in Kwame's death, Diane.'

'You make Terry as the murderer? I don't see that.'

'I never said Terry killed him. But when I spoke to him the day before, he fobbed me off. I went back with Kwame's sister to learn why. We found him that way.'

Diane drank some coffee. 'What're you into here, Kas? It sounds kinda big.'

'It *might* be,' I said, trying to inject my voice with some uncertainty.

'And what am I supposed to do if you get hurt or killed?'

'No chance. I'm staying low key, just gathering info.'

'Info on what? You're talking in riddles. Give me something meaty.'

I puffed out air. Over the years, Diane had done loads for me, personally and professionally: if she felt I was locking her out completely, I'd risk losing her for good.

'This is all off the record,' I said.

'Fair enough.'

'I think Kwame stole something off Terry, and it got him killed. That's why Terry lied to me. And it's why he topped himself.'

'What're we talking here? Drugs? Guns?'

'It's to do with missing women. Prostitutes and addicts, people low down the food chain who're easy to miss.'

'We're talking a sex ring?'

'Like I said, I'm still making enquiries, gathering evidence. I don't have the full picture yet. When I do, I'll be on the phone to you.'

She drank more coffee, ate maybe a fifth of her pastry; then she smiled.

'What's funny?'

'You're sounding like the old Kas.'

'Oh yeah?'

'Yeah. That truculent copper who couldn't let things go. You ever think about coming back, using those skills to help the team?'

It wasn't the first time Diane had asked me about a return to the Met. I gave the answer I gave before. 'No chance.'

'Reasons?'

'You remember how I was as a copper. My anger always held me back.'

'That's true. But maybe being a bit older and wiser will help keep fiery pants under control.'

'It's more than that, though. I really don't think I could do the job.'

'Instead, you're rocking this PI gig? That doesn't make sense.'

'It's hard to explain.'

'Try.'

I thought a moment. 'Day in, day out, police see the hardship, the suffering, the inequality on these streets. You want to help. But a lot of the time there's nothing you can really do to change things.'

'Go on?'

'The system's designed to keep things *un*equal. Why do you think they never ransacked a cesspit like Paradise? It's because it's in the public interest to keep the lowlifes in one place. Out of sight, out of mind. No wonder a lot of coppers just burn out.' I shook my head, aware that I'd ranted.

I expected Diane to counter back, but she seemed intrigued. 'I hear you. Every year I hear about another cop who's walked.'

'Anyone I'd know left recently?'

She thought. 'Ross Butler. Remember him?'

I did.

'Last year, he worked on a real nasty child sex case, had to interview victims, and go over a ton of smut. A few months before, Ross had gotten engaged and became a dad. Some of those shots stayed in his head. One day at work, he just lost it. They found him blubbing in the loo. Vicarious trauma they called it. He went off on sick and decided to throw in the towel. I hear he's working as an estate agent now.'

'Wow,' I said. 'I had Ross down as a die-hard copper.'

'Me too.' She lowered her mug. 'But you never can tell. Everyone has a limit.'

'How about you?' I said. 'What's your limit?'

'I've not found it yet.' She smiled, looked away pensively. 'I'm still proud I'm police. Want to know what your problem is, Kas?'

'Why not?'

'You take things too seriously. A sense of humour is important. Perspective too. You need to accept that you can't save the world. As a police officer, sometimes you can make a difference. A lot of the time though, you can't.'

'Yeah,' I said. 'Those are the times I struggle with.'

'Sure,' Diane said. 'But is doing what you're doing now any more rewarding?'

'Not financially. I've had to apply for a bouncer job to pay the rent.'

'Jeez.'

'If that fails, I'm thinking about becoming a vigilante, taking bad guys off the street. I'll wear a red helmet with a K in the middle and invoice the council for my efforts.'

'Idiot,' she said affectionately, and laughed, a full-bodied laugh that made Murphy look up and bark. A few more heads turned our way.

'So,' I said, 'what've you been doing for fun recently?'

'Well,' she said, 'if you must know, I've been dating.'

'Really?' My back stiffened. 'Who's the lucky man?'

'Men,' she said. 'There was a copper I was seeing briefly, but he neglected to mention his wife and kids at home, so I binned him. The new one's called Quentin. He works in finance, nothing to do with the Met. It's early days. But I kinda like him.'

'Lucky Quent.'

Diane blushed, just enough to tell me it was her who felt the lucky one. 'You should start dating,' she said. 'There's apps and things, ways to meet.'

'I've tried.'

'Any hits?'

'None. "Strapped-for-cash ex-copper seeks like-minded women for fun and games." I've no idea why they say no.'

'I'd tweak your strapline,' Diane said. 'But stick at it. I think you're ready to mingle.'

It was my turn to blush, this time at the memory of my last bit of mingling with Lisa, my go-to working girl.

'Look, Kas,' Diane said, 'speaking of work, I got to fly.' She slid the rest of her pastry over to me, took a serviette and wiped sugar from my lip.

As she stood, an idea popped into my head. 'One more favour.'

She hesitated.

'Can you plug Red Rose Productions into *CRIMINT*. See what comes up?'

She frowned. 'What's Red Rose Productions?'

'Just some phrase I heard the other day. It's probably nothing.'

She scribbled it down, then said, 'Take care, big man,' and took Murphy by the lead. 'And don't forget – you bell me if you get anything juicy. Hear?'

I told her I did and watched her and the dog leave.

Alone, I ate the remains of her pastry, looked at her empty seat, and the lipstick residue on her mug.

Quentin? Works in finance?

I hated him already.

Talking to Diane helped clarify what I already suspected – the police investigation into Kwame's murder was half-arsed. If it happened on Paradise, the rules were different.

But something else she'd said was rattling in my head too, a comment about our colleague, Ross. After seeing some harrowing footage, he quit the Met. Some images stay in your head. Those were her words.

Yesterday, when Patience and I broke into the café and found Terry's corpse, right before we bolted, she'd been staring at one of the photos on the wall.

She didn't know why it caught her attention.

But it had.

Some images stay in your head.

Had she seen something? Recognised someone?

Shot for other ideas, I decided to find out.

Chapter 10

I waited till dusk and the fall of a moody sky, then made my way back to Paradise under the cover of darkness.

The shutters were down to the front of Kinsella's Café, accompanied by a **Police: Do Not Enter** sign hung from the corrugated steel. I ignored this and went round the side like I had yesterday.

After a quick one-two, I hiked onto a wheelie bin, then shimmied up the drainpipe to the small window Patience and I climbed through.

The glass had been shattered, the hasp twisted open. By who? The police?

Craning, my phone's torch perched between my teeth, I lifted myself up and through, then tumbled down to the floor.

Like before, the cooking smells lingered; but the tang of death was gone.

Torch in hand, I came from the rear and in towards the kitchen and the café floor. The kitchen was ransacked, the fridge door hanging open, foodstuffs scattered, thawing in the cold. Cutlery, knives, spatulas, chopping boards were strewn over the work surfaces. The microwave had been wrenched from the wall.

I went into the seating area. Tables and chairs were tossed aside, the condiments and cutlery with them, the floor strewn with rugs and sleeping bags, shards of foil, blackened spoons, a crack-pipe and several used syringes. Further in, candles lay in cups and on saucers around the café floor. Paradise's addicts hadn't wasted time to scavenge the lair of their departed dealer.

A dull scratching by the entrance made me spin around.

'Who's there?' I said, flashing my torch towards the sound.

The scar faced junkie I'd walloped the other day emerged. He looked clammy, feverish. If he recognised me, he didn't let on.

'What're you doing here?' I said.

'I'm sick,' he said. 'Withdrawing. Hiding from the cold.'

'Anyone here with you?'

He shook his head. 'They all went to try an' score. I'm too ill. No one to get gear from anymore.'

I pointed towards the back window. 'Scram,' I said.

He staggered past, carrying a mixed smell of sweat and dirt, eyes bulging like ping-pong balls.

'Got any change, mate?' he said pathetically. 'Please. I'm rattlin'.'

Not looking, I dug out a tenner and tossed it in his direction, then waited for him to vanish.

I stood a moment, listening to the thrum of the wind, the kick of my heart, then moved in.

The spot by the griddle where Terry collapsed bore no remnants of him. Even so, I stepped around it, avoiding his imprint, as if there were a murder scene outline chalked to the floor.

In the main area of the café, I shuffled around upended furniture, moving towards the wall where the photos still hung, the only remaining items that hadn't been looted, perhaps because they bore no material value.

I couldn't remember which ones Patience had been looking at, so had no option but to capture the lot. I started snapping with my phone's camera, twenty-six pictures in total.

Although it was dark and my photography skills were limited, the phone had a flash and autofocus, and seemed to do an OK job. While I worked, I tried to suppress the memory of Terry's corpse, his waxy face and vacant eyes. What messed up things had those eyes seen before his ticket got stamped?

By the time I'd finished I was itching to leave. I shoved the phone away, headed for the window.

Halfway there, I stopped, looked at the staffroom door leading upwards. I wanted to take in the snuff film-set again.

As I pushed open the door and started up, the thread of fear spindled over my neck. Like before, it was dark, steeped in silence. But a faecal scent hung in the air too.

As I stepped onto the landing the smell intensified and made my guts turn. Inside the room, the stench became overpowering. I found the light, switched it on. Chaos met me.

The space had been used as a makeshift toilet, the withdrawing junkies expelling their loose guts on the floor. They'd given the desk and filing cabinets a going over, ransacking drawers, upending the bedframe, flinging Terry's papers everywhere, on the hunt for drugs. Any hope that this space could be salvaged for forensics was long gone. It was a sewer.

The only remnant from the snuff was the drapes, whisked from the cabinet and lying in a messy heap on the floor, the velvet fabric glistening like blood beneath the flimsy light.

Nineteen women breathed their last in this room. Nineteen

women screamed and begged as two monsters had their way. Now, as a final indignity, the space had been crapped over.

Repulsed, my heart turning somersaults, I climbed the stairs, clambered up to the window, and left the way I'd come.

Fifteen minutes later I was banging on Patience's door.

Eventually she answered, wearing Nike sliders, a Nike tracksuit, and a furtive frown. 'Kasper?'

'Sorry to turn up late,' I said.

'I was in bed. What's up?'

I need to show you some photos. Now.'

Her eyes narrowed. She knew I meant business.

'All right,' she said, 'come in.'

The hall was cluttered with mail, bin bags, and random junk packed into carrier bags. An electric meter box was propped open and tampered with to bodge the readings and keep from getting cut off.

'Kitchen's there,' Patience said, bolting the front door. 'First on the left.'

I turned into the space. It was a cramped box, with a semi-circular dinner table propped against the wall, covered with a plastic serving mat, and strewn with demand notices from energy suppliers and the council. The sink was leaky, plinking drops onto piles of plates and bowls. To my left there was a fridge, whirring loudly; right, a counter and a rusty kitchen sink. The air smelled foisted, like old dishcloths left out to dry.

'Get you anything?' Patience said. 'Tea? Water? I don't have no beer.'

I shook my head.

'So, what have you found?'

I pulled out my phone, went to the photos, handed it to her. 'I broke into Terry Kinsella's café.'

'Why'd you do that?'

'Last night, you were staring at those photos on his wall. I want to know why.'

'Hold up,' she said, raising her hands defensively. 'I was just waiting on you, man, looking at whatever there was to see.'

'In that case I've interrupted your evening for nothing.' I pointed at the phone. 'But I want you to examine each of these and tell me if anything sticks out.'

She looked at the phone again, started scrolling through, scrutinising each.

Apart from the whir from the fridge and the drip from the sink, the kitchen was silent.

A couple of minutes passed.

Then she drew breath. Her eyebrows hitched up.

'Him,' she said. 'He's the one I was looking at.'

I took the phone, studied the photo.

It showed Terry beside a slight Caucasian man, the two of them side-by-side in the café. The man looked young, mid-twenties, with buttery skin and a shock of honey-coloured hair. He looked every bit the Robert Redford understudy, and a far cry from what I was expecting.

'You're sure?' I said.

She nodded.

'Who is he?'

'Dunno.'

'Where do you recognise him from?'

'Dunno. Just something about him looks familiar. I told you this was stupid, Kasper.'

'Hold on.'

I studied the man.

His slight athletic frame, lips thin and red, eyes pale blue . . .

At the bottom right of the photo, there was writing. I expanded the image as much as I could.

It was an autographed message. I squinted to read:

Terry,
   Thanks for all you've done.
   Nate Willoughby

'Nate Willoughby,' I said. 'You heard that name before?'

'Nope,' Patience said.

Neither had I.

But I would.

I plugged the name into my phone's browser. It didn't take long to get a hit.

Nathan 'Nate' Willoughby was a British TV director. The three photos on Google showed a small, blond male, groomed, clean cut. Definitely the same man.

Energy surged in my chest. He was a filmmaker. A bloody filmmaker.

I looked at Patience.

'You reckon he could be the small man from the snuff?' she said.

'What do you think?'

She shrugged. 'But why's his photo on the wall of the fat man's café?'

'I don't know yet,' I said. 'But I intend to find out.'

There was a beat.

'All right then,' I said, 'first we need to—'

I didn't finish.

A slight cough came from the adjoining room. Patience had company. The cough sounded oddly familiar too.

Straight away, her face reddened.

I got to my feet, walked from the kitchen, went to the room the sound came from. It was a minuscule bathroom, containing a basin, toilet and bath, the curtain wrapped around it.

'Wait,' Patience said. 'I can explain—'

I pulled back the curtain. 'Well, well,' I said.

Suzi was hiding there. A lot of makeup was covering her face, and not a lot of clothing was covering the rest. Seeing me, her expression crumpled with embarrassment.

'Hey, Kas,' she said.

I should've predicted this. After seeing the two of them flirting at Dr Steiner's, it was only a matter of time before they hooked up.

'Suze,' I said, 'funny place to see you.'

And it was funny. On a different day, and in a different set of circumstances, I would've laughed.

But right then, I wasn't in the laughing mood.

Maybe it was the shoddy sleep and gallons of booze I'd put away; maybe it was being in Terry Kinsella's death-infused café twice in two days, or the anniversary of my daughter's death coming up, or just the whole lot frothing to the brim.

Whatever: right then, an anger fizzled up in my chest and I snapped.

'What's this?' I said, feeling my lips snarl. 'You two been having a secret pyjama party?'

'Easy, Kasper, man,' Patience said, behind me.

I turned, pointed. 'You're meant to be helping figure out what happened to your brother. Not cuddling up with *her*.' I gestured at Suzi with a head flick.

'It's not like that,' Patience said.

'So what *is* it like?'

She glowered. 'Yesterday, after seeing that fat man's dead body in the café . . . well, I was spooked. You didn't want to talk. So I called Suze, an' she came over. One thing led to another. And then—'

'And then.' I looked back at Suzi. She'd recovered from the shock, and now wore a tight, adversarial expression.

Stepping out of the shower and around me, she pulled a towel from the rail to cover her body and pointed a finger at my chest.

'Look, Kas,' she said, a steel to her voice I'd not heard before, 'I'm a big girl, and can hang out with whoever I—'

'No,' I interrupted, 'I don't want you near this.'

'What're you on about? Near what?'

'This estate, this thing we're investigating.' I pointed at Patience. 'And her. Just keep out of it.'

Suzi's expression sharpened. 'You're not my fucking dad. In case you've forgotten, he burned to death in a fire that was meant for you.'

I flinched. She must've seen it, for she put a hand to her mouth, but her eyes stared fierce.

'Stop this, man,' Patience said, placing a hand on my arm.

I tried to sweep it off, but her grip was iron.

'Get off me,' I said, eyeballing her. 'I mean it.'

'What's the big deal? You think I'm gonna hurt her? Corrupt her? Or make her go the way your daughter did?'

'Don't you ever mention my daughter,' I hissed, barging her hand away from me, each fibre of my body bristling.

114

Patience's eyes reddened. She turned her back and her shoulder trembled as she faced the damp-ridden wall.

My nails pinched into my palms, teeth ground together hard enough to hurt. A small voice told me that I'd overstepped. They were two kids, having fun.

I might've admitted as much, but Suzi spoke first. 'Just get out, Kasper,' she said, muscling between us. 'You're not welcome here.'

I felt the enmity in her eyes and knew I'd messed up.

'Fine,' I said, 'I'll see myself out.'

Chapter 11

The spat with Suzi and Patience left me far too edgy to sleep. Telling those girls how to live their lives was none of my business. I owed both an apology.

I also suspected Patience wouldn't want me investigating her brother's murder anymore, given her newfound dislike for me. Common sense dictated I should call things quits.

Problem was, I wasn't ready to do that. I'd made a giant leap tonight, identifying a possible suspect for the murders of Minka, Kwame, and maybe a heap of other women.

Nate Willoughby.

I stayed up late, scouring the web for information. I wanted him to have a track record making pornos and slasher flicks, but his brief IMDb page and a few remnant articles confirmed him to be a jobbing TV director rather than a major leaguer.

This was disappointing. Nothing gratuitous, nothing snuff related.

What's more, Nate had seemingly vanished from the public view in recent years.

Steeped in darkness, I came downstairs, brewed the first of

several strong coffees and then burrowed into whatever I could find of his back catalogue.

This consisted of a couple of soap episodes, a few early morning kids' shows, one or two domestic daytime-y dramas. Nearly everything was humdrum and inconsequential.

Before long I was bored, and considering calling it a night, when I stumbled on a stand-alone project he made ten odd years ago.

This hour-long documentary, written, narrated, and directed by Nate, was available to watch in multiple parts on YouTube. My fingers began to tingle as the title flashed up: *Paradise Lost*.

The focus was Paradise Estate, its fraught history, shocking crime rates, but also its resilient community and the quirky individuals living there. Undoubtedly the most ambitious work by Nate, the film romanticised the squalor through sparse, slow-moving close-ups: pensioners scrubbing graffiti off graves in the cemetery; teens playing football using cider cans as balls; addicts scrounging wheelie-bins; working girls kerb-crawling.

Juxtaposed against these were poignant exchanges with locals, activists, youth workers, squatters, even a meander through a community group for disadvantaged kids run by an altruistic husband-and-wife team.

I'm no critic, but there was talent on show here, less so in the interviews and oration, more in the Dickensian depictions, transforming the sere, hostile setting into something harsh yet beautiful. Here was the same art-house style that defined the snuff film. I was sure of it.

Nate's narration was spare, delivered laconically, the voice clipped and middle English. He appeared minimally, but when he did, his slick, deliberate moves, and those pale eyes and red lips struck the breath from me.

Two-thirds in, he had a brief exchange with a dishevelled Ghanian father of two young kids, describing how tough things were since his wife's death. I'd never met Colin Mensah, but his sharp jawbones and furtive eyes were familiar, and when his kids fell into frame, a boy and girl, the penny dropped. No wonder Nate's face rang a bell with Patience. She'd met him.

To blow out any doubts I'd found my man, *Paradise Lost* ended with a chirpy back-and-forth with the proprietor of a café synonymous with the estate. Gleefully, Terry Kinsella attempted to underplay the negative rep Paradise carried, describing locals as 'salt of the earth' and 'rough diamonds', before minimizing the crime stats, insisting the press '. . .were out to get decent folk like me.'

Decent? That scumbag couldn't spell the word.

What the hell had turned Nate Willoughby from making artsy-fartsy documentaries to snuff movies? Was *Paradise Lost* the kernel for a snuff movie enterprise?

The doorbell drew me from these thoughts. I hit pause, checked my watch, realised I'd been going all night. It was half seven AM, and a dingy light was already spreading its hooks across the sky.

An unhappy Diane was standing on the porch. This wasn't a social visit.

'What the hell you up to, big man?' she said, pointing.

I tried for a befuddled face, but feigning ignorance with this copper was no mean feat.

She stepped forward, said, 'Red Rose Productions. How'd you hear about it?'

I tensed. 'Why? What's come up?'

'What's come up is, I plugged the phrase into *CRIMINT* like you asked.'

119

She'd found something. 'And?'

'And, Red Rose Productions is the name used by a niche outfit the NCA would love to nail. They specialise in producing home movies. Films of a certain type. Till now, they've evaded capture. The only reason we heard of them is because a wanted sex offender living in Spain had a coronary while viewing one of their videos.'

'What was on this video?'

I had to ask, but already, I knew what she was going to say.

'A film of a woman.' She paused. 'A woman who appears to get murdered. It's made to look like flashy art.'

'You've seen it?'

'Enough to get a feel for it, yeah.'

I swallowed. It felt like I had a mouthful of glue. 'Who's the victim?'

'No idea.'

'Anything on the perps?'

'One's big, one's little. Both wear masks. The big one does most of the grunt work, tools, weapons, fists. The little one takes a more strategic role, so to speak, talking to the woman at the start, giving her a rose before tearing out her earrings.'

A carbon copy of the Minka snuff. I had to exert a great deal of effort to keep my face from crumbling.

'Well?' Diane said. 'That's me. Let's hear what you've got.'

I had two choices. Come clean, and spill. Or hold back.

If I took the former, told Diane everything, she'd be duty bound to step in, and take over. I couldn't have that, not yet.

'Sorry,' I said.

'Sorry? What's that supposed to mean?'

'It means I can't tell you.'

She shook her head, angry, shocked, hurt too. 'Kas, this isn't cheating husbands or unpaid parking violations. We're talking major crime. You're deep into this. Tell me what you know.'

'I swear, as soon as I have something concrete, I'm reaching out to you. But right now, I can't.'

'Christ, you're a stubborn pig-headed ass. This could cost us both. Hear?'

'Yeah,' I said, 'loud and clear.'

She turned and left. No goodbyes.

I closed the door, her words spinning in my head. She may've had a point. What the hell was I doing?

More coffee.

Over the next hour I trawled the internet further, determined to find Nate Willoughby. But there wasn't a website, a publicist, a Twitter, Facebook or Insta account or anything on social media.

Eventually, I located a small talent consortium in Soho that had represented him for a brief period many moons back. A bouncy sounding receptionist answered the call.

Donning a chipper voice, I introduced myself as Dale Kasper, and asked for the contact details of Nate Willoughby, an ex-client of theirs. She informed me of GDPR policy, that they weren't at liberty to give out client information, past nor present, blah blah.

'OK,' I said, 'what if I wrote an email for Nate, and you forward it on to him. Could that work?'

'I don't think so,' she said. 'Besides, he's been off our books for years. The email address we have may be wrong.'

'Rats,' I said, thinking fast, for she'd just revealed that they had an email. 'What say you ping him something from me on the off-chance?'

'Well . . .'

'I'll wash your car every weekend for a year?'

That earned a giggle. 'I haven't got a car. But I guess if you send an email to me now, I could forward it on to him.'

'You're one in a mill,' I said, took her details, and said goodbye.

Quickly, before she forgot about me, I drafted the following:

Dear Mr Willoughby,
My name is Dale Kasper. Not sure if you've heard, but a mutual friend, Terry Kinsella, passed recently. I'm collecting anecdotes for a memory book. Just wondered if you might have some free time to talk?

I put my mobile number at the bottom and hit send.

Then I leaned back, stared out the window, and faced facts.

I was out of ideas. Firing emails into the ether like this was like pissing in a storm.

I was headed for the kitchen to fetch some booze to mix with my coffee when the doorbell rang again. Diane no doubt, here for another stab.

Wrong. It was Suzi. A night's sleep didn't appear to have placated her, either.

'Hey, Suze,' I said, 'come out the cold,' and held the door open.

'No thanks,' she said. 'I won't be here long. I've just come to tell you how upset I am at how you acted last night.'

'Yeah,' I said, 'not my finest hour. I was meaning to call to straighten things out.'

'Don't bother.'

'Suze, I just lost it and—'

'I haven't finished. How you spoke to Patience was awful. There was me telling her how cool you were, and how much you'd helped me. Now she's hurt, and I look like an idiot.'

'I apologise,' I said. 'Try to understand, I'm in the middle of something big, and it's made me a little off-kilter.'

She shook her head. 'Right now, I don't want to see you. We need some space to figure out what we want to do.'

'So it's *we*,' I said. 'You and Patience a unit already?' There was reproach in my voice I hadn't intended. Was I jealous of a couple of kids?

'Not that it has anything to do with you, but yes, we're girlfriends.'

I took a moment, planning my next words.

'OK,' I said, 'I'll make it up to you. But look: Patience is caught up in some ugly stuff to do with her kid brother who got murdered. She's got a lot going on. It might not be the best time for you two to get involved. Can't you understand that?'

'What I understand is, the anniversary of your daughter's death is coming up, and you've never forgiven yourself for what happened. Well sorry, Kas, but you need to accept the truth. I'm not Rosie.'

That one stung.

'Look,' she said, quieter now, 'since Dad died, things have felt so shitty, and you and Dr Steiner have become my best friends. I want you to be happy for me. I've finally met someone I like. Don't you get it?'

I nodded, trying to think of something reparative to say.

I was still thinking when she said, 'Tell Dr Steiner I said hi,' and headed off.

'OK,' I said feebly, 'take care, Suze,' but there was no point. She was gone.

Chapter 12

Now, I was in an even bigger funk.

Diane was pissed at me. Suzi was pissed at me. Patience was pissed at me too.

And they all had pretty good reasons. Christ, if I wasn't such a big tough hard-nut, I could've cried.

What's more, I still didn't know what to do with this investigation. I had a name – Nate Willoughby – but no way of finding the bloke.

Yet again I considered what Diane said about going to the police. They had their tech, forensics, resources. For all I knew, Nate Willoughby might be on their radar.

But he might not be. And if they made assumptions about Paradise locals and screwed this up like they'd screwed up Kwame's murder investigation, I wouldn't forgive myself.

Times like this I revert to Page One in the Kasper Rulebook – when in a rut, seek solace in alcohol or violence.

I'd done enough of the former, but the latter sounded good. I pulled on my joggers and headed to Savages.

*

The boxing club stood on the site of a former meat abattoir, and to most passers-by I suspected it would've been more alluring in that previous incantation than now.

The windows were boarded up with chipboard, and there were at least three bullet holes in the masonry. Vast pine doors granted entry, like from some gothic horror movie that creaked as you opened them.

Inside, it was a tall-ceilinged, open-plan hall. A fighting ring to the far end, punch bags and free-weights dotted everywhere else. The reek of sweat was entrenched in the loose flooring and gamey air, and the clang of iron and thuds of punches echoed. If the council bothered to inspect the club, I suspected it would fail all manner of health and safety requirements. But of course, the council never would, in the same way they'd never demolish Paradise, for if they did, half its clientele would be spilling onto the streets.

There was a good crowd at Savages that afternoon, mostly teenagers and young adults from the flats, a couple of whom might go places if they stayed on the straight and narrow.

I jumped into some pad work with Ricky, my regular sparring partner whose speed and precision had increased in diametric opposition to my own.

In the films, pad work is seen as bread and butter, a way to loosen the muscles; in reality, chucking punches at a moving target is no mean feat. After twenty minutes my arms were trembling, and my eyes stung from the sweat.

As I stood by the wall waiting for my breathing to settle, I caught sight of a small, snappy little boxer working tricks on a heavy bag. Patience was clad in a sports bra and black shorts. Her skin glistened, her brow furrowed, and her punches were all mean and precise.

She must've sensed me checking her out, for a moment later she stopped, turned. Our eyes locked. Neither of us said anything.

But something must've been communicated, for a moment later we both simultaneously headed towards the ring.

I'd never sparred with a girl before, and was a little perturbed at the prospect. Pound for pound I outweighed Patience by a good fifty, and stood the best part of a foot taller. In fighting, weight invariably beats technique, and I didn't want to hurt her by accident.

Then again, I was a forlorn, sleep deprived man who felt every day of his forty-something years, where Patience was a whipper-snapper with a mean jab and a chip on her shoulder.

She came in hard, connecting a sneaky punch to the nose designed to rile more than floor. Technically she was adept, bobbing, feigning, with catapult speed and Michael Flatley feet. There was that temper too, innervating her muscles like a jump-start lead.

I shook off the stars and watched her ducking, weaving, using her diminutive size to sneak under my lumbering arms and connect another, and another.

If this was a street-fight, I'd just charge in and smother her. But boxing has rules. We had to play by them.

Before long we had a ringside gathering, including Jazz, an ex-steroid head I brought to Savages last year. Not wanting to lose face, I managed to land a few to Patience's ribs, made her snarl and pull back, but it was only momentarily, and she parried with her own counter blows.

Three rounds in, it was clear who the fitter boxer was. My vest clung to my body, my breathing was anaerobic, and the blood sang behind my eyes like a kazoo.

Patience's whole body was soaked, and her abdominals stood out like xylophone keys. Even though she was tired, there was no mistaking the grin, her mouthguard giving her the appearance of a pantomime horse.

'Call it quits?' she said.

'Only if you want to,' I said back.

'Just warmed up.' She smacked her gloves.

Three more rounds and my limbs were clay. I removed my mouth guard and pulled the plug.

'I'm done,' I said. 'Good fighting.'

She nodded. I could tell she'd gotten something out of her system. As had I.

I held out my gloves. She brought hers onto them with a wet smack.

Leaning on the ropes, I watched her head for the changing room, spitting out her mouth guard into a bucket.

From there, I went back home, and found some good news had landed in my inbox. Not to do with the case: it was a reply about that security guard job I'd applied for. The firm wanted me in for an interview. *Yowsah!*

My first instinct was to call Suzi.

But I held back. She'd asked for space, and I didn't want to dent our relationship more than I had done.

Instead, I made cheese on toast, drank an inch of Bushmills, and called Mani to fill him in on where I was with the case.

'This Nate Willoughby,' he said, 'you reckon he's the small man on the film?'

'Yes,' I said. 'I've got nothing on the big one yet. But I'm sure Terry Kinsella was working with them too. His job was to recruit the girls for this Red Rose outfit, bring them along, hold the camera steady while the other two did the killing.'

'A neat little operation.'

'Uh-huh. Until Kwame stole that camcorder from Kinsella's Café and tried making money. Then it got bloody.' I paused. 'The thing is, Mani, Terry's dead, and I have no idea where Nate Willoughby is, or anything for certain. Now might be the time to give all this to the police. I've got them evidence, the name of a suspect, plenty for them to investigate.'

'Hm,' Mani said. 'That'll piss Patience off.'

'Judging by the pounding she just gave me at Savages, she's already got an axe to grind with me. You hear how I put my foot in it with her and Suzi, right?'

'Yeah, she called me up last night, told me. She even used a couple of bad words describing you too.'

'Heavens above.'

Mani chuckled, a deep, sonorous sound. 'Give those two a bit of time. They both know you got a good heart, even if it sometimes gets lodged behind your pride.' I heard the snick of a lighter, the crackle of smoke. 'Anyway, whatever you do, I got your back. An' remember, Kasper – all this new information was found by you, not the police. You done good here.'

'Thanks, man.'

We let each other go, and I stared at my phone.

I'd done good.

Maybe.

So why was I feeling lousy again?

I stayed up late, drinking, my body tired, but my head refusing to shut up.

I looked at Minka Petrova's Polaroid photo, and the eighteen other women presumed dead.

I thought of Lisa, and working girls like her, caught in the trap of vice, all potential victims of Red Rose Productions.

I thought of Kwame and his father, two Londoners from the wrong part of town, killed way before their time.

I thought about Patience, Suzi, Diane, how I'd made a dog's breakfast of all our relationships.

Lastly, I thought of Rosie, my daughter, dead at fourteen. Still, a part of me couldn't believe she was gone.

A few hours later, half-cut and full of the blues, I accepted a hard truth: I wasn't up to this case. Time to let the pros take control.

I came close to ringing Diane, but stopped myself when I checked the time. Ten to midnight. She'd be snuggling up with Crispin or Quentin or whatever her new boyfriend's bloody name was. Last thing I wanted to hear was his voice in the background.

Instead, I sent her a text, asking if we could speak tomorrow.

There, decision made. Getting my life into order was my priority. From tomorrow, that's what I'd do.

I was pouring a final finger of whisky when my phone rang, a withheld number. Diane, no doubt. She'd probably just seen my text.

'Kasper,' I said, a little slurry.

'Is that the Dale Kasper who tried to contact me?' replied a clipped male.

Bones ground together in my spine. I knew the owner of this middle-English voice – I'd heard him before.

'Who's speaking, please?' I said.

'Nate Willoughby. An agency I was affiliated with years ago sent me your email. I was sorry to hear the news of Terry Kinsella's passing.'

'Me too,' I said, working hard to keep my voice relaxed. 'It came as a shock.'

'Indeed. What was the cause of death?'

'A drug OD.'

'Oh dear. Terry did indulge. But still, such a waste.'

'It was,' I said.

'Your email said you were pulling together anecdotes for a book?'

'That's right. It's nothing much. I'm just approaching people who knew Terry, asking them for titbits and memories.'

'Really.' He chuckled, then said: 'It's been a long time since I saw Terry. Even so, he wasn't the kind you forget easily. Yes, I'm sure I could think of something. And if I may say, what a thoughtful gesture this is of you, Mr Kasper. It says a lot about your character.'

'Just Kasper,' I said.

'Excuse me?'

'My name. People generally just call me Kasper. Like the ghost, but with a K.'

'In that case, call me Nate. Just Nate, with an N. Ha! I'm beginning to like you already.'

I smiled. That was the plan.

'So how should we do this? Shall I send you some comments to peruse through?'

'That's one option,' I said. 'Another is we meet in person?'

'Even better. Why don't you pop by the house tomorrow morning.'

'Tomorrow morning's good. Where are you based?'

He gave a northwest London address and I read it back to ensure I hadn't made a mistake.

'Drop by around half-ten,' he said.

'Will do,' I said, adding, 'looking forward to meeting you.'

'Oh, so am I, Kasper, so am I. Ciao.'

He went.

I sat rock still, holding the phone.

Stay objective, I told myself. Don't let your head run away.

Easier said than done.

I'd just established contact with the key suspect in this case, and had gotten invited round to his house, no less.

This was a massive inroad.

I brushed my teeth, switched off the lights and lay in bed, my body fizzling with anticipation.

See you tomorrow, Nate.

Chapter 13

Nine sharp the following morning, Diane called to find out what last night's text was all about. I'd predicted this and had my answer pre-rehearsed.

'It was to apologise. I've been a dick recently, taking info from you, but not giving back. Let me say sorry and—'

'Kas,' she butted in, 'are you going to fill me in on this Red Rose thing you're investigating?'

I hesitated. 'Afraid not.'

'Then there's nothing to discuss. And you're still a dick.'

She hung up before I could answer.

Fair enough.

I'd sort things out with her in due course. Right then, I had my sights set on the main prize: Nate Willoughby.

An hour later I was hiking up a steep slope towards Highgate Village, one of north London's most affluent pockets, and where he lived. I turned at the peak of the hill, took in a searing panoptical view across London that rose above the splodge of clouds. There was St Paul's, the Eye, the Shard; to the east, less than a mile from where I stood, but a world apart, the louring peaks of Paradise.

It'd been years since I'd last visited Highgate. Out-of-pocket PIs rarely do.

The place hadn't changed much though – still charming, leafy, unapologetically exclusive. Historic pubs and gourmet delis, independent bookshops, and pricey charity shops made up the high street; Burbs and Barbour seemed the attire of choice; haircuts were sensible, accents pukka, buggies huge, lips invariably huger. There was a famous private school at the head of the main parade; past that, a cemetery where Karl Marx and the bloke who invented the telephone were buried.

Amidst it all was Nate Willoughby. He lived in a two-storey Victorian house set back from the main strip of shops. The exterior was pointed terracotta redbrick, the windows large clear sashes showing into airy interiors. Surrounding the land was a waist-high gate and geometrically cut hedges. Apart from some charred brickwork around the guttering, fire damaged perhaps, I couldn't tell, everything was immaculate, polished to a tee.

An intercom was at the entrance. I pressed the button.

'Yes?' came a female voice, curt, no nonsense.

'I'm here to see Nate,' I replied.

'Who are you?'

'The name's Kasper.'

'Is he expecting you?'

'He is.'

A long pause. Then, without word, the gate buzzed open.

By the time I'd walked up the path, the front door had opened. I found myself face to face with the owner of the voice.

She was a small, sinewy woman. Mid-thirties, dressed in black pumps, black chinos, and a grey jersey. The face looked capable of smiling but in repose it wore a frown, making me think of an adult who hadn't laughed much as a kid.

A shapeless mop of mud-brown hair was parted down her scalp, frizzing around her ears and shoulders, and she was entirely without makeup, which drew out the bleachy paleness of her skin, and gave her a cold, ill kind of look.

The only colour came from her eyes. They were the clearest of blues and looked at me with a sort of double vision, so that they seemed to focus and were somewhere else too.

'I'm Tash,' she said. 'Nate's PA.'

'Are you two related?'

'Why?'

'Your eyes. They're similar, that's all.'

'I'm his sister.'

'It's a pleasure to meet you, Tash.'

She nibbled her lower lip, said, 'What do you want?'

'A mutual friend passed recently. Nate invited me round to chat about him.'

The lip nibbling continued, and the eyes drooped away. 'Nate never mentioned anything about a friend of—'

She didn't finish. From behind, a voice exclaimed, 'Is that him?'

She shuffled left. Suddenly, I was facing the man himself.

'Kasper! So nice to meet you.'

I'm not sure what I was expecting. A maniac wielding a sledge-hammer and wearing a frock of flayed skin would've been good, for that would be proof positive of what he was.

Instead, Nate Willoughby was a slight, pukka chap smiling a salesman's smile. Five-eight and ten stone at a push, he looked like he'd stepped out of a Ralph Lauren catalogue, wearing a pressed navy rollneck, sharp beige khakis and Sperry boat shoes. He had the same honey coloured hair as the man in the photos, brushed in a bushy side-sweep, and his skin had the glow of an infant's, smooth and creamy, lit by those electric eyes.

'Well,' he said, looking from my boots to my face, 'you're big, aren't you?'

'So I've been told.'

He reached past his sister, held out a hand. I took it. His fingers were manicured and icy. Minka Petrova's voice careered back: *Your hands are cold . . .*

'Tash,' Nate said, 'this is Mr Kasper,' then added, 'sorry, *just* Kasper,' and gave me a wink.

'You didn't say you had someone coming?' she said. 'I should know your plans, Nate.'

'It's fine, dearest, nothing to worry about.' He spoke to her slowly, like a parent to a child. 'This isn't business. Kasper's here to chat about a friend.'

She looked at me, her gaze furtive yet absent, as if something was bugging her but she couldn't remember what it was.

'Come in, Kasper, come in,' he said.

I obliged, following him into a hallway and a large reception area. The house was white, bright, and expansive. The floor was parquet, buffed to a high sheen. A flowery scent sweetened the air, as if there were rose petals sprinkled discreetly. Most of the wall space was adorned with movie posters, films by directors I'd mostly heard of – Fellini, Pasolini, Tarantino, Hitchcock – and resting on mantels were vintage looking cameras and reels of spool.

'Nice pad,' I said.

'Oh, thank you,' Nate said. 'We inherited the property from Mum and Dad, and I had it completely refurbished to my tastes.'

'Just the two of you here?'

'That's how we like it. Right, Tash?'

She shrugged, closed the door.

'Let's talk in my office,' Nate said. 'Can I get you tea? Coffee? Perhaps a beer if it's not too early?' He checked his watch. A Rolex.

'Beer sounds good.'

'Doesn't it? I think I'll join you.'

He swanned to the kitchen, leaving Tash and I alone. I considered making chit-chat, but there was something decidedly offish about her, and so we stood in awkward silence.

A long moment later Nate returned, two Peroni bottles to hand.

'This way,' he said, guiding me left, past a lounge and into a modern office sky lit by Velux windows.

He took a seat behind a desk, placed one bottle in front of him, the other near me. Then he rested his feet on the corner next to a slick Apple desktop, interlocked his hands over his snakish hips and affixed me with those eyes.

'Sorry about Tash. She can be a moody puss, but she means well.'

'No problem.' I took the seat opposite. 'She mentioned being your PA?'

He smiled an expensive smile. 'I call her that. It gives her a sense of purpose. Tash used to be our parents' PA. She's struggled since their deaths. Really, it's me assisting her. Little brother to the rescue. She has a few issues. Up here.' He tapped his brow demonstratively. 'You understand?'

I indicated I did.

'So,' he said, 'about Terry. Wretched news.'

I nodded. 'He had his vices, drugs and whatnot, but I never figured he'd do something like this.'

'You two were close?'

'On and off.' I wanted to keep this bit vague. 'I'm in the

building trade and did some work on his café a few years back. We hit it off. How'd you meet him?'

'It was a job too,' Nate said. 'I used to be a filmmaker. Terry appeared in a documentary I made some years back about Paradise, the crime-ridden estate where he lived and worked. You must be familiar with the place if you rubbed shoulders with Terry?'

'I know Paradise well,' I said.

Nate's eyes widened. 'Then you'll agree it isn't the most salubrious area?'

'There's an understatement.'

'Yet Paradise holds a stark beauty that fascinated me as a filmmaker. It's full of nooks and crannies, and all kinds of wonderful characters you couldn't dream up if you lived to a hundred. Terry being one. He featured in the doc. Did you see it?'

'Yup. Terry was dead proud of it.' I winced. 'Bad choice of words.'

Nate smiled. He had small teeth, symmetrical and white, in contrast with the redness of his lips. 'Terry was quite the character,' he said. 'Generous too. While we were filming, we would use his café as a kind of hub. I think he hoped I was going to whisk him to Hollywood, bless him.'

'Did the two of you stay in touch?'

'You mean after the project wrapped up? Oh no. We hardly had much in common. And not long after that, I gave up commercial filmmaking all together.'

'Really?' I said, a curve of curiosity to my voice. 'Sorry to hear that.'

'Don't be. Apart from that documentary, all I'd made were bland soaps and imbecile kids' programmes; fast-food for the public to gorge on, then forget. A filmmaker can make a decent living that way, but it was demeaning. My goal was to make art. I realised the error of my ways and quit before it sucked the life out of me.'

'That's a shame,' I said. 'I'm no expert, but I thought the Paradise doc showed flare.'

Nate's eyebrows hitched up again; he was clearly impressed. 'Well, that's nice of you to say. If only more people agreed. The consensus was it was too art-house and pretentious, and I should take a leaf from my parent's oeuvre and "sell-out".'

'Your parents were creatives too?'

'Of a sort. They worked in commercial advertising. The lowest denominator of artwork. Their output was superficial fodder that let them keep up with the Joneses, pay the mortgage, and send young Nate to boarding school. A few things they made showed some potential. The still behind you being one.'

I turned, looked. And stifled a gasp.

A framed black and white photo faced me, hung from the wall. It showed a slight girl, light haired, pale skinned, a white blouse and black skirt her only clothes. She was perched on a stool, her face partially turned, masked in sweeping shadow, two large hoop earrings dangling from her ears.

'I used to think the photo was tawdry,' Nate said, 'but I've grown to enjoy having her there, a nice reminder of who Mum and Dad were, and what they did.'

I tried to take in the whole image. But my attention was drawn towards the only colour in the photo which came from the girl's right hand. Hanging limply from her fingers like a smouldering cigarette was a single red rose.

'Rats!' Nate said, and I spun round.

He was mopping lager from his desktop with a hanky. Somehow, he'd toppled my Peroni bottle, half of which was gushing out.

'Tash!' he called. 'We've had a spillage!' Immediately she appeared, cloth in hand, and began dabbing up the frothy amber.

'Sorry, Kasper,' Nate said, 'I've got butterfingers.'

'No problem,' I said.

Tash mopped frantically until every drop was gone. 'I'll fetch you another,' she said, disappearing with her cloth and my bottle, reappearing with a fresh beer, careful to avoid my eyes as she placed it before me on a coaster.

'Thank you, lovely,' Nate said.

'I'll be outside,' Tash said, 'let me know if you need anything else.'

Nate waited until she was gone, took his bottle, held it up.

'To absent friends,' he said.

We clinked.

The beer tasted icy cold, but wasn't enough to steady my pulse. Nate however was the picture of serenity.

He placed his bottle on the desk, leaned forward, elbows on the desk. 'May I digress from Terry for a moment and ask *you* something, Kasper?'

'OK,' I said.

'How tall are you?'

'Six one, without my boots on.'

'What do you weigh?'

'Last time I checked, a little under sixteen stone.'

'A lot of that's muscle, I presume?'

'If I cut back on the lagers and fry-ups, there'd be more.'

'You said you're a builder? Are you working at the moment?'

'I'm in-between jobs, actually.' I paused. 'Why?'

'It's just . . .' He made an L-shape with each of his hands, joining the thumbs and forefingers to make a square, then brought the square to his right eye, shutting the left one, creating the impression that he was peering at a screen and framing me within it.

'Oh yes,' he said, 'you have a presence. Certain people do.' He moved his hands, left, right, keeping the square poised on me like a steady cam. 'The camera would like you, I'm certain . . .'

The makeshift screen held me in its focus. It was uncomfortable, like I was being gazed upon, objectified.

After a minute, I said, 'I can't help feeling I'm auditioning for something, Nate.'

He lowered his hands and beamed. 'But you are! You see, I still do a little consultation work. Casting. Advising. Making introductions. And there're a few projects I know of in the pipeline that have *you* written all over them.'

'What do you mean?'

'Acting, of course. I'm imagining you as the tough guy playing a counterpart to a femme fatale. You've got the physique, the menace, plus the,' he waved his hand, a sweeping gesture, 'the je ne sais quoi.'

'Hm,' I said. Unless I was mistaken, the killer I'd come here to ID was offering to find me work. I wasn't sure how to respond, and said, 'I'm not sure how to respond.'

'Why so?'

'Because acting's not something I've ever thought about.'

'Maybe *acting* isn't the right word,' Nate said. 'Consider it more like playing an exaggerated version of yourself. Remember how Guy Ritchie used real life hard men in his early films? I'm thinking along those lines. Just so you know, a few friends are coming over for a get together tomorrow night. Several work in the industry. I'd be happy to make introductions. If you'd like.'

He smiled again.

I smiled back.

We drank beer.

*

For the next half hour Nate and I continued our amiable exchange. He recounted stories about Terry's on-set tomfoolery, how he cracked lewd jokes, broke wind, and kept actors and crew fed, watered, entertained, and stoned with his high-class hashish. I have no idea how much of this was true, but Nate sounded convincing, and it gave me the chance to watch him in flow.

He clearly enjoyed his voice and the chance to use it, invariably talking about himself in the third person, with 'Nate said this,' this and 'Nate did that,' that, an odd affectation. Even so, there was something beguiling to the man, likable too, for he possessed an old-fashioned charm.

I scrutinised his body language and expressions, looking for clues to suggest a Mr Hyde lurking. But everything was so slick and stylised, from the musical cadence of his voice to the smile that ended each sentence like a perfectly placed full stop.

'And those are just a few of the memories I have of Terry,' he said. 'Maybe I—' he started, but was interrupted by his phone pinging importantly.

'Goodness,' he said, reading the message, 'is that the time! I must go.'

'No problem,' I said.

'I hope that's been of some use, Kasper?'

'Very much so.' I returned my notebook to my pocket, drained my beer. I'd done some groundwork, meeting the man, and had plenty to chew over.

'Thanks for seeing me, Nate,' I said, and stood.

'Thank *you*,' he replied earnestly. 'I've enjoyed every minute.'

I believed him too, for his eyes were sparkling, the irises no longer pale blue, but bold, azure.

He led me back through the house and to the front door.

Tash was sitting at the bottom of the stairs, knees bandied

together, hands clasped above them in a knot. At the sound of our footsteps, she peered up.

'Pleasure to meet you, Tash,' I said.

She gave a tetanic kind of smile, her eyes flickering like an unturned TV.

Nate shrugged and gave me an 'I told you so' wink.

I considered trying a bit of humour to crack Tash's armour but sensed it would be pointless. There was something unreachable to her.

'Take care, Kasper,' Nate said. 'Hope you can make the party tomorrow. It could be the start of a wonderful career.'

I told him I well might and opened the door.

Chapter 14

I walked down Highgate Hill, passing a leafy park, a hospital, but taking little in. A moment later I boarded a 41 heading home.

Seated on the lower deck, I looked out the condensation-smeared window, trying to make sense of what I'd learned about Nate Willoughby.

I couldn't. My thinking was as bleary as the glass.

Questions fired in all directions:

Who was he? What was the story about the photo his parents took of the girl with the red rose? What was up with his cranky sister, Tash? And what was this invite to find me screen work all about? Was he for real?

I hadn't a clue.

But one thing I did know – I'd found a killer. As this certainty sank in, my teeth ground together. At this rate, I'd need dentures before the case was up.

When a flat-capped geezer tossed a copy of the *Gazette* onto a seat, I reached over, keen for a cheery distraction.

As if. Front page was more on these two Met police officers, by now household names. A string of other serving coppers had also been accused of uploading salacious crime scene images onto specialist dark-web sites. Independent complaints were firing in all directions, and the commissioner was facing a battering.

By the time the bus reached my stop I'd read the whole report along with a dirge of other articles about violence, exploitation and mindless brutality. I wasn't sure what sickened me more: the stories, that they were considered newsworthy, or the fact that I'd read them.

That evening, I made pasta with pesto out the jar and a green salad tossed with dressing from a bottle, about the pinnacle of my culinary skills. As I was dishing up, Dr Steiner came from the lounge, a lit cigarette in one hand, the new Rankin in the other, and we ate together in the conservatory.

I used the term ate loosely in relation to the doctor. She had the appetite of a rodent, in part the consequence of two bouts of bowel cancer – the second requiring surgery and the fitting of a stoma she affectionately christened Mildred after an ex – and also her habit of smoking *while* eating, as if the very act somehow enhanced her dining experience.

Tonight, she wore black leggings, cherry Dr Martens 8-holes, and an oversized black t-shirt with the Smiths' *'Meat is Murder'* LP cover superimposed onto its front; her crop of grey hair was buzz cut round the sides, mauve lipstick was lacquered on her small, thin mouth, and her round framed specs, above which she had a tendency to stare querulously, were balanced on her beak of a nose.

After the meal I scraped the remnants from our plates into Tommy's dog-bowl while she put a Nick Cave record on the turntable. I'd never been a fan, finding his voice a little warble-y, his tone a bit dour, but Dr Steiner had made it her mission to educate me, and after a few listens I couldn't deny the bloke knew how to spin a tune.

She started telling me about a matinee she'd been to earlier at the Almeida Theatre, a play written by some Frenchman I'd never heard of. I tried to feign interest, but halfway through she stopped and stared a knowing stare.

'You're somewhere else.'

'Sorry,' I said. 'Weird day.'

'Care to tell me all about it?'

'I think I would,' I said, realising how much I needed to thaw. 'But don't say I didn't warn you.'

Over the years, I'd used Dr Steiner as a soundboard for all kinds of woes. She knew about my daughter's death, my self-destructive traits, my fiery temper, use of prostitutes, and pretty much everything else. Never had I felt judged.

But until now, I'd not had cause to tell her something as abhorrent as this case. Doing so left me feeling exposed.

Within ten minutes she'd smoked two Dunhills and I'd told her pretty much the whole shebang.

'What was your impression of this Nate Willoughby?' she said. 'He has me quite intrigued.'

'He wasn't what I was expecting.'

'In what way?'

'He was disarming. Welcoming me into his house, inviting me to his party to meet his friends. I know he's a killer. Christ, I've watched him murdering a defenceless woman. Even so, there was something likable to him.'

'Jimmy Saville was likable,' Dr Steiner said. 'They awarded him an OBE for charitable services. But that's often the way with men like this: you want to loathe them until you meet them, but then when you do, they're not the way you want them to be, and loathing them seems wrong.' She paused to smoke. 'And what do you make of his sister? Do you think she's complicit somehow?'

I thought back to Tash, her awkwardness. 'I don't know. She's . . . an enigma. They both are.'

'OK, let's try to unpick them. Why does Nate make snuff films in particular? Beneath that charm, what's driving him?'

'Maybe it's his parents,' I said. 'He had a photo hanging up, a girl holding a red rose, just like the rose in the snuff. His parents took that photo. He keeps it in the study as a reminder of them.'

Dr Steiner winced. 'And "zee parents" are always to blame, yes?' she said, in her Sigmund Freud voice.

I shrugged. 'You think there's more to it?'

'Perhaps his familial relationships propelled his pathology. But Mummy and Daddy issues alone can't explain this quantity of killing. What else could be spurring Nate to kill and kill again?'

I thought some more. 'Maybe it's the money he's making from selling these snuffs? Judging by his house and clobber, the snuff business is lucrative. Or maybe it's the praise he receives? Stroking his ego?'

'OK,' Dr Steiner said, her head tilted, in full-blown psychiatrist mode now, 'money and accolades bring surface rewards. But these could be achieved through less bloody means. Think. What inner need do these killings satisfy at the time he commits them? That's what draws him back.'

I took a long moment, reliving the snuff frame by frame. Nate taunting Minka with fake compliments, cupping her breasts, before ripping out her earrings; I could see his snake's tongue licking those blood red lips, and the libidinous thrill that flashed across his pale eyes like lightning as the big man held her down and beat her.

'Sex,' I said. 'He's doing it because he gets off on it.'

Dr Steiner gave an obliging nod. 'Now, we're getting some- where. Eros and Thanatos. Sex and death. The two are inextricably linked. At some juncture in Nate's life, his sexual appetites have been fused with sadism. Of this I'm sure. How much his sister knows remains to be seen.'

She paused to light a fresh smoke. By now, her ashtray was brimming, and Nick Cave was in full maudlin mode.

As she exhaled a cloud, I caught her expression. She was smiling.

'I've just recounted a story about a snuff movie enterprise, and you're looking bemused. Care to explain?'

She slotted her next cigarette into its holder. 'You expect me to be appalled by the barbarity inflicted on these women?'

'Aren't you appalled?'

'No. We're all savages, Kasper. Read Dickens' description of a public execution, and the zeal he saw in the crowd when the noose fell. Compare that with this ongoing case in the news, two policemen sharing crime scene photos with their dastardly chums. Our pull towards violence has never dwindled, only mutated through the technological age.'

I looked at my hands. Two of the knuckles throbbed from the punches I'd chucked in the past few days. 'Returning to Paradise has brought home a few truths about me and violence,' I said.

'Oh? How so?'

'As a kid, after I got locked in that basement, I learned to fight. My dad taught me the basics. Then I found boxing.' I looked up. 'I guess you're right, Dr Steiner. We are savages. I've always had this destructive side. It's part of who I am.'

'Yes,' she said, waiting for more.

'But the violence I know, and the kind on the snuff film are poles apart.'

'How? If you're to thwart Nate, it's important to recognise the differences between you and him.'

'For a start, I've never killed. I've wanted to, but always held back.' I paused. 'Plus, I really don't understand what kind of warped mind could do something like that to a defenceless woman. It's . . .' I struggled for the word.

'Yes?' Dr Steiner said.

'It's monstrous.'

Dr Steiner took a moment. 'This's interesting,' she said.

'Why?'

'Because you're talking about Nate as if he's not human. Therein lies a fatal mistake. I'm afraid he's as human as you or I. Read through transcripts from the Nuremburg Trials, and you'll find example after example of insipid humans who committed acts of unspeakably monstrosity. It's Nate's humanity, in the face of the monstrous things he does, that makes him all the scarier.'

We were distracted by Tommy mooching around our legs, a sign that he wanted to head up to bed. Dr Steiner reached down, cupped his head in her wizened hands. He made a doggy noise, then settled himself in his cushion bed by the bi-fold windows.

'It's late,' Dr Steiner said. 'Before I retire, I'll tell you a real-life story that might resonate. When I was a junior registrar not long out of med-school I had a rotation at Broadmoor, the high-security hospital. You've heard of the place, I presume?'

I indicated I had.

'Early on, I was asked to assess a patient. This man was a rapist of minors, detained indefinitely due to the risks he posed. I'd famil-iarised myself with his files. Over the course of a decade, he'd assaulted dozens of girls, luring them with false promises of money and sweets. His drive was lust, a paedophilic interest coupled with a sexual compulsion to inflict harm. On paper, he was a textbook psychopath – seductive, manipulative, remorseless. Psychological assessments showed him to lack empathy or understanding for the lives he'd ruined. He was proud of his achievements. I thought I was going to meet a real-life monster. I prepared myself for the challenge. To be honest, I was looking forward to it.'

'What happened? Did he live up to your expectations?'

'On the contrary. I was thoroughly disappointed.'

'I don't understand.'

'He was so *un*remarkable, Kasper. Garrulous, smug, banal, the kind of hapless man you'd chat to at a bus stop, then forget. By day he'd worked in a biscuit factory; at weekends, he'd volunteered with the local church. On the surface, everything about him was humdrum. He should've been a nobody. He was.

'Yet he had this capacity for cruelty, committed these awful crimes, and would've re-offended if released, of this there was no doubt. It left me chilled.'

'Why?'

'Because it proved to me that we fear all the wrong things. People like him and Nate aren't the monsters of folklore. They walk in our midst, and appear quite normal. "Evil is unspectacular and always human and shares our bed and eats at our table." So said Auden, and he knew more about these things than you or I.'

The record ended; the stylus clicked on the turner. I stared at the table.

'Well,' Dr Steiner said, 'you look even more disheartened than before.'

'You're not far off. Any advice?'

'Perhaps a sideline. Why not make amends with young Suzi?'

'She told you we fell out?'

'She called yesterday, rather upset.'

'I acted dumb, lost my temper with her and Patience.'

'You did. But it's not irredeemable. Suzi will hate me for saying this, but that girl thinks a great deal of you.' She placed a bony hand over mine. 'As do I.'

I felt warmth, a welcome tonic to the darkness in my head.

'So, what's next?' she said. 'Give everything to the police, presumably?'

'No. Nate's invited me to his party tomorrow night. I plan to go and keep looking for evidence.'

'Isn't there enough evidence already? What with the film, the photos, and now today's developments, surely there's plenty for the police to work with?'

I shook my head. 'The police have made enough cockups. I need solid proof that Nate is the man on that film, something that will put him and everyone he's working with away. Soon as I have it, I'm on the phone to the cops.'

'What if he cottons on to you first?'

'Can't see how he will. Right now, he thinks we're mates.'

'Well,' Dr Steiner said, 'I think it's unwise. You have considerable skill, but this is something exceptional. Remember what I've said. You must be wary. If needs be, don't hesitate to be merciless.'

'Merciless?' I made another incredulous face, trying to add humour, but it lost steam when I saw Dr Steiner's steely gaze.

'Haven't you been listening?' she said. 'These are cruel men you're after. You may need to be cruel back to survive.'

As I was thinking about this, she pushed up from her chair and went to the record player. Halfway there, she turned. Said, 'Oh, one other thing.'

I looked up, expecting a final biting observation to go to bed with.

'Your rent's late.'

Chapter 15

I returned to Nate Willoughby's house the following evening to find his soiree in full swing.

I'd come wearing a black shirt tucked into grey chinos and my old penny loafers polished like a honey-glazed roast. I'd brushed my hair back, had a shave, even slapped on some Cool Water, expecting the attenders to be highfalutin types.

In fact, they all seemed normal well-to-dos. The youngest were Nate's age, early-to-mid thirties, while others were older, fifties and sixties. The men wore jeans and well-cut blazers, scuffed brogues and pricey watches; the women, sparkly dresses and low-cut tops, with tasteful handbags, sparkly earrings, and sharp, insistent perfumes.

There were maybe fifty hemmed into the lounge and reception rooms, most bunched up in clusters, sipping flutes of prosecco, pecking at a buffet spread that looked like an object d'art. Lounge-y dance music played from the ceiling-mounted speakers, over which bursts of laughter popped like firecrackers. As I wandered through, I caught several stares.

Nate's lounge featured an immense orange sofa to one side and three voluminous green chairs adjacent. One wall was exposed

New York style brickwork, the others had two-tone grey and white wallpaper. Copies of *Esquire*, *The New Yorker*, *GQ* were strategically left out, alongside piles and piles of film periodicals, confirming that we were at the home of a cinephile.

The drink selection was arranged on a table by a fireplace. There was enough alcohol here to keep even the most ardent boozer sated. I took a bottle of Peroni, sensing more eyes studying me, like I was the new boy in class. If I still smoked, now would've been the time to light up and do my Bogart impersonation. Instead, I leaned beside the fireplace, smiled politely, and drank my drink.

At one end of the room there was an extended conservatory; right of that was an open-plan kitchen. The whole place was preened to perfection, much like Nate, who I spotted over a sea of heads.

He wore a white silk shirt unbuttoned midway, revealing a chiselled midriff and tufts of honeysuckle chest hair. He held a flute of fizz and was gesticulating with it as he spoke with a tall male with his back to me. This man was thick through the middle, his blazer squeezing around wide shoulders that pulled his sleeves above big hands.

A freezeframe from the snuff flashed in my skull – the two killers standing over Minka. The stark, almost comical size difference was a match. This was the big man. As the realisation sank in, the music seemed to slip into a minor key.

'Kasper!' Nate called out. He'd spotted me.

I headed over, navigating around bodies, my smile fixed. A moment later we were face-to-face.

'So glad you could make it!'

'Great party,' I said.

He nodded, said, 'There's people here I'd *love*,' drawing out the

154

vowel, making it sound like *laarve*, 'to introduce you to.' He turned to the big man. 'First, meet Simon. He's a sort of business partner. I told him about you earlier. He's been dying to meet you.'

Simon was taller than me. Six-four, but his girth made him seem even larger, a slab of beefsteak with the fat left on. His chin was wired with thick stubble, his eyes were small and gunpowder black, and he wore his hair swept back, a sharp widow's peak. Despite his silk shirt and blazer, he carried something tough and dogged about him, like a man who chewed rocks for breakfast.

'Nice to meet you,' I said.

We shook hands. His was a stonecutter's grip.

'And you,' he replied, the voice flat, expressionless. 'Nate reckons you'd be good on camera.'

'Possibly.'

'You had experience?'

'Nope.'

'Training?'

'Nope.'

He gave a sniff, like he smelled a gas leak.

Nate smiled. 'Si has particularly high standards.' He looked at me with a raised eyebrow. 'Have you got any defining features, Kasper? Something that would make you stand out to a casting director, perhaps?'

I put my drink on a sill, took hold of my upper left canine, and carefully wobbled the false tooth from the socket. When I was a teenager, a squabble turned ugly, and the original tooth got punched out. I'd worn this replacement the best party of thirty years. Pulling it out was my party trick. Not that I got invited to a lot of parties.

'Ta-da,' I said, smiling at them both, exposing the gap.

Nate clapped his hands. 'Marvellous!'

'Aw, thanks,' I said.

Simon stared, mirthlessly.

'Come, Kasper,' Nate said, stepping forward, taking my arm. 'Let me introduce you to a few more friends. Talk soon, Si.'

As I replaced the tooth, I glanced back over my shoulder at Simon, took a mental photo of him. He wouldn't be hard to forget.

Over the next hour, Nate shuttled me around his friends. I met Tarquin, Tamara, Ricky and Romilly, before I stopped trying to remember names and just went with the flow. They all seemed intrigued by me and shared an unyieldingly positive regard for Nate, who stayed with me the entire time, introducing me as if I was a show horse.

I kept Dr Steiner's words from last night close to mind, remembering that this was a cruel manipulator who would hide behind his charm. But like yesterday, Nate was endearing, possessing the rare knack of being able to move seamlessly in conversation, always staying attentive, and making you feel attended to.

After an hour I was dizzy from all the talking. Nate however was in his stride, brimming confidence.

'Here.' He handed me a beer, even though I was still working on another. 'Are you having a nice time?'

'Absolutely,' I said. 'A cracking bunch of friends you have.'

'I'm lucky, aren't I? Some I've known since childhood. Acquaintances of Mum and Dad's. Others are new friends. You being the newest.'

'I'm flattered,' I said, and looked around. 'But there's one person missing. Your sister.'

He looked bemused, like I'd made a joke. 'Poor Tash. She's upstairs, resting.'

'She can sleep through this noise?'

'She took a pill. Probably for the best. She gets disorientated when there's too much going on. It takes her back to the fire.'

'Fire?'

Nate's tongue flickered out, wetted his lip. 'A fire took our parents, Kasper, in this very house. It was a decade back. I assumed you knew.'

'Uh-uh,' I said, thinking fast. 'I had no idea.' A fire explained the blackened masonry I'd spotted outside the house, and why everything looked so squeaky clean and new in the interior. But it also opened a heap of new questions.

Nate said, 'Tash nearly died from smoke inhalation. Her brain was starved of oxygen, and the trauma has left mental scars too.'

'Christ,' I said, and drank a hefty gulp. 'Hardly surprising she's struggling now.'

For the briefest moment, Nate's smile wavered. His pale eyes darkened, the pupils dilated, and I swear I caught a glimpse of the raw emotion simmering beneath that cool exterior.

Then the spell evaporated, the irises paled, the smile crimped. He was the picture of serenity again.

'Come,' he said, 'there's more guests just arriving.'

Over the next hour I chatted away to a dozen more of Nate's friends, swapped the lager for prosecco, and bit the heads off several prawn hors d'oeuvres. Quickly, I realised two facts – I was useless at chitchat. And I couldn't handle my fizz.

Around ten, the music became harder, edgier; then the coke came out, chopped into fat lines on the tables, hoovered up with twenties. One gent offered Nate and me a toot.

Nate obliged, snorting his as neatly as the act permitted. Then he held the note my way.

I shook my head. 'Not my bag.'

'Quite right.' He flared his nostrils, smacked his lips. 'A filthy habit, reserved for special occasions.'

The marching powder must've been good, for his pupils had already turned to saucers.

'You're right about Tash though,' he yelled over the music. 'It really *isn't* surprising she has a few problems. She's riddled with guilt.'

'Why's that?'

'She blames herself for the fire. The night it happened she'd agreed to do some of our parents' admin, but she fell asleep in the lounge here, forgetting about a lit cigarette in the upstairs study. It wasn't her fault, not really. But the self-hatred runs deep. Bless her.' He licked his lips again.

I took a swig of prosecco and watched Nate over the rim. 'You seem to have coped OK,' I said.

He nodded. 'I have, haven't I. I've often wondered why that is.'

'Any ideas?'

'Maybe it's because Tash and I had different upbringings. She lived at home her whole childhood and went to school here in Highgate. Whereas I was sent to boarding school from my eleventh year. It toughened me up. But she never developed mettle. Instead, she was sheltered. Mollycoddled. She believed our parents could do no wrong.'

We were onto something here, I knew it, and the coke was making Nate loose-tongued.

'Your parents left quite a legacy,' I said.

He scoffed. 'They could've left far more if they'd tried. They were talented artists, with ideas. But like so many, they failed to push themselves. For art to mean something, it must provoke, stretch boundaries, strike fear. Don't you think?'

'I'm no artist, Nate. I'll leave the critiquing to you.' I took my flute, drank deeply, said, 'So, how do you fill your time these days?'

He beamed, as if he'd been waiting for someone to ask this question all night. 'Well, if you must know, I'm working on a new project.'

'I thought you said you'd retired from film making?'

'Oh, to all intents I have. But this is something else, quite special.'

'Care to tell?'

He tapped a nostril. 'Mum's the word, I'm afraid. But tomorrow morning I'll be making final preparations.'

I waited for more.

None came.

Nate smiled that smile, and said, 'Come, there's one or two more friends who've just arrived you simply must meet.'

Off we went again.

The next hour passed in a whirl, taken up with further inconsequential chats with Nate's pals. He snorted another line and kept me topped up.

Before long, the music got cranked up another notch, and the guests started dancing around the lounge, the coke giving them wings. A petite woman in a silky dress summoned Nate with a finger. The crowd separated like a parting sea as he joined her, his lips a fixed grin, his moves slick as a pro.

'You and me,' another pretty woman shouted into my ear, 'dance.'

I shook my head. 'You don't want to see that, love.'

She made a face and sashayed off.

It dawned on me that I should scoot. I'd plenty to think over, and if I stayed longer, I'd drink more, and then if I got shit-faced I'd risk messing up, maybe saying something that gave me away.

I caught Nate's eye, indicated that I was off. He made a sad face, followed by a "call me" sign with his hand to an ear.

As I came out from the lounge, jostling past bodies, I spotted Simon again over heads. He was in the kitchen, chewing on a chicken drumstick. Our eyes met. He gave a nod.

I moved into the hall towards the front door. The music and noise dampened, making me realise how tipsy I was. Some fresh air and a walk would do me good.

I was halfway out when I heard a familiar voice.

'Kasper.'

I turned.

Tash Willoughby was at the head of the staircase. She was barefoot, wearing light jeans and a creased lilac shirt. She was pale and drawn, and her expression seemed detached, as if she were lost inside a deep kind of stillness.

Slowly, she walked down the stairs. It was as if each step took forethought. She stopped near the bottom so that we were head level with each other and placed a hand on the banister.

'What are you doing here?' she said.

I pulled the door shut. 'Your brother invited me to the party.'

'But why?'

I shrugged. 'He wants us to be friends.'

'Friends?' she looked perplexed. 'No, no, you shouldn't have come.'

She kept nibbling her lower lip, and when she rubbed her mouth, I noticed her fingernails were gnarled and stubby, bitten to the quick.

'Are you OK?' I said.

She glanced at me, as if awoken from a fugue. 'Yes. Why?'

'Nate mentioned you don't like busy events.'

'Did he say that?'

I nodded.

She went back to nibbling. What was with this woman?

Time for a different tack. 'Mind me asking what you meant just now?'

'What?'

'You said that I shouldn't have come here.'

'Did I say that?'

'Yes.'

'I can't remember. It doesn't matter.'

But it did. And something was bothering me about her too. Her eyes weren't vacant as I'd originally thought, but were gazing past me, at a flat desert of time that stretched backwards and forwards as far as she could see.

Following my instinct, I stepped closer. She flinched.

'Is something wrong, Tash?'

She shook her head automatically. 'Nothing. I'm fine, thank you.'

I had the sense she wanted to talk, but if I pushed, I might freak her out and the shutters would slam shut.

I decided to pull back, let her take the lead.

'I'll be off, then,' I said, and turned for the door, took the handle.

'Stop,' she said.

I stopped.

Tentatively, she came down the last of the steps, shuffled forward, until she was just a couple of feet away, close enough to feel her cool, scentless breath. Her shoulders were trembling. As she bit her lip, the skin blanched white.

'Sorry,' she said, softer now. 'I'm not quite myself.'

'Don't worry.'

She shook her head. There was a guardedness to her, both opaque yet familiar to me too, that left me on edge.

She said, 'I have funny turns.'

'It's fine, Tash.'

'Is it?'

'What?'

'Fine?'

I didn't answer. My instincts, dulled from the drink, were suddenly on alert. Something had caught my eye.

Her shoulder movement must've caused the hair to part around the right of her face. The gap was slight, but enough to momentarily expose her neck, her jawbone, her ear . . .

Through the tissue of the earlobe ran a squiggly scar. Although old, there was no doubting what it was. Something had torn through the flesh with great force, ripping it apart. I didn't need to see her left earlobe to know it bore a similar scar.

Nausea rose and my inner world began to shudder. I found myself back in the snuff film, the hoop earrings ripped from Minka's ears, the gushing blood, her wrenching screams.

'Are you OK?' Tash said.

The prosecco was sloshing about in my belly. I had trouble catching my breath, and wanted out of that house, fast.

'Kasper?'

I looked at her. 'Sorry,' I said. 'I . . . must've had a bit too much to drink. Better go.'

She kept staring, and said, 'Well, nice to see you.'

I held out my hand. She hesitated, and then took it.

Her fingers were cold as stalagmites, but her pale eyes were suddenly alit like wildfire.

I could feel those eyes as I lumbered from the house, down the porch way, the cold seeming to heighten my shock and drunkenness; and I felt their presence as I zigzagged down Highgate Hill, stopping halfway to lean on a tree and vomit.

Chapter 16

The cab driver had it all sussed, putting the world to rights about migrants, religious fundamentalists, welfare scroungers, the cabinet reshuffle, football, women's football, whatever popped into his swollen blister of a head.

I'd flagged him down at the foot of Archway, as the thought of catching the bus home after puking my guts out didn't appeal. But after five minutes of his diatribe, I was regretting it.

'I mean in my day, a bloke was a bloke, a bird was a bird . . .'

I closed my eyes, switched off as best I could, and tried joining the dots.

Questions blasted my head like pinballs in an arcade. Who was Simon? How did he and Nate join forces? What about Nate's parents, Henry and Martha Willoughby? How did they fit into the story? And what the heck was going on with Tash Willoughby and her mutilated ears?

The main thing was, I'd identified the whole Red Rose Productions ensemble: Terry had been the behind-the-scenes scout; Simon was the muscle; Nate was the director. And unless I was mistaken, I was his new BFF.

I still didn't have hard evidence. But I was getting close, so close . . .

'Then on to these refugees comin' here, taking all our houses—'

'Stop the car,' I said. 'I'll walk the rest.'

I stayed up late, sitting on my bed, thinking.

The sports bag containing the camcorder lay on the floor. I tried to ignore it, but it seemed to be whispering, drawing me towards it.

Around three I whipped it out, stuck the SD card into my laptop and watched the snuff film from the beginning.

Nate stood next to Simon, both dressed head to toe in black, staring at Minka's violated body. Two men I'd sipped prosecco with at a party a few hours ago. Two cruel, sadistic killers.

The final line ricocheted in my head: *'See you next time.'*

I turned the film off, took a few steady breaths, then headed for the basin, splashed water onto my face, swished some around my mouth. The taste of vomit was gone, but the nausea remained in my guts.

Lying down sounded good right then, but I couldn't waste time. Nate was planning another film. *Something else, quite special.* That's what he'd said – the new project.

I booted up Google and started digging.

Before long I'd found a couple of archived pieces about the Willoughby fire ten years back, including a photo of the carcass, barely recognisable as the resplendent house Nate and Tash now occupied in Highgate. According to the articles, the flames claimed Henry and Martha in their upstairs bedroom, and smoke inhalation left their daughter Natasha fighting for life. As Nate said, the cause was thought to have been a cigarette. A tragedy, it was claimed.

It all sounded too neat. Could Nate have been responsible for the fire? A way to get his interfering parents out the way so that he could plough on with his snuff movies with impunity?

A bit more searching revealed information on the parents themselves. Two well-regarded advertising execs who went the extra mile for the community and were liked and respected by all. Until the fire, they lived a comfortable life.

But that's never the full story. What had life really been like for Nate and Tash growing up? He was sent to boarding school, while she was kept at home. Why? And what the heck was the significance of the red rose image?

By five a.m., my vision was a blur and my thoughts stuck together like bugs on a glue pad. Rest was what I needed.

I lay back on the bed, tried switching off.

As if. My head was a radio stuck between stations.

Hearing a friendly voice sounded good.

But I was short on friends. And at this hour, there was only person I could think to call.

She answered on the third ring. 'Hello, Dylan.'

'Sorry to call at this time, Lisa.'

'Have you found something? About Minka?'

'I'm getting closer to snaring the men responsible.'

'Good.'

'But that's not why I'm calling.'

'What do you mean?'

I heard the hesitance. 'I just wanted to speak to you.'

'Why?'

I took a heavy breath. 'Look, are you busy? I could come over—'

'It's not a good idea. Our relationship has become . . . complicated.'

'Right,' I said, and a final vestibule of hope seemed to calcify in my heart.

'What's the matter?' she said.

I took a long time to answer. 'I'm just feeling it a little tonight, babe. You know?'

She said she did; then she listened.

I told her everything, about my cock-ups with Diane, Suzi, Patience, how I was pushing people away when I needed them most; I told her I had a suspect for Minka's murder, knew his accomplice; I'd been at his home earlier, and had seen what he'd done to his sister, ripping her ears like Minka's, and I knew he was planning to do it again; I told her how my life was steeped in violence, from my childhood on Paradise up to last year when I faked a suicide to protect a grieving father.

It must've sounded crazy, the rantings of a madman. But when I'd finished, Lisa didn't say as much, try to dish out platitudes or TV therapy advice. I guessed our relationship had bypassed fakeries like this.

She just said, 'So, what will you do now?'

'I don't know.'

'This is risky. I want you to stop.'

'I can't, Lisa. These bastards are planning another film.'

'I'm scared. For you. Of what might happen.'

'I can take care of myself.'

'The violence and killing – it's too much.'

'That's why it must end.'

A long pause. I could hear the inhalation of her vape, and the crackle down the receiver as she exhaled. 'Maybe when this is over, we should both make changes.'

'Yeah,' I said. 'Let's promise that.'

'Now, I must go.'

'Thanks for listening. I appreciate it.'

We said goodbyes.

And in the silence, I stared dully at my phone.

Before long it was morning and I was still staring at the phone, none the wiser.

As the first rays of dawn poked through the blind, it occurred to me that tomorrow was the anniversary of Rosie's suicide. Since all this snuff movie madness, I'd hardly given my daughter much thought.

Now, memories of the morning she died hurtled back. Right before setting off, she'd asked me if she could stay home from school, as she wasn't feeling great. I wasn't long back from a night shift and wasn't feeling too clever either. I told her it wasn't a good idea, she should go in, take her mind off things, and we'd chat at teatime over fishfingers. Those were the last words I said to her. Bloody *fishfingers*.

Many times, I've analysed the image of her as she headed off, trying to figure out what was going on. She'd wanted to talk. But I hadn't let her. Instead, she'd departed with a guarded look I've punished myself for ever since.

Now, I realised I'd seen that expression before.

Where?

In Tash Willoughby. Last night, as we'd stood in the hallway of her house, and her torn ears were exposed.

Suddenly, my head lit up like a neon bar.

I had an idea. How to get Nate and Simon sent away. It was risky. But if it paid off, it'd be worth it.

I punched Mani's number into my phone. He answered, groggily. 'What's up?'

'Morning,' I said. 'I need you and Patience mobilised. Now.'

'Huh?' he said. 'It's early, man. What you got in mind?'

By the time I'd finished telling him, he was as awake as me.

Chapter 17

An hour later I was in the passenger side of Mani's Astra. Patience occupied the back seat. We were back in Highgate, around the corner from Nate Willoughby's house, and I'd just finishing telling them the finer details of my plan.

'That sounds nuts,' Patience said.

'Girl's got a point,' Mani added.

'No,' I said. 'It'll work.'

'You wanna reach out to this Nate Willoughby's sister, get her on side?' Patience said. 'All you know, the woman's crazier than her brother.'

'Tash isn't crazy,' I said. 'She's afraid.'

'You know this how?' Mani said.

'Last night, at the party, I could see she wanted to talk. She knows about Nate, but she's buried it. He's already mutilated her, made her believe she's nuts. I think he killed their parents, made her think she was to blame. She's scared to reach out because of what he'll do. But if I can get Tash alone, make her feel safe, I reckon I can convince her to help me.'

'You make it sound a cinch,' Mani said. 'How you plan to get her on side?'

I shrugged. 'I'll talk to her.'

'Talk? About what?'

'Leave that to me.'

I tried to catch Patience's eye through the mirror, but she was looking down, her brow furrowed into a sharp triangle.

'Nice sparring the other day,' I said. 'You gave me quite a whooping.'

'Took it easy on you, old man.'

'Maybe. I still owe you an apology.'

She didn't answer.

'The other night, my behaviour round yours after finding Suzi . . .' I looked at my hands. 'Well, I was out of line.'

She gave a minuscule shrug.

Mani looked over to her, grinning. 'That's the best apology you're getting out of this man. My suggestion? Take it.'

She shrugged again, but a bit more purposefully. And when I offered my hand she took it, squeezing till it hurt.

'Suzi says you two are an item now?'

'Kinda,' she said. 'We're taking it slow.'

'When're you next seeing her?'

'She's got an interview tomorrow for some art internship. I said I'd go with her, hang out a bit, then we'll have lunch.'

'Nice. I'm happy for you two. I mean it, kiddo. Now let's end this thing and get on with our lives.'

'For real.'

'Back to why we're here, Kasper,' Mani said. 'Say this woman does agree to help snare her brother. What then?'

'It's obvious,' I said. 'I'll take her to the police so she can testify.'

Patience kissed her teeth.

'I told you from the off,' I said. 'I'll find these men and make sure they can't hurt anyone else. But at some point, the police need to be involved. This is major crime we're talking about.'

Her frown did all the talking.

'So what do you need from us right now?' Mani said.

'You're going to be my surveillance.'

'Explain.'

'Last night, Nate said he was going out this morning to do some final prep for a new project he's working on. Unless I'm wrong, that project's his next snuff movie. Soon as he sets off, I want you two on him like a catsuit. I want to know where he goes, who he meets, and when he's headed back. You know what he looks like?'

Mani held up his phone. The photo of Nate from Kinsella's Café wall was on the screen. 'You're sure this guy's a killer?' he said. 'He looks like he should be in a boy-band.'

'I'm sure,' I said. 'OK. We're all set.'

'But Kasper,' Mani said, 'I never followed no one before. Any tips?'

'It's easy,' I said. 'Don't get seen.' I gave him a wink.

'Bah,' he said as I got out the car.

The sky was a muzzle of greys, thick, dismal, cold. I popped the collar on my leather and walked towards the High Street where I began window-shopping, killing time. A half an hour of that and I bought a coffee from a Costa and nursed it in the window seat.

A little after ten, my phone vibrated. Mani was talking on car loudspeaker, the engine purring in the background.

'Your man's just left the house,' he said, 'heading down the hill on foot.'

'He alone?'

'Yup.'

'Stay on him, Mani, and keep in touch.'

I left my coffee and bolted, my heart suddenly a hairball in my throat.

A minute later I caught sight of the Willoughby house. The lights were off. The place looked empty, with no signs of last night's party.

I caught my breath, then pressed the intercom buzzer, waited.

No lights, no movement.

I was about to try again when a curtain twitched.

I spoke into the intercom: 'Hello. It's Kasper. I think I left my phone here at last night's party. I'm such a dope. Can I come in?'

Again, faint movement in the curtains. Then the intercom crackled to life.

'Nate's not in,' Tash said, her voice a whisper.

'That's OK,' I said. 'Could you open the door? I know where to look for it.'

Another, longer pause.

Then the gate buzzed, and I was walking to the house.

A few feet away, the front door opened. Tash peered down.

'Hi,' I said.

She was barefoot and without make-up, wearing a long, shapeless black dress made from a silky fabric that swished around her thin ankles. Her face was a greyish white, a ceramic mask, those pale blue eyes the only colour.

'Nate never found anything,' she said. 'Maybe you should come back . . .'

I climbed the porch. She started, breathing shallow as I came into her space.

'What are you doing?' she said, stepping back.

'Listen carefully, Tash. First of all, you're safe. Two friends of mine are keeping tabs on your brother. If he comes back, they'll let me know.'

'I don't understand, what do you—'

'I'm a private investigator. I'm looking into the murder of a woman. The men responsible filmed the whole thing. I've watched it. I wish I hadn't.'

'Why are you telling me this?'

'Because one of the killers is Nate.'

She stared mutely. I studied her eyes, tried to harness something of her through them, but she pulled away.

'I'm sorry,' she said, 'you're mistaken.'

'I'm not. Just take a moment, think about it.'

'No.' She shook her head. 'Nate isn't like that. He loves me. You should go.'

I stayed where I was.

Her bottom lip quivered, like it wanted to speak. In response, she bit it.

'Please,' I said.

'You're wrong,' she said, her voice stuttering. 'Nate's taken care of me. Honestly, he's a good brother. He's—'

Gently, I placed my hand on her shoulder. She was shaking. I brushed her hair aside, just enough to expose her mutilated ear.

'He did the same to the woman on the film. Ripped out her earrings.'

Her eyes filled; tears streamed down. 'Nate said I did it to myself, in my sleep. I was having one of my flashbacks, about our parents, how I caused the fire. He woke me. I was covered in blood—'

'Lies.'

'No!'

'Talk to me, Tash.'

'I can't.'

But she could.

And did.

*

173

Tash went inside the house, then reappeared wearing boots and a knee-length Paddington bear duffle, toggled to the neck and with the hood up.

'Let's go for a walk,' she said, locked the front door and led the way.

I followed her back to the High Street, then right into a park characterised by undulating paths, bare shrubs and large trees that hung like skeleton hands; further back were tennis courts, children's play areas, a small bird sanctuary, bandstand, and a stately home. Not the obvious setting for what I planned to discuss, but needs must.

Tash kept quiet, her hands in her pockets, head bowed.

After a moment, she said, 'Do you have a cigarette?'

I shook my head. 'Want me to try to bum one off someone?'

'It's OK. Nate hates me smoking. After the fire . . .'

'He's got quite a grip over you, hasn't he?'

She didn't reply.

'What was it like?' I said. 'Growing up? When your parents were alive?'

She looked away. 'What do you mean? It was normal. We were a happy family.'

'At the party last night, Nate said the two of you had different upbringings. He was sent away to boarding school, you lived at home. Why was that?'

'Mum and Dad said boarding school would be good for Nate. Because of his potential.'

'He said you were mollycoddled as a result of staying at home.'

She slowed, glanced at me sternly; then she went for a smile and looked away, picked up her pace. 'Silly Nate. He says these things. You must've misunderstood.'

'He also suggested your parents' death was your fault.'

She stopped abruptly, looked up at me again. Her eyes glimmered with emotion. 'It *was* my fault.'

'Maybe.' I paused, cautious to not push too hard. 'Do you remember much about the fire?'

She shook her head. 'It's like a gap.'

'What can you tell me?'

'I wanted to help Mum and Dad to do some admin for one of their charity schemes. That's the kind of people they were. Kind. Generous. Did Nate mention that about them to you?'

I nodded, keen to keep her on subject.

'Anyway, I must've been more tired than I realised, and fell asleep in the lounge, leaving a cigarette burning upstairs. Next thing, I'm in the hospital, attached to machines.'

'Where was Nate when the fire happened?'

'I don't know. All I remember is waking up, and Nate telling me they were dead.'

I allowed some space, hoping for more.

When nothing came, I said, 'The fire wasn't your fault.'

She was biting her lip again.

'Nate's responsible. He framed you. A part of you knows that story about a cigarette is rubbish, designed to torment you.'

'No,' she said. 'No, no, that's completely wrong.'

'Your brother's a murderer, Tash. Killing your parents, mutilating you, crippling you with guilt, convincing you you're half-baked – he gets his kicks doing twisted things like this.'

'What are you talking about?'

Time to spell it out.

'Nate and his buddy Simon make snuff films. Know what those are?'

She shook her head.

'Real-life killings, made into movies. They get uploaded onto the dark web and people pay to view them.'

Her breath caught. 'No,' she said. 'I don't want to hear anymore.'

'Well tough. You need to. Those two are targeting sex workers who won't be missed. A prostitute I know helped me identify one victim, which led me to discover the photos of a load more. Nineteen women, Tash. All presumed dead.'

She looked at me sharply. 'Why are you telling me this now?'

'Because I'm putting Nate and Simon out of business. And I want you to help me.'

She gasped, covered her mouth, stepped back. An elderly couple ambled in front of us, out with their elderly Scotty dog, each of them oblivious.

For a second I thought Tash was about to leg it. Instead, she stood rigid.

I waited till the couple had gone; then, in a hushed voice, I said, 'I'm sorry. Christ knows how painful this must be.'

'Pain?' Tash removed the hand from her mouth, glowered. 'What do you know about pain?' Her voice was surprisingly hard.

'More than you think,' I said, and decided to take a gamble. 'Six years ago tomorrow, my daughter took her life. She was fourteen. Coming back from that's been the most painful thing in my life.'

Tash stared. Her eyes softened enough to tell me I'd reached something.

'I'm sorry,' she said.

'Yeah. Me too.'

'How will you mark the anniversary?'

I shrugged. 'I hadn't really thought about it. Maybe I'll go to Trafalgar Square. When Rosie was little, we liked to go to Nelson's Column and feed the birds.'

'Rosie. That was your daughter's name?'

'Yeah.'

'That's nice. Yes, that's nice . . .'

She brought her hands to her eyes. And wept.

I led her to a bench, as if I were guiding a blind person, sat next to her. It poured out from her silently.

'What do you want me to do?' she eventually said, rubbing her eyes with the balls of her palms.

'Cooperate.'

'Who with?'

'Me. And when the time's right, with the police.'

She shook her head, dabbed her runny nose with her sleeve. 'I'm not strong enough. I can't.'

'I'll support you.'

'Nate will convince them I'm crazy. They'll look at my health records and believe him.'

She had a point. 'What about evidence then? Can you find any?'

'What do you mean?'

'Nate will have a stockpile of items. Weapons. Mementos from the victims. Serial killers like to keep stuff. If we can find these and link him with the snuff, we can get him and Simon off the street before anyone else is hurt.'

A pair of paunchy gents in tracksuits sidled past, chatting amiably. One said to us, 'Morning.'

Soon as they'd passed, I said, 'Well?'

'I'm afraid,' Tash whispered.

'Me too. But I'm more afraid of what will happen if we don't act now.'

She looked at me. 'What do you mean?'

'Nate's planning another film.'

Her eyes grew bigger and bigger. Something passed between us, and I saw then that I was winning her over.

'Well?' I said.

'OK.'

'OK, what?'

'I'll help. I just need time, to think. My head hurts.'

'Think fast, Tash. If you don't come though, I'll have to find something else. But one way or another, it'll be curtains for Nate. Help me now, chances are the police will look on you favourably.'

She put a hand to her mouth. 'What do you mean?'

'The authorities may consider you as an accessory. But if you do this, I'll vouch for you, I swear it.'

Her breathing became short again, like she was hyperventilating. I'd pushed too far this time.

'Easy,' I said. 'You're OK.'

Gradually, she gained control.

I removed my business card, slid it along the bench.

'My number,' I said. 'I'll be waiting.'

'I don't have a mobile phone. Nate won't let me keep one.'

'Christ.'

'But I'll find a way to contact you.'

I believed her, too.

A buzzing in my pocket drew me away from her. It was Mani.

'Kasper, your man's on his way home. ETA ten minutes.'

'OK,' I said, and looked at Tash. 'He's heading back.'

She nodded, stood, returned her hands to the pockets of her duffle.

I walked her back to the house.

Chapter 18

Mani and Patience picked me up at the lights at the bottom of the hill.

'Well?' she said.

I looked through the car window at a McDonald's. A couple of toddler boys were fighting over an ice cream. In front of them was an overweight woman, their mum presumably. Right when we were pulling off, the ice cream plummeted, the white goo splodging on the paving. The last thing I saw was the boys howling and chucking fists.

'Kasper, man,' Mani said, 'don't go silent. How'd it go with the sister?'

'OK,' I said.

'Meaning?'

'She's thinking. But I reckon she's on board.'

'She believes you? That her brother's Ted Bundy?'

'Deep down, Tash knows what Nate is, and what he's capable of. She just needed to hear someone say it. Now, it's a case of letting the truth settle in.'

'I hope you're right,' Patience said. 'You're taking a risk here, man.'

I looked over. 'Something on your mind?'

'All I'm saying is, Tash and Nate are siblings, and blood's thicker than water. I should know. It was my brother's murder got me into all this.'

I didn't answer.

Mani braked at a red. He pulled out a cigarette, lit it, lowered the window, and blew out a plume of smoke.

'Where'd Nate go?' I said.

'Down Crouch End way, by cab,' he said. 'An upmarket area. I drove around. Patience followed him on foot.'

'What was he doing there?'

'Viewing some swanky house,' Patience said. 'He met an estate agent who showed them 'round.'

'Them?'

'Nate met up with someone. I got his picture here.' She handed me her Android with an image on the screen. 'He's familiar, right?'

It was a fuzzy still of Nate beside a larger, thicker man wearing a tightly fitting tracksuit. Familiar was an understatement.

'Big fella from the snuff?'

'Correct.' I handed her phone back. 'Goes by Simon. Can you tell me about this house he was viewing?'

'I can do one better,' Patience said. She tapped into her phone, handed it back. 'That's the place. I looked up the ad.'

A letting advertisement was on the screen. It was indeed a swanky townhouse converted from the site of a former recording studio. Floorplans revealed it to have two bedrooms, an open reception and – most tellingly – a sound-proofed studio to the rear.

My stomach lurched. 'This is his new film set.'

'Uh-huh,' Patience said. 'That's what I figured.'

And it had to be – but I was puzzled by this development too. Till now, Nate had kept everything centred around Paradise, where his depravity could be hidden amidst the squalor. Crouch End was trendy and high-profile. Why here?

'So, what happens next?' Mani said.

'Next,' I said, 'we wait.'

Before I could say anything more, a BMW beeped behind us. The lights were back to green.

'Shit,' Mani said.

He found bite and zapped away.

Mani dropped me off at home.

Now I was alone, Patience's remark nagged away at me. The girl had a point. This thing could backfire royally. Going over all the different ways made for unhappy thinking.

Fortunately, I had a useful distraction. My job interview was scheduled for that afternoon. I toyed with the idea of sacking it off: this investigation was too important, and something might come up.

But what the hell – I'd have my phone with me if Tash called, and it was an hour out of my day. So, I dusted off my only suit, and a little before two PM, found myself in a desolate industrial park in Hackney Wick, knocking on the door of a tatty static caravan.

The interior looked like student digs – Pot Noodle tubs in an overflowing bin, bottles of Tango and Pepsi strewn on the gnarly counters, a sink overflowing with dirty plates and cutlery. Cut-outs of topless women were tacked to the wall, and the place smelled of kebab, BO and the cold.

My interviewing panel, if you could call them that, consisted of two burly men who ticked all the cliché boxes for the east

London bouncer. Both had buzz-cut scalps and faces like fried pork loins. They wore steel toe-capped monkey boots, black combats and black bombers bearing the company insignia laminated on the rear – *Mash-Up Security*. Catchy.

They took seats beside each other. I perched on a stool opposite and they confirmed my particulars.

'Done security work before?' the one on the left said. Even from a distance, I could smell his breath – stale smoke and staler garlic.

'Oh, absolutely,' I answered. 'I worked in a rowdy pub for a few years.'

'Before that?'

'I was a copper.'

They shared a look.

The one on the right produced a clipboard, wrote something down.

'You look like you can handle yourself,' the other one said.

'Yes,' I said.

'But we're not looking for scrappers, unnerstand?' said the second. 'We're a professional service, no aggro. If that's you, sling it.'

'It isn't,' I said. 'I rely far more on my erudite wit than my fists.'

They looked at each other again. The one with the clipboard wrote something else, a heavy groove forming across his brow as he concentrated. Probably trying to spell erudite.

'All right,' the other one said. 'Here's a scenario. Know what scenario means?'

I told him I did.

'You're working the door of a club an' one of the dancers comes up an' says a fella's been sticking his hands where he's not meant to. What do you do?'

'OK,' I said. 'First up, I'd ensure there was no physical harm inflicted on the dancer. If there was, I'd have to call an ambulance and the police, and let them deal with the man in question, as technically that's an assault.'

'An' if the dancer weren't harmed? What then?'

'Then I'd need to jettison the man from the club myself.'

'Jettison. What's that mean?'

'Remove.'

'How?'

I smiled. 'Through the forcefulness of my character.'

They shared another look.

'All right. Question two . . .'

It went on this way. When the questions were done, the pair, who turned out to be brothers, Gary and Preston, took turns telling me a bit about the job.

To call them a security firm was misleading – *Mash-Up* was bog-standard bouncing at rough-end boozers and late-night skin-clubs, all cash-in-hand and ask-no-questions work.

By the end, I was pretty sure I'd talked myself out of a job offer. To be honest, I wasn't fussed. It didn't seem my cup of tea.

The brothers asked me to wait outside the cabin so they could discuss my answers. While they did, I checked my phone.

Nothing from Tash.

It'd only been a few hours. Stay cool, I told myself.

Yet already, the uncertainty was gnawing.

The door of the cabin opened abruptly.

One of the brothers – I forget which – stuck his head out.

'Can you start tomorrow night?' he said.

On the bus home, I decided it was high time to take Dr Steiner's advice and sort things out with Suzi.

'I told you not to ring,' she said.

'You did,' I replied, 'but I've chosen to ignore your plea, and lay myself at the mercy of your court. I acted like a knob, Suze. Sorry.'

An aged woman on a neighbouring seat frowned at my potty mouth. I gave a consolatory wink. She kept frowning.

'You *were* a knob,' Suzi said.

'Yes.'

'A lumbering gorilla, to be exact.' She was on a roll. 'But I guess you were coming from a good place. You're just looking out for me. Right?'

'Right,' I said. 'What if I take you and Patience out for milk-shakes? I'm now gainfully employed, after all, so I can afford it.'

'Huh?'

I told Suzi about the job interview and successful appointment, to which she started cackling.

'A bouncer!' she said. 'Oh, man.'

'A security enforcer, actually,' I corrected. 'There are important differences.'

'I'll bet. As it happens, I've got news too. I had an email from a little art studio out in the docklands. The manager's seen my work and asked me to come in tomorrow to discuss an internship this summer. It sounds like a good opportunity, Kas.'

'Patience mentioned something about that,' I said. 'Awesome.'

'Yeah, it's OK. I know we've not known each other long, but Patience really helps me go after things. I feel lucky to have met her.'

'I can tell. You've both got fighter spirit.'

'You're OK with us two, aren't you?'

'"Course I am,' I said, adding, 'you two make a cute couple.'

She laughed, and we let each other go.

★

That evening, a little after nine, my phone finally buzzed with the message I'd been waiting for.

The number was withheld, impossible to reply to. Adrenalin surged:

Kasper, I need to see you tomorrow.

It was Tash Willoughby. As the realisation landed, another text landed:

Trafalgar Square. I'll be there at 11.

A minute passed. Two.
The phone vibrated a final time. My teeth clenched:

You were right about Nate.

I was restless for the rest of the night.

Tomorrow, I had Rosie's anniversary. Now, I was due to meet Tash. The past and present were intersecting in ways beyond my understanding.

But I felt positive too. I had work lined up and was sorting things with Suzi. Best of all, I was getting close to nailing Nate Willoughby, exposing him, Simon, Red Rose Productions, and cracking open my first big case.

Never a natural optimist, I lay in bed with a sense that things were coming together, and tomorrow, they'd be at an end.

Big mistake.

Chapter 19

Trafalgar Square.

I'd been here since half eight in the morning, throwing chunks of bread at the pigeons, blowing on my hands to keep warm.

Six years back, round about this same time, my teenage daughter Rosie put herself under the tracks of a train. A split-second move that would end her life, and change mine forever.

After the inquest, the funeral, the scattering of her ashes and all that ceremonial crap, I used to sit like this in random places across the city, going over the morning of her death, trying to figure out what had gone wrong.

I'd fantasise about repealing the passage of time, rewriting the film of her life with a whole different ending. In this new version, I let her stay home from school. Over endless cups of tea we talked, got to the bottom of what was going on. We figured things out.

But these lines of thought just led to regret, fuel for this aimless rage that's simmered within me ever since.

A filthy pigeon shuffled close to my boot, pecking crumbs. The bird was withered, its iridescent plumage vanished beneath grime.

Soon, it would be gone.

Like Rosie.

The last time I saw her she was lying in an ICU ward, wired to life support machines, her face bloated, lips blue, eyes taped shut, dying an unnatural death.

I tried remembering the pretty girl she was. A feisty fourteen-year-old. Precocious. Going places, her English teacher said in her last school report.

Yeah, right.

If that train had been late, or we'd spoken, things might've been so, so different. Maybe Rosie would be alive, I'd still be a policeman, with Diane, and I wouldn't be sitting on a cold bench waiting for a snuff filmmaker's sister to turn up . . .

The pigeon pecked.

The memories swirled.

Six years.

'Jesus.'

I checked my watch. Half-ten.

Lapsing into these maudlin thoughts was a bad move with so much going on. I needed to focus, stay present.

I stood, my joints rigid, and began walking around the square, taking in the weathered granite of Nelson's Column and the small man at its pinnacle, gazing down imperiously. Tourists meandered past, holding phones aloft like props. Further back, a council cleaner was jet-spraying filth from the flagstones, avoiding a cluster of homeless people lying entombed in sleeping bags.

A few laps of walking, and I headed up the steps in the direction of the National Gallery. Entering the foyer, a warm blast of air hit me. I ascended a flight of stone steps and went into the first room, full of more tourists staring at paintings of important looking dead people.

Room two, more death, this time decapitated heads, exploit-ative nudity, public hangings and gallons of sex, gore, misery. A couple of minutes and I headed back out, preferring the cold to this.

During that brief jaunt in the gallery, the weather had turned even more blustery. Thick buffets of sharp air dashed across my face, blowing my hair this way and that.

I took a different bench on the square, checked my watch. Five to eleven. Not long.

Pigeons waddled past. I was beginning to recognise a few.

I glanced around, scanning faces, a knot tightening in my belly.

Tash might not turn up. Maybe after texting me, she got spooked or had a change of mind. A night to reflect on things can do that.

But her message was clear. She wanted to meet. She believed what I'd told her about Nate.

It went eleven.

Five-past.

Ten.

I kept checking for messages.

Nothing.

By half-past, I was starting to panic. Apart from turning up at the Highgate house, I had no way of reaching Tash. Had some-thing gone wrong?

I was re-reading her messages for the zillionth time when the world capsized. From my periphery, something hooked my attention.

What I was seeing didn't compute. A small, slim man walking towards me.

Not Tash Willoughby.

Nate. Swanning from Leicester Square, wearing a creamy white parka, slim black chinos and shiny brogues; Nate, lithe as a lasso, with hawkish eyes, the irises piquant blue, and his fair hair swishing like barley in the wind.

'Kasper,' he called out, 'over here.'

I stared, punch-drunk, pocketed the phone and got to my feet unsteadily.

He descended the steps for the square, heading for me. A few feet away, he said, 'Good to see you.'

'Hello, Nate,' I said, trying to keep things measured, not let confusion show.

'Slight change of plan, I'm afraid.'

'What do you mean?'

'Tash sends her apologies. She couldn't make it.' His eyes twinkled knowingly. 'She and I had a chat last night. We agreed I'd come in her place.'

He knew we were meeting today. How? Had he hurt her? Killed her? Did he know who I was, and what I knew about him?

'You look baffled,' he said. 'Let me explain.' He pulled from his pocket my business card, waved it like a trinket. It was the business card I'd given Tash yesterday.

First question answered. My identity as a PI was rumbled.

'How'd you find out?' I said.

'Guess.'

'Tash made a mistake, and you forced it out of her?'

He shook his head. 'I didn't make Tash do a thing.'

I couldn't believe what I was hearing. Did Tash willingly tell Nate about my visit yesterday? Had I misread her so much?

'Don't look aggrieved,' he said. 'This was bound to happen sooner or later.'

'What was?'

I kept staring; then, as the realisation sank in, my lungs tightened, my heart began to swell. 'You've known about me from the start?'

'Of course. And it's been thrilling to interact with you under this smoke and mirrors subterfuge. It's *so* Hitchcock – a flawed private investigator thinks he's cracking a case, but instead he gets thwarted, all on the anniversary of his daughter's suicide. Could you get any more *neo*-noir?'

My hands became fists. 'You've been playing me? Stringing me along?'

'Don't get angry. If anything, you should be thankful.'

'Why?'

'Because I could quite easily have killed you. That first morning when you came to the house, I put poison in your beer. The plan was to drug you and smother you. Simon was gunning for it. And I must admit, that would've been easier.'

'Instead, you knocked my drink over and spared me. Why?'

'Because it felt all wrong just to bump you off like a minor character in some B-movie. No, after meeting you in the flesh, I wanted a more fitting end. It's so serendipitous, meeting at this pivotal point in our lives.'

'Huh?'

'Serendipity. When chance events lead to good things. My life has been full of these fortuitous meetings.'

'Why's meeting me a good thing?'

'Ah,' he said, 'we'll come to that.'

Before I could ask more, he turned and walked in the direction of the column, gesturing with a head flick for me to follow.

I cantered to keep up, for my legs were suddenly rubber, and the cold seemed to have found hundreds of tiny holes in my skin. Nate on the other hand looked as sprightly as a spaniel.

I caught up beside him, said breathlessly, 'So you know about me? Let me ask about you.'

'Very well.'

'Why make snuff films?'

He tutted. 'Don't minimise my work into the realms of *snuff*. It's demeaning.'

'Is there a better word for what you're doing?'

'Art, Kasper. I'm making art.'

'You're for real?'

Nate pointed a thin finger at the sky. ' "I shall go so far that people will be seized with terror at the sight of each of my works." Egon Schiele said that about his paintings. His work was vilified as perverted smut. Now, he's heralded a genius. If you need proof, pop into the National. I believe they've got one or two of his works on loan.'

'Already had a look,' I said. 'Not my bag.'

Nate smiled. 'Maybe so. But no matter how gratuitous, what I'm doing carries power. In years to come, when you and I are worm food, Nate Willoughby's films will still be circulating.'

'You reckon?'

'With every ounce of my being. My works will be revered as horrific masterpieces, and I will live forever through them.'

I looked away. Sickening though he was, I suspected this last comment bore some truth.

But I couldn't let Nate know this. That would massage his ego, give him more power.

I said, 'The only people revering you will be nutjobs who get turned on seeing women sliced up. Is that the kind of fanbase you'd like?'

He shook his head. 'I'm catering to an existing market that bleeds into all walks of society. The appetite for this kind of work is rampant. You'd be amazed how many *un*-suspecting people enjoy my films.'

'Bullshit.'

'Really? You came to my party. You spoke to several friends. Did they leap out as nutjobs, as you put it?'

My mind flitted back to the collection of Nate Willoughby devotees gathered at his house. Were they all snuff film enthusiasts?

'The women,' I said, my voice tremulous, 'these prostitutes you butcher.'

'What of them?'

'Are they your friends too?'

'In a manner of speaking.'

'How?'

'I'm giving them some meaning in their otherwise empty lives. They're the dregs of society, nobodies. No one misses them. No one cares. What I'm doing is a worthy act, surely?'

'No!' I said, louder than intended. 'It's batshit crazy.'

A little girl strolling past looked up at me and giggled, before her mum glared and pulled her away.

'Kasper, please,' Nate said. 'Be civil. We can't talk if you act like a baboon.'

I took a few steady breaths, then said, 'Let's talk about your parents.'

Nate smirked. 'Must we?'

'Why kill them?'

'Who says I did?'

'Me. What happened? Did they cotton on to your sadism? Is that why they sent you to boarding school and kept Tash home?'

Like at the party, a flicker of something passed over Nate. 'You really haven't a clue what you're talking about,' he said quietly. 'My parents went up in smoke. They're history.'

'If they're history, then what's with the red rose symbolism in your films? It's a nod to the photo your parents took that's hanging in your study, right?'

He shook his head. 'The rose is an in joke.'

'Really? I thought jokes are meant to be funny.'

'Oh, it is funny. The whole charade is deliciously so. And when you finally see the big picture, you'll get the punch line. Tell me, when you watched my film, what was your first response?'

I looked at a scrap of crisp packet caught on a breeze. Focusing on it, I said, 'Repulsion. Anger. Disbelief.'

'Yes, yes, those are good. But was there not a part of you that was enthralled? The moment I ripped the woman's earrings out and she realises this isn't pretend – it's like Janet Leigh in the *Psycho* shower scene. Priceless. And what about when Si cuts her throat? It's hypnotic, seeing her ebb away like that. Did you know life could be so beautifully grotesque?'

'No,' I said, a little too fast. The truth was, I had been sickened, yet transfixed. Nate knew it.

'Speaking of Simon,' I said, 'what's his story?'

Nate smiled. 'Si's terrifying, isn't he? On the surface you'd never pair us. But likeminded people invariably find each other, and click.'

'How'd you lovebirds meet?'

'Serendipity again. For us, boarding school. The classic breeding ground for English savagery. We discovered a shared interest in the macabre. As young men, we made fledgling films involving animals. Around the time I was directing bland TV by day, he and I started to make sex flicks. Bondage. Humiliation. We shared our work and earned positive feedback. I knew this was an embryonic time. More would come.'

'Nineteen women came,' I said, 'all of them, murdered. Your little operation was going swimmingly until New Year's Day.'

'Correct,' Nate said. 'That boy broke into Terry's café and stole my camcorder. Then he tried to make money from it. The cheek!'

'That boy's name was Kwame Mensah,' I said. 'He was fourteen years old.'

'The same age as your teenage daughter,' Nate said, 'before she jumped in front of that train. Six years ago today, correct?'

Something snapped. I stepped forward, my fists raised.

Nate held up his hands, and his eyes widened. At first, I thought he was afraid; but his gaze was fixed, as was the smile. He wasn't scared at all.

'Steady,' he said, 'I'm only teasing. You don't want to cause a scene.'

I looked, saw a couple had stopped, and were staring warily. The man had his phone out, poised to start filming, and the woman was following suit. Around us, the square was teeming with life. That's why Nate wanted to meet in public. He knew he'd be safe, surrounded by witnesses with camera phones and have-a-go heroes willing to jump in and stop a lump like me from hurting someone as unassuming as him. Christ, he knew everything.

I lowered my hands, said, 'What do you want?'

'Well,' he said, 'first, I want my camcorder returned.'

'Why? It's an old machine, easily replaced.'

'Nevertheless, it holds sentimental value.'

'OK, that can be arranged. But there's heaps more evidence that'll put you away. What about the photos I found in the film-set? And everything you've told me? I could just ring the police, give them the lot.'

'Ah, yes. That takes me to my second request. Along with the camcorder, I want *you*.'

'Me?'

He nodded. 'I meant what I said the other day, Kasper. You'd be perfect in front of the camera. It's why I've kept you alive. At first, I wondered if you'd join my circle and participate. But behind that butch armour, you're far too virtuous. A man who's willing to walk down the mean streets but isn't truly mean.' He winked. 'Then it dawned on me – how about you adopt a different role? As the star of a film?'

'You're joking?'

He shook his head. 'For years I've been toying with the idea of using a male. Someone big. Imposing.'

This was getting weirder and weirder. 'And what's the plot of this film?'

He paused, tapped his lip with an index finger. 'You'll portray a version of yourself, this maudlin hulk of a PI who meets a sticky end.'

'Meaning I get tortured to death.' I went for a laugh, but it was limp.

Nate merely stared, eyes like stained glass.

'It will be beautiful, Kasper. Trust me.'

'Sounds fun. But no thanks.'

'It's up to you. But if we don't use you, I have others lined up. I plan to film tonight. Think about it.' He checked his Rolex. 'Well, this has been fun, but I need to dash.'

He started walking, and I sidestepped in front of him, blocking his way. For a moment his brow was against my chin, and I could smell his expensive skin products, flowery shampoo, and minty breath.

'Excuse me,' he said.

'You're over,' I growled. 'Confess. It'll be easier.'

'I think I'll pass, thank you.' He peered up, not blinking. For the briefest moment I could see through the windows of his eyes into the blackness of his soul.

'What's to stop me dragging you to the cop shop right now?'

'That would be unwise.'

'Why?'

'Do anything silly, and you'll suffer. I know how to hurt you.' The air left me like a brick to the chest. 'What're you on about?' He smiled.

Was he bluffing, playing more games? I couldn't tell.

While I was thinking, he said, 'I'll be in touch.'

For a moment my temper flared, and I felt a pull to flatten him.

But something held me back. Maybe I needed to process what I'd heard, to try to work out whether it was some trick. Or maybe, more simply, I was afraid.

'Ciao,' Nate said.

I listened to the click of his brogues as he sauntered past until that dampened, and he fell from view.

Chapter 20

I stayed by the fountain in the square, going over the exchange with Nate again and again, trying to figure out what the hell had just happened.

No idea. My head was a train wreck.

All I had was a resounding certainty – somewhere along the way, I'd messed up. There was me thinking I'd had the upper hand, when in fact Nate had been trailing me along the whole time.

How did he know so much about me? Through Terry? Tash? And how the hell did she factor into all this? Was she friend, foe, or dead?

Patience's remark came back, about blood being thicker than water. Were the Willoughbys working as a duo? Had I been hoodwinked by both?

Sod this. It was time to get the police involved. I'd call Diane, give her everything, let the powers that be take control before this hole got any deeper.

I pulled out my phone, intending to do just that.

But didn't.

Something rattled in my head. The comment Nate said before leaving:

'If you do anything silly, you'll suffer. I know how to hurt you.'

How could he hurt me?

With an awful crack, the realisation landed. By taking out someone I cared for.

With numb fingers, I scrolled to my contacts, starting with Dr Steiner, and hit call.

She answered.

Working hard to keep my voice steady and not get her concerned, I asked if she was OK; she informed me she was 'quite all right', as was Suzi, who was with Patience, who had texted an hour ago. When I called Mani, he said he was 'pretty cool' too. Diane answered, too, still sounding pissed at me for holding back, but very much alive.

I lowered the phone from my ear and stared at nothing. Was this part of Nate's plan, to drive me crazy with doubt? Who else could he hurt?

It was obvious. Lisa.

I called, and it went straight to voicemail.

I tried again.

Same.

Suddenly I was running for the tube, forcing a city bod to brake sharply on his Boris bike, pushing people out of my way like skittles, ignoring the curses and looks, the wind harsh, drying my blinkered eyes.

Forty minutes later I was striding into Paradise, passing the deluge of dumped litter and white goods left out to brittle in the cold.

As Lisa's block fell into view, my fear became panic, and by the time I'd barged through the broken front entrance and bundled up the stairs I was gasping.

I tried her door handle. Locked.

I banged on the frame with the code. No answer.

I booted the lock. It splintered but held.

Another hefty kick caused a fist-sized hole, and a third was like a mallet to balsa, enough to send the whole thing flying off its hinges, thudding inward. I heard a scream, stepped in, felt for a light switch, pulled the cord, took in the scene.

'Shit,' I said.

Lisa was on her bed, wearing silk knickers and a lacy bra. Next to her was a bald, pudgy, middle-aged man – presumably a client – stark-bollock naked. Both were staring at me as if I'd just beat up a granny.

'Dylan,' Lisa said, 'what the hell are you doing?'

'I thought . . .' I started, then faltered.

I took in the man's rhombus chin, his golf ball eyes and bulbous gut, wobbling as he caught his breath. He brought his knees to his chest to cover his shrivelling dignity.

Lisa was more composed. She put her feet on the carpet and stood, took a kimono from the dresser, wrapped herself in it, tied the cord.

'You've broken my door.'

'Sorry,' I said. 'I thought something had happened to you. I'll get this fixed.'

'What's going on?' the man said. 'You know this nutter, Lisa?'

She ignored him. 'Why have you done this, Dylan?' she said. 'I told you, stay away.'

'I know,' I said, feebly. 'I . . . panicked.'

'Panicked?' the man said. 'You scared the hell out of me!'

'Shut up!' I said, pointing, but keeping my eyes with her.

She was looking at me strangely. Her lips were tight, a flat expression, but the vessels in her dark eyes bulged red with reproach. 'You need to go,' she said.

I stepped closer. She recoiled.

A sour taste rose, and I was about to do as she asked, when something leapt out. On her face, beneath the left eye, a grey streak of a bruise, daubed like face-paint, puffy, angry looking, recent.

'Who gave you that?' I said, pointing at it. 'Him?' I turned my finger to the man again.

'Hey!' he said, his voice somewhere between a cry and a yell. 'I never did anything! I swear!'

Probably so. He looked far too puny to raise his hands. 'Someone else get rough?' I said. 'Tell me.'

Lisa shook her head. 'It's none of your business.'

She was right. It wasn't.

But by kicking her door in, bringing my chaos into her world, I'd made it so. The black eye proved how vulnerable she was. Now I couldn't leave things alone.

'C'mon,' I said. 'We're going.'

'What do you mean?' Lisa said. 'Going where?'

The man whimpered something else, but I ignored it. 'Away from here.' I reached for her hand.

'No.' She broke the grip.

'I'm not negotiating.'

'You can't make me, Dylan.'

'There's two nutjobs roaming around.'

'That's nothing to do with me.'

'Afraid it is. They know about me, and people I care for. And they're planning on making another of these films. Tonight, Lisa.'

She took a sharp intake of breath, put her hand over her mouth.

Quieter, I said, 'It won't be for long. But I can't let you stay here. I'm sorry. Now pack some stuff. I'll get us a cab.'

A stilted moment followed. Her eyes seemed to pulsate, the anger drawing back her skin, giving her a stark, sepulchre look. The only sound was the cold wind gusting in from the gaping doorway.

Then she looked down and nodded. 'OK,' she said. 'I'll do what you want.'

Lisa dressed silently in a tracksuit and trainers, then she placed various items into a holdall – underwear, spare clothes, toiletries, her vape, plus a collection of dog-eared photos from a drawer. I glanced at the top image and wished I hadn't. It showed a girl, Lisa as a teenager, slight, fair haired, stood with a dozen or so other kids and some grown-ups. She was dressed in dungarees. Smiling. The photo told of a backstory I didn't want to know about. I looked away.

Lisa zipped up the holdall, pulled on a puffer coat and her cap. She turned to me. 'I'm ready.'

'Then let's go,' I said. 'The cab's up the road.'

'What about me?' the man said, still on the bed, shivering now.

'You,' I said, 'get lost.'

An hour later we were back in Edmonton. The Uber driver kept the meter running, and Lisa and I walked up to Baba Petrova, standing in the open doorway of her house, smoking a roll-up.

I shook Baba's hand. Like before, her grip was strong, expression unflinching.

'This shouldn't be for long,' I said. 'Thank you.'

'No problem,' she said. 'Is there trouble?'

'Maybe. This is a precaution.'

'You need help?'

'Just keep this one safe.'

Lisa stared at me from beneath her cap. She'd wiped off her makeup.

'I'm sorry,' I said. 'When this is over, I'll make it up to you.'

She shrugged.

'What happened?' I said, pointing to her bruise again. 'Tell me, please.'

'A client, he became angry.' She shook her head. 'It happens sometimes.'

'Who is he?'

'Don't worry.'

'I can deal with him, make sure it doesn't happen again.'

'No.'

She pulled out her vape, tugged deeply, vanished in a curl of mist.

'I'll go,' I said, and turned.

'Wait,' she said.

I looked back.

She held out her hand. Straight away I took it. It felt like a child's, the fingers tiny.

'Don't do anything crazy, Dylan. Please.'

I told her I wouldn't, gave Baba a nod, and then headed to the cab.

As the driver pulled off, I looked over my shoulder through the rear window. Both women were standing kerb side, statuesque in the cold.

Another hour later I was back home with Diane and Dr Steiner. The three of us were sat in the lounge, staring at my laptop on the coffee table.

Today was Diane's day off, but after my harried call she'd cut short her afternoon date with her beau and zipped straight over.

At first, she'd been full of questions, as had Dr Steiner. When I put on the snuff film, that all ended. Nate was right: his work really did have the capacity to seize whoever was watching it.

There he was, holding the bloody earrings, giving directions to Simon as he dished out his punishing blows to Minka. They went on and on until the closing death cut when I shut my eyes. But the sound got through.

'See you next time . . .' Nate said.

My phone vibrated. We all jumped.

It was Mani, no doubt calling for an update.

Later, I thought. This took precedence. I cancelled the call, closed the laptop, looked at Dr Steiner, then Diane.

'You both OK?'

'Not especially,' Diane said.

'Ditto,' Dr Steiner said. 'You'd described the film. But seeing it is a different matter.' She pulled a Dunhill from her deck and lit up.

Diane pointed at the camcorder. 'How long you had that thing, Kas?'

'Since last weekend.'

She took this in. I could tell she was struggling to balance her professional duty against our history. Not only had I withheld evidence from a serious crime, but I'd also had her share confidential police reports relating to this case. Now she was in a compromised spot. It could cost her career.

'I knew you were into something heavy,' she finally said. 'But never knew *how* heavy. You ever think about bringing this to me before now?'

'Many times,' I answered. 'But I wanted hard evidence first, enough to secure a conviction against these bastards.'

'Have you got that evidence now?'

'No.'

'OK. Then let's hear what you *do* have and go from there.'

I gave Diane the condensed version, starting last weekend when I accepted the job, then identifying Nate, reaching out to Tash after the party, the turn of events that morning at Trafalgar Square and Nate's threat. While I spoke, Dr Steiner stroked Tommy's head from his pew next to her on the couch.

'You think Tash has been colluding with Nate the whole time?' Diane said.

'God knows. Whatever; I've been played. Somehow Nate's had a stack of info about me right from the start. He's cunning, and I let him get one over.' I looked at Dr Steiner. 'These men *are* cruel. You're right.'

'Invariably, I am,' she said. 'What happens now? Surely there's enough for the police to swoop in?'

'Let me see the photos first,' Diane said, 'the ones you found at Terry's.'

I handed them over and she started leafing through, taking her time, long enough for Dr Steiner to smoke one Dunhill and light another.

A few more minutes, and Diane held one of the Polaroids up. 'This is the victim from the film I've seen. I'm sure of it.'

'Minka's there too,' I said.

Diane placed the photos on the table by the laptop. 'I'm confused,' she said. 'If Nate's known the truth about you this whole time, why hasn't he killed you already?'

'That was his original plan. But he changed his mind. Now, he wants me alive.'

'Explain?'

'He wants me to return his camcorder and the film on it.' I cleared my throat. 'And he wants me to appear in tonight's snuff.'

'What?'

'You heard me right.'

'But why?'

'Haven't a clue.'

'But there will be a reason,' Dr Steiner said. 'In his warped mind, everything he's doing makes sense.'

Diane just stared, in full police mode now. 'And what do you think he meant when he said he knew how to hurt you?'

'Don't know. I thought he was going to target one of you. Then I figured he had a working girl in his sights, someone I know.'

'You know many working girls?'

I felt my cheeks flush. No getting around this. 'Yeah, a few.'

Diane's eyes narrowed. Something hardened in her.

'I mean, there's not many,' I added, trying to back-pedal. 'It's for a bit of company, no big deal.' I sounded pathetic. 'Maybe Nate was bluffing, a way to get me scared.'

'Maybe,' she said.

'Listen.' I leaned forward, splaying my hands on the coffee table. 'All that matters is getting Nate and Simon off the street. I did what I thought was right. It backfired. Now, we need to move fast.'

'We move when I say we do,' Diane said. 'This is a police matter. First up, I want more details. Tell me about the big man.'

'I don't know much. Nate said they met at school.'

Diane jotted this down. 'And Terry Kinsella was involved too?'

'Terry was the talent scout. Luring the girls, taking their photos, convincing them they'd appear in sex films, and letting those two use his loft room as the film set. When I turned up asking questions about Kwame's murder and flashing Minka's photo, Terry must've freaked and then killed himself before the law came knocking.'

'Maybe not,' Diane said, looking up. 'Terry's autopsy report came back. He died from asphyxiation brought on by vomit inhalation. Toxicology indicates drugs in his system.'

'Meaning he deliberately overdosed and puked, right?'

'Not necessarily. Sure, he'd had pills recently, benzos, but not enough to OD on. No, what tipped him over was another substance in his system, most likely GHB, the chem-sex drug, slipped into his tea. It's tasteless, a favourite amongst date rapists. And in these quantities, almost certain to kill. Does that sound like Terry's thing?'

'No,' I said, as the realisation fell together. 'But it does sound like Nate's. He told me he drugged my beer the first time we met.'

'There you go.'

'So Terry was murdered. That's what you're saying?'

'Could be Nate knew Terry was a blabbermouth, spiked his drink, killed him, and wrote a fake suicide note. Problem solved.'

'Indeed,' Dr Steiner said, lighting up again. 'What charming specimens these people are.'

I pointed at the camcorder. 'Is the film made on that similar to the Red Rose Productions snuff you saw?'

Diane nodded. 'Different woman, but the same masked pair, and definitely the same MO.'

'And the location's a match?'

'I'd say so. Metal bed fame, velvet drapes, little and large killers.'

'OK then,' I said. 'We've got enough for a case. Let's just move on it.'

Before Diane could answer, my phone was buzzing, a second call from Mani. I cancelled again, sending an automated message that I'd call back.

With a heavy shrug, Diane said, 'You're right, there's a case here, and we could bring Nate in for questioning. But in terms of a warrant and searching his home, there's not enough hard evidence linking him with these crimes. That camera could've belonged to anyone. The confession you heard today is your word against his. If it came to a prosecution, we'd need more for the CPS to buy it.'

'Shit,' I said.

'Whatever. The Met's taking over from here, Kas. Your input won't be needed any longer. Just drop it.'

'Agreed,' Dr Steiner said.

I nodded, a strange mix of relief and tension flooding me.

Tommy made a whimpering noise, a warning that he needed a pee.

'I'll take him to the garden, make us all a brew,' I said, and got up. Tommy scampered from the couch. 'When I come back, I suggest we head over to the cop-shop. The sooner I can get rid of this case and not have to think about Nate Willoughby anymore, the better.'

I went to the back of the house, filled the kettle, then slid open the conservatory bifold doors. Tommy zipped out to take care of essentials. I stood on the patio, shivering a little.

The sky was mushroom coloured, the air cold. A fresh skein of clouds hovered, flicking rain against the patio.

Alone, I realised my head wasn't just full; it was broiling over. Rosie's anniversary, Nate rocking up that morning, bursting in on Lisa like I had – I was exhausted. Any more and I'd pop.

As the kettle whistled, I stood there, trying to separate one thing from another.

But the whole thing was a tangled mess.

All I knew for certain was I needed out. It was making me ill.

Patience wouldn't be happy that I'd gone to the police, but she'd have to live with it. Hopefully, Lisa and Baba wouldn't get dragged through the wringer. And when it was over, we could all move on.

I called Tommy back in, slid the door closed, went to make the teas. I was stirring sugar into my cup when my phone went a third time.

It was Mani. This time I answered, putting him on loudspeaker.

'Hey, mate,' I said, taking a sip, 'sorry for not answering earlier. Been a hell of a day. I'm with Diane and—'

'Kasper,' he said, his breath heavy. 'You need to get to the hospital.'

'Why?' I said.

He told me.

The sound of my mug shattering on the floor made Tommy bark, and by the time Diane and Dr Steiner came out to find out why I was halfway through the door.

Chapter 21

The three of us bundled into Diane's Audi and she put her foot to the floor.

'Kas,' she said, 'want to tell me what the hell's going on?'

I looked at Dr Steiner, sat in the rear. 'You said you spoke to Suzi and Patience earlier?' I said.

'I said I'd *heard* from them,' she said. 'Why?'

'When was this?'

'This morning, around ten thirty. Patience texted, said they were going to Suzi's art internship meeting. What's happened?'

'Mani said there's been another stabbing.'

'A stabbing?' She covered her mouth. 'Not Suzi?'

'No. Patience.'

'Details.' Diane said. 'When? How?'

'I don't know any more than what I just told you.'

But I did. Already, it was dawning on me what Nate had meant, and how much trouble we were in.

'*I know how to hurt you.*'

Dr Steiner again was tapping her phone, trying Suzi's number;

a muscle twitched along her mandible as she lifted the receiver to her ear and heard what I knew she would.

Dead air.

I stormed it into A&E, barging through doors, past porters, pushing stretchers and trolleys out my way, the lights lurid, sounds disorientating. I cornered the first person I could find wearing scrubs, started firing questions. The poor bloke knew nothing about Patience.

Meantime, Diane and Dr Steiner did the sensible thing, approaching a reception desk. As Diane was showing her police ID, I bundled over. The receptionist looked at her computer screen, tapped her keyboard, called someone on a phone.

A moment later a short pudgy man in scrubs appeared and guided the three of us into a private room. Mani was there, leaning against a wall. His eyes were grave, skin like cigarette ash.

'Where's Patience, Mani?' I said.

'Intensive care,' he said. 'Hooked up to a machine.'

'How on earth did this happen?' Dr Steiner said.

He shrugged. 'Patience called me this morning, saying all's good, and she was hooking up with Suzi. Next thing I hear is from the hospital saying she got found maybe an hour ago, bleeding out.'

'Found where?' Diane said.

'Out east, on some industrial estate.' He looked at me. 'Patience was alone. No sign of Suzi.'

I felt a crumbling sensation, as if there were a landslide in my chest. Leaning a hand on the wall for support, I said, 'Suzi's not answering her phone, Mani.'

He breathed heavily, nostrils flaring.

The door opened. We turned as one.

A different man wearing scrubs came in. He was tall, with a young, round face and prematurely grey hair. A lanyard round his neck identified him as an A&E consultant. Behind him stood a rosy-cheeked nurse.

'I'm Dr Mike,' he said, polite but serious. 'Please, come with me.'

He ushered us through a corridor, towards another corridor, and into a secure ward full of cubicles separated by curtains. I could hear beeping from behind them, and smelled that mesh of processed food, cleaning products and clinical waste ubiquitous to hospitals.

'What can you tell us, Mike?' Dr Steiner said, talking with that familiarity medics share.

He shrugged. 'A single wound to the abdomen area. She's lost a great deal of blood. The blade penetrated the stomach and intestines. She's been in surgery and remains intubated and unconscious. I forget how many units of blood we gave her. She's still being transfused and may've suffered a minor stroke.'

'Oh, Lord,' Mani said. 'It's the same as Kwame.'

The doctor went on. I caught about half of what he said, and only understood a fraction of that.

'Cut to the chase,' I said. 'How bad is it?'

'Well,' he said, hesitating before continuing, 'it's bad.' He proceeded to list the things that could go wrong.

The list was long.

'Can she speak?'

'She's unconscious, ventilated, in an induced coma. So, no.'

'Did she say anything before losing consciousness?'

Dr Mike hesitated again. 'I believe she may've said something to the paramedics, but I—'

Diane flashed her ID. 'I'm police. I need to speak to those paramedics.'

He looked over his shoulder at the nurse. 'Connie, could you try and find them?'

'This way,' nurse Connie said. Diane followed.

Dr Mike turned to the three of us. 'Did you have any other questions?'

'Yeah,' I said. 'Can we see her?'

No matter how many times you've been to ICU wards, there's always that initial shock. It strikes like a bad smell, bypassing the brain, landing in the gut, and tapping into that primal fear of death that exists somewhere in all of us.

Dr Mike led us through. Dozens of patients lay in bays on opposite sides of the long rectangular space. Lights were dimmed, and staff hovered, checking readings, writing stuff down, speaking in hushed voices, as if they were at a funeral. I tried not to stare at the patients but couldn't help it. Wires and tubes, dials and beeping machines surrounded them. They looked ill, pale, and as still as death.

Patience was in a bay at the farthest end. A ginger haired policeman was sitting a few feet away from her. With crimes like these, officers got posted with the victim on the off chance they awoke and made a declaration that could lead to an arrest. But one look at Patience told me the probability of this was anorexic.

Her muscles and brawn were deflated, and her face was no longer lined with scorn, now prone and infantile, the skin waxy, a bloodless grey.

A tube ran from her mouth and ended at a ventilator hissing and sighing as it pumped her lungs. Her hospital gown, rolled up to her sternum, showed a thick wedge of bandage wrapped around her midriff, the place where a prizefighter's belt should've been.

I stepped closer. Her lips were dry and flaked; thin vessels embossed her eyelids; further down, her fingers were caked with blood around the cuticles, and there were grazes on two of the knuckles of her right hand.

'Oh Patience,' Mani said. He made a sign of the cross and bowed his head.

I looked at Dr Steiner. She was without expression; but her eyes, behind her glasses, were fierce.

'Those marks,' I said to Dr Mike, pointing to her knuckles. 'How'd she get them?'

'Not sure,' he said. 'I gather she's a boxer?'

'Yeah. So?'

'Maybe they're from training?'

'Could they be defence wounds?'

'It's possible.'

Something was wrong with this picture. Patience was an experienced fighter. If Nate or Simon had snuck up, she'd have recognised them, not let them close enough to stick her.

Then a disturbing thought landed, one I couldn't ignore.

Tash Willoughby. Meek, shuffling, as threatening as a care bear; enigmatic Tash, capable of disarming you with those vacant eyes and getting near enough to stab you with a blade.

'I'll leave you,' Dr Mike said, and a moment later we were alone.

We stared at Patience.

I had no idea what to say. A person I'd been chatting with yesterday lay lifeless. Six years ago, it had been the same with Rosie. Who did I piss off in a previous life to get lumbered with this?

I leaned down, took Patience's hand.

'Sorry,' I said. 'I'll get them for this.'

Nothing came back but the hiss of the ventilator.

A moment later, Diane returned, breathing hard.

'You speak to the paramedics?' I said.

She nodded.

'What did they say?'

'When they found Patience, she was still conscious, talking.'

'About what?' Dr Steiner said.

Diane didn't answer. Her face said it all.

'About Suzi being taken?' Dr Steiner said. 'Spit it out, girl.'

Diane nodded. 'Yeah.'

'What's that mean, Kasper?' Mani said.

I stared ahead, seeing nothing.

'It means Nate has her.'

Chapter 22

While Dr Steiner and Mani stayed at the hospital, Diane and I jumped back into her Audi and gunned it away.

'Where to?' she said.

'Crouch End.' I handed her the postcode Mani had scribbled down.

'Why?'

'Nate was viewing a property there yesterday; a place with a soundproofed studio. I think it's the site of his new film set.'

'Jesus.'

Fifteen minutes later she was parked up on a side road in sight of the house.

Patience's appraisal was on the money. It was a swanky modern premises set back on a quiet cul-de-sac.

'What's your plan?' Diane said.

'Find Suzi,' I said.

'You really think she's in there?'

'I don't know what I think. But Nate's killed a heap of women. Patience is on life support. Suzi is missing. You got any better ideas?'

'There's no warrant or any rights to enter.'

'So?'

'So, any evidence you find will be inadmissible.'

'You think I give a crap about evidence?'

Diane screwed her mouth up. 'I can't let you do this. I'm a police officer.'

I was thankful for the lift, but realised it would've been better to come alone. Diane had rules to work within; I didn't.

'Just go,' I said, 'forget all this.'

'No.'

I turned to face her. 'If you try to stop me, I'll push past.'

She fell silent, her focus on the dash. That last comment had hurt.

I swung my head away, looked outside. The mid-afternoon rain persisted, a steady drone, making the bougie houses and cars in drives gleam wetly.

'I'm not leaving you,' she said. 'But what am I meant to do? Just wait in the car, twiddling my thumbs?'

'No,' I said. 'If you want to help, then see what you can dig up about this Simon character. What he does, who he is.'

I opened the car door.

'Wait,' she said.

I looked back.

'Sod the job. It might be dangerous in there. I'm coming.'

Despite the push of wind and rain, I felt a warmth in my chest, but knew I couldn't allow this. 'No,' I said. 'You'll be more use here. Stay put. If you see anyone coming, call me.'

It made sense. She knew it.

'One more thing,' I said.

'What?'

'You got anything in the boot I could use for burglary?'

She puffed out air. 'Help yourself.'

I had a rummage. The only useful items were a mini-jack and a screwdriver. I left the former, pocketed the latter, then buttoned up my leather.

As I walked through the nagging rain, I tried to process what was taking place.

But in the last hour, a red mist had fallen over my vision, tainting everything.

I stopped outside the house, looked around. The weather was keeping passers-by at home. No one was peering at me from windows. Hopefully, most of the neighbours would be at work. And if they weren't, I'd have to deal with it.

Breaking and entering requires a certain level of knowledge, or else things can go askew. Accessing Kinsella's Café was one thing, but a place like this would have tight security. Thankfully, my years working as a copper had taught me some tricks of the trade.

I went to the side, had a quick nosey, then hiked up the gate and lobbed myself over and into the side passage, landing in a squat.

I gazed up, squinting through the rain. The first-floor windows looked the best entry point, two simple sashes. Using the drainpipe and sills, I clambered up and tried to see through the glass of the farthest window at what awaited inside.

Nothing. The curtains were drawn, the room, pitch darkness. Time to break in.

Sweat began to run down my face, mixing with the rain. I started with the screwdriver, trying to find purchase between the window and the wood in order to hoist it up. No luck. The wood was slippery, the tool rudimentary. A crowbar or claw hammer would've made wrenching it easy, but with this, I couldn't get the leverage needed.

After a few painstaking minutes, I gave up. The longer I stayed here, the greater the chances of getting seen.

That left two choices.

Come back later armed with some decent tools and get in slickly. Or do things the more rudimentary way.

It was a no-brainer. With the back of the screwdriver, I punched the glass. On my third blow it caved inward. The pane gave an ear-splitting crash as it shattered on the floor.

No alarms.

I felt inside, found the hasp, unlocked the window, and prised it up, expecting a wailing alarm to sound.

No noise.

I switched on my phone's torch, held it between my teeth and shuffled through, past the curtains, the beam flailing, light and shadow dancing off the walls.

A moment later I was in. Even in the gloom I sensed the house was unoccupied, with that cold feel of empty places.

But I had to be sure. I got to my feet, found a switch. Squinted as light flooded the interior.

It was a master bedroom that looked ready for the inspectors. The décor was minimal, a double bed, an armchair, a dresser, a bookshelf; walls were mauve, carpets pink; the sheets on the bed were creaseless and so tightly spread a penny would bounce off them.

From the floorplans, I recalled that the soundproofed studio was downstairs to the back of the property. Tempting as it was to gun down there, the copper in me told me it was wise to stay vigilant, search each room systematically.

I started with the wardrobe. Empty. The same for the dresser. I flung the mattress off the bed to be sure no one was hiding, scouring around before finally moving to the bookshelf, shuffling it away from the wall to check it wasn't concealing anything.

It wasn't.

Exasperated, I moved on to another bedroom, followed suit, then went to a bathroom. A large space, big ceilinged, spotlessly clean, devoid of life. Nothing to indicate Nate had stepped foot here.

When I headed for the stairs, all that changed.

Hanging from a wall by a banister was a framed photo. It was the same photo I'd seen in Nate's study taken by his parents, showing the girl with the red rose.

I gasped, tried ignoring it, carrying on, but that made its lure more potent, and I found my eyes were drawn to the fleshy red petals in her slim hand.

From there, logic fell away. I clattered downstairs, storming through a lavish reception, then right towards a rear door, air-proofed, the word **Studio** engraved in the frame.

With a trembling hand, I turned the handle. It opened. Nausea swirled, and my breath began to stagger.

It was pitch dark inside, the air warm and musty.

I flashed my torch. The space was low ceilinged, rammed with objects stacked up haphazardly. By casting the beam around, I tried to make things out. Cardboard boxes, dusty cabinets, a mixing desk. And what looked like a bed.

A light flashed from a corner, making me spin round. It was a motion detector, picking up an intruder. I needed to be gone.

But I stayed.

Something looked wrong.

I flashed the torch directly onto the bed again. Were those arms and legs, bound to each corner?

'No!'

I felt the wall for a light switch. A moment later the room became a blaze of colour. I took in the whole thing at once.

Then I screamed.

A naked woman was on the bed. Her hands and feet were bound to the posts, a now-familiar X-shape. A single red rose lay next to her cheek. Blood dripped from her neck.

I tried to control my breathing, but it was running away.

This wasn't Suzi. It wasn't Tash, either. Or anyone I recognised.

I moved closer, quelling the sickness in my throat, the pull to flee.

She had thick, mousy hair and a pert body. Her head was bowed, but the eyes were open. Staring sightlessly.

There was something unearthly to her too. Her skin was lacquered, unlike the deflated appearance of a corpse; the muscles were taut, not sagging as they should be in death.

Then I understood. This wasn't a human. It was a mannequin, some real-life imitation made to depict a murdered woman. A sick joke, meant for me.

'Bastard,' I hissed. I'd been played again.

I was halfway out when I heard the phone.

I scanned for the source. It came from the mannequin's right hand. A smartphone, grappled in her fingers.

I prised it away, answered a FaceTime call.

Nate appeared on the screen.

'Hello,' he said, smiling. 'My detectors indicated company. I presumed it would be you.'

'What is this?' I said, gripping the phone so tight my fingers hurt.

'This is me showing you who's in control.'

'You knew I was coming here?'

'I know everything about you, Kasper. Hence the doll. Bad joke. I bought her a few years ago. A mock-up of Janet Leigh in *Psycho*. But I've re-christened her Rosie. That was your daughter's name, wasn't it? Red Rosie. Ha.'

The only way to keep from hurling the phone against the wall was to say nothing, but it took an immeasurable force of will.

'You know,' Nate continued, 'it's a good job I'm fond of you. I could have had you arrested for burglary.'

'It's you who'll get arrested when the truth comes out.'

'And what will I be arrested for?'

'Try kidnapping, and assault with a deadly weapon. Patience Mensah was stabbed this morning.'

'How could I have stabbed anyone? As you might recall, this morning, you and I were strolling around Trafalgar Square like a couple of old chums. Thanks to you, I have a cast-iron alibi.'

He was right. I'd been part of his plan.

'Where's Suzi?' I said.

'Ah, the girl. She's with me. How she fares will very much depend on your behaviour over the next few hours. Now—'

'Where the hell is she? Your house?'

'Course not. Don't bother going there. She's in my new film-set, somewhere you won't find.'

'Suzi has nothing to do with this! What do you want, Nate?'

I knew the answer.

'I've told you: first, I want my camcorder. Second, I want to make a new film tonight, starring you. Now that we both have something the other one wants, I suspect you'll take my request seriously. We'll do the swap at one a.m. Keep this phone with you. I'll call later to confirm the details. In the meantime, don't do anything silly.'

'Wait!' I said. 'Just wait a damn minute!'

'What now?' He sounded exasperated.

'I need proof Suzi's alive.'

'You'll have to trust me.'

'For all I know she's dead already.'

He shook his head. 'You are persistent. Very well. A glimpse.'

He went off camera, and the screen went black. For a moment I thought he'd hung up, until I heard muffled voices, footsteps descending steps.

'Here we are,' he said, and I could see.

We were in an enclosed space, no windows, the walls glinting, reflecting the phone's light. It looked different to the original set at Kinsella's Café: darker, moodier, the acoustics tinny, as if it were the inside of a steel drum.

Then a gargling came off camera, like a water feature, the same gargling sound from the Minka snuff.

The image arced around, revealing a wrist, shackled to the corner post of a bedframe, hanging limp; then an arm, a neck, a face . . .

It was Suzi. Tied up. Blindfolded. The bed covers were drawn to her chin. Her lips were moving, mouthing silent words.

The camera shot swung to her right, stopping on a figure, a big male right of the bed. Clad in the same stocking mask and jet-black clothes from before. Simon. His fingers were interlocked beneath his barrel chest, and everything about him was still, apart from his eyes, moving up and down Suzi as if she were a meal.

'There,' Nate said, off camera. 'Proof of life.'

The floor seemed to quake, and my inner world was quaking with it, so much so that I could barely stand and had to lean against the wall.

'Please . . .' I said, while her lips kept moving.

'Please what? Come now, you're not going to beg, are you?'

'I'll tear your heart out if you hurt her!'

'Don't make threats. Upsetting me would not be helpful.' The humour was gone from his voice, replaced with a rasp.

'Suzi!' I bellowed. 'Suzi!'

She must've heard me, for her face twitched. I yelled again, and she started moving, left, right. When I kept on, the recognition struck home, and she started saying my name, soft at first, then loud awful cries.

'Kasper!'

'Suzi! It'll be OK!'

She started screaming. The sound was piercing, and sent shrill metallic echoes through the receiver, tearing through my eardrums, piercing my heart.

'Suzi!'

I kept shouting until I was hoarse, but it was useless. The last thing I saw was Simon grappling her arching body, pushing her torso down, a hand on her mouth, and then she fell from view completely and Nate reappeared.

'I'll ring you later,' he said, Suzi's muffled voice still audible. 'Remember, if I catch wind you've got the police involved in this, the girl's dead.'

'Hold on! Let me—'

This time he hung up.

Chapter 23

'Suzi's alive,' I said. 'Nate wants to do a swap. Her in exchange for the camcorder, and me.'

We were at Dr Steiner's house, Diane, Mani, the doctor and me, the four of us sitting around the kitchen table. The air was cloyed with cigarette smoke, thickened by our mood.

It was a few minutes to six. Earlier, after leaving the Crouch End house, I'd had Diane drive me over to Nate's Highgate house so I could break in and ransack the place, knowing in my heart it was pointless, and precisely what I'd find there.

Nothing. Suzi could be anywhere.

But wherever she was, she wasn't dead. Yet.

'Why's Nate so keen to have you in this film?' Diane said.

'I don't know. But he plans on doing the shoot tonight.'

'Good Lord,' Mani said, his head in his palm, a lit cigarette between the fingers of one hand, the other caressing the crucifix around his neck.

I stared at him. 'Don't tell me you're praying?'

'Wish I could,' he said. 'I can't find a connection with nothin' right now.'

'What's that mean?'

He looked at me, shook his head. 'People who are capable of doing these things . . .' he paused, finding his words: 'well, I just can't understand how the God I believe in lets them live on earth. It's made me question a lot of stuff I took for granted.'

Diane had been silent until now. 'Mind if I have one of those?' she said, indicating the deck of Dunhills.

Dr Steiner slid over the deck. It'd been years since I'd seen Diane partake, and the sight took me back to our early years, before smoking was frowned on, and we both liked a cheeky Embassy. For a second I considered joining in, but then Suzi's face came back, blindfolded, tied to the bed, and the thought made my guts clench.

'Any more info on the sister, Tash?' Dr Steiner said.

I shook my head.

'How about possible locations for the new film-set?'

'It's not Terry's café, the Crouch End place, and it's not Nate's house.'

I took a moment, remembering the video call I'd had with Nate earlier, seeing Suzi bound and blindfolded. 'It's somewhere secluded, without windows, below ground I think.'

'Why do you think that?' Diane said.

'I heard him descending some steps.'

'That hardly narrows it down,' Dr Steiner said.

'I know.'

Mani smacked the table. 'So, we've got nothing. Meanwhile, Patience is on life support, and Suzi is in hell. We need to get the police involved. No other choice now, we've done all we can. They've got helicopters, sniffer dogs, the works. Let them take over. Simple as.' He looked at Diane. 'Can you make that call?'

I expected her to be all over this. Instead, Diane drew in a lungful of smoke, held it, and let it drift out. 'No,' she said, 'we can't let the police take over.'

My hands became fists. She knew something. 'Why not, Diane?'

'While you were breaking into properties, I did as you asked, made some calls, focused my attention on this Simon character. And I got a hit.'

'A hit?' I said.

'Intake records from Nate's boarding school show one S. McFee in his same year.'

'Nate said they met at boarding school,' I said. 'What else you got?'

'When Henry and Martha Willoughby died in the house fire, S. McFee's name came up again. Only by then he was a uniformed copper, one of the first responders to the scene. Since then, he's risen through the ranks. These days, he's made detective grade.'

By now, Diane looked like she'd chewed some turned meat.

'He's in the Met?'

She nodded.

I kept quiet. Anger seethed in me. It was all slotting together.

'Another psycho in uniform,' Mani said.

'To join the ranks,' Dr Steiner added.

In confirmation, Diane held up her phone. A photo was on the screen, a Met portrait of a uniformed, heavyset officer with regalia pinned to his lapel. Stubble barbed his chin, and his eyes were black pellet holes.

'Is that the man you met at Nate's party?'

'Yes.'

'No wonder Nate's been one step ahead,' Mani said. 'His best mate's a fed.'

'Correct,' Diane said grimly. 'This means we can't go to the police with this evidence. Simon will be monitoring the air-waves. He'll know what we're up to.'

'And Suzi's dead for sure,' I said.

The silence stretched out before us.

'Then we need to find Suzi ourselves,' Dr Steiner said. 'It's the only way. Ideas, people. Has Nate got any alternative accommodation? Flats somewhere?'

'He's got plenty of cash,' Diane said. 'I checked tax returns. Over the past few years there's also been a large amount of traceless income from offshore accounts. My guess, this is the money he makes through selling his snuffs. But apart from the property in Highgate and the place in Crouch End, both of which Kas broke into, there's no homes I could find in his or Tash's names.'

'What about Simon?'

'Negative. He lives with his wife and kids out in Harlow. A quiet suburban double life. No way he'd be able to build a torture chamber under their noses.'

'So, what can we do?' Dr Steiner said, her voice rising.

I shook my head, tried to put everything together, consider the options.

But the clock was ticking, and doors were slamming. The only certainty was this whole mess was my fault. If Suzi stood a chance, it had to be me who fixed it.

As this realisation took grip, my body started shaking.

'Chill, Kas,' Diane said, placing a hand on my shoulder. 'You've got that crazy look.'

I dashed her away. 'Too late to chill.'

'You need to stay calm. Going nuts won't help Suzi.'

She had a point. My head was all over the place.

But not so much that I couldn't see the truth – there was only one way out of this quagmire.

'I've got to play by Nate's rules,' I said.

'Rules?' Dr Steiner snapped. 'You really are a fool, Kasper.'

I stared at her, shocked. Her eyes were flint.

'I warned you against this case, but you wouldn't listen. This isn't a game. There aren't rules. The only way Suzi will live is if you take her back, by whatever means.'

'Will you both drop this Liam Neeson crap!' Diane said. 'We need to stay rational!'

'Not anymore,' Mani said. 'You still haven't figured out what we're dealing with.'

Diane glared, pointed at him. 'Don't you get all holy on me, train driver!'

'Then don't you knock the truth staring you in the face, detective!' he countered, pointing back. 'This is evil. Plain an' simple.'

We all stared at Mani. His voice, his demeanour had changed.

Diane's eyes went back to me. 'So how far *are* you willing to go?'

I tried to come up with an answer.

After an age, I said, 'These are cruel men. I'll need to be cruel back to survive.' I looked at Dr Steiner. 'Right?'

Her lips pursed. 'Right,' she said.

I stood, pulled my leather off the chair. 'You all need to back off now. You've done enough. Let me handle things.' I headed for the front door.

'Handle what?' Diane said. 'Kas, where're you going?' She came after me, grappled a handful of my sleeve. 'Don't. We need to work together.'

I pulled away.

'Kas!' she shouted. 'Wait!'

But I was gone.

Chapter 24

I t was dark now, the rain heavy, careening down the arch of my nose and through the collar of my leather as I pounded the pavement.

In the last ten minutes the shaking in my body had gone up a notch, as if I were having an allergic reaction. I'd never known anything like it.

To steady myself, I headed to my father's old allotment on the periphery of Paradise. I'd rented this small patch of land since his death, paying a nominal fee to the council for the dubious luxury.

Each allotment was in a state of disrepair, and mine was undoubtedly the most forlorn – a ramshackle hut stood precariously on a rectangular mulchy plot of lawn, encaged by rusty wire fencing netted with weeds and shrubs. It was dismal, secluded, but right then it matched my inner world.

I sat on a stool in the hut doorway, sheltered beneath the flimsy plastic awning, took a bottle of Bushmills kept on the sill, poured some into a stained teacup and drank.

Until last year I had a handgun in the hut as well, loaded with a single bullet, ready to fire. In the grey aftermath of my daughter's suicide, having the weapon was a comfort, a surety that death was close.

But I'd never quite managed to use it. And last spring I'd disposed of the bullet, and subsequently, the gun.

Now I wished I hadn't. Even with only one bullet, it would've come in handy. At least I could take out Nate or Simon.

But could I really kill?

I filled the cup with a second finger, necked that, spilling more than I drank.

My phone buzzed. I looked at it, expecting Nate.

Instead, it was a message from Mash-Up Security:

First shift is tonight. 8pm.
Don't be late!

My new job. I could've laughed. Right then, it seemed entirely unimportant.

More drink, more spilling. My sodden body wouldn't stop shaking. But rather than feeling cold, I was pent up, full of spiked energy, the reality of my hopelessness beating like a call to arms.

Suzi was hostage.

She was blindfolded, tied to a bed.

Terrified.

Visualizing her, my mind started to fragment and journey inwards. I closed my eyes, felt myself sway, then fall. Memories cascaded like light through a prism, and I looked for something to distract me.

Eventually, I found an encounter with Rosie, my daughter, aged five.

It's Friday, past midnight. I'm not long back from a twilight shift working as a beat copper. I've slept on the settee these past few days following my latest spat with Carol. I'm tired, cold, ready to call it a night when I hear Rosie from her bedroom.

'Dad!'

At first there's irritation, realising my night isn't through just yet.

Then I go to her boxy room, push open the door. Any ill feeling fades. She's sitting upright, lips parted, her brown eyes huge and focused on me. Although the room is steeped in navy darkness, thin rays of moonlight slant through the curtain, enough for me to see her clearly. Her breathing is fast, audible over the baseline of urban noises thrumming through the city.

'Why're you awake?' I say.

'I heard something.'

'Heard what?'

'The wolf.'

'Him again?' Rosie, a voracious reader, has recently been introduced to the fairy-tale of Red Riding Hood. Although she loves the story and voices I put on, the imagery of the manipulative wolf impersonating the little girl's grandmother seems to have triggered a deep-rooted fear that rears its horns in dreams.

I crouch by the bed, start to stroke her curly gold hair with my big hand. Her scalp is hot, brow clammy.

'You're safe,' I say. 'No wolves here.'

'How do you know?'

'It's my job.'

'What would you do if a wolf came for me?'

'I'd fight it away.'

'What if it tried to scratch me? Or eat me?'

'I wouldn't let it.'

'What if it killed me? What then?'

I hesitate. This is the first time I've heard Rosie talk about death with such candour. Till now, it hadn't occurred to me that these are concepts children of five appreciate.

'Would you kill it back?' she says.

'Yeah,' I say. 'I guess I would.'

'Promise?'

'Promise.'

I place my hands on her shoulders and gently push her back onto the mattress, then pull the blanket up to her chin and kiss her forehead. I kneel by her head and carry on stroking her hair.

'What are we doing tomorrow?' she says.

'It's Saturday. What do you want to do?'

'Can we feed the pigeons? At Nelson's Column?'

I smile. 'Course we can.'

And we did.

The buzz of my phone drew me back sharply to the present. I checked the screen, expecting Nate.

It was Mani calling.

'Kasper.' His voice sounded funny, like he was far away. 'Can you speak?'

'Yeah,' I said. 'What's up?'

'Look, man, Patience died.'

I didn't flinch, didn't say anything, just stared between my knees at a clod of muddy earth.

'You still there?'

'I'm here,' I said. 'When?'

'About ten minutes ago. Dr Mike called from the hospital, said her vitals changed and her heart just stopped. Nothin' they could do. She's at peace now. With her family.'

'Did she say anything?'

'She never woke up.'

We were silent. The awning eddied under the rain.

'Diane's out looking for you. She thinks you're gonna do something crazy.'

I didn't reply.

'Are you?'

'Am I what?'

'Gonna do something crazy?'

'I don't know what I'm going to do.'

'Well, whatever you decide, don't do it yet. Let me pick you up. This involves me as much as you.'

'No,' I said. 'When Nate calls later, I'm finishing this alone.'

'How are you planning on doing that?'

I breathed heavily. 'That's my problem, Mani. This is on me.'

'You scrap that talk. It's on those two killers, understand?' His voice was raw with emotion.

'Yeah,' I said, dully. 'Got to go, mate.'

I hung up, necked whiskey from the bottle, looked up at the blackening sky, and the tentacles of cloud spreading across the moon.

Mani was right. I should stay put. Let my nerves settle.

But Diane was looking for me. She'd been to my allotment before, knew it was my hideout. If she caught me up, she'd do whatever she could to stop me.

So what was I going to do?

Two options presented themselves. The first: play ball with Nate and do the swap, me for Suzi, a life for a life. If it meant she'd live, I was OK with dying.

But Dr Steiner was right. Nate couldn't be trusted. Why would he let Suzi live? She could identify him and Simon. Safer for Nate just to kill her.

That meant option two: take her back and eliminate Nate,

Simon, and whoever else was involved. Punch their tickets. Send them to hell.

Kill them.

Patience wanted it. Baba wanted it.

And in a dark corner of my heart, I wanted it too.

As this certainty took hold, the shaking started up again, buzzing through me like a ripsaw, sending specks of fire caroming across my reddening sight. I tried telling myself it wasn't real, I was stressed, my body was playing ticks; but the sensation was overwhelming, something dark and crazy coming from within.

'I'm not crazy,' I said.

Silence answered.

I hit the Bushmills again. But even the booze wasn't working. I was shaking uncontrollably, and my head screamed with implacable fury.

Suddenly I was standing, mobilized, ready for action.

Nate didn't want to do the swap for a few hours. Where was I to go? I couldn't stay at the allotment, and if I didn't find something to keep me occupied, I'd pop.

Then I realised the perfect way to fill some time had already been delivered.

Before I could weigh things up, I took my phone, texted the security guard brothers:

I'm on my way.

I locked the allotment and headed back into the rain, my trembling hands thrust in my pockets, and my thinking a long way from good.

Chapter 25

*S*ecrets, located off the Hackney Road, was an 'Exclusive Gentleman's Club', if the sign above its black awning was to be believed. Judging by the clientele queuing up, however, there was a shortage of gentlemen frequenting it on this pissy Saturday night. Most were shifty looking middle-agers wearing Stone Island shirts, Reebok Classics and lechy grins.

The brothers were outside, clad in bomber jackets and combats bunched into steel-capped boots. They spotted me. Neither looked pleased.

'Time do you call this?' the rounder of the two said, looking at his watch.

'Sorry,' I said. 'Got held up.'

His brother stepped closer, looked me down, up. 'You OK? You look a bit not right.'

'I'm fine.'

They shared another look. Then the smaller one said, 'I'm watching you,' and the other gave me a baseball cap with the company logo, *MASH-UP*, emblazoned on its font, along with an ID badge to pin to my coat. They'd misspelled my name CASPER.

'Where do you want me?' I said.

In unison, they pointed inside the club.

The interior of *Secrets* was even less gentlemanly, and a world away from exclusive. My guess, the place hadn't been decorated since the seventies: the walls were chipped Artex, the floor peeling vinyl and rotten cork; chart pop wailed from the speakers, and the air was muggy and fetid, smelling of stale beer, stale bodies, cheap perfumes and blocked drains.

To the left there was a bar; right, tables and chairs; in the middle beneath a rotating glow-ball was a stage on which three peroxide blondes wearing nothing but thongs and heels gyrated around ceiling-height poles, smiling humourless smiles as the entirely male audience gazed up like kids at a magic show.

I wandered around. A few other girls were taking orders, serving drinks while men offered chat-ups and rolled notes into bras. In response, the girls laughed obsequiously, flashing assets, giving come-ons, their accents invariably eastern European.

How many were Minka Petrovas in the making, I wondered?

I leaned by the bar, asked a stocky barman for a glass of water. As I drank it, I checked the phone Nate was to contact me on. No messages.

Staring at the phone's screen, the sight of Suzi bound to that bed hurtled back. I tried to shake it away, focused on the stage, the dancers, the men in the audience, anything to keep me distracted.

But now the image had landed it wouldn't shift, and I could feel the anger ticking inside.

If I could just figure out where Nate had her, this mess could be over. I'd head there, surprise the crap out of everyone, and do what needed to be done.

Unless of course she was already dead. What then?

I shook my head. I couldn't think that way.

I glugged the water, felt it spill round my mouth.

This place was damn hot. I loosened my collar. The music, the lights, the thrusting hips and rapacious grins were meshing into a nasty collage, ugly and foul. A ferrous taste fizzed up my throat. I drained my glass, tried to wash it away, but it stuck.

I caught the barman, asked for a top up.

As he refilled my glass, I concentrated on breathing. In. Out. Relax.

It worked.

For a bit.

But the thoughts lingered, and I couldn't control where they'd take me. Beads of sweat started running down my forehead. I held out my glass for more water.

I've no idea how long I was standing there at the bar, drinking water, checking the phone, trying to hold it all in. A hand on my shoulder made me start.

It was the barman. Shouting.

'What?' I said, leaning in.

'I said you're wanted! Outside!'

I headed for the door, stepped onto the street, took in the scene.

The brothers were at the front of the queue, trying to contain some low-level argy-bargy. A short bald man wanted to come in. He'd clearly had a skin-full, and his mates kept egging him on. I moved closer.

'You sayin' my money's not good enough for this dump?' He pointed a signet-ringed finger. 'Lemme in!'

'Not tonight, sir,' one of the brothers said.

'Think you've had a bit too much to drink,' added the other.

The man kept on.

I went to his flank, stood there. His scalp was salted with rain and dandruff; fat swelled around his neck like sausage meat.

His mates began sizing me up. After a moment he must've sensed something, as he stopped blabbing, turned, looked up at me.

'Who've we here?' he said, and looked at my ID card. 'The friendly ghost, is it?'

'You should head home,' I said.

He sniggered. Booze wafted from his breath. 'Gonna make me?'

'If I have to.'

His pupils narrowed; his mouth screwed up. Then he half turned, said, 'Maybe you're right, I should go.'

'Thank you.'

But instead of walking, he spun round, and did something stupid.

He hawked and spat at me.

Most of it dribbled onto his chin, but a few flecks landed on my cheek and neck. And it was like paraffin to a fire.

A single right to his face was enough. His head plummeted back like a snapped flower stem, and he staggered, flailing his arms, his legs spaghetti, before he slipped and fell onto the rain-soaked pavement.

The crowd fell quiet, staring. 'See that?' someone said. 'Bouncer just decked him!'

One of the man's mates tried to lift him, but he was too heavy, and instead they both collided in a heap.

I looked at my fist, shocked at what I'd done.

But I didn't have time to think. Two of the man's mates moved in. One tried a right that telegraphed wildly and gave plenty of time to step into the blow. I grabbed his jacket, swung him round, hurled him onto the road, forcing a black cab to brake hard. The man lay there, sprawled, stunned.

The other one had his fists raised. He was trying to decide what to do.

'Come on,' I said.

He bolted.

I stood there. The red mist was all over me. I blinked to see through it and take in the scene.

The man I'd punched was sitting on his knees. Bloody spit drooled from his nose. It was broken, dripping onto his polo shirt.

His mate I'd chucked to the road was shuffling over, nursing his elbow, looking confused.

'Give us the hat back,' one of the brothers said to me, 'and get lost,' said the other. 'You're fired,' they said as one.

Fair enough.

I lobbed them the cap and ID, and started walking, my ears clicking with each step, the mist not seeming to shift.

My knuckles throbbed, but I didn't register pain. I didn't feel anything really, regret, shame, fear. Just chaos.

I breathed into the sensation, felt it build in my body, crackling. When I breathed out, it was like I'd placed my hands on an exposed powerline.

A voice in my head said I wasn't myself, and I didn't know what I was doing.

'I don't know what I'm doing.'

A woman walking past gave a funny stare.

I kept walking, splashing through puddles.

It was dumb coming out tonight. What had I been thinking? Nate would be calling soon. If I was to save Suzi, I needed to get prepped, not start fights.

I tried to slow, but I couldn't stop my feet from moving, or prevent the images blasting across my skull.

Rosie, dead on a mortuary slab.

Patience, dead on a hospital bed.

Minka, bound, battered, her slit throat spilling her last.

Suzi, tortured and killed.

I thudded my head with both palms.

As I did, another woman in heavy make-up shuffled awkwardly around.

'Suzi?' I said to her. 'Do you know where she is?'

She veered back, shooing me away as if I were a rabid dog.

Jesus, I needed to get away from people.

Keep walking.

Left foot, right foot.

Splash. Splash.

I can't say how long I kept on like this, or where exactly I went. But at some point, I decided I needed some booze.

I went into an offy, bought some tins, a couple of miniatures.

Outside, a few homeless people were bumming fags and change. I was giving coins to one when a glancing blow floored me.

Next thing I was on my front. My head pounded. Shock more than pain.

I rolled over.

Three men stood there. The same three from the skin bar. They must've followed me. Waiting to attack.

'Think you're hard now, punk?' one said.

'Let's teach him a proper lesson,' said another.

That's when I lost my shit.

Pure instinct, I kicked the nearest square in the balls.

He made a high wheeze and caved in like a collapsing deckchair.

I dived forward on my front, avoiding the stamps from the others, and scrambled to my feet.

My eyes locked with the short one whose nose I busted earlier. He had a beer bottle in his right hand, inverted, ready to use as a weapon. His mates did too. They were grinning.

I grinned back. The redness buzzed like a swarm of crimson hornets. All sense had gone, replaced with that pull for violence. I wanted to annihilate these men, to throw each of their ugly faces into the pavement, smash noses, cave teeth, ruin them. The wanting was physical, coursing through my limbs like a force.

They charged. I charged. And where they were drunk and sloppy, I was a bull on heat. One caught a punch to my mouth, and I tasted hot, coppery blood, but that only fuelled me.

We tumbled down onto the pavement and I heard grunts and cries as bodies hit the flags. I didn't hold back, walloping them with punches, knees and head buts, again and again.

I don't know how long this went on. Eventually though, they stopped fighting.

I got to my feet, stood there. All three lay sprawled and groaning. The short one was sputtering, his broken nose frothy with fresh blood.

I got hold of his collar, lifted. He said, 'Hey!'

I slammed him against a lamppost. The back of his head clanged.

'Let go of him!' a woman said.

'Call the police!' someone else said.

One of the other four got up, tried to lock my arms to my sides. I released the short man, broke the grip easily, turned and shoved the assailant away.

While I had my back to the short one, he tried to slip past on all fours. I caught him by the collar, yanked him back, lifted, slammed him into the lamppost again. He pushed at my face with his hands.

'Stop that,' I said.

He kept pushing. I slammed him again. He stopped.

'Please,' he managed, his breath coming in grunts.

I stepped back, keeping him upward with my left hand under his chin. I punched his cheek with my right. He put his hands up to protect his face.

I punched his stomach. His hands fell there.

I punched his face again. He whimpered. Bloody spit trailed from his mouth. I could smell urine where he must've pissed himself. He was disgusting.

He tried covering his face and midriff with both hands but was too broken. Instead, he started crying. I punched his liver, then his face, then went for the ribs.

With each blow, firecrackers were popping inside me, innervating my muscles with electricity. Right then, this man was Nate Willoughby. I could see him, and I wanted to kill him. To mash his face and dump his corpse in some ignominious grave where no one would remember him. I punched his gut, harder.

'My God,' a woman shrieked. 'Leave him alone!'

The man's right eye was completely shut now, and his nose a pool of red. I kept on.

Suddenly something hit me on the back of my left shoulder. I ignored it.

It happened again, sending a shockwave of numbness through my arm, and then another hard blow stuck me in the crook of my legs, buckling me.

I let go of the man, turned. Three uniformed police, with their batons extended. They were shouting. Behind them, a police van, the blues on.

246

'Police! Stop!'

A crowd had gathered, fifteen, twenty people, several filming on phones. Even the shopkeeper from the offy was videoing, while the homeless folk watched with gleeful faces while drinking the cans and miniatures I'd dropped.

I looked at one of the police. 'Where's Suzi?' I said. 'Have you seen her?'

The puppyish officer turned to his colleagues and shrugged. Then they stepped in as one, and it hit home how much trouble I was in.

'Wait,' I said. 'This is wrong.'

No good.

'Suzi,' I said. 'Oh, Suzi.'

'You're under arrest.'

An awful weariness seized control, and I collapsed.

Hands grappled my wrists and the cuffs clinked on.

'No!' I said again. 'I need to be somewhere tonight!'

They ignored me.

A hand under each pit, and I was being lifted, bundled into the rear of a secure police-van so they could take me away.

Chapter 26

'Listen to me! I can't be here!'

I'd yelled, kicked and pounded my shoulders against the interior of the van the entire journey.

Pointless. The police were doing what they were trained to do, ignoring my pleas, treating me like the berserker my actions showed me to be.

Eventually I gave up, slumped down in a heap, lamented with several loud moans.

The van bumped and swerved through Saturday night traffic. After an age, I heard it park up. The engine died.

A rattle of keys and the back door opened. Five officers piled in and yanked me out, two grappling my arms, two my legs, the fifth holding my head. When I writhed, they pulled my handcuffed wrists upwards, a pressure grip that hurt like hell, and bundled me into the rear of the station to face the music.

I kept on trying to talk my way out of this, but they were having none of it. And why would they? I'd just battered a bunch of men, gave one a serious hiding. There was a ton of witnesses. Game over, Kasper.

But I had to try. Suzi's life depended on it.

What would Nate do when I failed to answer his call? Maybe delay tonight's snuff?

Or maybe not. Maybe they'd just crack on, using Suzi as the star of the show.

'Please!' I said. 'You don't understand!'

Onwards, through doors, corridors, more doors, and then we were in a wide, airless custody area. Simultaneously, the officers dropped me to my knees, leaving the handcuffs on, and stepped away. I looked around, taking it in.

I'd never been to this cop shop, but when you've worked for the Met, all the stations look alike. Chairs, bolted to the floor. Coppers escorting remand prisoners to cells. Centrepiece, an elevated desk, partitioned off by a cloudy Perspex screen.

From behind the screen, a heavyset custody sergeant came forward. 'Dylan Kasperick?' He spoke without looking up.

'Yeah,' I said, standing unsteadily, walking towards him. 'Listen, this whole thing's a mistake, you need to—'

Like an Old Bailey judge, he held up a hand, and started to read the report. 'You've been arrested for several public order offences, the most serious of which is an assault.'

'Fine,' I said. 'Book me. But I need to get out of here.'

'Afraid not.'

'Arsehole!' I said, and nutted the glass.

Not clever.

First, my head pounded. Second, the uniforms were all over me again, even rougher than before, arms up my back, reapplying the pressure grip, pushing my thumbs back this time for good measure.

'All right, all right!' I yelled.

Keeping me pinioned, a fifth copper took my possessions from my pockets and put them in a plastic bag – my phone, the phone

Nate was to ring me on, my wallet, belt, shoelaces, watch, keys – while the desk sergeant told me I'd be shown to a cell.

This time I didn't try to interject. No bloody point.

Only when he said, 'Just try to calm down, Kasper, all right?' did I look up.

The face was oddly familiar – a few more lines, a lot less hair – but I recognised those sallow cheeks and kind, tired eyes. Then I read the name on his lanyard – Dave Cromby – I remembered.

Two decades back, we did our basic training together in Hendon. It seemed a different life.

'All right, Dave,' I said, and my eyes misted.

He nodded.

A wedding band was on his finger, and a family photo of a woman and two kids was pinned to his desk. He had a decent paunch round his middle, no doubt from countless tasty home cooked meals, and lines round his mouth from smiling. Life had been good to Dave. He'd worked hard and reaped the rewards.

In that moment, our differences seemed painfully stark.

'Dave,' I said. 'Is there any way I'm getting out of here tonight?'

He shook his head. 'I'll arrange for you to speak to the duty brief. But you're not going any time soon. The victim's pressing charges. There were witnesses, including several police officers. You'll need to be interviewed before there's talk of bail.' He paused. 'What the hell happened?'

I came close to answering, telling him everything, but instead refrained. Any peep about snuff films and Nate Willoughby and Simon would find out. Nate had been crystal clear: if I squealed to the police, Suzi was done for.

'Can't talk, Dave,' I said.

He sighed. 'Well, if you change your mind—'

'Just get me that duty solicitor.'

251

'OK,' he said, back in official mode. 'A bit of time will let you calm down.'

'I'm calm now.'

He shrugged, turned his back.

The uniforms took me into a lift that descended one flight underground, and from there, they walked me to a corridor of eight cells. A smell filled the narrow interior, the rank mix of sweat, testosterone and regret.

All the cells had heavy steel doors, with only a letterbox to peer through. As we passed one, its occupant hissed out, 'The fuck you lookin' at?'

No one answered.

The interior of my cell was bog standard – a windowless square room with a cot-bed, a basin and a seat-less loo. No ventilation apart from the door slit. Etched in the metal walls were people's names, dates, gang tags and all kinds of profanities. A small fluorescent strip light flickered on the ceiling. Inside its casing lay the corpses of insects, baked and shrivelled, like sultanas.

The door slammed closed. I heard the clink-clank of keys followed by the dull thud of footsteps.

I went to check the time but realised I couldn't even do that. They'd taken my bloody watch.

My guess, it was coming up to half ten. Nate wanted to do the exchange at one. Three and a half hours.

I sat on the cot.

Time passed.

Now, the red mist had lifted, I could see things dismally clear.

My life was one of those melting ice caps you hear about, broken at sea, the chunks floating in different directions. Nothing would come together. Everything was hopeless.

The cause?

Me.

I punched the cell wall. The sound thudded and echoed back.

I wished I'd never gone to that boxing fight with Mani.

I wished I'd followed my instincts and walked away from this whole thing.

I wished I'd taken everything to Diane, let the police handle things.

I wished I wished I wished.

I thumped the wall again. 'Idiot,' I said.

'Stupid.'

Thump.

'Bloody.'

Thump.

'Idiot.'

My hand screamed. Fresh blood pooled round the knuckles.

I heaved, the sound reverberating and bouncing back, as if these cell walls themselves were confirming the truth, that all was lost, and Suzi would surely die.

Then the first tear fell, plopping down onto my fist, the salt-water stinging the fresh wounds. I became a seven-year-old again, locked away in that dark basement out on Paradise, crying, powerless, tears raining down onto my knuckles, bloody as they were now from punching the door, my sobs echoing off the metal walls . . .

I looked up.

Echoes.

Metal walls.

Paradise.

That's when I got it.

Maybe it was the stress levels, the booze, the blows to the head

I'd taken that night, or the whole lot shaking up my perception. Whatever, suddenly, an idea had appeared.

When Suzi was screaming, the sound echoed.

Just like my cries echoing in this police cell now.

The sound was distinctive. I'd heard it before.

Where? As a seven-year-old kid, when I'd screamed for help in a basement. A basement on Paradise.

'Paradise is full of nooks and crannies.' That's what Nate said the first time we met. He knew the estate intimately.

As did I.

Was Suzi being held in a basement on Paradise like the one I'd been locked in?

It seemed crazy, based only on a feeling. But I had to find out.

I was already on my feet, about to scream for the guard.

No need.

The rattle of keys, the turning of a lock, and the door swung open.

Chapter 27

I figured it'd be the duty solicitor or a screw coming to offer me a phone call.

Instead, there stood custody sergeant, Dave Cromby. 'Come on, Kasper,' he said, 'this way.'

Something in his eyes told me to keep schtum and do as I was told.

I followed him out of the cell, back down the corridor, up the lift, through the processing area and to a small interview room. Inside was Diane, sitting behind the table.

'Ten minutes,' Dave said, and then to Diane, 'I'll speak to you afterwards, DI McAteer,' giving her a strange, knowing look.

I took the seat opposite her.

As soon as the door shut, I said, 'How'd you know I was here?'

'Dave Cromby,' she replied, 'that friendly desk sergeant called me fifteen minutes ago. He remembered we had something way back when, and was kind enough to let me know you were in custody, under caution.'

'I need to get out of here, Diane,' I said.

'You should've thought of that before you got nicked for beating seven shades out of some undesirables.'

'I think I know where Suzi is.'

She paused. 'Go on?'

'There's these hidden basement flats on Paradise, out east of the estate.'

'Like the one you were locked in as a kid?'

I nodded. 'I reckon Nate's got access to one of those basements to use as his film-set. They're perfect – secluded, soundproofed. If we can figure out the address, we can get to Suzi.'

'Why would Nate make his new film-set so close to the old one?'

'Because he's obsessed with Paradise. I haven't figured out why. But that house in Crouch End was just a decoy, him trying to throw me off the scent.'

Diane's eyebrows raised.

'What?' I said.

'Something came up. After what you just told me, I think it's important.'

'Tell me.'

'While you were busy getting arrested, I made a few more enquiries about locations. Anywhere Nate might be holding Suzi.'

My heart thudded. 'What did you find?'

'Terry Kinsella's name again,' she said, 'or more specifically, his late mother's.'

'Irene Kinsella? She's been dead years. You've got me.'

Diane half smiled. 'Irene was a local legend. During the eighties, and the right-to-buy era, she bought up a bunch of flats dotted around Paradise, then used them to house vulnerable folks. That's the kind of person she was, right?'

'Right,' I said, thinking back to the warm, indomitably kind woman, poles apart from Terry.

'Anyway, when Irene passed, Terry inherited everything, including the flats. Land Registry confirmed it. He evicted the tenants and kept the addresses under aliases, using them for cash-in-hand rentals and storage for drugs and stolen goods. Police turned a blind eye because at least it was keeping the crime all localised to Paradise, and out of public view.'

Further proof of the stigma and neglect those from Paradise endured from those supposed to protect them. I could feel my blood temperature rise, but knew I couldn't get side-tracked. Not while there was so much at stake. Instead, my mind bolted back to Terry's office, the letters I'd found addressed to various men and women with Paradise postcodes. This was all making sense.

'These flats,' I said, 'do any have basements?'

Diane whipped out her notebook, flipped to a list of addresses scribbled down.

'At least two, maybe three for sure.'

'Then Suzi's in one of those basements.'

'Don't get carried away. It's a possibility.'

'I know it sounds nuts. But I'll bet my life Suzi's there. Christ, I could kiss you, Diane.'

'None of that,' she said, standing up. 'That was the easy bit. Now, I need to figure out how to get you released.'

She headed for the door.

Ten long minutes later she returned with Sergeant Dave again. They stared down at me admonishingly, like I'd been caught with a hand in the biscuit tin.

'You're free to go, Kasper,' Dave said.

I was baffled. 'What about the man I assaulted? The charges?'

'Oh, I wouldn't worry about all that,' Dave said, a smile flickering over his face. 'I just got off the phone with him at the hospital where they've reset his nose. I advised him that we've got probable cause that he's a serial groper and coke dealer, and we're planning on pursuing these charges unless he rescinds his allegations. Lo-and-behold he's had a profound change of heart. All the charges against you have been dropped.'

'Is he a groper and dealer?' I said.

'Who cares?' Diane said. 'It put the heebie-jeebies up him, and that's what counts. Thanks to Dave here, there's no record of you being nicked. You're free.'

'There you go,' Dave said. 'Run along.'

He held up a clear plastic bag containing my stuff.

I stood, took it. My heart seemed to have swollen to twice its size.

'Good to see you again, Kasper,' he said, shaking my hand briefly as I scurried past for the door. 'Don't come back. OK?'

Diane and I thundered out of the police station.

The rain had stopped, but the wind felt sharp and volatile, scudding across my face.

Her Audi was parked up in a bay. Mani and Dr Steiner were in the back. As I approached, I made out the Lonsdale sport bag containing the camcorder ensconced between them.

I got in the shotgun seat, leaned over to face them. 'Thanks for coming,' I said, 'and for bringing that.' I pointed at the bag.

'Glad to have it out my house,' Dr Steiner said.

Mani eyed my bruised face and pulped fists. 'Sound of things, you've had an eventful time.'

'I'll fill you in later, mate.' I gave a moment. 'Sorry about Patience.'

He nodded. There was nothing more to say.

Diane fired the engine, pulled out. I looked at her.

'Thank you, too,' I said. 'If it weren't for you, I'd be stuck in there.'

'I'm a police officer, Kas. But I'm a human too. I don't want to see people I care about get hurt. None of this lone ranger crap. I'm helping.'

'It might cost you your job.'

'And I'm still in. Whatever it takes.'

'That's the spirit,' Dr Steiner said.

'Roger that,' added Mani.

I considered him again in the rear view. Heavy lines and a heavier demeanour replaced the usual cheer, and his crucifix necklace was notably absent.

'Tell us what you know?' Dr Steiner said.

I summarised my theory – Suzi was on Paradise, being held in one of Terry Kinsella's properties.

'You got the addresses of these flats?' Mani said.

'Yup,' Diane said. 'There's a few possible ones with basements.'

We hit Hackney Road's weekend traffic, stop-starting as the hipsters and lager boys spilled from the pubs and staggered roadside. Diane beeped, growling her engine.

'Has Nate called yet?' Dr Steiner said.

'No,' I said, looking at the phone he'd given me. 'But he will.'

'When he does, have you worked out what to say?'

'I'll tell him I'll do the exchange like he wants it: me and the camcorder for Suzi. It needs to be somewhere open so that I feel safe, and Suzi can make a clear run once I'm captive.'

'You don't honestly believe he'll bring her, do you?'

'Nope. He doesn't have any intention of letting Suzi live. He'll want to manipulate me into coming out, and then take me prisoner too. But Suzi not being with them could work in our favour.'

'Meaning?'

'While I stall Nate and Simon, you three can rescue her.'

'I don't think that's a great plan, Kas,' Diane said, revving hard to beat a set of lights. 'What if you're wrong about Suzi's location and she's not in one of those basements?'

'She has to be, Diane.'

'OK, say she is? What if the sister Tash – or someone else for that matter – is guarding her, and they put up a fight?'

'Then you take them out.'

'You mean, kill them?'

'I mean, do whatever it takes.'

We hit the A roads, Diane put her foot down, and a few minutes later, we were crossing into Haringey.

'There,' I said, and we all looked.

Ahead, the clouds were writhing like grey fire, and then the jagged silhouette of Paradise fell into view against the conflagration of the night.

Chapter 28

Nate called a few minutes after midnight. We were in Diane's Audi, parked up on a gravel slope on the periphery of the estate.

Before answering, I stepped from the vehicle and stood a few feet away so that I was out of earshot.

'Well, hello,' he said, his voice as clean and smooth as a paper-knife. 'Are you OK? The tension must've been killing you.'

'I'm fine,' I said. 'And I'm on for the swap. How's Suzi?'

'Resting.'

'And Tash? Where's she?'

'My sister is none of your concern.'

'Let me talk to Suzi.'

'Not this time.'

'How am I to trust you, Nate?'

'By remembering who's holding the cards.'

'There're no cards. If Suzi dies, I've got nothing left to live for. You know about me, the things I've already lost. Hurt her and I'll pursue you to hell.'

'You are bogged with sentiment, aren't you? Take my word for it, Kasper: life's much freer when you don't care.'

'Screw you.'

'Maybe this is more trouble than it's worth. The girl's a beauty. Feisty too. Perhaps we should just use her.'

'In that case, you'll be looking over your shoulder the rest of your life.'

I must've been shouting or gesticulating, as I could feel Dr Steiner's steely eyes on me. I looked to the car. Sure enough, she was shaking her head slowly, deliberately, indicating for me to calm it.

She was right. I wanted to peel back Nate's arrogance, and for him to misread aggression as desperation; but I didn't want to provoke him into doing something awful.

'Sorry,' I said, tempering my voice. 'I'm a little rattled.'

'Understandable. Rest assured, follow orders and the girl will go free.' He chuckled. 'How're you feeling about your screen debut later?'

'Can't wait.'

'Oh, neither can I. We've got a long night planned. Now let's finalise the details. Where to do our handover. I was thinking we might meet somewhere discreet. How about—'

'Discreet is fine,' I cut in, 'as long as it's outside.'

Nate winced. 'Outside? But it's a beastly night.'

'Maybe so. But I need to see with my own eyes that Suzi's free before I hand myself over. It's outside, or I'm out.'

A long pause.

'How about Paradise Cemetery,' Nate finally said. 'You know it, I assume?'

'I *do*,' I said, taken aback by this suggestion. 'It's where my father was cremated, and my daughter.'

'Excellent. Then it seems fitting that the cemetery should be one of the last places you see.'

I thought about this. The cemetery was derelict and open-planned, ideal for what I wanted; it was also in the shadow of the estate, which kicked out any lingering doubts that Suzi was somewhere there too.

'Fine,' I said. 'Paradise Cemetery it is.'

'Good,' Nate said. 'I'm trusting you.'

'Just like I'm trusting you. I'm the one who should be worried.'

'You should,' he said. 'Remember that if you start getting ideas.'

The silence pounded.

In truth, I knew Nate had no intention of following through on what we'd agreed to.

Then again, neither had I.

'It's settled,' he said. 'One a.m. If I sense anything amiss, the girl dies. I'll film Simon slicing her to ribbons and send you the whole thing to watch. Ciao for now.'

I thought he'd hung up when he added, 'And Kasper?'

'What?'

'Conserve your energy. You'll need it. We have a surprise in store for you.'

After the call, I had to take a moment to steady my nerves.

Dr Steiner exited the Audi, said, 'That didn't look easy.'

'I feel like I've aged a decade,' I said.

'You think he bought it?' Diane said, stepping out too, along with Mani.

'Yeah,' I said, 'I think so.'

I checked my watch. Quarter past midnight. Forty-five minutes to go.

Mani lit a Marlboro, offered the deck round. Dr Steiner took one, as did Diane.

'So what now?' she said.

'I'll head to the cemetery,' I said. 'While I'm there, you three search those flats. Don't worry about me. Just get Suzi and call the police.'

Diane sucked deeply on her filter, scowled at the taste, but persevered, then said, 'You worked out how you're going to keep those two entertained while we're looking?'

'I'll improvise.'

'What about when they figure out you've tricked them? You crossed that bridge yet?'

'Same answer. But one way or another, this ends tonight. If it looks like the plan's going south, I'll take Nate and Simon with me before I go.'

'You mean you'll kill them,' Dr Steiner said, a statement, not a question.

We all looked at her. Her eyes glimmered behind her spectacles.

'Yes,' I said. 'I'll kill them.'

She inhaled smoke, held it in. 'Good,' she said, as it curled outward. 'Then you're ready.'

No one spoke.

In that moment I considered the three of them, my team of allies – an up-and-coming London Met detective; an acerbic retired psychiatrist; a TFL tube driver who'd lost his faith – and was struck by how innocuous a trio they were.

But right then they were my best friends. I knew I could rely on them with my life, and more importantly, Suzi's.

'If I don't make it back,' I said, 'tell Suzi I'm sorry she got caught up in this.'

'But you *will* make it back,' Dr Steiner said.

I reached over, took her small hand. Diane came to my left,

Mani to my right. They put their arms around Dr Steiner and me, and we stood there, linked, breathing the same cold air, thinking the same dark thoughts.

'We're doing this for Kwame,' Mani said. 'And Patience.'

'And for Suzi,' Dr Steiner said.

'And all the other women who've been butchered,' Diane added.

And for my daughter, I thought. One way or another, things always came back to Rosie.

We parted. I slung the gym-bag on my shoulder and looked at them a final time. 'See you later.'

'You better had,' Diane said.

They got into her Audi, drove off. I waited until they were out of sight.

Then I started walking to the cemetery.

Chapter 29

Paradise Cemetery covered a large plot of undulating lands about the size of Tottenham Hotspurs' football ground. It was circumnavigated by rusty iron railings and jagged shrubs and trees, and held hundreds and hundreds of graves, at the centre of which there was an oval-sharped crematorium.

The cemetery had two entrances: one at the northern tip of the housing estate; one to the rear that was adjacent to the parade of shops where Kinsella's Café stood. I headed in this way, my hands thrust deep in the pockets of my leather, the rustle of the bag and my breathing the only sound.

A gibbous moon was waxing overhead, casting just enough light for me to see where I was walking. But inside the cemetery, the illumination was blocked by the overhanging trees, and I was swathed in a darkness so thick and absolute it seemed to be viscous.

I switched on my phone's torch. The beam dazzled off the graves, the light drawing out the pigment of marble and weather-beaten stone, glossy from the rain.

As I headed in the vague direction of the crematorium, my boots squelched in the mud, and I wondered whose bones were beneath me. There are some people who make a habit of visiting cemeteries and thinking like this. By immersing themselves in death, they believe that they might acquire a deeper knowledge about its mysteries.

It's a pull I understand. In the aftermath of Rosie's suicide and cremation, I'd drift into these very grounds, wandering aimlessly, considering my own life and whether it was worth living.

My torch dashed across more epigraphs, picking out names, dates, dedications. I read a few. The youngest person was a four-year-old girl, Tonya Adamson, who died in March 1978; the oldest, Sid Cohen, passed only last year, aged a-hundred-and-three.

I kept on, an edge of fear sharpening against my back. At one point I stumbled over a stone that must've warped in the grass. I caught my balance, but the torch beam flailed, and then my knee splodged in the boggy earth. I took a moment to steady, my breathing harsh, each exhalation appearing like a vaporous ghost, vanishing, then reappearing before my eyes.

Before long, the crematorium emerged, its domed outline fuzzy in the dark. I stopped maybe fifty yards away, checked my watch. Five to one.

I listened. Nothing.

I shone my torch beam skyward like a flare so I would be easy to spot. The only answer was darkness and silence.

Then I saw it – three flashes, just to the right of dead ahead.

'Stay there!' I called out. 'I'm coming to you!'

A fourth flash signalled.

I kept my pace steady, not wanting to slip again, although as I drew close my heart was riding, and the air felt thin and dry, as if I were walking at altitude.

The crematorium dome was clearer now, tinged white,

glinting in the moonlight like a varnished bone. In front, the out-lines of two men, one small, one large, incongruous, and instantly recognisable.

A few yards away, Nate called, 'That's close enough.'

I stopped.

A large torch flashed on next to him, far more powerful than mine, and I squinted at the harsh beam. The light was mounted on stilts, beaming like a gaslight, illuminating the scene. Now, I could see them vividly.

Nate was clad in the same parka he'd been wearing that morning at Trafalgar Square. His skin was alabaster white, coloured by those red lips and pale, limpid eyes, like depthless icy water.

Simon was head-to-toe in black: black steel toecaps, black combats, and a black hoody that clung to his vast frame. He seemed impervious to the cold, his face expressionless, a strip of butcher paper with two bullet holes.

'Well,' Nate said, looking around, 'here we are. You came alone?'

'That's what you wanted.'

'Are you armed?'

'No.'

'Prove it. Drop the bag. Open your coat. Raise your hands.'

I did, the wind billowing out the hem of my leather.

'Search him, Si.'

Simon stepped forward, came to my flank, sniffing the cold air around my body. His hands began patting me down, strong hands, the fingertips like drill bits, capable of great force. Although I couldn't see his face, I could feel him brooding with cold dark rage.

'He's clean, Nate,' he said, stepping back.

'Good,' Nate said. 'Now, the camcorder please.'

'It's in the bag,' I said.

'Give it to Simon.'

I crouched down, lifted the bag, turned, and gave it to Simon.

He unzipped it, rummaged, and pulled out the camcorder.

Nate exhaled audibly. His pupils became abnormally wide. My guess; he'd had a line or two of coke before heading out.

Using his own handheld torch, Simon checked the SD card and the serial number. 'This is it,' he said.

'Check it works,' Nate said, his tongue flicking between his teeth.

Simon hit power. Lights flashed on the camcorder screen.

'All good.'

The capillaries in Nate's eyes crackled light bolts of lightning. It wasn't just the snuff film that held importance. It was the camcorder itself. Why?

'Thank you, Kasper,' he said. 'You kept to your word.'

'Where's Suzi?' I said.

Nate grinned. 'Slight change of plan.' From the pocket of his parka, he produced an iPad. 'She's here in spirit, but not in the flesh.' He held the screen up.

Suzi appeared. Like before, she was bound to the bed, strapped with the same blindfold, prone. A clock by her head indicated the time and date – this was a live feed.

'You were meant to bring *her*,' I said, raising my voice. 'Not a bloody machine. A swap – that's what we agreed. Me for Suzi.' I turned, as if I was about to scoot.

But I wasn't going anywhere. Simon had placed the camcorder on top of the bag and had gravitated to my flank, blocking my path. 'Not so fast, fucker,' he hissed.

'Kasper, please,' Nate said, a consoling curve in his voice. 'Let's not be silly. I couldn't bring the girl. It wouldn't have been fair to release her here in the cold. She'd be too vulnerable in her current state.'

I looked back. 'Current state? What do you mean?'

'After our call earlier, she got upset. Simon tried to calm her, and she bit him. He had to retaliate. Then we gave her a sedative.'

I stared at Suzi on the screen again. Her head movements seemed sluggish, and there was a purplish smudge around her lip. She'd been struck with blunt force.

I looked at Simon. He was grinning.

'What did you do to her?'

'Nothing much,' he said. 'I was just being nice.'

I forced myself to separate from the hatred and the desire to clobber him, but it took an immense force of will, and my body buzzed from the effort.

'So,' Nate said, 'the new plan is, you turn yourself over to us, and then the girl will be released afterwards at a safe place.'

'No way,' I said. 'How can I trust you?'

'You have my word.'

'Bullshit.'

'The alternative is she dies now.'

Now? Again, I looked at the screen, and Suzi. In the background, that strange bubbling sound again.

'Is someone with her? Or are you bluffing?'

Nate smiled, propped the iPad against a grave, in clear view. 'All will be revealed.' From his pocket he removed a small receptacle beaker and a flask. He uncapped the flask, poured some liquid into the beaker.

'So,' he said, 'first things first, I need you to drink this.'

I stared. 'What is it?'

'Not poison, if that's what you're thinking. Just something to calm you down. I know about that fiery temper of yours.'

'No thanks.'

'I'm afraid I insist on it. Trust me, in a little while you'll be glad for any medication you can get your hands on.'

He stepped forward, stopped a foot or so away, held out the beaker. I looked at it. The solution was clear.

'Let me guess,' I said, 'GHB? The stuff you spiked Terry with?'

Simon sniggered.

'Drink,' Nate said. 'A last tipple, before the fun begins.'

I looked into his eyes. There was no turning back now.

'I'm going to make you immortal, Kasper,' he whispered, like we were the only two people on earth.

Careful not to touch his fingers, I took the beaker.

'Slainte,' I said, put it to my lips, and downed it in one.

Chapter 30

For a while we just stood there – Nate in front of me, Simon to my rear – no one saying a thing.

Then Nate looked down at the camcorder lying on the bag. 'Isn't life strange,' he said.

'What do you mean?'

'All this aggravation started because of that harmless object. But like I said this morning, these events have proven serendipitous. If the camcorder hadn't been stolen, you wouldn't have appeared. We'd be strangers, oblivious to one another's lives.'

'Sounds good to me.'

'I disagree. Despite the bother you've caused, I'm genuinely glad we met.'

'Why?'

'Because you're fascinating, Kasper. Beneath that butch, Mitchum-esque exterior, you're a textbook flawed hero.'

'That so?'

'Indeed. You're fighting the good fight, like all heroes must, but you're bedevilled by frailties and flaws, and the capacity to be hoodwinked.' His tongue darted out, and he smiled.

'Nate,' Simon growled. 'Shall I take him now?'

'Si's keen to get you away.' Nate removed from his parka a set of handcuffs. 'Are you ready to put these on?'

I looked at the iPad screen. Suzi remained tied to the bed, blindfolded, prone.

'No,' I said. 'I'd rather talk a while longer if you don't mind.'

From my right, Simon came into view. 'I'll hurt this idiot,' he said.

I looked up, saw his eyes, knew he'd happily get physical.

But I couldn't let him cuff me, not until I was sure Suzi was safe. Keep Nate talking. It was the only way.

'Before I give myself over,' I said, 'can I ask a question? Something that's been bugging me?'

Nate tilted his head. 'Go on.'

'When we first met, you seemed a normal, friendly kind of fellow.'

'Thank you.'

'So how are you able to do what you do to these women?'

'Hm,' he said, dreamily. 'I used to wonder the same thing myself.'

'And what did you conclude?'

He tapped his lip. 'Tell me, when you eat a steak do you picture the cow being slaughtered? When you fight, do you think how you're reinforcing societal violence?' He shook his head. ''Course not. You just switch off and enjoy the moment.'

'You're saying you just switch off too, and get on with killing? No, it's not that simple.'

'It is, really. Humans aren't compassionate. We're savages. Most would rather film an atrocity and upload it for likes rather than step in to prevent it. We live in the age of desensitization, Kasper. My parents understood this. As do I. No, once the woman is on the bed, she's a prop, there to be used. Simple as that.'

I swallowed dryly.

Nate's mouth became a smile so thin you could cut yourself on it.

Don't let him take control, I thought. Keep him talking. 'And what about afterwards? When they're dead?'

'Meaning?'

'The bodies, Nate. How do you dispose of them?'

'Now you want to know all my secrets.' He paused. 'It isn't as hard as you'd think. After death, the blood congeals. Flesh becomes meat, and meat can be carved. How many times have you walked past sacks of offal outside restaurants and thought nothing of it? Late at night, Simon drops a bag here, another there. The binmen take them. Nobody misses these women. We pick them carefully, you know.'

A sickly taste swirled in my belly. Was it repulsion, the stuff he'd given me to drink, or both? I couldn't tell, but it was making me weaken, and Suzi remained captive. If she wasn't found, I'd have to take these two down. Time to rock the cart.

'Know what I think?'

'Do tell?' Nate said.

'You two are nothing more than a pair of serial killers who get horny torturing women. Remember, I've seen the Minka snuff, the look in your eyes. You might call it art. But really, you're bog-standard sadists. A failed filmmaker and a crooked copper. Both of you are pathetic.'

Simon growled. I turned to face him square. Enmity radiated from his coal black eyes.

'What's wrong?' I said. 'You think I'm not onto you, Detective Simon McFee, with your nice little family setup as a front? What do you reckon your wife and kids would make of all this if they found out?'

His body seemed to swell with rage, while his expression coiled inwards, like a wire spring, ready to explode. 'How did you find out who I was?'

'What does it matter? I'll be dead soon. But you'll go on. A serving officer paid to uphold the law. How'd you become what you are? Were you teased at the boarding school where you met Nate? Did Daddy not give you enough cuddles?'

I braced as he moved in, but Nate said, 'Stop, Si!' and he froze.

Staring down, his fist raised, Simon said, 'I like hurting people. Being a policeman helps me get away with it. I don't think about it anymore than that.'

'There you go,' Nate said, chuckling. 'Si understands. Violence is as inherent as the birds and the bees. You know it's true, Kasper. The same pull churns in you. What separates us is, you try to suppress it. Whereas we've embraced it.'

I looked back at Nate. His pale cheeks were blossoming red, and his eyes were louring.

'Perhaps it does churn in me,' I said, remembering the dark thrill as I'd beaten up the men earlier. 'But with you, that pull runs even deeper. And it's linked with your parents and the past, right? C'mon, Nate. I'll be dead soon. Tell me what happened? Spill the beans.'

'There's no beans to spill. The sins of my parents are history.'

'What sins? What did you mean when you said they understood the age of desensitization we're in?'

Nate shook his head. 'I know what you're up to. Stalling for time. Trying to prevent the inevitable. It won't work. You're finished. Si, shall we?'

'Let's go,' Simon said.

'No!' I said, holding up my hands.

Nate winced. 'Please. No more delay tactics.'

Simon stepped towards me. When I turned sideways, he stopped and grinned.

'Don't,' I said, shuffling back, squelching in the mud.

I glanced at the iPad. Suzi was still there. Panic fizzed in me. Maybe she wasn't in one of Terry's flats? Maybe she was somewhere far from here, and I'd got this thing all wrong?

'Look, just release the girl,' I said. 'Then I'm yours.'

'You're ours already,' Simon said, placing his torch on the ground by the camcorder, freeing both his hands. 'We can do it the hard way if you want.'

I kept back-stepping, my eyes fixed on him, not paying attention to my footing.

Bad move. I slipped in a patch of uneven soil, dropped to my ankle, my legs suddenly like butter, my gait swaying.

'Oh, Kasper,' Nate said, his voice sounding far away. 'Why fight? You know how this story ends.'

'Nooo!' I said, the vowels stretching out, my voice not quite mine anymore.

He laughed. 'Look, Si, he's delirious. Oh, we're going to have fun later.'

I pushed myself up, saw Simon coming. I put a grave between us. He came right. I circled left. He came that way, and I did the same, keeping the distance.

The fear was on me now. I had to take this pair down. Problem was, I wasn't sure I had the strength for it.

Simon lunged, and I pulled back. His fingers scraped over my hand, nails tearing the skin.

As we moved, I saw our shadows dance off graves like stick men on a cave wall. Amidst it all I tried to keep Nate in my line of sight, making sure he didn't try to flank me.

Another grab from Simon, and this time I stepped in, jabbed

his nose, one-two, then retreated. For some that would've been game over, but it felt like I was hitting the bow of a battleship, and the blows seemed to only rile him.

But decades of boxing had taught me a thing or two about tenacity. If I persisted, working the jab like Patience had with me when we sparred, even a hardy opponent like Simon could be toppled.

He came again and I kept on, aiming for the same spot on his face. The bloke was strong, but he was a wrestler, not a boxer, and his feet gave his moves away. Keep precise, working those jabs and holding the distance, and I reckoned I could put him out.

He lunged again, and I parried with another combination. Blood flowered from both nostrils, coating his chin, slickening the stubble.

He looked more shocked than hurt. 'You broke my nose,' he growled, and reached into his back pocket, pulled out a combat knife – army issue by the looks of it – with a serrated edge and curved tip. 'I'll cut you with this. And after, I'll go after that pretty detective friend of yours. Diane. Did she tell you about me?'

My heart lurched. What did he mean?

No time to think. He slashed at my face, missing by inches.

'Don't hurt him badly, Si,' Nate said. 'We need him looking good for the film, remember.'

Simon seemed less bothered. He slashed again, this time at my neck. I leapt back, heard the blade whistle through air. He kept on, alternating the blade between hands, his reflexes rattlesnake fast.

A third attempt nicked my shoulder, tearing leather. I reached for the wound, and a fourth dashed over my chest, ripping through the jacket and finding skin. Heat rose, and I could feel blood spill out like warm gravy.

'Ouch,' Nate said.

I didn't look at the gash, but knew it was sizable, enough to put me in trouble if untreated.

Simon grinned. 'Keep fighting,' he said. 'Just makes it more fun.'

And I believed he was enjoying himself. But the knife made him over-confident. That could work to my advantage.

He came again, going for my neck, lunging like a fencer. I swerved left and he slid forward in the mud, momentarily exposed. It allowed me to grab the knife hand, twist hard to the left, elongating his arm. He snarled, tried to parry. Before he could I fell onto the arm with my left elbow, combining strength and body weight to maximise the impact.

Something crunched and Simon screamed, both sounds in unison. Immediately his arm went floppy, and the knife clattered against a grave.

He fell to one knee, cradling his broken limb. Spittle flew through his clenched teeth. 'Gonna kill you!'

Not if I could help it. I charged, punching his face, toppling him back. As he lay starshaped, I reached out to where the camcorder lay a few feet from us.

'No!' Nate screamed.

I looked at him. 'Want your precious camcorder?'

Hard as I could, I plunged it into Simon's face. Once, twice, three times.

Plastic and metal disintegrated, shards flying like embers on a fire. A final smash and the camcorder was all but obliterated. I tossed the ruined casing aside, scrambled back.

Simon rolled over, clutching his face with his good hand. Blood ran through his fingers. He let out a guttural groan.

'Stay down,' I said.

But he staggered up, lowered his hand, looked at me.

I choked a gasp.

He was a mess, torn up, disfigured; eyes red, face glistening, his mouth a ghoulish maw.

I considered running but my legs weren't behaving themselves, and I knew if I fell with my back to him I'd be done for. Instead, I braced for combat.

He lumbered, and I jabbed at his face, two, three decent blows, but he was rabid, and the punches didn't slow him. He caught me a wild roundhouse fist across the cheek that sent me into the wet grass, my head thudding against a grave.

The false tooth rolled in my mouth. My vision went grey. I opened my eyes, tried to focus.

Above, Simon was advancing.

I lumbered to my knees, slipped in mud. I tried shuffling back. but another grave was in the way. Using it as a support, I made it to a stand, raised my fists.

Too late. He was on me.

I managed to land an uppercut, but it didn't touch the sides. Simon was a ton of bricks on my chest, his vast thighs pinning my arms, letting his good hand get access to my face.

He walloped me, beating his fist onto my face like a deranged ape pulping a melon. Blood filled my mouth. I fought for breath, but the dimmer was already turning.

He raised his fist again, high above his head. An opening appeared.

Hard, without aiming, I punched towards his heart.

It must've connected, for he heaved and toppled right, clutching his chest, releasing enough pressure for me to wriggle from beneath him.

I pushed to my feet, gulping air, rubbing blood from my bleary eyes.

Nate was in the shadow of the crematorium. He was clutching the iPad, and his expression was a tangle of anger. Something was wrong. What was it? Suzi?

No time to find out. Simon still wasn't out for the count.

He pushed to his feet, staggered forward. His wounds were catching up, and he was stooping, breathing hard; but his eyes were livid, and I knew this could only end one of two ways.

Before he could charge, I rushed to his flank.

He pivoted, and I turned with him. He kept moving, but I was faster, able to move in, grapple onto his back, my right arm around his neck. He growled, tried to shake me off.

I held firm, wrapped my legs around his middle to keep purchase. My plan was to get my left hand to the back of his head and lock my right against my forearm. That way, I could strangle the fucker.

But his strength was immense. With his good hand, he reached back, grabbing, clawing, trying to flip me over. I kept hold, my legs straining. With him disabled I was able to stay firm. He started punching blindly, trying for my mouth, my eyes. I smelled blood and sweat. I rammed my head into his back to protect myself. Blindly, I reached up, felt for his pulped face, found his nostrils, dug my fingers in, wrenched. He screamed. I screamed.

I felt his chin strain upwards. Just an inch, but enough to move my right forearm against his neck.

Then I squeezed.

The muscles in his neck bulged like an over-pumped inner-tube. I could hear his heart pound through his chest. He dug into my forearm with his fingers. I kept hold.

A noise like a cawing crow came from him, and I felt him hobble and try to keep balance. My muscles howled, but I kept the pressure. Everything I had was in that arm.

Then the world seemed to tumble. He must've lost his footing, and we were falling.

A wet crunch, and I felt his head snap back.

We were on the ground. I crawled on top of him. With what little strength I still had, I pushed up, ready to fight.

No need. Simon was done for.

He must've slipped in the mud and landed on a gravestone. His head was in a position no living person can achieve, a strange oblique angle, a jag of white bone poking through the skin. Eyes wide, tongue hanging limp from his mangled face like a cut of meat.

'Simon?' Nate said.

I turned.

He was about ten feet away, in front of the crematorium wall. 'What have you done?'

'He's dead,' I said. 'Now let Suzi go.'

'No need.' Nate dropped the iPad so I could see the screen. 'She's gone. See.'

Gone?

Sure enough, the bed frame Suzi had been bound to was unoccupied.

Relief surged through me, a warm, euphoric rush. They'd found her.

'What's funny?' Nate said.

'Huh?' I was laughing. I tried to stop but couldn't. My head was swimming.

The drug I'd had must've had a hallucinogenic quality, for when I looked at Nate again his eyes seemed to stretch out from his face like laser strobes.

He reached into his pocket, removed an object. It was an axon taser, police issue, the kind with multiple cartridges.

I tried to move out the way, but my legs had sunk into

quicksand, and I couldn't stop bloody laughing. Before I could do anything, Nate fired.

That shut me up.

The probes pierced my chest right above the breastbone, and a deep fat fryer exploded beneath the skin. The pain was excruciating. I keeled over, tossing like a tortured snake, my nerve endings on fire, vision ablaze with sheet lightning.

After what felt a lifetime, it ceased. I clutched my knees to my belly, smelled burned hair, fried blood.

Through fuggy, tear-streaked eyes, I could see Nate.

'You found her,' he said.

I tried to answer, but nothing worked.

'She'll always hate you. Remember that.'

I tried to roll away, but my body wasn't having it.

Then he blasted me again.

As I wrangled and writhed, random people flashed across my mind – Suzi. Rosie. Minka, Patience – a tableau of faces bleeding together like a watercolour left out in the rain. I knew it was over for me. But I didn't care. Suzi was alive. At least I'd done one good thing in this cruel world . . .

What happened next probably only took a few seconds, but in my frazzled head it stretched into a slow-motion scene.

The taser stopped.

Somewhere, tyres shrieked. Voices I recognised.

I forced my eyes open.

Nate was rigid, a look of horror on his face. Next to him was Mani, his hand gripping the butt of Simon's combat knife, the blade deep in the meaty spot between Nate's shoulder and neck.

Mani released the knife, staggered back. Its hilt protruded from Nate like a wobbly tombstone. Blood splurged around it, soaking his parka.

The taser fell from Nate's hand. He clutched the butt of the combat knife, tried to remove it. No luck. It was wedged in. A low, curdling groan came from him.

I was sure he was about to collapse.

Instead, he floundered back, past Mani, in the direction of the crematorium.

'Stop, Willoughby!' Diane's voice. 'You're under arrest!'

But Nate didn't stop. Instead, he fled into the darkness.

My vision was fading fast now, shadows closing in.

'Stay awake! Mani said, close to my head. 'Don't you die on me, Kasper.'

'Kas!' Diane's voice. 'You'll be OK.'

'Suzi,' I managed. 'Where?'

'Dr Steiner has her.'

'She's safe,' another voice said, female, familiar. 'We're alive.'

We?

I made myself look.

There was Mani and Diane.

And Tash Willoughby. She looked awful, her hair matted, skin sallow, eyes ginormous.

'Alive,' I said, and my lids peeled shut.

And then I didn't hear anything. Or see anything. Or imagine anything, except the blackness that collapsed inward.

Chapter 31

Something was beeping.

I opened my eyes.

I wasn't in Paradise Cemetery anymore. I was lying on a bed.

More beeps. The sound came from a machine. I think I was attached to it.

Dr Steiner and Mani were there. They were looking at me. Was I still asleep?

I shut my eyes again.

And slept.

Later, the same beeping drew me back.

This time I tried moving.

It felt like I'd eaten a Swiss army knife.

I looked right. Dr Steiner and Mani were still there.

I made to say something, but the nerve endings in my face didn't seem to be attached to my brain.

'What,' I managed, 'what ha—'

'You're OK,' Mani said. 'This is a hospital, case you hadn't realised. You've been unconscious over a day. That machine thing is just checking your heart's not doin' anything it shouldn't.'

'You've been in the wars,' Dr Steiner added. 'Three cracked ribs, a fractured cheek, several broken teeth, and nasty slices across your shoulder and chest they've stitched up. The taser shots made you tachycardic too. But you'll live.'

'Suzi?' I croaked.

'She's here, too, on a different ward. She's being treated for shock and superficial injuries, mild dehydration.'

Mani nodded. 'Suzi's OK, man. We got her back, just like we said we would.'

'Can I see her?'

'Not yet,' Dr Steiner said. 'The police are talking with both of them.'

'Both?'

'Tash Willoughby is here too.'

I took this in. Doing so took a little longer than it should've.

'Now that you're awake,' Dr Steiner went on, 'the police will want to take a statement. But now, rest.'

She was right. This brief exchange had left me depleted.

But my mind wouldn't sit still.

'Tash,' I said. 'Where was she?'

Mani shrugged. 'In that basement, with Suzi. She was gagged and blindfolded, tied up in the toilet, and scared out her wits. She was in a bad way. Even so, she insisted we go to the cemetery to help you.'

At the mention of the cemetery, the image of Mani returned, right after he'd plunged the knife into Nate.

'Where is he?' I said. 'Nate?'

'Dead,' Mani said.

I swallowed.

286

Dr Steiner said, 'He was found by police. Or what was left of him. He'd jumped from the peak of one of the towers on Paradise. A long fall.'

'Suicide?'

'He must've known the game was up.'

She reached over, held a beaker and straw to my lips. 'How about some water?'

I drank. It trickled down icily, stinging a little, but tasted cool and good.

'Diane,' I said. 'Where's she?'

'Where do you think? Off helping the police get to grips with the investigation. This thing's big, Kasper. We're talking corrupt cops, serial killers, the dark web. There was evidence in that basement. Loads of films copied to hard drives. Photos. Weapons. An address book too, containing names.'

'Names?'

'A black book,' Dr Steiner said. 'Diane thinks the names are people on the Red Rose Productions mailing list from all corners of the world. It's a treasure trove of snuff enthusiasts who'll be getting a knock on the door from Interpol.'

Before I could ask anything else, the curtain drew back. In came a buxom nurse with rosy cheeks and fastidious eyes.

'Well,' she said haughtily, 'look who's awake. How are we?'

I cleared my throat and was about to tell her *we* were OK when she came to the bed and started heaving me up to a seated position, two clammy hands grappling under my pits like crowbars.

I winced.

'My,' she said, 'we're a big boy, aren't we.'

'So they say,' I managed, the pain bellowing inside.

She carried on manoeuvring me, by which point I was

panting, my heart beating like a Duracell bunny. 'There,' she said. 'Better, yes?'

Not waiting for an answer, she proceeded to check my blood pressure, pulse, oxygen saturation, then removed a saline drip bag connected to a cannula and replace it with another and enquired about urges to relieve myself from every orifice.

Satisfied, she made some notes on a clipboard at the end of my bed and trotted off to the next bay.

When I looked at Dr Steiner and Mani, they were both smiling.

'When can I get out of here?' I said.

'Not till the doctor's given the OK,' Dr Steiner said. 'I've brought you some clothes and toiletries. Try to be a good boy and obey Hattie Jakes' orders.'

'Jesus Christ.'

'There's something else,' Mani said. He got up, looked around, then drew back the curtain and sat back down. 'We found this in that basement too. Hidden beneath the floorboards.'

He lifted a small, plain black rucksack by his chair, opened it. The bag contained cash, bound in bundles, a whole heap.

'How much?' I said.

'I stopped counting when I reached fifty K. Looks like a get-away stash.'

He closed the bag, returned it beneath him. 'Police don't know about this. Me an' Diane agreed the money should be yours.'

'Mine?'

'If you don't want it, donate it to charity or whatever. But you earned it, Kasper. You cracked the case wide open. I'll keep it till you're out. Then decide.'

'Well,' Dr Steiner said, 'at least you'll be able to pay your rent now.'

And despite the pain, I laughed.

Dr Steiner and Mani left, and for the rest of the afternoon I flitted in and out of consciousness.

Sometimes my mind was alert, and in these moments, I tried piecing together the events chronologically.

I was mostly able to do this, but there were foggy points, things I didn't understand – about Nate, how he'd met his fate; about Tash, what had happened to her; and about a third person, whether there really was someone else involved?

Before long, I was woozy with it all.

For now, I had to accept the not knowing.

My eyes shut.

Teatime, a young, pale, stressed looking junior doctor swung by my bed. He checked my bits just like the nurse had, told me my vitals were OK, the knife wound was healing OK, and I'd be medically fit for discharge come the morning.

'OK?' he said.

Before I'd had time to answer, he vaporized.

A little later still, my favourite nurse reappeared holding a tray of something I presumed was food, and which she insisted I eat, 'if we're to get some strength back into those big muscles.'

I made it through half before the nausea came. Before I knew it, I was hurling into a cardboard sick bowl she held to my mouth. When I'd finished, she rubbed my back consolingly.

'There, there,' she said, and took the tray and the puke away.

I tried reading a novel donated to the ward's benevolent stock, a private detective story by that woman who wrote the kid wizard series, but nothing was going in. Instead, I gave the hospital FM a go, using the earpieces attached to the bed, but the saccharine pop gave me a headache.

Eventually, I accepted I wasn't in the mood for stimulation and just lay there.

At some point I nodded off again, only to be awoken by a hand in mine. It was dark. I assumed it was the nurse again, here to give me some meds.

But it was Suzi, sitting by my bed.

She was dressed in a hospital gown and disposable slippers. A cannula was stuck into the crook of her arm, its tube attached to a saline drip mounted on a device she must've wheeled with her. She was without makeup and looked pale and young and quite beautiful.

'Hey,' she said.

'Hey back,' I said. 'Good to see you.'

She nodded.

I didn't ask questions. I didn't need to.

Instead I just listened while she told me what had happened.

The day before yesterday, she and Patience headed off together to discuss the summer art internship opportunity she'd been contacted about. The address was an industrial estate out in Docklands. While Suzi checked her portfolio, Patience went to find the interviewer, who claimed to have a studio on the site.

'When Patience didn't come back, I went looking. I found her slumped on the floor. She was bleeding, trying to warn me. I couldn't make out what she was saying. She looked terrified. Then someone grabbed me, a man, huge and strong. He shoved me into a vehicle, blindfolded me, forced me to drink something that made everything go fuzzy. He took me to a basement. I remember being tied to a bed, and hearing voices.'

'How many voices?' I said.

'Don't know.'

'Did you recognise any?'

She shook her head.

'All men? Or females too?'

'Maybe. It's a blur, Kas.'

'Do you remember hearing my voice?' I said. 'I was shouting your name when I was talking to one of them on video call.'

She nodded. 'I thought you'd come to save me. But then your voice went away. I tried to fight. The big one held me down. He was so strong. He hit me. Later, he put a finger in my mouth. I bit it. He punched my face, told me I was going to die, and they were going to film it, and I believed him, I—' Her breath caught, and she was quiet.

I shut my eyes, but that only made the image of Simon groping and assaulting Suzi worse. Nate's voice returned, his final words:

She'll always hate you. Remember that.

Perhaps. Suzi's entanglement in this case came down to me. More had happened to her in that basement, I knew it, and what she'd shared was only the start. She was tough, but this was hardcore stuff, and it would need to come out eventually.

But not now. Instead, she kept hold of my hand, and a moment later she was crying, and I was crying, and she leaned forward and put her arms around me, her face burrowed into my neck.

'I'm so sorry, darling,' I whispered.

She gripped me tighter.

Chapter 32

The following morning, two plain-clothes detectives visited me for a statement.

I was trying my best to plough through enough of my breakfast to avoid the wrath of my delectable nurse, back on shift that morning with a vengeance. The meal consisted of a beaker of tepid tea, an anaemic slice of toast and a tangerine that resembled an orange golf ball.

Despite the food, I felt heaps better. A night's sleep had cleared my head, my wounds weren't so angry, and I was beginning to feel normal again. I was also damn keen to go home, but knew if I attempted to rush these detectives, they'd stretch things even more, just to show who's the boss.

London Met detectives invariably look like you'd expect London Met detectives to look, opting either for the sharp-edged Line of Duty ensemble, or the scuffed, stubbly Sweeney effect. This morning, I had one of each.

Detective Ribby – the female of the pair – wore ice-picker heels and a razor-sharp beige mac complete with epaulettes and doubled-breasted buttons; Detective Jones, the male, had on distressed Wranglers and a Carnaby Street Harrington jacket with the collar suitably popped. Both shared beady eyes, saccharine smiles, and that nameless authority those in their profession carry.

Although I wasn't under investigation or caution, they gave the usual spiel, that anything I told them could be used in evidence, if I wanted a legal representative that could be arranged—

I said I was fine.

Jones drew the curtains, and they took seats.

'So, Mr Kasperick,' Ribby said, 'start from the beginning?'

I went back to the Friday before last, meeting Patience at the boxing match, hearing her suspicions about her brother's killing and the film she'd found in his drawer. I told them we'd identified Nate Willoughby from the photo on Terry Kinsella's wall, and I'd decided that, before going to the police, I wanted to gather enough evidence to put the killers away.

'You realise you took the law into your own hands?' Ribby said.

I shrugged. 'Patience didn't want the police involved. She was my client. With hindsight, I'd have done a few things different, but the outcome turned out right: two killers were snared, and a snuff movie enterprise got brought to its knees.'

They scribbled things down, asked more questions. I answered diligently, only becoming cautious when it came to Diane's involvement, for she still had a career, and I didn't want anything to jeopardise it.

'I used Diane as a soundboard,' I said, 'but I kept her at arm's length.'

'You mean you deceived her in order to extract information?' Ribby said.

'In a manner of speaking, yes.'

'Did she indicate that she knew Simon McFee was a serving detective?'

'She might've mentioned it.'

'How about whether she'd met him personally?'

'Not sure,' I said, keeping a poker face, but remembering Simon at the cemetery, his comment about Diane, *Did she tell you about me?*

'Had Diane met him personally?' I asked.

'We're not sure,' Ribby said brusquely. 'Let us ask the questions. Why was she on Paradise Estate with you two nights ago?'

I shrugged again. 'I'd figured out that Nate Willoughby was holding Suzi in a basement flat on Paradise. The flat was owned by the late Terry Kinsella who Willoughby was pals with. I asked Diane and a couple of friends to search the flat without revealing what they might find. My bad.'

The two detectives shared a look. This was hokum – they knew Diane was heavily involved, and as a serving officer, she should be laid on the coals for not following due process.

But they also knew this was a sensitive investigation, one that had untapped major police corruption, not to mention a litany of ineptitudes that would reflect badly for the already hobbling Met. Best to move on.

Next, to the circumstances of the deaths of the two Red Rose perpetrators.

'Detective Simon McFee,' Ribby said, scowling at his name. 'How did he come to die?'

'We were fighting,' I said. 'I jumped onto his back. He fell and broke his neck.'

'What are your thoughts on his death?'

'Very little.'

'Are you glad?'

'I'm not saddened, if that's what you mean.'

'And Nate Willoughby?'

'What about him?'

'What's your memory of him at the cemetery?'

'It's patchy.'

'Meaning?'

'He drugged me, and then tasered me.' I paused. 'I gather he threw himself off a building?'

'Yes,' Ribby said.

'Care to share the details?'

'No.'

'Fair enough. How's his sister, Tash?'

The detectives shared another look. 'She's under observation,' Ribby said.

'But not under arrest?'

'Correct. We're not bringing charges against her.'

'And have you got suspicions about any third parties who might've been involved? I gather there may've been a book of names that—'

'And that's of no concern to you, Mr Kasperick.'

They asked a few more detail-y things, mainly to do with the order of events, who did what, when, how. By the time I'd finished I'd owned up to a list of chargeable offences – withholding information, tampering with evidence, breaking, entering, perverting justice, maybe manslaughter over Simon's death. If they'd wanted to, they could've chucked the book.

Instead, Ribby closed her notepad and nodded. 'Very good.'

Clearly, their priority was to keep me sweet. If I started blabbing to the press, the whole thing could turn into Krakatoa for the Met. I guessed it was a case of quid pro quo: they'd overlook any wrongdoing on my team's part; in return, I'd stay tight-lipped about how the police had allowed Red Rose Productions to exist under their noses for years, and with a serving detective as one of its cadre.

Sure enough, Ribby said, 'On behalf of the Metropolitan Police, we'd be grateful for your discretion. This story is set to blow up in the next twenty-four hours. I'd suggest lying low.' She held my eye contact a little longer than was customary, ensuring I understood what she was saying.

'Oh yes,' I said. 'You can rely on me.'

They both shook my hand, and I watched them leave the ward.

Any remnants of an appetite had diminished. I pushed my breakfast tray aside and brought my knees to my chest.

Nate's death was a suicide.

No charges were being brought against Tash.

No third person had been implicated.

It didn't stack up as neatly as I'd have liked. But the main players were taken out. That's what mattered.

From the end of the ward, I caught sight of my nurse. She was helping an elderly gent from the toilet, and staring at my uneaten breakfast, her eyes like rocks of plutonium, radiating disapproval. Fast, I picked up a piece of toast, took a demonstrative bite.

As she turned, I hid the rest under my pillow.

Getting discharged from hospital was a lengthy affair. I needed all number of tests, had to have my stitches checked, and then waited forty-five minutes for a goody bag of pills and a letter to give to my GP who I hadn't seen in years.

Two p.m., I got the green light. The clothes I'd come in with were soiled with dirt and blood, and my father's trusty leather was done for, with a large gash across the front. I made do with an old Spurs tracksuit Dr Steiner had fished out from my meagre wardrobe and some Reeboks.

Before heading home, I passed by Suzi's ward, and asked a

nurse where she was. It appeared a night's sleep had been good for Suzi too, and she looked half-human, although she was still wired up to a drip.

'Hey,' she said as I came up.

'Hey, back,' I said.

She smiled; but it faded.

'I'm getting out,' I said.

'Lucky you. They're keeping me here a bit longer. Observations and a psych assessment.'

'And then?'

She shrugged. 'I figured I'll get away, maybe go to Ireland and stay with my aunty. The police say the press are going to be all over this. I've already had some emails from journalists offering me exclusives.'

'Jeez,' I said, 'how'd they get your details?'

'Social media. I'd uploaded my CV to some platforms, looking for jobs. That's how they reckon that man who kidnapped me found who I was. Dumb, right?'

'Not dumb,' I said. 'You weren't to know you were being targeted.'

I looked around. The ward was much like the one I'd been on, off-white lino flooring, fluorescent strip lighting.

'Must be boring here,' I said. 'Anyone to talk to?'

'The staff are quite nice,' Suzi said. 'And there's her. But she doesn't say too much.' Surreptitiously, her eyes flitted right.

Tash Willoughby was seated on a bed at the end of the ward, her knees scrunched to her chest. There was a policeman with her, sitting on a chair.

Tash was wearing a light pink tunic and milky green pants, standard hospital clothing. Her skin was pale, her expression vacant. Even from a distance, I could see there was bruising around her arms and face, grey-yellow islets; graze marks scudded her mouth from a gag, and her wrists were riven with purplish banding, the kind that handcuff restraints leave.

'Give me a minute,' I said to Suzi, and wandered over, giving the officer a nod.

Tash looked up. At first she looked disorientated, like a cat dazzled with a torch. Then her pale eyes focused.

'Hi,' she said.

'How're you bearing up?'

'Surviving. You?'

'Same.'

'Nate's dead.'

'I heard.'

We fell quiet. Machines thrummed and beeped in the background. From a curtained bay, a man was talking loudly in Arabic.

'I'm sorry, Kasper.'

'Me too.'

She nibbled her lip. 'You were right. About everything. The police found films. So many films. Of murders. They're saying Nate killed our parents. He drugged me and started the fire. All this time he made me think it was my fault.'

'Yup.'

'Then he and Simon killed all these women, just like you said, too. They filmed it, and made money from it . . .' The lip nibbles became harder. 'Do you hate me?'

'Why would you think that?'

'Because I messed up. Nate knew I'd been speaking to you. He found your business card on me and made me talk.'

'Nate knew who I was long before I met you. He fooled both of us.'

She didn't seem to hear. 'My whole life I've been so stupid. Letting people deceive me.'

'If anyone was stupid in all this, it was me.'

I stepped closer. The officer was watching us, a little more attentively.

I said, 'I gather you insisted on my friends coming to the cemetery to help me.'

'Yes.'

'If they hadn't, Nate would've killed me for sure. You saved my life.'

'And you saved mine.'

The officer cleared his throat. 'Can I help you, sir?' he said.

I shook my head. 'Just passing by.'

Talking with Tash like this wasn't smart, given we were both involved in a live murder case. 'Better go,' I said.

'Yes,' she said. 'Thank you, Kasper. If we don't speak again, good luck with what comes next.'

'What about you?' I said. 'What's next?'

She looked at the crumpled mattress and didn't answer, just shook her head.

I went back to Suzi, said goodbye. She stood on tiptoes and kissed my cheek.

'Keep in touch, Kas.'

I told her I would and walked to the lift. As the doors were opening, I glanced back.

At the end of the ward, Tash Willoughby sat on her mattress hugging her knees.

She wasn't looking at the mattress anymore. She was looking at me.

My plan was to head straight home and duvet dive.

But as I hobbled through the car park, I spotted Diane's Audi in a bay. She was in the driver's side, dressed down, a tracksuit, sunglasses, baseball cap, but she still looked hot, like a celeb out doing the shopping. She waved me over and I got in the shotgun seat.

'Lift home?' she said.

'You got time?'

'Got loads of that. I'm suspended, pending investigation.' She fired the engine.

For a few minutes we didn't speak. I stared from the window, at the grey throng of mid-afternoon traffic.

When she stopped at a set of lights, I said: 'The suspension's just a formality, Diane. You know that, right?'

'Hope so,' she said. 'What did you say to the detectives who took your statement?'

'Nothing that would implicate you.'

'You don't need to protect me. I'm a big girl. If I lose my career over this, I'm to blame.'

I looked over. 'You knew Simon more than you let on, didn't you?'

Her expression stayed hard.

'That morning we met, and you showed me Kwame's murder case file, you mentioned that you'd been seeing a copper. It never occurred to me that it was Simon.' I paused. 'When did you clock that he was the same Simon from the snuffs?'

'When I watched the film you had, something looked familiar. But I guess I tried ignoring it, convincing myself a police officer couldn't be capable of this. Then, when I learned his name, there was no getting away from it.'

I nodded, recalling how stony faced she'd looked at Dr Steiner's when she revealed who Simon was to us, and what he did for a living.

'How come you never told me?'

Her knuckles whitened on the wheel. 'I don't know. I mean, I'd only been seeing him a couple of weeks. And he seemed pretty normal.'

'Monsters always do seem normal,' I said, remembering my conversation with Dr Steiner on this very topic. 'Christ, Diane, how do you think this looks?'

'I know, Kas, and if it comes out, I'm fried. But I was ashamed to tell you. To think I was attracted to a man who'd torture and kill . . . it makes me sick. I panicked you'd assume I was covering for the bastard, or that I was even involved somehow.'

'Were you?'

'What?'

'Covering for Simon? Or involved somehow? I'm pretty sure there were more people in on this. And from the get-go, you were keen for me to stop the investigation, weren't you? For all I know, maybe you were on Nate's payroll too.'

She shot me a glowering look. 'How fucking dare you. I've put my career and life on the line for you, and you're seriously asking me that?'

'It'd make sense. Nate knew a heap of personal stuff about me, and that had to come from someone. Could be you wanted to protect your career, so gave your ex Simon titbits?'

I thought she was about to slam the brakes and boot me out. But she kept driving, and muttered under her breath, 'Jesus.'

I shook my head, looked back at the window.

'Sorry,' I said. 'I don't know what I'm thinking right now. I guess we're all in a bit of shock.'

'Oh yeah,' she said, 'we're in shock, all right,' her voice tight with sarcasm.

'For what it's worth, the police don't seem to know about your involvement with Simon. They might suspect it, but without proof, it's just that. A suspicion.'

'Will you tell them?'

'No.'

'Thank you.'

For the next couple of minutes, we were quiet.

Diane said, 'I'm guessing you want to hear what happened while you were at the cemetery?'

'Only if you want to tell it.'

'Like you guessed, Suzi was holed up in one of Terry Kinsella's properties out to the east of Paradise. It was the second flat we searched. The basement had been turned into a torture chamber film-set. Suzi was bound to the bed. I heard a whimper from an adjoining toilet, found Tash in there, bound, gagged, blindfolded, scared shitless.'

'But no signs of a third person?'

'None. Apart from the door we came through, the only escape route was a small window vent. You'd have to be tiny to squeeze through that.'

'I hear there was a trove of evidence down there too.'

'Correct,' Diane said. 'Weapons, films, mementos from the victims, you name it.'

'And a black book of snuff movie-fan contacts?'

'A veritable collection. We're talking email addresses, purchase downloads, dates films were sent to customers, the full shebang. Suffice to say the NCA are having a field day. Expect a lot of arrests on the back of this. There were copies of all of Nate's films, and one showing his parents getting smoked too in an arson. He probably meant for Tash to die in that fire. But she made it.'

I nodded. 'Yeah, she did.'

Diane pulled up at a zebra crossing. An old lady with a shopper ambled across.

'Nate's suicide,' I said. 'What are the details?'

'Far as I can tell, it's straightforward. A blood trail from his injury traced his final movements. Appears he staggered from the cemetery into Paradise, went into the tallest block, got the lift to the top, took the fire exit to the roof, and then went over.'

'You sure it's Nate who fell? Checked the DNA and prints?'

'This isn't CSI. It was him. Dental records proved it.'

'Anything suspicious about the jump?'

Diane puffed air. 'The man fell twenty-four floors. You've seen enough jumpers. There wasn't enough of him left to get suspicious over. You're sounding kinda paranoid here, big man.'

'Maybe I am. I just can't quite buy the idea that it was just Nate and Simon working, and no one else.'

'You may be right.'

I looked over.

'Forensics have followed up every lead. Turns out on the night Minka Petrova was murdered, Terry Kinsella was spotted at a snooker hall three miles east from Paradise. There's a half dozen witnesses swearing blind he was there the exact time she was getting sliced up.'

'You're saying Terry *wasn't* the person behind the camera?'

'Looks that way.'

'Then who was?'

'Most likely it'll be one of these names we've got in Nate's contact list. Don't worry, Kas, we'll get them.'

Outside, a cab driver was exchanging words with a traffic

warden who'd just printed him a ticket. Judging by expressions, neither was complimenting the other.

'Suzi described the kidnapping,' I said. 'She was targeted.'

'Yup. Our tech guys found some fake emails Nate sent. He was looking for ways to hurt you right from the start.'

'He knew so much about me. How?'

'My guess, Terry tipped Nate off about you after you visited him, and Simon used his police contacts to dig stuff up. Nate knew you'd come snooping. And he figured you'd approach his sister for help too.'

I let this simmer. It made sense. Terry knew I'd been a copper, and as a detective, Simon would've been able to access certain information about my life and career. But Nate seemed to know me intimately too. Could all this have come from police files alone?

'I guess we'll never know the full details of what Nate knew, or how he operated,' I said. 'The man was a psychopath.'

'Correct. A dead psychopath, who took his secrets with him.'

'What do you make of Tash?'

'She's obviously a few strawberries short of a fruit salad. The press will probably demonise her, make her out to be an accomplice.'

'That's not what I mean.'

'If you're asking do I think she was in on her brother's killing spree? All I can tell you is what I saw. She was in that flat, tied up, in a bad way. Despite this, she insisted we find you.'

I stayed quiet.

'What?' she said.

'Probably nothing. I just can't see why Nate kept her alive, that's all.'

'Now you think *she's* the third person in all this, instead of me?'

'I'm not saying that. I don't know if there was a third person at all. I just can't work that woman out. It bugs me.'

It was Diane's turn to go quiet.

While driving, she reached to the back seat for an A4 envelope, handed it over. 'If it bugs you now,' she said, 'you'll hate these. Look.'

I pulled out maybe a dozen photocopied printouts, blurry, heavily pixelated, taken from height through an unfocused lens.

'What are those?'

'CCTV images. All from near the Docklands site where Suzi was kidnapped. Straight after Patience's stabbing, I requested them. Forensics pinged them over to me yesterday, not realising I'd been suspended. By the time they'd retracted them, I'd had a peek and taken copies. They're poor quality and would never stand up in court. But they make interesting viewing. What's your first impression?'

I leafed through the dozen images. Some were indiscernible, others showed an empty pavement, a street, passing traffic, all fuzzy. In one, there was a partial sight of Suzi walking next to Patience, both recognisable for their low-slung tracksuits; another, from a different angle, had someone slumped, Patience, and someone else crouched by her, Suzi; another had Suzi being choke-held by a much bigger person – Simon, without question, with a parked van to their rear.

The last image made me cough involuntarily. Suzi being pulled by Simon into the van, her legs bicycling in mid-air.

I forced my feelings to one side and studied the image. The van had reversed. The driver's seat was occupied by a slight figure whose face was indistinguishable.

It couldn't have been Terry, for he was dead by then. And Nate was with me at Trafalgar Square at that precise moment.

'Well?' Diane said. 'Any ideas?'

'Someone else helped them. This proves it.'

'Looks that way. But who?'

I shook my head.

'Kas,' Diane said, 'don't go weird on me again. You've got that expression.'

'Sorry,' I said. 'My head's a jumble.'

'Well, it's going to get worse, trust me. The Met are making an official statement first thing tomorrow. This story's going to explode. And there's a good chance both our names will explode with it.'

Another set of lights flashed amber. Diane slowed, pulled the handbrake.

'You spoke with Mani?' she said.

I nodded. 'I don't reckon he's handling things well.'

'Not surprising. All this death and carnage – it's big stuff. Did he say anything about a bag found at the basement, and what was in it?'

'He might've mentioned something.'

'Good. I never saw a thing.'

'Right,' I said. 'Well, regarding this thing you never saw – you should have a cut of it.'

'Negative,' she said. 'From here on in I'm distancing myself from this case, and everything to do with it.' She paused, looked at me in the mirror. 'That includes you, Kas.'

'Me? Why?'

'Various reasons.'

I waited.

As the lights changed, she hit the indicator, pulled up to a bay on the left, slipped into neutral, and looked at me square. 'Because to be honest, Mani's not the only one not handling things well.

This case, the violence, the fact that I was dating one of the killers – well, it's got to me. First time in my career it's happened. I'll be OK. But I need a change of scene.'

'Meaning?' I said, but I knew the answer coming.

'I've put in for a transfer. Assuming I manage to keep my job, I want to leave London, maybe try living in Brighton or somewhere by the seaside.'

I swallowed. 'What about your new man, Quentin? Is he coming too?'

'Oh, him,' she said. 'After he heard about this case and how I'm in the middle of it, he freaked and called it a day with me.'

'Sorry.'

'Don't be. The guy was turning out to be a floppy lettuce. I've never had much luck with men, have I?'

Regret expanded in my chest, a hollow feeling. 'You mentioned *reasons* for going,' I said. 'What else?'

Diane nodded. 'That stuff about you using prostitutes . . .'

I sighed. 'Yeah, I figured that would come back to bite.'

'It was a shock, that's all. I guess I always figured we might get back together some day. Now, after all these revelations, I'm not sure. I think we've both made some lousy choices recently, and could do with a bit of distance to work out what we feel.'

'Sorry,' I said, looking at the dash. 'For what it's worth, those women didn't mean anything, and—'

'Don't you see, Kas, that makes it even worse. "Those women" are crapped on and forced to degrade themselves. You've reinforced their existences to get your rocks off. Can't you see why it bothers me?'

I didn't answer. But I got it.

'Look,' she said, 'it's none of my business what you get up to. But you asked.'

I looked out the window again. It was raining lightly, and the sky was carpeted grey.

'I think I'll walk the last bit,' I said.

'Thought you'd say something like that,' Diane said. 'You sure I can't drive you? You're meant to be recuperating.'

'It's fine,' I said. 'Fresh air will do some good.' I opened the door.

'Wait,' she said.

I looked.

She leaned over, and before I knew it, she'd kissed my cheek.

'I don't think I deserved that.'

'You didn't,' she said, 'but there you go. Rest up, hear?'

I told her I would, then stood in the drizzle and watched her drive off.

But I couldn't rest.

Despite the codeines I munched, the drink I put away, my head wouldn't sit still.

Why?

Lots of reasons.

Guilt, over the trauma Suzi, Mani and Diane were burdened with. Anger over what Diane said about my use of prostitutes, the fact that she'd been seeing Simon and kept it hidden. Uncertainty about whether there was anyone else involved, or if my head was just playing tricks.

But that wasn't all.

I didn't think I was easily shocked.

Wrong.

The barbarity of this past fortnight had left its imprint on me too.

What I'd learned about other humans, what they were capable

of – what *I* was capable of – had changed me in ways I couldn't fathom.

A little after midnight, my phone vibrated:

Thank you for coming to see me today.
Tash

I stared at the text a long time, then took another painkiller, closed my eyes, and fell into a heavy, restless, unquiet sleep.

Chapter 33

Diane's prediction about the Met response was bang on. The following morning, an official statement on the killings was broadcast on national TV. Before a packed hall of tabloid hacks and photographers, the deputy commissioner, a greying, monosyllabic, wholly uninspiring man, confirmed the identities of Nate Willoughby, a filmmaker, and Simon McFee, a serving officer, as prime suspects in a murder conspiracy of '. . .an unprecedented nature'. He included details of the torture chamber at Paradise and confirmed that a number of women were thought to have been victims, and their deaths filmed for circulation. Names would be confirmed in due course.

'And for now,' he said, 'we request sufficient time and space to pursue our lines of enquiry. Thank you.'

On the back of this the press went to town, seeking every grubby detail for the lascivious public to gorge on, and using this case as further ammo to assault the flailing Met. Over the next few days, headlines like *PARADISE RIPPERS SLAY WORKING GIRLS UNDER POLICE NOSES* and *DEMON FILM DIR-ECTOR AND KILLER COP SNUFF CONSPIRACY* were across the front of the tabloids; a slew of exclusives appeared, about the vice trade on Paradise and the disenfranchised population who lived there; there were interviews with migrants, all insisting they'd reported concerns to the police about missing daughters, wives, and sisters, to be unanimously stonewalled.

Despite his crimes, Nate became a figure of fascination, this slight, charming, unlikely serial killer. Former TV colleagues came forth, giving soundbites about his 'peculiar ways' on location, but offering no insights into his psyche, just that he 'was always a gentleman', with that 'friendly smile and startling eyes'.

In contrast, Simon was reviled, and became an effigy for the abuses inflicted by those with power; for many, he was the final nail in the coffin of the Met's reputation. His wife, seemingly unaware of his double life, fled the capital with their children, and their home in Harlow was pelted with eggs and paint. If it ever came out that Diane had been dating him, I had no doubt that her life would go down the khazi too.

Four days in, the rumours about Nate's black book of contacts were leaked. Amongst this clandestine membership, which stretched to Latin America and the Middle East, there were media moguls, creative execs, and, most disturbingly, other coppers, including the two officers already in the headlines for circulating gory crime scene photos.

'I pledge to root out all the rotten apples on the force,' the London mayor stated outside his offices that same afternoon. 'The Met will be the capital's jewel again.'

Good luck there, mate.

Speculation about who else was named in Nate's black book spread, and names ricocheted around social media. I Googled a few, found photos. Three faces I recognised from Nate's house party. One was a teacher, one an accountant, one a civil servant – all united by a predilection for torture porn.

As a result, there was a resurgent interest in all things snuff. A litany of lowlifes came forth on platforms, claiming to have Red Rose films in their possession, which they were willing to share for the right price. People paid, and it dawned on me that Nate's prediction was true: in death, his work lived on, crystallising his name forever.

TV psychologists analysed Nate's commercial work, claiming to have found hidden symbolism hinting at his psychopathic temperament, and there was talk of a bidding war between streaming channels for firsts dibs on the true-crime series. By the end of the week, I was sick of hearing about Nate. I just wanted to forget about him.

One small blessing was that my identity stayed out of the limelight. The Met took all the credit for finding Nate and Simon, with no mention of any have-a-go gumshoes. Suzi fared less well. Post discharge, she was bombarded with tabloid offers, chat show invites, exorbitant book requests. She eschewed them all, and Dr Steiner and I kept her shielded long enough to arrange transport so she could stay with her aunt in rural Ireland.

The only person I hadn't heard from was Lisa. I'd sent her a text from hospital, reassuring her that the culprits who'd killed Minka were dealt with, and she was safe. She'd sent back a smiley face.

Since then, there'd been nothing. Perhaps her silence should be taken as a wish to be left alone?

I considered doing this, came close.

But it didn't sit right. I'd smashed in her door, frogmarched her from her flat, caused her a royal headache. Things had been left untidily between us, and I committed to see her one last time.

The morning of Suzi's flight to Ireland, Mani dropped by the house. His expression remained sunken, skin sallow, eyes droopy with fatigue. The crucifix necklace remained absent, and he reeked of cigarettes.

A backpack was slung over his shoulder. I recognised it from the hospital.

After lighting a Marlboro, he slid it over to me.

'I finished totting it up,' he said. 'In total, there's a few quid short of ninety-eight grand.'

'Yikes,' I said. 'That's a lot of dough.'

'For real.'

'I don't think I should have this, mate.'

Mani shrugged. 'Money don't have owners, Kasper. Just spenders. Take it. Patience would've wanted you to. You did what she asked.'

'*You* did too,' I said. 'If memory serves me right, it was you who stuck the knife in Nate Willoughby.'

Mani's eyes greyed with compunction. 'Maybe,' he said. 'But I don't want it.'

I opened the backpack. I'd never seen such a vast sum.

'Looks like Monopoly money,' I said, and zipped it up, placed it on the floor between my feet. 'I want to pay for Kwame's and Patience's funerals,' I said.

'Figured you would.' Mani said. 'I want them cremated together. We could take the ashes to the inter-borough fight happening next Friday. Patience was meant to box that night. What do you think?'

'I think that's good.'

He smoked, looked somewhere else.

'How are you bearing up, mate?' I said. 'Really?'

He shrugged. 'You know.'

'Want to talk about it?'

He shrugged again. 'All this stuff in the news, it's brought home what we did, how big it is. Before, I had a clear view of things. God was the centre of my universe. Let thy will be done an' all that. But my faith's been tested, man. Those men, what they did to those women, and Kwame, and Patience . . . and what *I* did at that cemetery, stabbing that man . . . it's changed me. Understand?'

I told him I did.

'I wanted to kill him. Stabbing him, it felt good.' He shook his head. 'Me and God, we got some things to figure out.'

'I hope you manage to,' I said.

He stubbed out the smoke. Then he leaned over, grasped my shoulder. 'Thanks, Kasper,' he said.

'How about a beer?'

'Now you're talking,' he said, and managed a grin.

After Mani left, I cleared away our bottles, showered, dressed, took several bundles of the cash, and headed to the bank. Through direct transfer, I wired my ex-wife Carol a few thousand, sent another few to a pastoral fund set up at my daughter's school, and a final few as an anonymous donor for the upkeep of Savages Boxing Club.

Back home, I settled my overdue rent with Dr Steiner and gave her enough to cover the next twelve months. She looked at the cash contemptuously and placed the notes in her kitchen safe above the cooker.

'Well,' she said, 'that will keep me stocked up with cigarettes for a while.'

'It will,' I said. 'Now, let's have some fun.'

A cab drove us to the South Bank. I paid top dollar for us to see a play Dr Steiner picked out at The Globe Theatre.

I'd never been to the place before or seen much Shakespeare for that matter. On the strength of this show, I won't rush out for a repeat. We stood in the open-air pit beneath a dismal cloud of sky and stared at a stage. Men and women wearing tights and wielding swords bounded on and started saying things.

From what I could ascertain, the story concerned a general who, after killing his sons, cooked them in a pie that he then fed to their unsuspecting mother. Gore started flowing early, and was disturbingly convincing; enough to make the audience squeal.

The subtleties flew over my head, but maybe that's because I wasn't in the mood. Everyone else in the audience looked enthralled though, so it must've been good, and when my phone buzzed, several stares of reproach were shot my way. These theatre-goers. So prudish.

As soon as we left the theatre, Dr Steiner lit up a Dunhill. 'Wasn't that marvellous,' she said.

The nastiness of the past couple of weeks didn't appear to have left a dent in her. Clearly, she was made of hardier stuff than me.

'Glad you liked it,' I said.

'You seemed slightly distracted, dear.'

'With hindsight, something less bloody might've been preferable.'

'Hm.'

We strolled along the bank; to our left were skateboarders zipping beneath the National Theatre, ahead was a swell of tourists, buskers, office types; right, the Thames, dark, filthy, blustered, backlit by a pale band of January light.

Dr Steiner said, 'So what now, pray?'

'How about a drink for my long-suffering landlady?'

'Very good. Mine's a Bloody Mary.'

I laughed, and she slipped her non-smoking hand into the crook of my arm.

★

316

We cabbed it home. Around nine, Dr Steiner retired to bed with her book, and I fed an indignant Tommy a snack and switched my phone on.

The buzzing in the theatre had been a text from Tash Willoughby, asking to speak. I took a moment, then poured a couple of fingers of Bushmills and rang her from the conservatory.

'I feel like I'm going crazy,' she said, her breath crackling. 'The doctors at the hospital have put me on these other pills. They say they're for my nerves. I should only take them when things get bad.'

'Aren't the pills helping?' I said.

'I've already had the lot and feel worse than ever. It's like everyone's staring at me, thinking I'm a killer.'

I sipped my drink.

She proceeded to tell me about the past few days. After more police interviews, she'd been discharged from the hospital and was given a chaperone to a B'n'B, as the house in Highgate had been turned upside down. She'd been holed up ever since, sitting in a room with the curtains drawn, watching the news about her brother unfurl.

'It's hardly surprising you're feeling paranoid,' I said. 'You need to get out.'

'Paranoid? My God, is that what I am? Is the TV going to talk to me, and little green men appear through the walls?'

'Poor choice of words.'

'It's true though. I need to get out of this awful room. And I shouldn't be offloading to you. I'm the last person you want to speak to. My brother tried to kill you, for God's sake.'

'It's OK.'

She sighed. 'Why don't you hate me? After what Nate did to you and your friends . . . to all those women . . .'

317

'You're not Nate.'

'People think I am. They think I knew what he was doing.'

I kept silent.

Her breath became audible. 'I can't . . .' she gasped, 'I can't . . .'

Then she started crying, harsh, arid sounds that came from deep within. I let it ride out, knowing there'd be plenty more to come.

Eventually she regained enough control to say, 'Will you help me? I know I shouldn't ask, but I don't have anyone else.'

'How?'

'I need to go to the house to get some clothes and toiletries. But I'm scared to do anything alone.'

I thought about this, finishing my drink while I did.

'Well?'

'OK,' I said. 'We'll go tomorrow if you like.'

She gave me her address. I said I'd be there at lunchtime.

Chapter 34

Nine the following morning I rang the priciest funeral directors northeast London had to offer and paid a sizable deposit for two cremations, side-by-side, one for Patience, one for Kwame, to take place next week.

Then, after some deliberation, I sent Lisa a text:

Hey. This case on Paradise has brought some money my way.
I'd like to share some with you and Baba.
You both deserve it.

I wasn't sure if this was the right thing to do. But I wanted to do something and figured they could both use some cash. Plus, it was a good excuse to see Lisa.

Twenty minutes later, she called.

'Hello, Dylan.' Her soft, husky voice was like a warm blanket.

I asked how she'd been.

'Stressed. Police and newspaper people are around Paradise. Customers are scared to visit. I think this is the end for me here.'

'What do you mean?'

'I've decided to leave London. Start afresh.'

'A bit of money will come in handy, won't it?'

'You are kind.' She cleared her throat awkwardly.

'What is it?' I said.

'Baba, Minka's sister, wants to visit Paradise to pay respects to her. I tried to tell her it is not a good idea. But she says she must. She asked if you can be there. Maybe we can all meet in person?'

I hesitated. Going back to Paradise wasn't my idea of a good time.

But this wasn't about me.

'When were you thinking?' I said.

'Are you free later today?'

'Lunchtime I'm tied up. How about in the afternoon?'

'Good,' Lisa said. 'I will tell Baba. She will be pleased to see you again.' She paused. 'So will I.'

Before heading out, I counted two piles of cash, ten grand in each. I wasn't sure how I came to this amount, but figured it was enough to give Lissa and Baba a head-start on whatever came next.

I stowed the money in the inside pockets of a tatty old windbreaker. Then I gobbled a couple of painkillers, called an Uber, and was pulling up to Tash's B'n'B a few minutes before noon.

She was outside, sitting on the steps, wearing black pumps, navy trousers, and her duffle coat, with her knees hugged to her chest. She'd lost weight, much of it around her face and upper body, making her skin dry and pale, like sugar paper, and her eyes appear abnormally large.

I tried to pick up on a cue in her expression, but like before, she was like a pastel sketch, the lines undefined, smudgy, impossible to discern.

'Thanks for coming,' she said.

I nodded. 'Ready?'

'I think so.'

We cabbed it to Highgate. When we got to the house, I gave the driver a couple of scores, told him to wait and keep the meter ticking.

I was expecting media folk to be flocking around, but apart from a few tassels of police tape, nothing suggested this had been the home of one of Britain's worst serial killers.

Inside was another story. Forensic officers often lack finesse when searching for evidence, but even by their standards, they'd really gone to town here.

Cupboards, drawers, shelves, cabinets were gutted, the contents strewn across surfaces like rubble. Footprints muddied the parquet floor, and the air, once crisp with floral diffusers, smelled musty and stale.

Tash took it in. 'The police did this?'

'Mostly,' I said. 'I broke in and had a rummage too, looking for Suzi.'

She nodded.

'Where do you want to start?'

'My bedroom.'

She took light steps ahead, half on tiptoe, head bowed, as if her thoughts were far away. I followed, keeping her in tow, staying alert.

The landing was cluttered with bedding, ornaments, Nate's movie memorabilia, the old-school posters all removed from their frames, tossed about. Tash moved around the debris and towards a room at the end of the hall, taking dainty steps, like a ballerina. Carpets had been stripped up, revealing blackened pine boards, reminders of the fire that pulverised the house and Henry and Martha Willoughby a decade back.

Tash's bedroom was a tip, the drawers, the wardrobe, the dresser all emptied, underwear and personal items rifled through. She fished out a holdall, placed it onto the bed, and began putting various items inside, books, clothes, pyjamas, plus a bunch of photos, creased and gnarled. She moved with a neatness that seemed to defy the clutter, and kept mute throughout.

For fifteen awkward minutes I stood in the doorway, aware of this silence and my own presence. I felt clunky, uncomfortable, with a dull thud in my head and a gnawing pull to leave. I was meant to be recuperating and distancing myself from all things Willoughby. Yet here I was, at Nate's house, with his sister. Why?

Maybe because a missing piece of the jigsaw was still playing hide and seek. Every time I caught a glimpse of it, it fell out of view.

To compound this, my chest wound was throbbing worse than it had in days, my nerves probably intensifying the pain. If I wasn't meeting Lisa and Baba later, I'd have headed home after this and rested. Instead, I dug around my pocket, found the codeine strip, popped a couple more.

As I waited for the pills to kick in, Tash walked from the bedroom, the holdall full.

'Got everything?'

'There's one more item I need,' she said. 'This way.'

I followed her downstairs, towards the back of the house and the study where I'd first spoken to Nate.

Like everywhere else it was ransacked, the mahogany desk emptied, the PC gone, leaving only a bunch of cables dangling like entrails.

What did Tash want from this room? All I could see were remnants of her brother.

Then she walked past me to the wall facing the desk. 'This,' she said. 'I don't think it should go to waste. Do you?'

It was the black and white photo of the girl holding a red rose. Like the other pictures in the house, it had been removed from its frame, the print left bare, curling like parchment against the wall.

Even so, it lost none of its impact.

'This girl was a friend of mine,' Tash said. 'Did Nate tell you that?'

I looked at Tash, back at the print. 'No,' I said. 'He didn't.'

'She used to come to Mum and Dad's project for disadvantaged kids. I thought we'd stay friends forever. But she vanished. Such a shame.'

'Where was this project run from?' I said.

'Paradise Estate, silly. You knew, didn't you?'

'No,' I said, and stared at the print closer, seeing it in a new light. As I did, remnants from Nate's *Paradise Lost* documentary came back, the clip of a community project for local kids, the couple who ran it, a husband-and-wife team.

Not just any team. Henry and Martha Willoughby. How'd I missed it?

'Dad took that photo,' Tash said. 'She's pretty, don't you think?'

I studied the rose in the girl's hand, bold against the whiteness of her thin fingers. Then I moved up her arm, took in the rest of her. Until now, I'd been so caught up with the rose, I hadn't really considered who she was.

I'm not sure I agreed she was pretty: beautiful was better, with deep-set eyes, her elliptic smile draped in shadow, making her seem older, worldlier than her slight body suggested.

As I continued to take the image in, a warmth rose from my

belly. The painkillers were taking effect. And with the sensation came a light breeze. It seemed to whistle past my ears, drifting into my skull, releasing a source of tension I hadn't realised I'd been holding onto.

'Jesus,' I said.

I was still staring at the photo when I realised Tash was beside me, saying, 'Kasper, I'm ready to go.'

I looked at her.

She repeated herself, adding, 'Are you OK?'

'Uh-huh,' I said. I'd been lost in my head. 'Sure, let's get out of here.'

We exited by the front door, walked up the porch. The cab driver was still there, his car engine purring to keep the interior warm. I put Tash's holdall in the boot, and as we got back into the car, she said, 'Where are you going now?'

'Paradise.'

'Why?'

'For a meeting I arranged.'

She nodded, minuscule head movements.

'You could come with me?'

'To Paradise?' She looked incredulous. 'I don't know—'

'You're right. It's the last place you'd want to go.'

The driver, a grizzly Mediterranean fellow with a thick mono-brow, looked over impatiently. 'Where to, mate?' he asked.

I gave him the address of Tash's B'n'B.

She took several breaths and rubbed her runny nose. 'Hold on,' she said. 'I mean, you're right, I don't want to go back to Paradise ever again.' She dabbed her cheek with the hem of her sleeve. 'But I don't want to go back to that B'n'B either, not all by myself. And you're the only friend I have.' Another pause. 'Maybe I can wait for you? Somewhere nearby?'

'It's not the nicest part of London, Tash.'

'I know. Is there a place close by where I can wait?'

There was a dingy boozer called the Duke's Head a stone's throw from the estate, but I wouldn't board a rodent there.

Then an idea landed. 'Tell you what,' I said. 'You like the great outdoors?'

'I think so. Why?'

'You'll see,' I said, and gave the driver the address to my father's allotment.

As he slipped into first, I reached for my phone, called Diane.

'Kas?' She answered a little stiffly. 'What's up? I thought we'd covered everything.'

'Yeah, I thought so too. But I need a favour. It's important.'

'Go on.'

I told her.

Chapter 35

The tour of my dad's allotment took less than a minute.

'It's hardly The Ritz,' I said, 'but there's worse places to hang out, I guess.'

'It's fine,' Tash said. 'I'll wait for you here.' She looked around. 'Did you come here? After your daughter?'

'Quite a lot. I still do.'

'I can see why. No one's about. It's peaceful.' She paused. 'You know, meeting you has been the one good thing to come out of all this for me.'

'There's a word for that,' I said. 'Nate used it.'

'What word?'

'It means when you find something unexpected that turns out to be good. I can't remember what it is.'

'Try not to think about it,' she said. 'Then it'll come to you.'

She gazed up at the crooked outline of Paradise. I considered her demeanour. She was no longer tearful, but bore a quiet equanimity, as if she'd finally located something that had been eluding her.

'Who are you meeting?' she said.

327

No point lying. 'Two women. Both were affected by everything that's happened.'

'Will you tell them I'm sorry? For what my brother did. Please.'

'You could tell them yourself.'

'I can't. I just . . . can't.'

'OK. Leave it with me.'

Before setting off, I unlocked the hut, showed Tash where the light switch and kettle were along with the fan heater and blankets. On the windowsill was the bottle of tablets I'd lifted from Terry Kinsella's café.

I glanced over my shoulder, noticed Tash had spotted them too. Without remarking on it, I reached for the bottle, and put it in my coat pocket.

'Call if there's anything,' I said.

She nodded and took the stool beneath the awning.

At the gate, I glanced back. She was gazing at me.

From there, I walked to Paradise.

Since the news of the killings, the estate felt like a no-man's land. The blocks were coated with a greyish patina of grime and dust, as if necrosis had set into the bricks and mortar, while the fading light deepened the shadows, drawing out the decline.

Lisa and Baba were waiting for me beneath the shelter of a tawny block of flats. Lisa was dressed down again, a look that had become familiar – All-Star pumps, fitted jeans, a puffer coat. The bruise was still visible beneath her eye.

Baba was in work clothes, scuffed boots, paint spattered jeans, a Nike windbreaker. She was holding a large bouquet of white roses. As I came up, she offered a hand. As before, her grip was a vice.

'Kasper,' she said.

I nodded.

Lisa stood on tiptoes and kissed my cheek. 'Hello, Dylan.'

'Howdy,' I replied.

'Thank you,' Baba said, 'for finding the men who killed Minka.' Her pronunciation wasn't clunky like before. My guess was she'd been rehearsing what to say.

'You're welcome,' I said.

She looked around the estate, said, 'Please show me where Minka died.'

I led them north, away from the easterly townhouses where the basement film-set was, past the alleyway where Kwame was stabbed, the square where Terry claimed to have witnessed the fray, and in the direction of Kinsella's Café. Noise and lights emitted from some flats, and I could hear dancehall music from another; even so, there was an emptiness to the estate, a haemorrhaging caused by the years of suffering and deprivation, and which Nate Willoughby's murders finally tore open for the world to see.

Fresh police tape had been wrapped across the corrugated gating to the front of Kinsella's Cafe, and a deluge of litter lay scattered around, drink cans, sandwich wrappers, cigarette boxes, the debris from media types and onlookers who'd come to ogle. Someone had spray-painted **PSYCHO KILLA** on the corrugated front in garish red letters, but there were no press or weirdos lurking. Like the rest of Paradise, the place was lifeless: a lonely place to live; a dismal place to die.

Baba placed the flowers outside the café. They'd probably get pinched or stamped on within an hour, but I didn't see much point in telling her this.

She bowed her head, stepped back. We stood there.

The only sounds were the whistling wind, and a tin can rattling somewhere against the paving.

*

Lisa suggested we go back to hers. I was glad for this, as I didn't much fancy getting out large sums of cash in plain view.

And so, ten minutes later we were walking up the familiar flight of stairs of her block. The door I'd kicked in had been taped up, but the lock and hasp were splintered off the hinge, unsecure, and Lisa gained entry by shuffling it inwards.

The interior of the bedsit felt alien. Gone were the faux leather cushions, the leopard skin rug, everything now packaged in the multitude of cardboard boxes stacked up by the window. All that was left out was the bed and settee, stripped bare.

I looked at Lisa. 'You're leaving so soon?' My voice echoed through the space.

'Tomorrow,' she said.

'Where to?'

She shrugged, sat on the mattress. 'I don't know yet.'

Baba leaned by the wall. She pulled out a pouch of tobacco, intimated to Lisa whether it was OK to smoke. Lisa said it was; in turn, she pulled out her vape. A moment later the room was clouded with fumes.

I sat on the settee, withdrew the two bundles of cash.

Baba stared at the money. The cigarette hung between her lips.

'Here,' I said, tossing one of the bundles over.

She caught it in one hand, looked at it as if it was some delicate artefact.

'Do whatever you want with that,' I said. 'Spend it, give it to your family, get a bigger place to live in, blow it at the casino. It's yours.'

She made the cash disappear. I placed the second bunch for Lisa on a cushion next to me.

'Just for the record though, Baba,' I added, 'I didn't kill the two men who murdered Minka. One fell and broke his neck. The other went off a building.'

'But they're dead?' Lisa said.

I looked at her. 'Yes,' I said. 'They're dead.'

'This is all that matters,' Baba said.

'If you say so.' I paused. 'But there's others out there who were involved too.'

A silence beat through the smoky room.

'What do you mean?' Baba said.

'There *were* others, Baba,' Lisa answered. 'The fat man, Terry. And the people in this black book. It's been in the newspapers. I read about it.'

'Yup,' I said, 'you're right. There's lots of people on the Red Rose mailing list. And Terry had his foot in this, no question.' I paused. 'But I don't think he was a main player in the way I first thought. There was someone else too.'

Baba kept staring, her eyes inky black and unwavering. 'What will you do?' she said. 'Carry on looking?'

I shrugged. 'This is a police matter. They're calling the shots, not me.'

She nodded.

'But part of me wants to keep on,' I said, 'until every one of those bastards is brought to justice. Make them answer for what they did. You understand, don't you?'

Baba's brow became triangular lines, like wings of a bird of prey. Then she pulled on the cigarette again and vanished within the fug.

'Anyway,' I said, 'the main thing is, Nate Willoughby and Simon McFee are finished. Now, I think we all need a holiday.'

'Good idea,' Lisa said, smiling.

I smiled back.

Baba remained stony faced.

'How about a drink?' Lisa said. 'I have some brandy?'

Baba checked her watch. 'I must go.'

'OK,' Lisa said. 'I'll see you out—'

'Let me,' I said to Lisa, and got up from the settee. 'You pour us two brandies.'

I led Baba through the busted door from the bedsit, and the two of us walked single file down the narrow stairs, pushed through the broken main door to the block, and stood outside.

It was evening now, bleak, dark, the air painfully cold.

'There's something I need to tell you, Baba' I said.

She waited.

In a couple of sentences, I passed on Tash Willoughby's apology. Baba stood in silence. The only movement came from her eyes, blinking occasionally.

After finishing, she offered her hand a final time.

As we shook, I looked up.

Lisa was watching from her window. She was holding two glasses.

The bedsit still smelled heavily of cigarette smoke, and the sweet blackcurrant of Lisa's vape.

As soon as I'd returned the door back into place, she handed me a brandy. 'What were you two talking about?' she said.

'I had a message to give to Baba,' I said, returning to the settee beside the second bundle of cash. 'Tash Willoughby, Nate's sister, asked me to apologise to you both. Not that it'll make much good.'

'Are you and this Tash friends now?' There was surprise in Lisa's voice.

'I wouldn't stretch to that,' I said. 'But circumstances have brought us into each other's worlds. In fact, she's waiting for me at my allotment right this minute.'

Lisa took a small sip from her glass. 'Does that mean you need to go to her now?'

'Not unless you want me gone straight away?'

She smiled, staring at the brandy, then me. 'No. It's nice having you here, Dylan. This might be the last time. Relax.'

I rested my glass on the floor. The beat had picked up in my head, making things a little fuzzy.

It must've shown, for Lisa sat next to me, shuffled close, said, 'Are you OK?'

'I'm fine,' I said. 'Just a headache.'

She placed her glass on the floor beside mine and rested her hands on my shoulders. Her fingers began kneading, tapping out knots, releasing tension deftly.

'Wow,' I said, exhaling. 'That's nice.'

'You are stressed,' she said. 'Try to unwind.'

I reached up, placed a hand on hers. 'Serendipity,' I said.

'What?'

'It's a fancy word I was trying to remember earlier. Soon as you touched me, it just landed in my head. How about that.'

'What does it mean?'

'It's like a happy coincidence, I think. When one set of events reveals something else that turns out to be good. I'm sure it happens more often than you'd think.'

'Hm,' she said. 'Why are you thinking about that now?'

'Because this whole thing's been full of serendipity. Nate realised it long before I did. I reckon he was expecting me to join the dots quicker. Guess I was a bit slow.'

Her fingers kept moving, but the pressure was lighter. 'What you said to Baba earlier, about there being more people involved. Did you mean it?'

'Yes,' I said.

'Who is it? The sister? Tash? Is that why you're spending time with her?'

I shook my head. 'Until a couple of hours ago, I had my suspicions about Tash.'

'Not anymore?'

'No. Now I think she was one of the biggest victims in all of this.'

'Really?'

'Uh-huh.'

Lisa kept on with the massage, pushing, releasing, working with a pianist's precision.

'Maybe I'll fly somewhere hot next week,' I said. 'Lie on a beach, sip ice cold beers, forget all this.'

'Yes,' she whispered in my ear. 'I could come too.'

I felt a stirring in my belly, a rumbling in my loins. I turned, looked.

She was inches away, her eyes large, tumescent, drawing me close. She really was beautiful.

'Normally, when you give me money,' she said, gesturing towards the bundle of cash, 'I give you something in return.'

I smiled. 'Yeah,' I said, 'that's true.'

She stroked my cheek.

I took her hand, held it.

'But I don't want that from you, Lisa.'

She gave a playful frown. 'Maybe I can change your mind?'

Her other hand slid down my chest.

'I don't think so,' I said, taking that one too. 'But there's something else I want from you instead.'

'Tell me,' she whispered. 'Anything.'

I gave her hands a little squeeze, and something in my face must've given it away, for suddenly her eyes narrowed, and she wasn't so beautiful anymore.

'How about you tell me what made you become such a cold-blooded bitch.'

Chapter 36

'What are you talking about, Dylan?'

I shook my head. 'Face facts, Lisa. You're up to your eyeballs in these killings. Now it's time for you to come clean.'

She took her hands from mine and placed them into her lap, one in the other. 'Have you gone mad? I don't know what you mean.'

'Yeah, you do. The clues were all there. I can't believe it's taken me this long to see them.'

'See them? I haven't done anything wrong.'

I sighed. 'There's a photo taken by Nate's parents, Henry and Martha Willoughby. It shows a girl holding a red rose. She attended their community project for disadvantaged kids here on Paradise. Tash was friends with her. The first time I met Nate, he pointed the photo out to me. I think he was trying to tantalise me, wanting me to recognise who it was before he killed me. But I missed it. So, he kept me alive.'

'Missed what?'

'The girl's you, Lisa. As a teenager. I was too caught up by the rose to see the rest of her properly.'

337

Lisa swallowed. 'Dylan, please. It could've been anyone in that photo.'

I shook my head. 'They say love is blindness. Maybe lust is too. And I've been blinded by my feelings for you. It's so obvious now.'

'What is?'

'Henry and Martha Willoughby were the original Red Rose Productions. You attended their group for disadvantaged kids here on Paradise. And they violated you.'

She said nothing.

'My guess, they had a side income from dealing kiddy porn. They subjected you to God knows what, captured it on film and photographs, and circulated the lot among a network of like-minded perverts. It made you hell-bent on revenge. Am I warm?'

She gave a tight little laugh. 'You realise how mad you sound?'

'I've not even started yet.' I got to my feet. 'I'm going to tell you what I know or have theorised. Then I want you to fill in the blanks.' I started walking in a small circle. 'At first, I assumed Terry was finding the women for Nate and Simon to kill. It made sense to think that. Terry knew Nate from that documentary he'd made; he'd tried to fob me off with a bullshit story about witnessing Kwame's murder; he'd had photos of nineteen women in his drawer, all presumed dead; and he died in mysterious cir-cumstances. Clearly, he was involved.'

'There you go,' Lisa said. 'Terry was guilty. Nothing to do with me.'

'Afraid not,' I said, 'at least, not like you're suggesting. Sure, Terry knew what Nate and Simon were doing. He let them use his properties. But he wasn't involved like I first assumed. In fact, the night Minka got murdered, Terry was in a snooker hall, three miles away. It couldn't have been him behind the camera.'

'Dylan, stop this at once.'

I ignored her. '*You* could've befriended others on the game and sold them a line about a way to earn some fast cash filming a porno. A working girl would've been an ideal person to earn their trust. *You* were the talent scout for Nate and Simon.'

'You honestly think *I* found the girls that were killed?'

I just stared.

Lisa didn't move; but her hands were locked together, pinched white.

'There's plenty more,' I said. 'See, my friend Diane who's on the Met discovered Terry owned a bunch of flats around Paradise. It's how we found the basement where Suzi and Tash were being held.'

'So?'

'So, what I didn't realise until I called that same friend today is that *this* bedsit flat, the one we're in now, was Terry's too.'

Lisa shrugged. 'I rented it from him. What does that prove?'

'It proves there's a link between you and Terry. It proves you're a liar.'

'I never lied.'

'Then why didn't you tell me this crummy dive was his?'

'I don't know. It didn't seem important.'

'I've got another explanation. I reckon it's because you had to keep any connection between you and Nate separate from me. Am I right?'

I didn't wait for an answer.

'Here's how I reckon it went down. Over the years, you built up a loyal customer base, me included. Whatever abuses you'd suffered in the past, you'd tried to bury. But that all changed a decade back. Nate was commissioned to make a documentary on Paradise. It's how he met Terry. But I didn't clock that it was how he re-connected with you too. Suddenly, you saw him, and all the trauma his parents put you through came flooding back. Am I getting warm?'

She looked at me sharply. 'Please,' she said, her voice tremulous, 'please stop.'

'I wish I could. But it's like watching a snuff film: once you've seen it, you can't un-see it. And now I've figured this bit out, everything else makes sense.'

'What do you mean?'

'Right from the get-go, I was confiding in you, Lisa. And you were feeding Nate everything. That's how he knew so much about me, the people I cared for, the personal stuff about my daughter. It's how he guessed I'd reach out to Tash. And it's how he knew my weak spot was Suzi. I suspected everyone. The police. Tash. Baba. Even my ex, Diane. But no one else could've known this. No one, except *you*.'

She reached into her coat pocket, pulled out her vape, put it to her mouth, drew heavily.

'Well?' I said.

'OK,' she said.

'OK what?'

'I knew Nate. Like you said, he came to make that film all those years ago. One morning, he noticed me paying Terry my rent for this flat. He approached me, said he remembered who I was. I told him he was mistaken. But I recognised him. The last time I'd seen him he'd been an eleven-year-old, watching what his parents did to me. Now he was a grown man.'

'What did he want?'

'At first, I assumed he was interested in me for my body. That's what most men are after.' She shrugged. 'But Nate wasn't like most men.'

'What do you mean?'

'You met him. He wasn't turned on by sex. At least not in the normal way. What aroused Nate was pain. Seeing the pain inflicted on me by his parents had planted the seed.'

'Sex and death,' I said, remembering Dr Steiner's ominous insight into Nate's warped psyche. 'The two are inextricably linked.'

Lisa nodded. 'Nate kept saying how fate had brought our lives together, and we could help each other. Meeting me was meant to be – serendipity, that word you used.'

Now we were getting somewhere.

'What did you do after hearing all this?'

'At first, nothing. I tried to forget him. But the anger in me had been fired up. You understand this kind of anger, Dylan. After what happened to your daughter, I know you do.'

'Yes.'

'I went back to Nate. And this time I told him everything.'

'What did you tell him?'

'My life story. How I came to this country from Romania aged fourteen, me and my stepfather, both on fake passports, illegals. My mother had died the year before. We were here to start a new life in London. My dream was to be a model, like Kate Moss. I could've made it. I was beautiful. My stepfather found us a place to rent in Paradise. Our landlord was Irene Kinsella, Terry's mother, a nice woman.'

'Yes, she was,' I said.

'Irene knew we were illegals, but turned a blind eye, helped us get documents. I enrolled in school under my new English name – Lisa. I tried making friends. But I was lonely. My English was not so good.

'A few months later, I noticed posters around the estate.

A summer group for local kids. I asked my stepfather if I could go. He said yes.'

She rummaged in her bag, pulled out a Polaroid and held it up. It was the same one I'd glanced at before, and showed a sprightly, attractive teenage girl, Lisa without doubt, stood with a bunch of boys and girls of similar age. At the back of the group, two adults I'd come to recognise: Henry and Martha Willoughby. Successful advertising execs by day; smut merchants behind closed doors. And next to their parents, a pale girl and fair-haired boy, both children recognisable by their startling blue eyes – Nate and Tash.

Lisa looked down at the photo. 'Henry and Martha had money. They wanted to use it to help kids like us. They said we were the flowers of Paradise. I was so excited.

'Quickly, I became friends with their daughter, Tash. She was my age, a quiet girl. Nate was a few years younger. He used to hover in the background, watching.

'After a few days, Tash invited me back to her big posh house in Highgate. My stepfather encouraged this. Henry and Martha were good people, he said. They could help us. I did my best, tried to impress them. And they responded, paid me compliments, told me I was talented, the reddest rose of all the flowers of Paradise. I believed every word. Ha!'

I rubbed my eyes. A steel belt seemed to be tightening round my forehead, fuzzing my concentration. But I couldn't lose focus, not until it'd all come out.

'What happened next?' I said. 'When did you realise what they were?'

'After a week or so, Henry said he'd spoken with Martha, and they wanted to help my career. They both worked in advertising and had all kinds of links in the entertainment world. Of course, I said yes.'

'What kind of help were they offering?'

'At first, building my portfolio, taking photos.'

'Photos?'

'Me, wearing kids' clothes. Sportswear. Having fun. Martha said the photos were OK, but they could be improved if I worked a little bit harder.'

'How?'

'They had a photography studio setup at the house, the same room Nate used as his study. Martha brought in other girls and boys from the group. To begin, we were doing silly things, playing. But then she suggested I do other things with them. Taking items of clothing off the boys, making poses with the girls. Martha said it was normal. I trusted her. Henry photographed everything.

'Before long, Martha asked me to do things with sex toys. Costumes. And every time, she gave me a red rose to hold, like in the photo you saw. That was their calling card – they worked in advertising and knew how to make things stick in the audiences' mind. Sometimes she appeared on camera too, wearing a mask, nothing else. She had me do things to her. Awful things.

'Soon, Henry swapped the camera for a camcorder, making videos. It was the same camcorder Nate used to make his films years later. Henry would start rolling, and watch, naked. It aroused him. Then he came into the frame and joined in. I thought I had to do these things, Henry and Martha were being kind, helping my career. I was so, *so* stupid.' Her breathing had become staccato.

'Did you tell anyone?'

She paused. 'They said if I did, they'd get my stepfather and me arrested and kicked out of the country.'

'Did Tash know what was going on?'

Lisa shook her head. 'Tash knew nothing. They kept her far away. She thought her parents could do no wrong. She was a fool.'

'But Nate found out. And it planted that seed you mentioned. Right?'

'He said he used to spy on them through the cracks in the door. It was all feeding into his imagination, the start of what he became.'

I massaged my scalp, but a ball of pain kept pulsing relentlessly. 'Henry and Martha picked you well, didn't they?'

'What do you mean?'

'A poor voiceless kid, easy to control and victimise.'

She nodded. 'They had all the power.'

'How long did it carry on?'

'Months and months.'

'What happened to end it?'

'I became pregnant. Maybe it was Henry's, or maybe one of the other kids from the group. I don't know.'

I waited while she drew on the vape.

'I was fifteen. If my stepfather found out, he'd have been furious. I thought it would be better to fix it myself.'

'How?'

'I went to see Henry and Martha alone, at night, at their big house. They were surprised, and happy at first. I told them I was pregnant, and they needed to help me get rid of the baby. Otherwise, I'd report them to the authorities. That was a mistake. Making threats. It made them angry.'

'What happened?'

'They took me into the photography studio. They said it was to talk properly and avoid waking Tash and Nate. I thought they were going to help me. They gave me some hot chocolate. It must've been drugged. When it took effect, they tied me up. They started filming, stripped me. Beat me. Mutilated me.'

'How?'

Rather than answer, Lisa reached for her clip-on earrings and pulled both off simultaneously, a sharp movement.

I gasped.

Both lobes bore faint squiggly scars running from the centre to the bottom of the ear, warping the skin.

'They were going to kill me, I'm sure. But Nate walked in. He picked up my earrings, shouted at them to stop. He'd seen what they were doing. I ran for my life. Henry and Martha were furious.'

'That's why they sent him to boarding school?'

'To try to keep him away from everything. Out of sight, out of mind.'

'Instead, he met Simon, and the two became far worse than his parents.'

We fell into silence.

'The pregnancy,' I said. 'What happened?'

'I miscarried that night. Shock will do that. Somehow, I made it home. I told my stepfather I'd been attacked. Not long after, we moved from Paradise, to forget. Like you moved away as a little boy, Dylan, yes?'

I nodded.

'And believe me, I tried to forget. But the nightmares and flashbacks haunted me. And the self-hatred. What happened was my fault – that's what I believed. I thought I was worthless. My dreams were over.'

'What happened?'

'As I grew, I fell in with a bad crowd. I had no respect for myself, and started working in strip bars and massage parlours, mixing with bad people. My stepfather threw me out. A year later, he died of cardiac failure. A broken heart.

'Before long I was a working girl. I came back to Paradise, drawn to the darkness, the place where it all started. Henry and Martha had stopped the community group, but I knew they'd still be out there somewhere, hurting other kids.

'By then, Irene Kinsella was dead. She'd left everything to Terry, her loser son. He rented me this flat. I started seeing men from it, men like you, Dylan. The years went by. I was imprisoned in this life.' She paused. 'I knew I'd have to confront what Henry and Martha did to me eventually. I just didn't know how. So, when Nate came into my life, it really was serendipity.'

I nodded. 'And after hearing all this, what did Nate suggest?'

She smiled. 'That we make a film. By then, Nate had been to film school. His parents had wanted him to go into advertising, follow their path. Nate had real talent though, wanted to make serious work. He thought his whole family were pathetic. Henry, Martha, Tash – if they were out the way, he'd receive the house, their wealth, and would be able to do whatever he wanted.'

'And what did Nate want to do?'

'To make something shocking.'

'The real-life killing of his parents and sister?'

'Yes.'

'What did you think about this idea?'

'I thought Nate was deranged. But I also saw how serious he was. And he was offering me a way to get revenge on the people who'd ruined me. How could I refuse?'

'Whose idea was it to start the fire?'

'Simon's. As a policeman, he knew how to avoid suspicion. It worked.'

'Let's hear it.'

'The night we did it, Henry and Martha had gone to bed early. Tash went over to do some paperwork. We drugged her, then made it look like she'd been smoking a cigarette and that started the blaze. Nate captured the whole thing, from the fire being started, the flames catching, right to the finale. He made it look slick, like a movie. At one point you can see Henry and Martha pounding on their bedroom window, screaming, howling. The last thing they saw was me beside Nate, waving from their garden, holding up a red rose. Their son, next to the girl they ruined. It's what they deserved – a painful death.' Lisa smiled again at the memory and looked at me. 'Are you shocked, Dylan?'

'Not really,' I said. 'Last year, I met a bumbling professor who'd bludgeoned two psychopathic men to death for what they'd done to his family. Rage can make normal people do monstrous things.'

'You understand.'

'To a degree. What happened next?'

'The plan worked. But our only complication was Tash. She lived.'

'She certainly did,' I said. 'And you had Nate punish her, mutilate her, and made her believe the fire was her fault.'

'Yes,' Lisa said. 'But Tash had to pay too, don't you see? For her stupidity. Her blindness. And that should've been the end of it.'

'It *should've*,' I said. 'Instead, Nate and Simon took Red Rose Productions to a whole new level. Nineteen snuff films, Lisa. Innocent working girls. All slain. Explain that to me.'

Lisa sighed. 'That was Nate's idea too. He said the video of his parents' dying was a masterpiece. He wanted to make more.'

'What did you think to this?'

'That it was foolish and reckless. But Nate said the money

would pour in. I told him to prove it, so he uploaded the film to a pay-per-view website on the dark web.'

'And?'

'He was right. We made thousands and split it between us. I'd never seen so much money. There's a hunger for this kind of work, Dylan. Sex and death – it's what people want to see. And they're willing to pay for it. Nate understood this. His parents did. And eventually, so did I.'

'So, you went into business together?'

'We agreed to do a second film. Only this time, we'd kill someone who wouldn't be missed. A working girl from Paradise was the obvious choice.'

'That's where you came in?'

'Yes.'

'And Terry?'

'Terry provided us the room above his café to use. It was prefect, located in the heart of Paradise, and somewhere the police never came. My job was to find us a girl. It was easy. Her name was Tammy. She was new to the area, with no ties or family. She admired me, a big sister figure. I said to her, "Do you want to make some easy money appearing in a sex film?" Of course, she did. I took her photo, showed Nate, and brought her to the café at night. We went upstairs, met Nate and Simon.

'Nate tied her to the bed. He set up the same old camcorder his parents used, told the girl to put on the same earrings that'd been ripped from my ears. Then he started filming from a tripod. Nate and Simon put on masks. They talked with her. Made jokes. Nate placed a red rose on her pillow. She was relaxed.

'Then he ripped out the earrings. He held them up for me to see while she screamed. And he and Simon killed her. I handed them weapons. I couldn't believe what I was doing. But then when the money came in from that film, I knew we were onto something big. This could be my ticket out of Paradise. How could I refuse?'

My eyes closed, and I breathed through the sounds in my head.

'How'd Terry respond when he learned his café had been used as a snuff film-set?'

Lisa gave a sniff of contempt. 'Terry got a cut of the money. That was enough for him. He was spineless, no threat.'

'Agreed,' I said.

'But when you appeared, Dylan, asking questions, that changed. Now, we were in danger.'

'One thing I don't get,' I said, looking at her. 'When I first came to you, I showed you Minka's photo. You could've said you didn't know anything about her or sent me on a wild goose chase. Instead, you introduced me to Baba, helped me identify who Minka was. That led me to Nate. Why?'

Lisa shrugged. 'To protect myself. By then, things were getting risky. First, that boy broke into the café and stole the camcorder. Next, Baba appeared asking question about Minka. And then you showed up too, with photos from the film. It was only a matter of time before you'd pull Red Rose Productions apart and find Nate. I needed you to think I was innocent, and so decided to help you.'

I was impressed – she'd duped me good and proper. 'How could you be so sure I'd pull Red Rose Productions apart?'

She looked at me strangely, like I'd made a bad joke. 'Come on, Dylan. I know the kind of man you are. You wouldn't give up on something like this.'

'So, the only option was to make me think we were allies and lead me to Nate.'

'Yes.'

'For him to then kill me?'

She didn't answer.

'But Nate didn't kill me,' I said. 'He planned to poison me, but changed his mind at the last moment, and decided to keep me alive.'

Lisa nodded. 'After you went to see him, he became fascinated with *you*, just like he had with me.'

'Why?'

'He said you were a classic movie detective, tricked by a femme fatale.'

'That femme fatale is you?'

'Yes. Nate decided he had to make a film of your death. I warned him this was a bad idea. But Nate always knew best.'

'What about Tash? How was she to feature in all this?'

'Feature?' Lisa gave a light, derisive sniff. 'Tash would've been killed too.'

'Why?'

'She was living on borrowed time. Nate kept her alive to amuse himself. She helped maintain the image of the caring brother. But she is weak.'

'She's not weak,' I said. 'She's a victim in all this.'

'No,' Lisa said, her voice rising. 'Haven't you been listening? *I* am the victim.'

I let that one pass, said, 'You do realise you've just confessed to major crime. Everything you've told me could put you away.'

'How?' Lisa said. 'You don't have proof of anything.'

I thought about this. 'You're right. As things stand, we're just two adults having a conversation in a dingy bedsit.' I looked through the window, at the black cloud roiling over the horizon, and back at her. 'But I *know*, Lisa. I know you're guilty.'

'*I'm* not guilty,' she said, pointing at her chest repeatedly.

'Nate's parents were. Henry and Martha. I'm the product of what they did.'

'Afraid not.'

'Dylan, please,' she said. 'My motive was the money we made, plain and simple. I just found the girls. I didn't hurt them. I couldn't hurt anyone. I hate violence. You know me. Please, my love.'

Memories flooded back, the two of us lying spoons in the breathy afterglow of sex, feeling her warmth, her pain, knowing we were alike.

For a moment I pitied her, and I wanted to believe her so much. I wanted *her* too, a dark, lustful longing to seize her hips, kiss her neck, and take her a final time.

Then she lifted the vape, inhaled. The fluid gargled. A trace memory hurtled back, and another piece of the puzzle slotted in place. For here it was – the water feature sound from the films. I saw Lisa there behind the camera, watching as Minka got tortured. Any warmth I felt disintegrated. Time to set this straight.

'Sorry,' I said, 'but you're still holding back.'

She exhaled a thick cloud. 'What do you mean?'

'I mean, you're the most twisted person in this whole thing.'

'I'm not!' Lisa said. 'I am a vic—'

'A victim?' I was starting to feel hot, edgy, not quite in control. 'Drop the act, sweetheart. Money may've been your motivation at first. But before long, you were getting your rocks off on the killings as much as Nate and Simon. And you got a heap of blood on your hands protecting yourself along the way.'

'Blood?' She tilted her head and looked at me quizzically. 'Whose blood?'

I held up my hand and counted off four fingers: 'Kwame Mensah. Terry Kinsella. Patience Mensah. Nate Willoughby. Four people. All dead.'

'Yes. So?'

'They were murdered.' I pointed at her. 'By *you*.'

She stared. Her mouth opened an inch; then her face grew tight.

'So how about you quit playing the sympathy card and finish the fucking story the way it happened.'

Chapter 37

My headache had grown claws.

I tried ignoring it, but that just seemed to make it worse, a dry scraping behind my eyes.

Lisa must've noticed. 'Dylan,' she said, 'you're not well. It must be your injuries affecting your mind. What you're saying is crazy. You think *I* killed four people?'

I nodded.

'I admit I was involved. I wanted revenge against Henry and Martha for what they did. I helped kill them. And then I found the girls for Nate and Simon to use in their films for the money. But they were the killers. Not me.'

'Lies.'

'How can you say this? What evidence do you have?'

I gathered my thoughts. She stared up from the settee.

'Let's start with Kwame,' I said. 'He was left to die in an alley-way on Paradise. Terry was the star witness, claiming he saw a bunch of kids chase and stab Kwame. As a result, that became the line of enquiry.

'But it was full of holes. Any decent copper could've told you the facts didn't add up. The police report showed no defence wounds, no suggestions Kwame tried to fight back. He knew his killer and wasn't scared of them. Whoever it was must've been pretty slight to fit down that alleyway and knife him.

'That killer was *you*, Lisa. Here's how I reckon it happened. Kwame, the opportunist thief, stole the camcorder from Terry's café, watched what was on it, went to Terry and tried to black-mail him. Terry got spooked, told you, and you decided to deal with Kwame yourself.

'My guess: you told Terry to arrange a payment to Kwame – cash for the camcorder. Kwame was expecting Terry to turn up. Instead, you appeared. Perhaps he'd seen you around and liked you. He was a teenage boy, for Christ's sake, and you're easy to like. You got him in that alley and stuck him. As he was dying, you searched him for the camcorder.

'Only he didn't have it. He'd double-crossed you too. I bet that really pissed you off. Huh?'

She didn't answer.

'Then there was Terry. After I turned up at his café, pulled his witness statement apart and showed him the photo of Minka, he would've been bricking it. Like you said, he was spineless, and would have squealed under pressure. He had to die too. But Nate couldn't send Simon to bump him off. Terry would've been frosty around him. But you – the tart with a heart – he had a soft spot for.

'So, after I went to see you and told you what I was investigat-ing, you headed to the café, spiked his tea with some GHB, the tasteless chem-sex drug. Combined with the sedatives Terry liked to gobble, that was enough to send him over the edge. Then you left a bogus suicide note and planted a bunch of photos of all your victims in the film-set, knowing I'd find them and would suspect Terry of being the talent scout. You even left the photo of Terry and Nate hanging on the wall, figuring I'd join the dots and work out Nate was significant. It all helped lead me to Nate, created the impression that Terry was guilty, and distanced you from the whole damn thing. Pretty clever, Lisa.'

Her lips remained tight.

'Killing Patience was harder. But by then, things were getting messy. Nate had decided to keep me alive for his next snuff film. You knew I was dangerous. And you needed a way to keep me under control. But how were you to do it?

'Easy. Through Suzi. I'd told you about her, how we were close. You knew about my daughter, and that I'd do whatever it took, including sacrificing myself, to keep Suzi from coming to harm.

'So, Nate sent Suzi an email about some art internship opportunity and invited her for an interview. While Nate was surprising me at Trafalgar Square, you and Simon headed over to the site to nab her. Sure enough, Suzi turned up.

'But she had Patience with her. That put a spanner in the works. When Patience came snooping, you appeared, introduced yourself. Patience would've been disarmed, not expecting trouble, especially from someone as unlikely as you. You stabbed her in the gut, the same way you murdered her kid brother. You thought she'd go out just as quick too.

'But Patience was a trained fighter. And before she fell, she got a decent punch in. It left that bruise on your face. You had me believe a punter did it. Nice try.'

Lisa touched the greyish mouse below her eye that still bore a shadow.

'With Patience dying, Simon grabbed Suzi, and the two of you sped off. Only problem, you got snapped on CCTV. The image quality is poor, but if you know who to look for, it's clear who was driving.' I pointed at Lisa's chest.

'But your last victim was the real kicker. Nate Willoughby. When your plans went south at the cemetery and Suzi and Tash got rescued, you knew the game was up. Simon was dead, but if Nate squealed, you were both going down for a long time. He had to die.

'The police are happy with the idea that he committed suicide. Well, I'm not. Here's how I think it happened.

'Nate fled the cemetery. He'd been stabbed and would've been in hysterics. He called you, and you said to meet up on a tower block on Paradise where it was secluded. My guess, you calmed him down, convinced him it'd be OK. You're good at making people feel OK, Lisa. Christ, you did it enough with me.

'Then you killed him. I don't know how. My guess, you stabbed him too. After, you pushed his corpse off the top of the tower. With a fall like that, Nate would've been mincemeat. There's no way to tell the cause of death. Everyone assumed he took his life. But you murdered him, and the others. And you won't get away with it.'

By now, she had regained some composure, and was sitting neatly, symmetrically, her hands in her lap, eyes on me. Part of me didn't want to look at her; but I couldn't take my eyes away.

'Impossible,' she said.

'Why is it?'

'I was at Baba's on Saturday when all this happened. Remember, you took me there for my safety. How could I have killed anyone?'

I shook my head. 'I had a word with Baba just now. Guess what? You went missing from hers for much of Saturday, and came back in the small hours a little out of sorts. She was embarrassed to tell me, as I'd asked her to keep you safe. She tried to stop you going, but you were pretty determined to get gone. Now I know why.'

Lisa didn't answer, but her pupils expanded, huge, black, like freshly poured tarmac.

'*You* were in that basement with Suzi and Tash,' I said. 'They were both blindfolded. Neither would've seen you or known anything about you. But I could hear you, Lisa. Off camera. Smoking that vape. *You* were keeping guard, waiting, while Nate and Simon went to the cemetery to fetch me. Once they brought me back, *you* were going to be the one who killed me, and Tash, and Suzi, all of it filmed on the same camcorder that captured your suffering years ago. Nate said I was due a surprise. He wasn't wrong.'

'No, Dylan,' Lisa said, her voice rising in pitch. 'No more.'

I waved down her protest. 'Christ, when you heard my friends breaking into that basement film-set and realised the game was up, you must've really freaked out. There was a small window. I'm guessing that's how you escaped. It must've been a scramble, as you left a heap of evidence, Nate's black book of contacts, plus your getaway money.' I pointed at the ten grand bundle, still on the settee. 'Does this cash look familiar?'

Lisa ignored the money. Her eyes were zeroed on me.

'That takes us to the present,' I said.

'What do you mean?'

'I mean, what were you planning on doing tonight?'

I looked at my glass of brandy on the floor, untouched. 'There's a little more than brandy in there. Let me guess. GHB? Your drug of choice.'

She didn't answer. But her eyes gave her away.

'Were you going to drug me, kill me and flee?' I looked at her boxed up possessions, and back at her. 'It could've worked. Maybe you'd have faked my suicide. With someone like me, my history, it would've fit.'

'Yes,' Lisa said. 'It would.'

'And Tash?' I said. 'She's waiting for me now, alone, on my allotment. What would you have done about her?'

'I'd have killed her too,' Lisa snapped. 'And made it look like you did it. With this.'

She reached for her bag. If there was a gun in there, I'd have been done for.

Instead, she pulled out a small knife.

I recognised it immediately. It was the kitchen knife used in the snuff film to cut Minka's throat. The metal glinted dully.

For a moment I was sure she was going to come at me with it.

I might've outweighed her, but I was still recuperating, and she was boxed into a hole, desperate.

But she didn't make a move. She just placed the knife beside her on the settee, and we kept staring at each other in the cold, empty room.

'No,' she said, her hands suddenly grappling her knees. 'This isn't how it's meant to end.'

'Sorry.'

'No!' Her dark eyes blazed. 'Stop this!'

'Why should I?'

'Because there's no point.'

'I'm afraid there is.'

'Nate is dead. Simon is dead. No more films will be made. No more girls will die. I'm leaving. You win, Dylan. Just stop!'

'I can't.'

'I have more money saved. I'll pay you.'

'I've got plenty already, thanks.'

Her lower lip quivered, but her eyes were on fire. Pointing at me, she said, 'You think you're clever. Some action-man superhero who swans into town and gets all the bad guys. Bullshit. You're guilty too. As guilty as Henry and Martha and every man who's ever stepped foot in this flat to use my body. It's because of men like you that I exist. And now you try to pin murder on me. How dare you! I'm the victim here! Me!' She pointed at her chest, a stabbing motion.

I started back, rocked by what I'd heard.

'She'll always hate you,' I said.

'What?' Lisa said.

'It was the last thing Nate said to me. I assumed he meant Suzi. But he meant you. Didn't he?'

'Please, Dylan,' she continued, softer now, 'do this for me, and I won't hate you. We've both made mistakes. You and I have lost so much. We should move on, and pretend it never happened.'

'It's that simple?'

'It can be.'

I took some heavy breaths. My chest was doing funny things, and my throat had constricted. 'You want to know what I think?'

She went for a smile. 'What?'

'You're right. We've both suffered, and both made mistakes.'

'Yes,' she said, more freely.

'But that doesn't exonerate you. Life dealt you a shitty hand. But you made your choices. Revenge and the money you were making were what drew you into this. But you got off on the killings too, Lisa. Seeing those women die turned you on. And now you need to answer for it.'

Silence clung in the air like a final breath.

She said, 'Have you told the police about me?'

'Not yet. My detective friend Diane knows I'm here, but I

didn't say why. Right now, no one knows the details, apart from us two. We're just two people having a conversation.'

'So, what happens now?'

'I can't decide. Any ideas?'

Leaving the knife on the settee, she stood, came towards me, arms outstretched. I could smell her skin cream and the blackcurrant vape on her breath.

'Please, Dylan. This doesn't need to come out.'

'You reckon?'

'Yes. Our secret.'

And I must admit, despite everything I was tempted.

But not tempted enough.

'Come to the police,' I said. 'I'll make sure you get treated fair.'

Lisa stepped back. Her arms flopped to her side. 'No,' she said. 'I will not.'

'Are you sure that's wise?'

'Why would I confess? There's no evidence. You're not a policeman. You're not really a man at all, Dylan. You just live on the fringes. A nobody, same as me. Like you said, we're just two people having a conversation.' She smiled. A sour, victorious smile I didn't much like.

'You're right,' I said, 'I can't force you to do a thing. But there's other things I could do.'

'What things?'

'For starters, I could still tell the police everything. Even if there isn't enough to put you away, they could make life unpleasant. You'd get interviewed. Your status and ID would be checked. All the men you've got on your books would be screened. They'd go through your belongings. Then they'd probably deport you.'

She shrugged. 'I'm leaving the country anyway. Is that the best you can do?'

'I'm just thinking out loud. Maybe I'll go to the press. I'll give them your name, description, tell them the whole lot. This is a hot crime story. They'd be all over you.

'Or maybe I'll tell Baba everything and suggest you two thrash it out? I asked her to wait for me. It wouldn't take long to nip down and fill her in on your part in her sister's murder. How do you think she'd respond?'

Lisa's eyes bulged and she went to the window. I knew what she'd be seeing – Baba, stood outside like a sentry.

While Lisa was there, I reached for the knife on the settee and said, 'Or perhaps I should deal with you myself? Rough justice. I'll do to you what you did to them.'

Lisa turned fast and stared at the blade. A ripple of fear crossed her face.

'You'll kill me?' she said. 'Is that what you're saying?'

I didn't answer.

'No, Dylan, you'd never do this. You're not a murderer.'

'You'd be amazed at the things I've learned about myself recently, and what I'm capable of doing. Maybe you're right. I can't kill you. Till recently, I'd have been sure that was the case. Now though, I won't make any promises.'

I shut my eyes a moment; then looked at her squarely. 'But you need to realise I won't let this go. One way or another, you're finished.'

It was her turn to pause.

'So that's it,' she said.

'Pretty much.'

Then an idea dropped into my head.

Before I'd thought it through, I said, 'There's another option, of course.'

She waited.

From my coat pocket, I pulled out the pill bottle I'd taken from my allotment hut earlier. Lisa stared at it. Recognition gleamed across her eyes.

'I lifted these from Terry's when I found his body,' I placed the bottle on the floor by my glass of brandy. 'At the time, I didn't know why I kept them. Maybe it was a sixth sense that they'd come in handy later.'

Her eyes averted to me, then the pills, back and forth. 'I don't understand.'

'There's still a dozen or so left. A handful and whatever's in that brandy should be plenty.'

'You're serious?'

I didn't answer.

She laughed, high-pitched and forced, then stopped abruptly.

I looked at my phone. I'd been here well over an hour.

'It's time for me to go,' I said.

'Go where?' Her breathing was hoarse. 'Sit down. We're not finished yet.'

'I think we are.'

'Wait. Let's figure this out!'

'There's nothing to figure out.' I took the bundle of cash off the settee, returned it to my pocket along with the knife. 'I guess you won't be needing these.'

She fired me a look, eyes like lava, spiting indignation.

I zipped up my coat and walked away from her. 'If you decide you want to go to the police, call me.'

'And if I don't? What then?'

'Then I'll know you've taken a different option.'

I shuffled open the splintered door. A blast of cold air hit my face.

'I could just run,' she said.

I turned back. 'You won't run.'

'How are you so sure?'

'Because I'll come after you. And you know the kind of man I am.'

Baba was waiting for me beside the pillar of a block. Hearing my footsteps, she came forward from the shadows.

'Here,' I said, 'and tossed her the second bundle of cash. 'This could do with a new home.'

She stared at the money, and at me. 'Why?' she said.

'Long story.'

'Do you want me to stay longer?'

'No.'

She glanced up at Lisa's bedsit window. I followed.

The blind was drawn, but the lights were on, and there was vague movement behind it, a slight shadowy figure, pacing.

'What is going on, Kasper?' Baba said.

It was a reasonable question. 'If you really want to know, then I'll tell you.' I paused. 'But I don't reckon you really do want to know.'

She took a long time with this, her brow etched with concentration. Then she said, 'I trust you.'

We shook hands a last time and let each other go.

I walked through Paradise the way I'd come, heading for the southern entrance. The temperature seemed to have dropped into minus figures, and the cold brought out the desolation of this place, the inhumanity it bore witness to.

At some point this whole estate should be scaled, the bricks, mortar, the remnants of Paradise obliterated. Good riddance.

But the ghosts would remain. Kwame. Patience. Minka. Nineteen women.

And Lisa.

Nothing could justify the actions she'd taken. She'd manipulated, coerced, watched people get tortured, killed, committed murder herself. And yet she was right: in all this, she'd been a victim too.

Something else she said was bothering me, about the other perpetrators in this story. Men who paid for her and yearned for the anonymity of the cheap fuck; men who reinforced the status quo that let women be trampled on, sliced up, bagged and dumped.

Men like me. Did I have a part to play in what happened too?

I kept on, pushing against the flits of cutting wind, my eyes watering, my whole body tremulous. A few minutes later I turned the corner onto the allotment grounds and my plot fell into view.

No light or movement came from the hut. I couldn't see Tash anywhere.

A cold dread rose like water filling a well, and that strange, resigned look she wore earlier came back . . .

I pulled open the gate, scampered close. Those few seconds stretched out, and I was quite certain she was dead.

I flashed my phone's torch beam forward, made out the hut, its door partially open. There was a pair of legs, a body, slumped on the stool.

I must've yelled something, for suddenly Tash stood, a marionette pulled upright, eyes stark, mouth wide open in surprise.

She was alive.

And I felt a fool.

'What is it?' she said. 'Kasper?'

I tried to speak, but all that came was a sickly croak.

'Are you OK?' She came close.

'I thought . . .' I managed, 'Jesus, I panicked and—'

'I was just dozing,' she said. 'This hut, with the heater on, it's cosy.'

A surge of emotions gushed forth. My eyes were watering uncontrollably now. I put a hand to my mouth when I felt my lips start to go.

'It's OK,' she said. 'I'm fine.'

I nodded.

'Did you do what you needed to?'

'Think so.'

'Want to talk about it?'

'No.'

She turned, switched off the electric heater, closed the hut door, and locked it with my key. Then she buttoned up her duffle coat, came beside me and linked an arm in mine.

'Then let's go.'

Chapter 38

I t was the following Friday.

Mani and I were at the February inter-borough boxing bout. The community hall was packed, a raucous affair, much like the one we attended four weeks back when Patience was alive and this whole nasty business kicked off.

A bigger crowd had flocked into the venue tonight, the bog-standard beer-bellied men plus a few journos and media hacks. The compere, a portly geezer with a smoker's rasp and chipmunk cheeks, introduced the fighters through a crackly mic, and promised us '. . . a blindin' night'.

But before the first punches were thrown, Mani was asked out. He stepped into the ring, took the mic, and talked about Patience and Kwame, whose ashes he carried together in an urn.

'Paradise produced the two kids I'm holding in this,' he said, gesturing to the urn. 'Paradise killed them too.' His crucifix necklace, recently returned, glinted against the lights. 'Those kids both should've been here tonight. Don't let no one here forget them. Enjoy the fights.'

Applause followed, firm but respectful. Mani shook hands with people as he returned to his seat.

Then the bell clanged, the first fight started, the mood went up a notch, the shouting and jeering really ramping up.

Over the next hour, the two of us watched a couple of brawly three-rounders, downed a few lagers, tried to join in the furore. But I guess we were both somewhere else, a sombre place, and neither could get into the cut and thrust of fighting the way we wanted.

I assumed my mood was partly the result of fatigue, for the day had been a busy one. That morning I'd rented a hire car and driven Tash Willoughby to a therapeutic community in rural Wiltshire: the start of a month-long residential stay, and the beginning of a long recovery journey. The six-bed converted mansion was staffed by mental health professionals who all had heaps of letters after their names. Food was organic, the drinking water sourced from local springs. On a different day, I'd have fancied a stint there too.

The drive was my first time behind the wheel since I left the Met. Stop-starting on the North Circular, pushing against the angry tide of rush hour traffic, I was reminded why my preference remained for two wheels rather than four.

Even so, I was happy for Tash, and for the chance to help get her settled.

Before heading back, I said to her, 'Call me if you want a chat.'

She'd just deposited her belongings into her room, and we were outside in the gravel car park. 'I don't think we're allowed phones,' she said. 'This is meant to be an immersive experience. No WIFI, no contact with the outside.'

'Oh,' I said. 'How about smoke signals? Carrier pigeon?'

Her pale eyes shone, and her smile seemed genuine.

We stared at each other; then she said: 'You suspected me, didn't you? Of being involved in the killings, and helping Nate?'

I looked at my boots.

'It's OK,' she said. 'I'd have thought the same too. After you came to see me at the house, Nate just seemed to know about you. He and Simon blindfolded me, drugged me, and took me away. I was sure I'd die. But I never told them about you. I swear.'

'I know, Tash,' I said. 'It's OK.'

'What's upsetting me is, long before you appeared, a part of me *did* know what Nate was doing. In the same way a part of me knew what my parents were doing too. I just chose not to see any of it, because it was too painful. Does that make me as bad as them?'

'No,' I said. 'You were used. And all this needs to come out.'

She nodded.

'It's good you're talking openly like this. Secrets can drive us crazy.'

'Secrets,' Tash said. 'Have you got many of those, Kasper?'

'Plenty.'

'Yes, I believe you do. Last week, while I was waiting for you at your allotment, something happened, didn't it? I wanted to ask what it was. But I knew I shouldn't. That maybe I didn't really want to know.'

Despite the cold, I felt my cheeks blanch from a rush of heat.

In that moment, I came close to telling Tash the truth, how her old friend, Lisa, was at the centre of this bloody mess.

But I stayed tight lipped. What would've been the point of adding to her turmoil?

'Whatever you *did* do,' Tash continued, 'I know it was for the good.'

I stared at her. 'How do you know this?'

'Because you're a good man, Dylan Kasper. Remember that.'

We shared a slight and awkward hug, and I got back in the car and left this leafy corner of the country, back towards the city with a lot to think about.

A bell clanged, drawing me back. The ref had just stepped into a clinch, separating another pair of ungainly welterweights at the end of the round. The fighters took to their corners and the placard girls appeared, garnering whoops and cheers.

'You seem a little quiet, Kasper?' Mani said. 'You OK?'

I nodded. 'A little weary. But alive.'

'I hear you. The fights are different to last time, huh.'

I was about to say that maybe the fighting hadn't changed, but *we* were different, but my voice was drowned out by the opponents exchanging a burst of clumsy close-range blows, and the crowd going full throttle, egging them on, demanding the knockout.

I reached for my beer under my chair. Today's *Gazette* lay beside it. I'd already read the paper front to back, but had kept it in case I wanted to read it again.

The Willoughby case remained a hot topic, but it was dwindling to the middle pages. Other, more prescient stories were starting to occupy the public's appetites.

Front page was a report on further cuts and the closure of more community drop-ins for youths; page two, scandals in the cabinet, with accusations of misogyny and porn viewing in parliament doing the rounds; page three, another fatal stabbing in Paradise, more kids killing kids, the usual stuff.

A two-paragraph snippet at the foot of the article was the bit that caught me. The decomposing body of a woman had been found in a bedsitter out on Paradise. Suicide was the suspected cause of death.

There was no description or an I.D., or details about how she'd done it.

She was a nobody.

After reading the piece that morning, I felt nothing.

But a little later, the emotions had erupted, too many to name.

Even now, I struggle to explain my actions. Had they been proportionate, a measured response? Or had I descended to Lisa's level?

All I knew was that somewhere deep within the shadows of my heart, a line had been crossed. Tash calling me a good man seemed to only magnify the indelible stains these events had left. I didn't know who I was anymore, or what I'd become.

I do know that I gained no satisfaction from learning of Lisa's death.

But I didn't regret the news either.

One of the fighters landed a corker of a southpaw, and his opponent flailed, punch drunk. As the ref ended the bout, I shouted in Mani's ear I needed to pop out for some air. He gave a nod.

Outside, the night was cold, lit by a sickle moon. A helicopter whirred above, its flashlight beaming left and right, as if seeking out meaning in the blackness.

I found a corner spot away from the noise, pulled out my phone and dialled Suzi.

'How're you doing?' I said.

She told me she was good, still in Ireland with her aunt. 'How was Patience's funeral? I wanted to come back, but the press are still on at me.'

'For a funeral, it was OK,' I said. 'Mani's got her ashes. We figured we'd scatter them when you get back.'

'Thanks,' she said. 'You know, all this has made me think about my future, what I want to do. I know Patience hated the police, but that's because she only had bad experiences with them.'

'So?'

'So, I've done some research. And when I get back to London and turn eighteen, maybe I'll sign up.'

'With the Met, you mean?'

'Yeah, why not.'

I puffed out air.

'You don't think I'm up to it?'

I gave this question some serious thought; then I answered truthfully. 'I reckon you'd make a great copper, Suze. And I'd be scared shitless for you.'

We chatted some more. Near the end, she said, 'You sound different. What's wrong?'

'Nothing much. My voice is croaky from shouting at the fighters.'

'That's not it. You sound like you got the weight of the world on you.' She paused. 'You know I'm not mad at you, right?'

'Yeah,' I said, a little stiltedly.

'Then stop feeling sorry for yourself.'

'Who says I am?'

'Me. It's not a good look. Only dickheads feel sorry for themselves.'

'Fair enough,' I said, and laughed, the first time in a while.

We set a time to speak tomorrow, and I told her I better go back to Mani. I could hear the compere bellowing into the mic, and the noise from the crowd had risen again. The next fighters were coming on.

I went back into the hall, jostling past bodies towards my seat. But as the heat and lurid lights, and the reek of sweat and lager all struck me, I stopped and just took in the scene in the ring. Two fresh-faced kids about to knock seven shades out of each other, with the crowd going nuts in anticipation.

In that moment I knew I'd had my fill.

I caught Mani's eye, indicated I was going. He nodded. I suspected he'd be off soon too.

I left alone, hands slunk into my pockets, collar turned up, back into the night. After the hall doors had slammed shut and I was halfway home, the smacks of punches were still audible, along with the jeers and hollers for more.

THE END

Acknowledgements

Thanks to –

Jack Butler and Rosie Margesson of Wildfire Books; Gordon Wise at Curtis Brown; Russel McLean, freelance editor; Jo Malone, Scott Maynard, Sam Tobin, Rob Parker; and to my wife and son.

If you enjoyed A KILLING IN PARADISE and want to know where Kasper's story began, THE NEXT TO DIE is available in paperback now

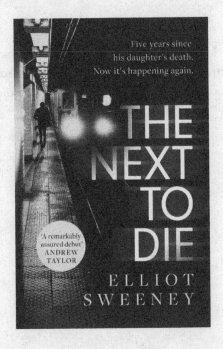